BLOODLINE

Warren Murphy

A TOM DOHERTY ASSOCIATES BOOK
NEW YORK

This is a work of fiction. All of the characters, organizations, and events portrayed in this novel are either products of the author's imagination or are used fictitiously.

BLOODLINE

Copyright © 2015 by Warren Murphy

All rights reserved.

A Forge Book
Published by Tom Doherty Associates
175 Fifth Avenue
New York, NY 10010

www.tor-forge.com

Forge® is a registered trademark of Macmillan Publishing Group, LLC.

ISBN 978-0-7653-7797-5

Our books may be purchased in bulk for promotional, educational, or business use. Please contact your local bookseller or the Macmillan Corporate and Premium Sales Department at 1-800-221-7945, extension 5442, or by e-mail at MacmillanSpecialMarkets@macmillan.com.

First Edition: November 2015
First Mass Market Edition: December 2016

Printed in the United States of America

0 9 8 7 6 5 4 3 2 1

To all the people who traveled this road, too.

To Dawn and Molly and Elizabeth and Margaret and Tony and especially Dick Sapir, the best partner ever, and to Deidre, Megan, Brian, Ardath, and Devin— best kids (and critics) ever.

Acknowledgments

The acknowledgments owed from some sixty years of writing would demand a book of their own. So here are just a few of the people who made a difference in my life and by putting up with me, had a hand in this work: Andy Ettinger, Henry Bolte, Ron Semple, Bob Waldron, Bob Randisi, Rick Myers, Ted Joy, Steve Needham, Richard Curtis, E. R. Boffa, Mark Coles, the remarkable Neil Bagozzi family, Patsy and Chrissie, Sheriff Bill and Mary Chambers, Merc and Asli, Jim Mullaney, Will Murray, Mary Higgins Clark and Larry Block, K. S. Brooks, Bob Napier, Tom Whelan, and every cocktail waitress and bartender in the Western world—each of them indispensable.

Let us all persevere enough to hang around until the pub closes.

NIGHT OF THE SICILIAN VESPERS:

A Sicilian revolt in 1282 against Charles I, the French King of Naples and Sicily. After killing French soldiers in Palermo while they attended religious Vespers services on Easter Monday, native Sicilians massacred 2,000 French inhabitants of the town.

—Desk Encyclopedia

BLOODLINE

PROLOGUE

June 6, 1918

They had been driving toward the front all day long, a thousand-truck-long caravan racing at top speed through the rain and unexpected cold of an early June day, through Paris and a dozen, two dozen, who-knew-how-many small towns and smaller villages, past the broken, spent French Army, past even more desperate peasants and villagers trying to escape the onrushing Huns, all the way toward the small village known as Château Thierry.

It was past dark when they finally stopped. They climbed down from their trucks, cursing and joking, standing around in the building rain, waiting for a hot meal they all knew would never come. Then, sometime after midnight, still stiff and sore, they moved up to the line.

Private Tommy Falcone—U.S. Marines, Second Brigade, First American Division—as empty of heart as he was of stomach, moved along with the others. He was frightened and wished that he were somewhere else. Anywhere else would do.

The damnedest part of it, he reflected grimly, was that, strictly speaking, he did not have to be there. He had not been drafted; he had enlisted and he now considered that the damnedest, dumbest, stupidest thing he had ever done yet in his short life.

Papa was right.

It had not been funny at the time, but now Tommy smiled ruefully as he remembered the scene in their apartment when he had told his father he was enlisting.

"Never," his father had said.

"Mario has enlisted."

"Your brother is a priest. He has God looking out for him. Who will look out for you?"

"I am almost nineteen, Papa. It is time I started looking out for myself."

"You are still *nasamorba*. A snotnose. Grow up first. *Then* go kill Germans."

Tommy's mother had contributed her opinion by weeping constantly for seventy-two hours, but in the end, Tommy Falcone had walked into the Marine office and enlisted. What had seemed a good idea at the time, now that he was here, now seemed the act of an idiot bent on suicide.

It was so dark here in the trenches that Tommy could barely see or hear the man in front of him. It was important to be quiet, they had been told. They were going to surprise the Boche as soon as it was light. The Marines had come stripped for action: no extra clothing, no extra packs, just what they were wearing—their rifles, their bayonets, and small combat packs.

Tommy Falcone checked his equipment and again wished he were not there.

The night dragged. When it came his turn, Tommy tried to sleep but could not. He was too tired, too excited, too scared. He wished that he had carried his rosary with him, the one Mama had given him when he had left their apartment back in New York City. But he didn't have it. He was a man now, he had told himself at the time. He had no need for God. All he needed were his fellow Marines and a little bit of luck.

He said a Hail Mary anyway. Then an Our Father. Then a Glory Be. He said them over and over, gradually drawing comfort from their almost-mesmerizing grace.

Mario would approve, he thought. Mario was also somewhere in France this night. He was a battlefield chaplain with the army, and if Tommy knew his brother at all, he would be in the thick of whatever fighting there was. Tommy thought of his brother, then the neighborhood, his friends, his parents, all the pretty young girls he had yearned to have. He said some more prayers, anything to take his mind off what was coming.

This trench is not the worst place in the world to be. If I had to, I could stay here for days. Perhaps even months. I'll bet there are places in the world where backward peoples live in trenches, spend their whole lives in them. We could do the same.

He thought idly about suggesting this to one of his superior officers, but before he could find one, the war intruded again on his life.

The sky in the east was turning gray. Tommy could hear the soft clicks as Marines down the line from him fixed their bayonets onto the ends of their rifles. Without waiting for orders, Tommy did the same. A moment later, a sergeant appeared, scurrying along the floor of the trench like some nervous water bug, telling each of them that it was almost time. "Ten minutes," he said. "Maybe fifteen. Just be ready to go when the whistle blows."

It wasn't so bad, Tommy thought. He had been told that this would be the worst time, the waiting, and he had gotten through it okay. He crossed himself and turned to look at the two Marines next to him. They both grinned but did not speak.

Those are nervous smiles. They are as frightened as I am.

After what seemed only a few seconds, the whistle blew and Tommy and the others scrambled up out of the trench. They marched forward in a line that stretched as far as he could see in the gray mist, half-crouched, their rifles held at port arms.

It was quiet, eerily so. A hundred yards ahead of them was a wooded area. That would be their first objective, and then beyond that there was supposed to be a wheat field and, beyond that, another woods. They were to get as far as the second woods if they could and then dig in there and hold.

The sun raced into the sky, driving away the clouds and turning the grass of the meadow they were crossing a blood red. Ahead and to the left, Tommy saw a small farm building that looked too small to be a barn and too crude to be a house. He watched it as he moved. One step. Two steps. The morning was alive with the sounds of singing birds.

Three steps.

The building erupted, shooting noisy bursts of flame across the field. Tommy went to his knees, then onto his belly. He was ready to stop, to dig in. He had done enough for one day. He thought about it, but then somebody was beating on his helmet with a stick. He looked up and saw some officer whom he had only seen once before. He was cursing at Tommy, and Tommy reluctantly got to his feet again.

He turned to grin at the officer, to show him that he was all right, but the officer was already moving away, shuffling low toward the next Marine who had taken cover prematurely.

Tommy watched the officer move and admired his confident self-control, wondering if he would ever be able to do the same. As he watched, the officer split in half just above the waist and his intestines snaked out onto the ground.

Tommy knew he should be horrified, but all he could think was that it was amazing how much of the stuff there was. The officer's legs ran on a few steps before collapsing, and the man's upper half fell to the ground, crying and cursing and then shrieking with pain.

Tommy turned back to face the woods. The silence that had accompanied the men across the fields was gone, replaced by a universe of total noise, so loud, so pure, that silence had never existed in its world. He could see flashing, like swarms of fireflies, in the woods ahead of him. Tommy glanced back and saw other Marines trying to move forward. Some were succeeding; most were not. Their screams hung in the air.

I'm going to die out here. Like a hen in a barnyard. And no one will even know my name.

He covered his head with his hands, curled into a ball, and remembered how his parents had come to the New York pier to see him off on the troopship to France.

"I didn't want you to be a Marine," his father had said.

"I know."

"Be a good one."

A good one. A good one. A good one.

Tommy rose to his knees and looked ahead toward the flashes. They had to be machine guns, he decided. Behind him, his fellow Marines were scattered, leaderless, many already killed or injured. Tommy rose to his feet and charged, screaming, like some wild Indian he had read about when he was a kid. He would never know why he did it; he just knew it was the only thing he could do.

Then he was into the woods and facing two men behind a machine gun. They were in dirty gray and seemed tired, exhausted, and even at a distance they looked as if they had not washed in a year. Tommy shot the first one through the head and watched his brains explode. Then he stuck the other man in the chest with his bayonet, just below his right nipple, and pulled the blade diagonally down toward the man's left hip. The German was still standing, grasping fearfully at the cut in his belly, but he did not go down, so Tommy shot him too.

At first Tommy Falcone had been all alone in the woods, the only Marine there, but that quickly changed, and for what seemed like a long, long time, Tommy slashed and shot and killed because nobody told him not to. Then somebody blew a whistle and Tommy stopped.

The Marines regrouped. Some drank water from their canteens. Others had found bottles of wine among the dead Germans. Somebody handed Tommy a half-filled bottle, and he thirstily chugged most of it before passing it on. He felt good. He never remembered having felt so alive before. It was glorious.

On the other side of the woods was the wheat field, the stalks of grain standing waist-high and colored a rich golden brown. In among the wheat were mixed thousands and thousands of brilliantly red poppies.

They started forward again, through the wheat field, marching steadily, waiting for the Germans to fire. Tommy hummed to himself as he went, a flat, unmelodious old Sicilian folk song he had heard growing up. He wished he could remember the words so he could sing aloud.

It would be stupid to sing. But why not? I am Falcone the Magnificent. I am invincible.

He had not gone far, only a third of the way across the field, when the Germans started firing again and he felt a slight burning in his arm. He looked down and saw blood, and it took him a moment to realize he had been shot. He stopped and looked around for someone to help him. He turned and then felt a thump, like a kick, in his side. He looked down and saw another hole in his uniform. He tried to remain standing but could not. He fell and could not rise.

All day long he lay there. Twice more bullets thudded into his exposed side. People stumbled over him. Two Marines died, gurgling in their throats, not a dozen yards away. The day grew hot, unbearably so, and he wished that it were cool so he could die comfortably. He had always hated sweating. Then it thundered and rained and it grew cold and Tommy wished it would be hot again. Sometime after noon, the pain near his hip grew unbearable and he began screaming. By sunset, he was too tired, too weak, even to scream anymore. When the moon rose, two stretcher bearers found him and started to carry him off. The motion reignited the pain and he began screaming all over again.

They stopped back inside the first woods, and some-one came over to him and asked his name and wanted to know where he hurt. Between screams, Tommy told him. Then Tommy could see something flashing in the moon-light. He cringed and tried to pull back from whatever it was.

The other man laughed. "Big, tough Marine, afraid of needles."

Then in a kinder voice: "Don't worry. This won't hurt you. It'll make the pain go away. It'll make you feel better."

Feel better. That sounds like a good idea.

"What is it?" he croaked from between parched lips.

"Morphine," the other man said. "It means 'sleep.'"

In New York City, as the war wound down, life went on.

- *Enrico Caruso sang in* Rigoletto *at the Metropolitan Opera House, then to raise money for the war effort, sang in regular concerts at which his rendition of "Over There" never failed to bring down the house.*

- Dere Mable, *a comic collection of letters from the front, became a best seller.*

- *A young artist named Norman Rockwell painted covers for* The Saturday Evening Post *magazine.*

- *And on October 24, 1918, a sixteen-year-old Russian immigrant named Maier Suchowljansky was returning home from his job as an apprentice tool and die maker when he heard screams from a deserted tenement building on the fringe of the Jewish neighborhood where he lived. He rushed inside and found a naked prostitute and a partly clad teenage boy whom he had often seen on the streets. The prostitute was being beaten and kicked by her pimp, a swarthy, sharply dressed Italian in his early twenties, and when the good-looking young boy—who had been enjoying the prostitute's services—tried to protect her, the older man advanced on him too. Suchowljansky grabbed a wrench he carried in a belt around his waist and slugged the Italian man over the head. As he went reeling, three policemen, called by neighbors, rushed into the room. Sgt. Tony Falcone, who led the police detail, told the prostitute to find a new neighborhood and ordered the three males brought to headquarters. Riding there in the police wagon, the swarthy young Italian man, whose name was Salvatore Lucania, slipped a twenty-dollar bill into Falcone's hand. Falcone slapped his face and stuck the bill into Lucania's mouth. "You'll pay for that," Lucania snarled. "Quiet, pimp, or it'll be worse," Falcone responded. At the precinct, several hours later after a few telephone calls were made, Lucania was released and, because of his age, so was the boy whose name was Benjamin Siegel. Suchowljansky was held for two days, then fined two dollars for disorderly conduct. He never went back to the tool and die works.*

Nilo

PART ONE

CHAPTER I

May 1919

The sirocco was blowing hot and fierce out of the heart of the Sahara desert, hopping quickly across the short span of the Mediterranean that separated Africa from Sicily, up the face of the Sicilian mountains, down the other side, and on out into the Gulf of Castellammare.

Danilo Sesta stood in the bow of the *tonnara* boat and stared back over the purple and blue and peacock-green waters into the heart of the hot wind, back toward the town of Castellammare del Golfo.

He did not much care for work, rising early, laboring until after dark, forced into the company of loud and stupid men, but still, he thought life was good.

And someday it will be perfect.

The tunny were running well this spring, and even though he was just eighteen, he was making a man's wages. For now. But when the fishing season ended in the autumn, he would be the first to lose his job, and that would not be so good. Perhaps he would go to America. It was cold there, he had been told, and he would not have the sun and the heat that he loved. But there would be work. He would grow rich, as did all who went to America.

And then when he was old—forty or so—he would

come back to Castellammare del Golfo and build himself
a fine villa and stock it with many fine things to eat—
he was always hungry—and many beautiful women:
women of every color and sort, but all of them very, very
bellissima.

"Hey, Nilo." A voice behind him spoke his nickname.

Nilo turned around and smiled. "What, Fredo?" he
asked.

Fredo motioned him to come closer. He was perhaps
a dozen years older than Nilo, a short, sturdily built man
who looked like one of the Saracen lords who had ruled
this island so many hundreds of years before.

"We've work to do," Fredo said.

He was looking down into the *mattanza,* the "chamber
of death" as it was called, the small room made of fishing
nets and hung in the sea between the two boats of the
tonnara.

Nilo was puzzled. He moved closer to the older man.
They were not supposed to be fishing this day, not
collecting the tunny or spigola or dolphins or swordfish
or sharks that had swum into the chamber, there to be
speared and hauled aboard either of the *tonnara* boats.

Indeed, there were only four of them out on the water:
Nilo, Fredo, and, on the other boat, the two Selvini
brothers, Paolo and Enzo. The others of the *tonnara* crew
were all ashore, helping to celebrate the wedding of the
fleet owner's daughter, and only the four of them had
been left behind to clean up the boats and to protect the
nets from vandals or thieves.

Nilo did not like the other three, but he had found them
useful. They drank too much, and when they did, they
were careless with their money and some of it found its
way into Nilo's pockets. He justified this by thinking, *As*

well into my pocket as into the purse of some waitress or prostitute.

"I did not think we were to do any fishing this day," Nilo told Fredo.

Fredo smiled at the boy and put his arm around him. Nilo was handsome, almost to the point of prettiness. He had large chocolate eyes with thick black lashes, pouting lips, and a slim boyish body. At night, several times when the boats had been at sea overnight, Fredo had lain down next to him, gently brushing the boy's back. Nilo had pretended to remain asleep, ignoring him, as if he had not noticed.

"That is not the kind of work I mean," Fredo said.

Nilo looked at him for a moment, then shrank back. He had the fleeting fear that Fredo knew Nilo had been stealing his money and that of the other crew members. He tried to tell himself that it was only his imagination.

"What do you mean?" Nilo asked. He tried to move sideways carefully to the rack where the great long gaffs that they used to haul in the fish were stowed.

Fredo laughed softly, almost shyly.

"Have I ever told you how beautiful you are?" Fredo asked.

Nilo stopped. He said nothing.

"I dream of you all the time," Fredo said. "You and nothing else."

Nilo laughed and then spat into the sea.

"I thought you were a man, Fredo," he said. He was just out of arm's reach of the gaffing poles.

"I *am* a man, and as a man, I must have you."

Nilo felt a shiver run up and down his spine. Where were Paolo and Enzo? He needed help. Fredo was too big, too strong. There was no place to run to. No help could be expected from the wedding guests until late this night at the earliest. And despite the way he made his living, Nilo could not swim. The water had always frightened him.

Nilo called the names of the other two men. "Paolo! Enzo!"

Now it was Fredo's turn to laugh.

"It will do no good, little thief," he said. "They feel the same as I. And we have all paid in advance. With all the money you have lifted from our pockets."

The two brothers appeared just then in the corner of Nilo's vision, and he turned toward them, but with just a glance, he could see that what Fredo had said was true.

Nilo fought them to keep them from catching him. And he fought them while the brothers held him down while Fredo carefully, methodically violated him. He fought them when Paolo entered him, and he fought when Enzo did the same. By then he was bleeding terribly and he felt as though his flesh had been gashed open, just as he had gashed open so many of the fish that they had hauled in from the *mattanza*.

They let him lie there on the deck, unconscious, after that. Then, in the heat of the dying late afternoon, they came into him again and again and again, drinking and laughing and singing songs of the sea.

When the sun went down and darkness covered the waters and they were done with him, the three men threw Nilo into the sea, counting on the predators that always swam around the *tonnara* boats to finish him off.

IT WAS SPRING AGAIN. Tommy Falcone knew that before he even opened his eyes. He could smell it on the air: a scent dense with lilacs and some other unidentified heavy, sweet flowers, an aroma that somehow managed even to gently, subtly overpower the sick, septic smell of the hospital all around him. Tommy could tell it, too, from the very texture of the air. It felt warm and moist, soft, pleasant, comforting. The worst was over.

He opened his eyes slowly. The operations were over, they had told him. No more going under the knife. His body would repair itself now, they said, and in a few short months—six at the outside—by Christmas, he would be well enough to go home. Tommy smiled to himself. He almost felt like singing. But he could not do that. It would disturb the other men on the ward, other men far sicker than he, many of them with no hope of ever really recovering, no hope of ever going home.

Tommy's eyes were open all the way. Then he remembered. He was not on the ward anymore. He looked around him. They had moved him the previous evening. He was in a private room, a room to himself. He stretched, felt a twinge of pain from the exertion, and laughed anyway. It was the first time in over a year that he had slept in a room by himself. God, he loved it. He loved life.

There was a robe lying across the end of his bed. He put it on, limped to the window, and looked out. There was an immense green lawn that seemed to stretch on and on forever, spotted here and there by clumps of trees. Tommy laughed again. In his neighborhood in New York City, ten thousand people—maybe twenty thousand— would live in that amount of space, but here there was nothing except for a few robins tugging at their breakfast worms and a couple of squirrels playing a frenetic game of tail-chasing.

The feeding robins reminded him that he was hungry.

For some reason, even that thought amused him, and he laughed again and began to think he had turned into an idiot who thought everything was funny. He wondered how soon breakfast would be served. He turned and walked carefully to the door. Walking was still a new experience to him. He had spent months in bed while his liver, his kidney, his stomach, and his hip bones were being carefully rebuilt, and even now, after all the surgeries had been deemed successful, he walked slowly and cautiously. He made it to the door and turned the knob. It did not open. He went back to the bed to sit down and ponder this bit of information.

He looked again toward the world beyond the window and noticed for the first time that the window had bars on it. For a moment, Tommy fought back a rapidly rising panic. Then the door opened.

A nurse came through carrying a breakfast tray. She was old and almost ugly, but she had a cheery manner and she showed her teeth when she smiled.

"Good morning, Tommy. It's a beautiful day out, isn't it? How are we feeling this morning?"

Tommy noticed that she had not bothered to close the door behind her.

"I'm fine," he said carefully.

"Is something wrong, Tommy?" the nurse asked. "You don't sound like yourself this morning. And look what I've brought you. Remember last night? I asked you what you'd like and here it is. Eggs. Pancakes. Bacon. Even orange juice. And lots of coffee."

"Thanks," Tommy said without enthusiasm. "That sounds good. Real good." He paused. "Is there some special reason why I'm in here?" he asked. "And why there are bars on the windows? And the door's locked?"

The old woman smiled at him reassuringly.

"Doctor will be in after breakfast," she said. "He'll answer all your questions for you then."

Then she was gone and Tommy heard the door click locked behind her. It was only after she had left that he realized she had forgotten to give him his shot.

He was tempted to call after her but decided not to. He would wait until the doctor came.

He tried to eat his breakfast. The nurse was right: it was all the things he liked, but nevertheless he had no appetite. He was feeling too restless to sit down and eat.

"GOOD MORNING, TOMMY," voice said. It had a slight southern drawl.

Tommy opened his eyes slowly. Had he fallen asleep? It did not seem likely and yet he must have.

He twisted around until he was sitting on the edge of his bed. The man perched on a chair next to the bed was dressed in the uniform of a U.S. Navy medical officer. It took Tommy a moment to get beyond the uniform, and then he noticed the man himself: he looked young, not much more than Tommy's own twenty years.

He nodded briskly at Tommy and said, "I'm Doctor Singer. We haven't met before."

"I don't feel so good, sir," Tommy said.

The doctor half-smiled.

"I've been reading your records," he said. "It says that you were a very brave man at Belleau Wood."

"I don't remember, sir. I just remember being scared. I guess all I did was what I had to do to stay alive. And not let my pals or the corps down."

"In my book, that adds up to brave."

"Thank you, sir," Tommy answered.

"Now you're going to have to be even more brave."

"Sir?"

"We made a mistake," the doctor said. "We're going to try to correct it."

Tommy felt panic beginning to grab at him.

"I don't understand, sir."

Doctor Singer pulled the chair over to the side of Tommy's bed and sat near the younger man.

"I'm not going to feed you a lot of nonsense," he said. "We've given you too much morphine over too long a period of time."

Tommy's panic swelled. He could feel his temples pounding. Growing up on the streets of New York's Little Italy, he had seen enough of what morphine could do to be scared.

"Am I a drug addict?" he asked slowly.

Singer shook his head. "I wouldn't call it that. I prefer to call it a 'morphinist.'"

"What's that mean, sir?"

"It means that I don't think that you have the temperament to be a drug addict," Singer said. "It means that I think I can cure you."

"How, sir?"

The doctor hesitated.

"For one thing, we've been steadily decreasing the amount of morphine we've been giving you. We've taken you down from nearly five grains a day about six weeks ago to just a little more than one grain a day now."

"That sounds good," Tommy said. "I hadn't noticed."

"That's another thing that makes me hopeful."

"What do we do next?" Tommy asked.

"We've already done it. As of this morning, we've taken you off all drugs altogether."

Tommy had heard before about what that meant, heard it on the streets of his neighborhood.

"Cold turkey from here on in?" he said.

"Yes," Doctor Singer answered. "The next couple of days might be pretty hard on you."

NILO SESTA WANTED TO DIE. He wanted nothing more than release. Release from his pain. Release from his shame. He could not live anymore. He wasn't a man. Not after what had been done to him. He was not a man and he was worse than a woman.

Nilo let himself sink deep into the sea. It made no difference. The sea was warm and inviting. The Gulf of Castellammare would take him into its bosom, hold him there, not let anyone hurt him anymore, not let anyone shame him anymore.

Nilo sank until he could go no farther. He was too buoyant. His body was rejecting its watery grave. His body wanted to breathe fresh clean air. Nilo wanted to open his mouth and let his lungs fill with water and sink even deeper down into oblivion. He wanted to, but he could not make himself do it. He began rising, rising not because he wanted to but because of his body's own natural buoyancy.

Something brushed briefly against Nilo's leg, something big and wide and rough. The boy shuddered. Sinking peacefully to the bottom of the bay and dying gently was one thing, but being bitten and hacked and chewed to death bit by bit, piece by piece, by sharks or barracuda was something else again. Nilo kicked out at whatever had bumped into him and began frantically flailing his arms. He rose even faster than he had before. Once he began rising, his body took over from his mind: it had determined to live, regardless of what Nilo's brain had been planning. He kicked even harder.

Nilo broke the surface of the sea at first without even knowing it. He took in huge gulps of air before he realized that he was breathing again. His eyes feasted on the moon and stars, as he thought that they had never been more beautiful, that life had never been more precious.

He trod water unthinking for almost a minute before he remembered that he did not know how to swim, before he remembered that to fall into the sea was automatically to drown, to die. The thought panicked him, and he began flailing the water again frantically, desperate for rescue and yet not desperate enough to call out for help lest Fredo or the Selvini brothers hear him and turn back to finish the job they had begun.

In his flailing, Nilo turned in a complete circle, and as he started halfway around again, he noticed only a few meters away the dark silhouette of the two *tonnara* boats riding high in the water.

Nilo forced himself to calmness. He could not stop his fear, but he could control it, prevent it from becoming panic. He tried treading water again and found that it worked. He was able to remain upright, in place. The only problem now, he realized, was how to get to the boats to keep from drowning.

But if he went back to the boats, Nilo told himself, he would be delivering himself once more into the hands of his assailants, and that was certain death. He would have to, somehow, get to shore. But that too was impossible. The shore was a mile away at its nearest point. He could never reach it.

He felt panic rising in his throat like a swollen lump of flesh, and he fought to keep from retching. Perhaps, he told himself, if he could get to the side of one of the *tonnara* boats and somehow hold on until the rest of the fishing crew returned from the wedding celebration, then maybe he could be rescued.

Nilo forced the top part of his body to lean in the water, toward the boats, and then tried to use his hands and arms to move forward, just as he had seen swimmers do. The distance was not great, but it seemed to take an eternity to traverse.

When he finally reached Fredo's boat, he searched desperately for a safe handhold until he came upon the anchor line dangling overboard. He grabbed the coarse rope and held on with a fierce determination.

I am alive, God damn their souls. I am alive.

Time came and went. Minutes passed, then hours. Nilo could hear the sounds of drunken revelry from the three crewmen aboard the boat above his head, and while he waited, his determination just to survive grew and changed into an even more powerful desire for revenge.

Finally, Nilo grew aware of a change in the activity on the boat. He listened carefully for what was being said but could not make out the words. Then he knew what was happening. Paolo and Enzo were leaving the *tonnara* and taking one of the smaller rowboats to go back to shore to meet the partying fishermen after they returned from the wedding.

Nilo waited for the Selvini brothers to leave. A few minutes later, he heard snoring from above his head. Fredo had gone to sleep. Or passed out. Slowly, Nilo worked himself around the boat until he reached the stern, where he could hoist his upper body onto the gunwale and then pull himself completely onto the deck. He lay there on the wet cold wood, gasping and puffing, fearful that he would wake Fredo and yet not really caring if he did so. But Fredo did not wake.

Nilo crawled forward to the rack where the gaffs were kept and only then stood up. Most gaffs were hammered into a hook, but throughout the fishing season, Nilo had been using a straight spear with a sharp bladed barbed end. He quickly found that tool in the rack.

He crossed the small deck in three quick steps and positioned himself over the thin pallet where Fredo slept. Nilo gently prodded the older man with the point of his weapon.

Fredo stirred and Nilo prodded again.

"Who is it?" Fredo demanded thickly. "What do you want?"

Nilo did not answer at first. Then he said, "You, Fredo. I want you."

Fredo sat up, still not fully aware of what was going on. Nilo did not give him a chance to say anything. He drove the gaff hard between Fredo's legs. His aim was sure.

As neatly neutered as any capon or gelding, Fredo screamed, a horrible mixture of pain and anguish. He grabbed at the place where his manhood had been. Nilo laughed and slammed the end of the gaff pole into Fredo's face. The burly man collapsed back into unconsciousness, and Nilo trussed him up with heavy fishing lines until the older man was immobilized. He took his folding knife from his pocket and slowly began to carve away on Fredo. For the first five minutes, the fisherman screamed, begging for mercy, begging for death, begging for Jesus and Joseph and Mary to help him.

By the time his screaming had stopped, there was hardly a strip of skin more than three inches wide anywhere on Fredo's body that had not been sliced by Nilo's knife.

The necessary deed done, Nilo sat back on the gunwale

and quietly contemplated his work. Fredo was dead now or soon would be. That left Paolo and Enzo Selvini. The brothers would be more difficult, watching out for each other, protecting one another.

For them, I will need a weapon more powerful than a knife or a hook.

Nilo began looking through all the cabinets and lockers of the two boats. Occasionally, he had seen the owner on board carrying a *lupara*—a sawed-off shotgun—and that was what he was searching for. He finally found it hidden under the captain's bunk. Now all he had to do was to get ashore and run Paolo and Enzo to ground.

Another dinghy was tied up to the other *tonnara* boat, and carefully holding the shotgun out of the water, he worked his way across the nets to the other fishing boat, clambered into the rowboat, locked the oars in place, and began pulling for shore.

TOMMY FALCONE COULD NOT STOP YAWNING. He tried and could not do it and became very annoyed with himself.

He rose from his bed and began pacing the floor of the hospital room. It was early afternoon now, and Doctor Singer and the homely nurse and a pair of burly orderlies had been coming and going all day.

He wondered where they were now and decided they were off drinking coffee somewhere. Or smoking. He wished he could get out of the room and see for himself.

So far, one day, and it had not been so bad. Maybe the doctor was right. Maybe he was not really a drug addict. Just a "morphinist." Whatever that was. The doctor had to be right. He was not ever going to be a drug addict. It wouldn't be fair, especially since it was not his fault. He had never asked for the morphine. They had just shoved the needle in him and kept pumping him full of the stuff all during that horrible three-day trip back from Belleau Wood to the hospital in Paris and then, afterward, during all the operations. It was not his fault.

God, but his nose was runny. He had lost track of how many handkerchiefs he had used already today, and now he needed another. He was amazed at how many disgusting fluids could come out of the human body, and he wondered how doctors and nurses could stand seeing it all.

A new set of handkerchiefs came, and somebody—an orderly and nurse he had not seen before—asked him how he was feeling, and Tommy told them that he felt just fine, really okay, there was no trouble.

He walked over to the window and looked out. Other patients were outside now, walking on the great green lawn, being pushed about in wheelchairs. He crossed himself and thanked God that he was not one of those poor souls who would never walk again. What kind of life did they have to look forward to? He considered himself lucky. All he had to do was to get through the next couple of days and then he would be free.

The breeze coming in through the window was surprisingly hot. Tommy felt weak and began to sweat. He shut the window and moved over to his bed and lay down on it. In a moment, the heat passed and Tommy felt cold. He started to shiver and his teeth chattered. That had not happened since he was a little kid. Tommy curled himself up in a ball, wrapping himself in blankets and burying his head in his pillow. He got colder and colder, and just when he thought he could not stand it anymore he felt a flash of heat pass through his body.

Tommy threw off the covers and got up, sitting on the

edge of his bed. He sat quietly for a moment, feeling almost at peace with himself. Then his nose began running again. He dabbed away at it frantically, blowing into a handkerchief and disgusting himself with the mucus that filled the small piece of cloth and spread out over his hand. Annoyed, Tommy wiped his hand on his bedsheet, but his damned nose was already running again.

He tried to sit quietly, to fight down the rising panic, the ever-increasing disgust with his own body. When he thought he had things almost under control, something happened to his breathing. He could not get enough air. Nothing was coming through his nose.

It was probably normal, he thought. Probably to be expected.

He tried breathing through his mouth, but that did not do any good, either. His breath came in short, jerky gasps, and he suddenly knew, beyond any doubt, that he was going to die. He began to cry. He wanted to call for help. He wanted more morphine.

That'll make this go away. I know it.

But he would not let himself call out. He concentrated hard on his breathing, working to make it normal, and to his surprise, he succeeded.

Then the chills started again. Tommy went back to the window, to the steam radiator in front of it, and tried to turn the heat valve. It did not work. Back to the bed, curling up in blankets, burying his head under his pillow, Tommy fell asleep.

He awoke with a start, fully and instantly awake. It was dark outside. His room was dark. The hospital around him was deathly silent except for some moans and screams somewhere far in the distance.

Tommy lay in bed for a moment, almost at peace with himself, and then began yawning again. The yawns grew bigger, more frequent, more demanding. In five minutes' time, they had become so overpowering that it felt as if all the muscles in his neck were being stretched and pulled apart. He thought that this must be what a man feels when he is being hanged.

His jaws ached and then went on, beyond aching, to pure pain. Tommy began to shiver again. It was cold, so cold. The yawning stopped and he began to sneeze.

The first sneeze was not so bad. The second was a little worse. By the tenth—or was it the twentieth?—he felt as if his lungs were being ripped out through his mouth. His chest was heaving and the back of his head was aching, feeling as if it were being banged against a brick wall harder and harder with each sneeze. That too stopped just before dawn.

Tommy walked to the window to watch the sunrise. He tried to feel a moment of peace. He would have, too, except for the chills that he felt and the fact that his eyes would not stop watering.

He thought it still had not been too bad. And it had been a long time now. A week at least.

He wondered how much longer it would be until the withdrawal period was over.

He was considering that very question when he began to suffocate. Suddenly Tommy knew he was dying. Somebody had grabbed hold of his throat, from behind, and was collapsing the air passage. He let out a strangled cry for help and tried to turn to see who had hold of him.

Whoever it was had cleverly hidden himself, because there was no one in sight. Tommy began to cry and, when that did no good, to scream.

Someone came. He could never remember who. They moved him to his bed and stretched him out, covering him with two blankets. After a while, the suffocating feeling passed and Tommy sat up. Outside, birds were singing.

Tommy got up and began to walk to the window. He had gone no more than three steps when he felt a stabbing pain in his left foot. He hopped back to his bed and sat down. The pain was beginning to spread, sending spears of agony up his leg and into his groin. In a few minutes, his entire left leg was pulsating in wave after wave of stabbing cramps. Gradually they subsided, and Tommy, who had been biting his lips to keep from crying out, muttered a quick Hail Mary. It was the first time he had prayed since France, since he had been shot and carted back to the field hospital. After more than an hour, the pain in his left leg showed no sign of slackening. Then it was joined by pulsating cramps in his other leg as well. Then, as suddenly as it had begun, the pain was gone.

Tommy sat quietly, afraid that if he moved even a muscle, he would start the whole thing over again. The door opened and the homely nurse came in again. He knew he had not seen her in weeks, maybe months, and today, she looked especially beautiful.

"Good morning, Tommy," she said. "It's a beautiful day out, isn't it? Did you manage to get any sleep last night?"

"Where have you been?" he demanded. "I've been waiting for you for weeks."

She shook her head sadly. "I only work the day shift, Tommy. I was here with you yesterday. And I'll be here for you today. And as many days as I have to be."

Tommy looked at her through bloodshot eyes.

She's lying. It's been two weeks at least. Of course, she's lying. But I won't let on that I know.

"How much longer?" he asked. "How much longer does this go on?"

She shook her head. "I don't think it will be too long. And you'll be glad when it's all done. You'll feel much better. Now eat your breakfast. I know about growing boys like you. I raised two of my own. So eat up."

Meekly, Tommy obeyed. When he was done, the nurse removed his tray and Doctor Singer appeared at the door. Tommy was rising to greet him when the pain kicked him in the stomach. It was totally unexpected. It felt like a knife tearing through his guts while at the same time someone tightened a belt around him until he was squeezed into the shape of a barbell.

Singer helped Tommy stretch out on the bed, but it did no good. The pain grew worse and worse. The chills began again and then the sweats. The bedclothes, after a few minutes, looked as if they had been left out in the rain. The pains in his belly would not stop. Tommy turned on his side, trying to make it go away or at least abate. It did not help and, as he turned back, he could feel his breakfast coming up. He tried to hold it down but was unable to. Bits of egg and pancake and sausage and pineapple, all embedded in a thick yellow-green bile, erupted from him. Tommy jerked back, trying to miss the doctor, but was not successful.

When the doctor wiped Tommy's face with a towel, the diarrhea started. And the chills again.

Tommy began to cry. He wanted more than anything to beg for another shot of morphine, anything to ease the pain, the suffering. But he would not let himself beg. He told himself that he would wait five minutes and then ask for it.

And when the five minutes were up, he made the same bargain with himself again. *Wait five more minutes and then ask.*

Periods of sheer agony alternated all day long with moments of respite. The physical pain kept getting worse and worse; the times of reprieve were never long enough.

When lunch came, Tommy tried to make himself eat, but as he brought the food to his mouth, its aroma set off another bout of vomiting and stomach spasms. He finally gave up the effort. He made himself drink a glass of water, but that only made the pain worse.

He tried then to make himself sleep, thinking that he could pass the worst of the time that way. But sleep never came. Instead, he began twitching all over, the muscles from one end of him to the other going into frantic spasms.

When the nurse came back to help, Tommy realized he had an erection and he turned on his side so she would not notice. She stroked his back and he ejaculated.

That seemed to ease the spasms in his legs, and the nurse left. Then the next wave of stomach cramps attacked.

It kept up all day, a constant replaying of the previous agonies.

Again and again, Tommy decided that in five minutes he would beg for a shot of morphine. Again and again, he delayed the begging. Again and again, he prayed. Again and again, he suffered.

At sunrise the next morning, there came one of those moments of near tranquility. Tommy felt little discomfort and went to the window once more to watch the dawn. But while he was looking outside, his vision doubled, then tripled, and then dissolved to a totally meaningless blur.

Tommy closed his eyes and cried. Then he called out. But not for morphine. He called out for his brother, Mario.

Then the pain came back, and he crawled across the

floor to return to his bed, where he lay in his own vomit and wept and shivered.

One day.

Another day. And another.

On the evening of the fourth day, Tommy Falcone fell asleep.

NILO SESTA WOKE WITH A START. His tongue was thick in his mouth and he ached in every part of his body. The ache between his buttocks turned to pain and he wanted to cry out. But that would not do. A man, even an eighteen-year-old man, did not cry—at least, not because of physical pain. A broken heart, yes. Other things, perhaps. But not for physical pain.

Nilo carefully scanned the nearby shore. He was still in the rowboat he had taken the night before. He must have fallen asleep at the oars, and the boat had run aground on a deserted portion of beach. Perhaps he had passed out. He remembered what happened—the shame of it, the pain of it—and for a moment he said a prayer that it had all been a bad dream.

But it had not been. Nilo knew that and there was no use pretending.

Slowly, Nilo remembered Fredo and what he had done to the burly fisherman. He half-smiled at the memory.

The sun was coming up, far off to his right. He had drifted to the west during the night, drifted away from Castellammare and the men he had to kill. That was bad.

By now every fisherman along the coast must have learned that Fredo was dead, and they would all be looking for him, them and the Carabinieri and all of Fredo's family.

I should have thrown his body overboard. Then no one

would know what happened to him and I could have moved freely. I must be more careful in the future.

It was too late to worry about it. Nilo leaned forward in the small boat and carefully unwrapped the shotgun that he had bound in a piece of canvas sailcloth. He inspected it and then, satisfied, rewrapped it. He had no love for guns, but sometimes they were necessary. He remembered Fredo. The fisherman had loved guns, fondled and caressed them as other men might touch a woman. But not him, not Nilo. *At least, not until now. But who knows? This gun may become my closest friend.*

Nilo set the oars, eyed one of the old Saracen watchtowers more than a mile away, and began drawing slowly toward it. After a few minutes, he realized he was hungry. This surprised him. Thirsty he could understand: the body demanded water regardless of what indignities it had suffered. Thirst could not be controlled. But hunger was something else again. What he had gone through the day and night before should have driven all hunger from him, but it had not. Nilo thought of his mother's kitchen, thought of the good things she cooked there, and wanted more than anything to be back in those familiar surroundings. It was not that he was babied or pampered. On the contrary: Nilo was an only child and often his mother and father seemed to treat him with disdain and indifference, causing him occasionally to wonder if he had been left with the Sestas as an infant and adopted.

Nilo beached the boat, then hid it between some huge sentinel-like rocks at the water's edge. He climbed the hill leading to the road, moving rapidly in the early morning sun. If he was where he thought himself to be, he should make it back to Castellammare by noon, even allowing for keeping out of sight and moving through the brush away from the main road.

As he moved along, Nilo began to hum a tune, something he had known since infancy from hearing his mother, an old folk song that from its curiously flat melody must have been brought across the water by some of Sicily's Arab invaders.

The farther he went, the more he noticed—as he rarely ever had before—the intense beauty of his home island. The trail he was following was edged in vines and cacti. Off to the side were clumps of bamboo and small stands of blue-green olive trees. The air around him hummed with the songs of massive yellow-banded bees, and thousands of butterflies seemed almost to provide a guard of honor for him. A little way off, Nilo could hear the faint whir of hummingbirds going about their lives, collecting sweet nectar from the flowers that bloomed here in every color and shade imaginable. The sun moved higher into the sky, and the air around him grew more and more heavily perfumed with the scents of thyme and other wild herbs.

It could have been paradise, Nilo thought, and could remember no time when he had felt more intensely alive. *I have been treated like a woman and yet my heart is light.*

It might, to some, seem strange, but Nilo understood the reason for it very well. He was Castellammarese. In other places, in other times, he would not have been expected to feel the way he did. But here, among the hills of western Sicily, there was no need for pretense. Especially in Castellammare del Golfo. The town, all said, had an evil reputation, even for Sicily. Somebody had once told him that eight out of ten men in the town had spent time in prison and that one out of three had taken another's life. Those things might or might not be true, Nilo thought, but in his hometown there was, at least, no hypocrisy that prevented one from taking pleasure from a righteous killing. He had killed once already and was about to do it twice more.

As he walked, Nilo meditated about the pleasure of delivering death to someone who richly deserved it, then hummed another song, this one happier than the last.

Once the parish priest—and at this thought Nilo crossed himself—had tried to take him for the priesthood. Nilo was a good boy, he had said, and could go far in the church. But Nilo's father would not allow it. The elder Sesta had some private quarrel with God, and he had sworn that he would rather be eternally damned than have any child of his go over to the enemy's side.

It was a memory from childhood.

And now I am no longer a child. My childhood has ended.

He hardly noticed that he had arrived at the hill overlooking Castellammare. Trying to keep out of sight, he started down toward the center of town. Almost without guidance from him, his feet automatically led him along the various *viccolos,* the dark and narrow alleyways, leading to his home.

It was fortunate that they had. And it was equally fortunate that his feet stopped him before he turned into the last shadowed way.

Nilo stopped and unwrapped the *lupara* and moved forward with caution. His eyes, he later told himself, must have been directed by San Giuseppuzzi, his favorite saint, father of Jesus, protector of the family, patron and advocate of lost causes. Because ahead of him, their backs toward him and facing Nilo's house, were Enzo and Paolo Selvini. Each held a shotgun in his hand. They must have been waiting for him, waiting to shoot him down as he came out of the door of his house.

Nilo walked slowly up behind them and spoke each of their names once, softly. They turned and Nilo fired. One shell for each brother. They went down, crying and cursing. Nilo carefully picked up their guns. Dead men had no use for guns.

TOMMY FALCONE CAME BACK to life slowly.

Someone was wiping his forehead, not saying anything, not trying to be gentle. He could feel that the hand holding the cloth to his face was big and rough. Still, Tommy was grateful. He tried to open his eyes but had difficulty. They felt as if they had been glued shut. He moved slightly and immediately a ripple of nausea flowed up from his stomach.

The ripple became a wave and Tommy wanted to vomit. He tried, but nothing came. His body was wracked by shudders. He felt his bowels loosen and then he slipped back into oblivion.

Consciousness came back with a start. One moment Tommy was somewhere else, somewhere in some gentle dreamworld, and then he was awake and lying in his bed. He tried to sit up but could not. He was strapped down on the bed.

"Hello," he said tentatively.

"Hello, Tommy," somebody answered. "Welcome back."

He knew the voice and then remembered the hands that had been wiping his brow.

He tried to open his eyes but quickly gave up. The daylight was too bright; it pierced his brain, stabbing right through his eyeballs. Whoever was beside him got up and walked away. Tommy heard the curtains being drawn, and even through his closed eyelids he could feel the room growing darker.

"You can open your eyes now, Tommy," the voice said.

"Mario?" he asked. "Peppino?"

"It's me, Tommy," the voice said.

He opened his eyes slowly this time. Slowly they focused on the figure next to the bed, the man clothed in the familiar black cassock of the Catholic priest. He was not as tall as Tommy and was bulkier through the shoulders, and his hair was already thinning, but no one could have missed the brotherly resemblance between the two men.

"It *is* you," Tommy said. "Does that mean I'm alive?"

He heard his brother's familiar chuckle.

"If you can call what you've been through 'living,' " Mario said, "then you're alive."

Tommy considered that for a moment before speaking.

"Mama. Papa," he said. "Do they know what's happened to me?"

Mario shook his head. "They don't know, Tommy," he said.

"Oh, Mario. I'm so ashamed of myself." He began to cry.

The priest wiped his forehead and eyes with a fresh white cloth until he stopped crying.

"I know," he said. "I know, Tommy. Now the hard part starts."

Tommy stopped crying. He glared at his brother with a rapidly welling hatred.

" 'Hard part'? And just what the hell do you think this has been? A vacation? 'Hard part'? Don't start preaching at me about saving my soul, you high-and-mighty son of a bitch," he shouted. "What do you know about it? Get out of here and leave me alone. You're no brother of mine."

The priest stood next to his brother's bed, looking as if he wanted to speak, but he kept his silence, turned, and walked from the room.

Tommy closed his eyes but heard the sound of his brother's shoes thudding on the floor. Priest's shoes, Tommy thought, with cheap rubber heels that would last till the Second Coming of Christ.

But as the sound faded away, he opened his eyes and realized his brother had done nothing wrong. He called out Mario's name, and when there was no answer, he began screaming curses, and when that did no good, he began crying. He cried himself to sleep. When he woke up again, Mario was there.

"I'm sorry," Tommy said. "I'm really sorry that I'm a dope addict. More than you can know."

"I know," Mario said. "I know, Tommy. And there's more to come."

Tommy held his temper this time.

"He doesn't know," another voice said. "We haven't had a chance to talk."

Tommy turned to the new speaker, Doctor Singer, who stood in the open doorway.

"Good morning, sir," Tommy said. He felt tongue-tied, at a loss for words, and blurted out, "I'm sorry if I vomited on you. Did it really happen? I'm sort of confused."

Singer laughed. "It happened, but forget it, Marine. It goes with the job. And it's not morning anymore. It's afternoon."

"It feels like morning to me," Tommy said. He turned to his brother. "You've been here a long time?"

The priest looked toward Doctor Singer before nodding. "On and off, since just after you were injured."

"Why don't I remember?" Tommy asked. "I don't remember seeing you."

"There's a lot you won't remember," Singer said. "That's normal."

Mario held his brother's hand. "And I've been here the whole last week."

"Why didn't you come in and help me?"

The priest smiled. "He wouldn't let me," he said, nodding toward the doctor. Tommy turned to look at him.

"You had to beat it on your own," Singer said. "No help, no crutches."

"Did I beat it? Is it over?"

"For now."

"Excuse me, sir," Tommy said quickly, "but what does that mean, 'for now'?"

"You've broken the chemical dependency," Singer said calmly, "but remember, deep inside yourself, you're a morphine addict. You always will be. Now you didn't get that way because of your own decisions. We did it to you. So I think you can stay free of the stuff. If you want to. A lot of people can't."

"I want to," Tommy said.

"Well, that's a start." The doctor turned his gaze toward the priest. "I understand you're willing to take him under your wing for the next six months."

Mario nodded.

"And you used to be a boxer?"

"Yes."

"Good. You can slap him around if he needs it."

Mario smiled. "I always could," he said.

"Not on your best day," Tommy grumbled with a grin of his own.

"You've made those arrangements we talked about?" Singer asked the priest.

"I have."

"Good, Padre. Good. Come by my office later. I'll have his discharge papers all ready for you."

Singer turned toward the door.

"Doctor? One question?" Tommy said.

"Yes."

"Where am I?"

"You're still in France, Sergeant. A U.S. Army hospital. But you're going back to the States."

"Sergeant?" Tommy said. "I'm a private."

"You were promoted."

Tommy looked toward his brother. "Two sergeants in one family." He saw the doctor's puzzled look. "My father," he said. "A police sergeant."

"I was a chaplain captain," Mario said. "I outrank both of you."

Tommy laughed heartily for the first time in months that he could remember. "Tell that to Papa," he said.

NILO SESTA STOOD for a moment, looking down at the bodies of the two Selvini brothers, surprised at the quantity of blood that poured from their bodies, streaming now, forming a puddle halfway across the alley.

Nobody could ever pay him back for what had happened to him on the *tonnara* boat, but Fredo and the Selvinis had made a down payment.

Above him, Nilo heard a wooden window shutter open slowly. He looked up at the window, saw an old woman there, and smiled. Soon, very soon, everyone in Castellammare del Golfo would know what had been done and who had done it. Everyone would know except the police, because no one would speak to them about it.

He thought for a moment about urinating on the men's bodies.

That will make me as much an animal as they. And they are not worthy of my urine. He reached into the pockets of their loose-fitting pants, but neither man had any money.

Cradling all three shotguns in one arm, he walked quickly, almost defiantly, across the street, through the front door of his home.

NILO WAS TRYING TO CONSOLE his mother when his father came home, obviously summoned from his job in the nearby stone quarry, because it was still the middle of the afternoon.

The old man drew his son into another room, where Nilo told him all that had happened.

The old man nodded, then said, "You must flee. You must leave right away and go somewhere else to seek your fortune. If you do not, you will be killed. No matter how just your reasons, the law of the feud demands that you die."

"Yes, Papa," Nilo said, his spirits momentarily crushed. "But how? Where will I go?"

His father said, "To America. We have family there. Your mother's brother has a good job in New York City. They will help."

Nilo nodded. He had been hearing about his uncle Tony for as long as he could remember. Occasionally, Uncle Tony even sent them a little money.

"Hide in the cellar," his father told him. "I will return shortly."

Nilo knew better than to ask questions. He took one

of the shotguns and went down into the dirt-walled room while his father scurried from the house.

Just an hour later, he was following the old man out the front door of the house. The bodies, he saw, had already been removed. Father and son hurried down the alley, then turned up toward the rocky headland that skirted the beach west of town.

It was a hard walk, scrambling over hills much of the time. Nilo carried with him an old basket his mother had prepared, filled with his meager wardrobe: two pairs of pants and three rough work shirts.

They walked briskly, passing long lines of high stone walls that seemed to have been built for no purpose. Finally they reached a clearing, and up ahead Nilo saw a pink palazzo sheltered on one side and on the rear by steep overhanging cliffs.

The elder Sesta stopped and looked his boy over. Finally, he nodded. "You are wrinkled but presentable. Fortunately, you have not blood on you."

He hesitated, then held his son's shoulders. Already, Nilo was taller than he. "You look every inch a man," the father said gently.

"I feel that way, too, Papa," Nilo said. "Who have we come to see?"

"A big man. Don Salvatore Maranzano. I did him a favor once. He will protect you."

"Is he of the Mafia, Papa?"

"Such things are the gossip of women. It is enough to know that he is powerful here and he is powerful in the United States."

Without warning, his father pulled the boy to him and kissed him sadly.

"I have never been much of a father to you," he said. "Some men, sometimes . . . fatherhood is not . . ." He hesitated, seemingly unable to get out the words he wanted to say. Nilo saw that the man's eyes were wet, and he fought back tears himself.

"Don't cry, Papa. I will come back."

He saw disbelief in his father's eyes.

"Or better yet, Papa, you and Mama—you will come to America and live with me. I will be very rich and very famous. You will see. Then you can come and live with me in *my* palazzo."

His father smiled. "I wish that for you, Danilo. I wish that for you with all my heart."

IN THE GATHERING GLOOM OF NIGHT, the palazzo looked like an old relic, but up close, it was obvious to Nilo that it had been immaculately maintained by a sensitive, loving hand.

A rough-looking servant must have been waiting for Nilo and his father to arrive, for they had only to rap once on the door before it swung open for them.

The servant led them along a cloistered walkway, around a central courtyard filled with heady-smelling flowers, and into a large, sparsely furnished room. The room glowed with the light of hundreds of candles. Along the walls were original oil paintings, both large and small, showing scenes from the lives of Jesus and his saints.

To one side was a long, carved, Spanish-style dining table heaped with foods of a variety and richness Nilo had never even dreamed of before, and seated at the table were two people: a woman who was strikingly beautiful, though well past first youth, and a man wearing the simple black cassock of a religious.

The man rose to greet them. To Nilo, he looked about fifty. He was handsome and his expression was pleasant enough, but he had cautious eyes and thin, tight lips that looked as if they would never knowingly entertain a smile. He nodded respectfully to Nilo's father and then turned to the boy. This must be the powerful Don Salvatore Maranzano, Nilo thought. *But why would a powerful man dress in priest's robes?*

"Nemo est tam fortis quin rei novitate perturbetur," the man said.

Nilo did not understand what had been said or what his response was supposed to be. The man laughed; despite his dour visage, it was a warm, friendly laugh, and Nilo felt heartened. *This man means me no harm.*

"Ah, Nilo," the man said, "I see you do not know the language of our forefathers, the Romans."

"No, sir."

The man smiled. "What I spoke was from the words of Julius Caesar. You have heard of him, I trust?"

"I think so, sir."

From the corner of his eye, Nilo was watching the woman, who seemed to be enjoying her companion's dialogue with the boy. Nilo thought he had never seen a more desirable woman in his life. He wanted to have her, her and the house with all its beauty. He wanted that and to be able to speak of Julius Caesar, too. He was just beginning to realize exactly how many things in life he truly wanted.

And this priest who is not a priest has them all, he thought. *So why not me? Perhaps without wanting to, Fredo and the Selvini brothers have done me a favor. I hope it is so. That will be even better than pissing on their dead bodies.*

"It is from Caesar's book of war commentaries," the man said. "Caesar says: 'No one is so courageous as not to be upset by an unexpected turn of events.' What do you think of that?"

Nilo hesitated and glanced toward his father, who was standing off to the side, uncomfortably twisting his hat in his hands.

"Go ahead, boy; speak," the man said.

"Well, sir," Nilo said, "it seems just like common sense. Unless it means something I don't understand."

"What it means is that you should not feel bad about being afraid right now. That fear will pass."

"But I am not afraid, sir," Nilo said.

"No. I guess you're not." The man laughed yet again, then turned to the elder Sesta.

"You have done a good job of raising the boy," he said. "I am in your debt. Danilo will stay here with me tonight. Tomorrow he shall start on his journey."

Nilo's father hesitated, and the man in the priest's robe said soothingly, "Do not worry yourself. He will be among his kind. I myself am returning to New York soon and I will look after the fortunes of all us Castellammarese. You may count on it."

"Yes, Don Salvatore," the old man said. He came forward and put his arms around his son.

"Live a good life, boy," he said.

"I will, Papa. I will be very good," Nilo said.

Don Salvatore Maranzano laughed again.

A warm spring breeze blew through the open windows.

• *In New York City, Ignazio Saietta was beginning to dream great dreams. For more than twenty years, working under the name of "Lupo the Wolf," he had been squeezing money under threat of violence from Italian immigrants in the city, and his Black Hand extortion racket had become the city's most profitable. This was because Lupo had earned his reputation as one of the most bloodthirsty killers in city history, and police one day would find in his stable at 323 East 107th Street the bodies of sixty people, murdered by Lupo when they would not pay up.*

For the last few years, Lupo had been expanding his business into loan-sharking, prostitution, hijacking, and robbery, but his big intellectual moment came in 1919 when he decided that counterfeiting would be an even easier way to make money than extortion was.

The Secret Service caught him, and Lupo was sentenced to thirty years in prison. Control of his rackets passed into the hands of one of his chief lieutenants, Giuseppe Masseria, a chubby, cherubic-looking man whose innocent appearance masked the fact that he was as cold-blooded a killer as Lupo ever was. As "Joe the Boss," Masseria quickly became New York City's crime overlord. Anyone foolish enough to oppose him was left dead in the streets.

- *The Eighteenth Amendment to the Constitution prohibiting the manufacture or sale of alcohol in the United States was approved.*
- *The best-selling book in America was* The Four Horsemen of the Apocalypse.

CHAPTER 2

Winter 1919–1920

Standing on the deck of the rusting old steamer, Nilo stared down at the fog-dappled pier below him and shivered. It was Christmas, but back home the holidays were mild and bright and sunny, and here in New York there was only cold and darkness. He shivered again. Despite the heavy Melton peacoat he wore, he was not used to the chill and doubted if he ever would be.

I'd better learn. This place is my home from now on.

He shivered again, this time not so much from the wild and bitter December wind as from excitement. Thirty feet below him the New World began—his new world, at least. He began pacing back and forth on the wooden deck, beating himself with his arms, trying to keep warm.

"Getting anxious?" a voice asked from the darkness behind him.

Nilo turned quickly. Despite all the thousands of miles he had come from Castellammare, he had not gotten the fear of reprisal out of his head. He still jumped at every shadow, winced at every unexpected noise.

He relaxed when he saw Rocco. Unlike most of the crew, who were Sicilian and therefore, in Nilo's mind, potential allies of the devil, Rocco was an easygoing young man from Naples, slow to anger, quick to laugh.

"A little bit," Nilo admitted. "I've been waiting up here for permission to go ashore."

"And when you do, it's good-bye to the ship, eh?"

Nilo shrugged.

"If you're leaving anyway, why wait for permission?" Rocco asked. "Why not just leave and be done with it?"

Nilo shrugged again. He had told Don Salvatore Maranzano—he of the priest's cassock and the magnificent palazzo—that he would work on one of his ships to pay his passage to New York and that he would obey the rules and keep his nose clean once he got there. Don Salvatore said he had helped many to go to America, many who might not be permitted to enter if they had had to pass through formal immigration control . . . even many who were on the run from the law in their own countries. And not one of them had been caught, Don Salvatore preached, just so long as they had followed his advice. As for those who had not followed his advice? Don Salvatore had just elaborately extended his hands, palms up, by way of explanation.

Not from fear but out of common sense, Nilo had decided he would wait for permission to leave the ship.

"I'll wait," he told the other man.

"You are a strange one, Nilo," the other man said, and put an arm around Nilo's shoulder. Nilo cringed and Rocco laughed.

"You see? Three nights we have made love, yes? And now? Now you do not even wish to speak to me, yes?"

Nilo did not answer immediately. His eyes were still cast down below toward the dock, toward New York City, toward his new world. He had boarded the ship in Naples, coasted along the Mediterranean, then east through Suez to India and Shanghai and Japan, then east across the Pacific and through the Panama Canal to Havana and now to New York. He had traveled farther and seen more than he would have thought possible a year before.

During the voyage, many men on the ship had looked at Nilo with lustful eyes, but Rocco had made it clear that Nilo was under his protection and the other men had left him alone. Nilo had expected that there would be a price to pay for this, and there was. He and Rocco had made love. He had thought he would never do that with a man, not after what had happened on the *tonnara*. But where there was no violence, it was not so bad. And when a man was shut away from women for weeks, months without end—then what other choice was there? Men needed sex. It was best with women, but if not—well, sometimes it was necessary. Especially when it provided Nilo with protection from those who would treat him like an animal.

He heard Rocco laugh again.

"Do not worry, my friend," he said. "What happens between sailors does not count on shore. It has always been so. Besides, it was a very long voyage."

Nilo had another reason for hoping to depart the ship soon. During the long months of the voyage, he had carefully watched at night to learn where the other sailors hid their money while they were on duty, and just an hour ago he had sneaked through the bunkroom, stealing a little bit from every sailor's pile. All told, he had lifted almost $150, although none of it from Rocco. By the time the sailors found out about it, he wanted to be long gone.

Rocco said, "I have a message for you."

Nilo raised his eyebrows quizzically.

"Mr. Maranzano—Don Salvatore to you—was impressed with your hard work during this voyage." At Nilo's expression of surprise, the older man laughed.

"You wonder, how did he know about your hard work, and the answer is simple. Most simple. I told him. It was my job to keep him informed of your progress, and so I wrote him from every port and told him that you were doing very well."

"Why should he care about me?" Nilo asked.

Rocco put his arm on Nilo's shoulder once again; this time Nilo did not cringe.

"Maybe he's just kind. Anyway, he said to give you this if you survived the voyage," Rocco said, and handed Nilo a small folded piece of cardboard. "It is the address of his New York City office. I believe he sells real estate, among other things. He said that when you need work or advice or money to call him. He knows how hard it is to get started in New York. Especially if you're Sicilian."

Nilo jammed the cardboard into his pocket and murmured his thanks.

"Good. Now the news you've been waiting for. The captain says you are finished on this ship. Free to go. Welcome to America."

Nilo stood uncertainly for a moment, not sure what to do next. Then he mumbled a quick thank-you and hurried below deck to gather up his seabag. But when he came back onto the deck, Rocco was still there.

"Do you know where you are going?" he asked.

"I have an address," Nilo said.

"Ah, but you cannot read, can you? Not even a simple address. Is that not right?"

For a moment Nilo considered lying and then told the truth.

"No," he said. "Not English. I cannot read. Or write."

"You Sicilians are all alike," Rocco said with a laugh. "Then how will you get where you are going?" Rocco demanded. "Have you ever been in New York before?"

"No. But I thought I would take a taxi. Taxi drivers can read. They know New York. They will take me where I want to go."

"Of course they will. After they swindle you out of every penny you have somehow gathered up."

"I wouldn't let them do that," Nilo said in a flat voice.

Rocco studied him for a moment. Nilo was just nineteen and still almost pretty, even though six months of hard work and regular eating at sea had packed meat and muscle onto his bones.

"No, I guess you wouldn't," Rocco said finally. He pulled a massive old pocket watch from his peacoat and looked at it.

"Listen, boy, I've got some time, so let me help. I'll get you to your address. It will be my welcome-to-America Christmas present for you."

Despite the freezing weather, Rocco insisted upon walking so Nilo could get a look at his new city, and it took more than an hour before they turned off Spring Street and down Crosby.

Nilo was amazed at how many people were out in the street. In Sicily, after dark, only criminals and ghosts could feel at home in the narrow streets.

Rocco watched the building numbers closely, and when they reached the corner of Broome Street he pointed at a redbrick building of four stories that housed a grocery and a barbershop on the ground floor.

"You are here," Rocco said.

"Thank you," Nilo answered. "I hope I see you again."

"You never will," Rocco answered. "I am just a simple sailor whose life is at sea. But I'm sure I will hear of you. Merry Christmas."

As Rocco walked quickly away, Nilo went into the building, hoisted his seabag on his shoulder, and started up the stairs. The apartment he wanted was on the top floor. Throughout the building, he could hear people singing and instruments playing and the smell of food cooking and loud laughter. Women's laughter. Nilo suddenly felt very homesick. He took a deep breath, then knocked, loud and long.

The door opened slowly, and a tired, happy-looking man who appeared to be in his mid-forties looked out. In the room behind him, Nilo could see an enormous Christmas tree, gaily decorated and lit with flickering live candles. He had never seen a Christmas tree before, and he stared at it until the man cleared his throat and Nilo looked back at him. The man's eyes seemed familiar to Nilo, but the thick muscular shoulders, discernible under his heavily starched white shirt, gave the impression of a man not to be trifled with. The pleasant look on his face had also seemed to fade, as if he had been expecting someone else and did not bother to hide his disappointment at seeing Nilo.

"Excuse me for intruding," the young man said quickly in his Sicilian dialect. "I am looking for Anthony Falcone."

"And who wants him?" the man demanded. He seemed to reach behind the door for something. There was a mirror at the end of the long entryway to the apartment, and in it Nilo could see the man put his hand on a revolver that hung from a holster draped over a strange-looking piece of furniture. It did not surprise Nilo; in his hometown, doors were often answered gun in hand.

"I do," he answered crisply.

"And who are you?"

"I am the son of his younger sister, Maria," Nilo said.

The man at the door looked at Nilo hard for a few long seconds, then said softly, "I'll be damned." He shouted aloud over his shoulder, "Hey, it's little Danilo, all grown up and come to America," and then stepped forward to embrace his nephew.

IT WAS AS IF THEY HAD BEEN EXPECTING him and planned a party for his arrival, Nilo thought later. His uncle Tony ushered him into a large kitchen, where a big metal-topped table had been set with five places and platters were heaped with food.

He was introduced to his aunt Anna and then his cousin Justina. They both looked disappointed, too, although in the case of Justina it was harder to discern, since she was simply the most beautiful girl Nilo had ever seen and disappointment did not rest naturally on her face. She was probably a little younger than Nilo and dressed in a long skirt and white blouse that did nothing to hide her bosom. While his aunt Anna hugged and fussed over him, Nilo had trouble taking his eyes off Justina, who sat watching him. She had light skin and wide-set green eyes. She seemed to measure him with interest but glanced down shyly at the table whenever their eyes happened to meet.

"I am sorry," Nilo told his aunt, gesturing around the kitchen. "I have interrupted you."

"Nonsense," his uncle said. "We've always got room at *this* inn," then led him into a bedroom, showed him a closet where he could hang his clothes and a bathroom where he could wash up.

"Take your time," Uncle Tony said. "We'll hold supper for you." Nilo felt better after he had washed up and changed into clean clothes, but he was taken aback when he reentered the kitchen and saw a priest sitting with the rest of the family at the table. The priest was a burly young man with large, meaty hands. His hair was already thinning, even though he could not yet be thirty years of age.

Nilo had grown up regarding priests as part of the official government and therefore not totally to be trusted. *Why is he here? Have they called him in to question me, to find out if I am really Danilo Sesta?*

He nodded uncomfortably toward the man in the clerical collar, but the man bounded to his feet, came to Nilo, and threw his arm around him. Nilo's discomfort must have been obvious, because he could see a broad smile cross Justina's beautiful face.

The smile annoyed him. *She is looking at me as if I were not a man but a child. And I am clearly older than she is.*

"Father, I . . ."

"Forget 'Father.' I am your cousin, Mario," the priest answered. "And I am starved after serving Mass all day and all night. So sit down and let us eat before the food gets cold and Mama tells us it is all spoiled."

After months of eating unappetizing shipboard gruel, Nilo found the meal a feast beyond imagining. At first he was uncomfortable, eating in the presence of a priest, but Father Mario, who waved a drumstick around in one hand to punctuate his conversation—which seemed oddly to concern itself mostly with professional prizefighting— put him quickly at ease. Especially when he pulled Nilo up from the table and helped him arrange his fists in a boxing position, then demonstrated for his father, Nilo's uncle Tony, a devastating left-right combination to Nilo's stomach, which had apparently decked some hapless pugilist somewhere. Even though the priest pulled his punches and did not really hit him, Nilo was surprised and a little shocked at the display. He learned only later in the dinner that Father Mario, before taking the vows of priesthood, had been a boxer of some local renown, even winning eight professional prizefights. Apparently, at the nearby church where he was assigned, he had begun a boxing team for local boys.

"Fighting? In church?" Nilo asked with surprise.

"See, Papa?" Mario said. "That's what the monsignor thinks, too. But I think if I can get the kids to fight inside a ring, maybe I can cut down the amount they'll be fighting in the streets."

"Good luck," the priest's father said, with a dismissive wave of his hand. "Most of those mugs are Irishers. They'll be fighting in the street anyway. Irishmen were born brawling in the streets."

"That's the trouble with you, Papa. You're stuck in the old ways of thinking. Wake up. In a couple of days, this'll be the 1920s." He looked back toward Nilo. "I might get you over there to the church, too," the priest said. "You look to me like you might be able to handle yourself pretty well."

Nilo blushed. As he mumbled a response, Mario asked, "You ever fight?"

Not unless you count the three men I killed before leaving home, Nilo thought, but answered instead with a simple shake of his head.

"Well, plenty of time to learn," Father Mario said. "I taught my brother Tommy; I can teach you."

"Will you all leave the boy alone?" Aunt Anna said. "All this talk of fighting. It's like living with gladiators. Stop talking. Eat, eat."

After sitting with the family for a while, Nilo figured out the reason for their disappointment. Apparently, the Falcones' other son, Tommy, who had been injured in the war, was expected home any day, and when they heard

Nilo's knock on the door they had hoped, although without real expectation, that Tommy had returned early in time for the holiday.

For his part, surrounded by the warmth of a family for perhaps the first time in his life, Nilo spoke of his boyhood in Sicily. He was amused to learn that Justina's command of Italian was spotty, and Father Mario and the Falcone parents served as translators so the two young people knew what each other was talking about.

He did not tell them the real reason for his leaving home, commenting only that he thought it was time for him to get out into the world. When later in the dinner he found out that Tony Falcone was a New York policeman—which explained the gun hanging in the hallway—he knew he had acted wisely in keeping his secrets to himself.

After they had eaten and drunk wine and dark Italian coffee and then more wine, they all went inside to the living room, where Tony Falcone lit even more candles on the ceiling-high Christmas tree that took up half the room. When Nilo sat on the sofa, Justina shyly approached him and handed him a gift-wrapped box.

Her smile lit her face and his heart. "For you," she said. "For Christmas. From all of us."

"But . . . I have nothing for any of you."

"You're here. That's gift enough for Italians. We're big on family," Father Mario said heartily.

"Open it, open it," Justina insisted.

Nilo opened the box. Inside was a white shirt and a dark blue tie. It was the first dress shirt and tie he had ever owned.

"I don't know what to say. You did not even know I was coming." He looked around at all of them. His uncle Tony said, "We really bought it for Tommy. But we'll get him another one."

"Oh, Papa," Justina said. "You take all the fun out of it." She looked at Nilo for support, but he only shook his head.

"No," he said. "It's all fun."

Near midnight, when Father Mario was getting ready to leave, Nilo asked if they knew a nearby hotel or place where he could rent a room, but his aunt and uncle would have none of it.

"I have money," he insisted.

"Good," Aunt Anna said. "Hang on to it; you'll need it."

"You have money," said Tony, "but we have room. What kind of family are we if we turn you out into the street?"

"You can stay in Tommy's room," Justina said, and her father added, "And when Tommy gets home, then we'll see how things work out."

LATER, NILO LAY IN TOMMY FALCONE'S BED, exulting in the silence. He had been aboard ship so long that the drone of the ship's powerful engines was a constant, day and night, and the ear became so adapted to it that the mind eventually forgot to recognize it as noise. But here now, it was like being back in Sicily. The apartment was still, and from the street below, at this early morning hour, came not a sound. He could hear his own breathing, and that realization brought a smile to his face.

America, he had decided, was a wonderful country. His uncle was a simple policeman, but he lived like a king, wearing a suit, with a priest in the family, living in an apartment that had three bedrooms. No one in Sicily, save for the Mafia and the politicians, lived like that.

It is what I will do. I will become the best of Americans and I will be rich and honored like my uncle Tony.

He wanted to dwell on that, to roll around in his mind the thought of how well the New York Falcones lived, but he was very tired. And besides, it was difficult to think of anything else except Justina. The thought that she was now in her own room, lying in a bed only a scant few feet from him, almost made him ache with anticipation.

Maybe she is awake, too, thinking of me. Someday, someday . . .

He could not finish the thought; it would have been ungrateful to his uncle. He fell asleep and dreamed of her.

IN EXPECTATION OF HIS SON'S RETURN home, Tony Falcone had arranged with other detectives to cover his shifts so he was off for the entire week between Christmas and New Year's. Justina was also on vacation from school, so the two of them were free to act as Nilo's guides to New York City.

For two busy days, the three of them traveled around their neighborhood and the rest of the city, showing Nilo the landmarks, the Statue of Liberty, Chinatown, Greenwich Village, Madison Square Garden, Central Park, even a tour of Tony's police precinct. Aunt Anna was dutifully invited to join them on their outings but regularly refused. She seemed always to have something to do, either in the kitchen or at the neighborhood parish.

They were two days of wonderment for Nilo. He had known the United States was big, but until he saw the buildings of New York City he had not realized just how big it was or just how far he had come from his little hometown in Sicily. He also savored the opportunity to be near Justina—in fact, often wishing that Uncle Tony might find something else to do so the two young people could spend some time alone, but that clearly was not to be. Still, they were two wonderful days.

On the third day, Tommy Falcone returned home.

FROM WHAT HE HAD BEEN TOLD about Tommy's wounds, Nilo had expected some kind of crippled war veteran, but the young man he met looked the picture of health. He was a little older than Nilo and a little bigger, and like everyone else in the family he seemed sincerely happy to meet a relative from the old country. While neighbors kept streaming into the Falcone apartment to welcome Tommy home from the war, his American cousin always took pains to make sure that Nilo was not left out and was always included as part of the Falcone family.

This is what it must be like to have an older brother, Nilo thought. *And it would be hard to find a better one.*

Or a better family than the Falcones, for that matter. While they celebrated Tommy's return home, they never forgot Nilo, the guest in their house.

After a couple of days rest, Tommy took over the tour-guide duties from his father and Justina, and while they had shown Nilo the tourist attractions, Tommy promised to show the young Sicilian "the real city." He walked Nilo around lower Manhattan and pointed out the railroad yards where as a young boy he stole coal, the piers where the neighborhood kids would go to smoke cigarettes and not be found out, and where they would cool off by illegally swimming in the polluted river.

Not too far from the Falcones' apartment, he showed Nilo a neighborhood that even to the foreigner's eye was clearly a decrepit, dangerous slum.

"People live here?"

"And die," Tommy answered. "This is the Five Points. For a hundred years, the worst spot in the city. When my father was a rookie cop, he used to patrol here."

"Rookie?" Nilo said.

"Young. A beginner. Like you. You're a rookie American," Tommy said with a grin. "Everything here was crooked. There were almost three hundred saloons and more whorehouses and dance halls than that. The whole place was run by the most vicious gangs in New York."

"And now?"

"Now it looks a little better. From what I hear, the mobs around here are dying out because there's not that much business for them. But I still wouldn't want to live here." He looked around. "When we were kids, we used to come over, just to watch the weird drunks and women and just the general filth."

He stopped and pointed to an empty lot down the block. "There used to be a brewery there. It made beer once and then they closed it down, I guess because it was too filthy. So they made it into a tenement, and the police said that they figure five thousand people were killed inside the building over the years. The cops used to have to go in forty or fifty strong or they'd never come out alive. When they got ready to tear it down, they forced everybody out of the building. Some of the kids who came out had never been out of the building before. They were afraid of the sunlight 'cause they'd never seen the sun."

"You are making a joke with me, aren't you?"

"No, Nilo, I'm not. That's the way it was. Things are better now. They get better all the time."

"I hope so," Nilo said grimly. "You make living in America sound like being in hell."

They wandered together over to Father Mario's church

in Greenwich Village and found the young priest in a large basement recreation room that had been outfitted with a boxing ring. Stripped to an undershirt and priestly black pants, he was in the ring, a heavily muscled formidable figure wearing boxing gloves and showing a half-dozen awkward looking young teenagers the way to move around the ring.

"Hey, Tommy," he called out. "Nilo." He beckoned them forward to the boxing ring and told the boys, "This is my kid brother, Tommy. He used to be a punk just like all of you. And the good-looking one's my cousin, Nilo."

He looked down from the ring and grinned. "What say, Tommy? You remember anything I taught you?"

"How could I forget? You pounded it into my head hard enough."

The priest beckoned him up to the ring. "Well, come on, then. Let's give these kids an exhibition." He kicked a pair of boxing gloves from the ring in his brother's direction.

"I don't know," Tommy said.

"Afraid?" The priest was grinning.

"I just don't want all those young guys to find out what a sissy their priest really is," Tommy answered.

Father Mario turned away and faced the teenagers, who were clustered in a corner of the ring. When he did, Tommy slipped off his heavy coat, pulled on the boxing gloves, and nodded for Nilo to tie the laces.

Nilo heard Mario talking to the boys. "My brother here was a big war hero. When the Germans found out he was coming to Europe, they all started throwing their guns away and surrendering. But some of them were too slow, and he managed to kill ten thousand of them with his bare hands before they declared the armistice. But I guess he left all his fight over there. Or somewhere else."

By the time Father Mario finished his sarcastic speech, Tommy was in the ring. He stepped behind the priest and touched him on the shoulder. When the priest turned, Tommy tapped him on the nose and with a big grin said, "Bang. You're dead."

Nilo watched in growing wonder as the two brothers lit into each other. The teenagers stepped out onto the ring apron to get out of their way. Tommy was taller and faster than Mario, but the stocky priest was clearly more skilled. He just kept boring ahead, flicking away Tommy's left jab with a slap of a glove, or taking the punches on his shoulders. Inside close, he worked over Tommy's midsection with flurries of punches that drew a pained grunt from Tommy each time one landed cleanly.

It looked as if they were killing each other, and Nilo glanced toward the teenagers, hoping one of them would jump into the ring and break up the fight. But no one moved, and finally Nilo, while feeling very much the outsider, clambered up onto the ring apron to get ready to try to separate the fighters. Mario was hurting Tommy. Nilo's hand closed over the knife in his pocket. If he had to, he would use it to scare the priest off.

But before he could make a move, Tommy yelled, "Enough, enough, you maniac," and both fighters dropped their guards, tossed their arms about each other in warm hugs, and began laughing aloud.

They're laughing, Nilo thought. *Back home, a fight like this, even between brothers, would start a blood feud that could last for generations. And these two crazies are laughing about it.*

"You're still pretty fast," the priest told his brother. "But you're out of shape."

"And you still move like a truck," Tommy said. Rubbing his jaw, he added, "And hit like one."

Mario grinned and then hugged his brother again. "I'm glad you're home, Tommy."

"You have a peculiar way of showing it." He paused a moment and leaned closer to his brother so he could speak softly. "We're going to go get a beer. You want to come with us?"

Mario shook his head. "I'd better not," he said. "The collar and all, you know. A lot of the parish thinks I'm punch-drunk already. Find me in a tavern swilling beer and that'd be the last straw. But go ahead. Have a good time. I'll see you at dinner Sunday." He nodded toward Nilo, then turned back to the younger fighters.

"I taught him all he knows," Nilo heard him say. "And if you do what I say, you'll be that good and even better. Now all of you get back here in the ring."

WHEN THEY WALKED AWAY from the church, Tommy coughed and Nilo saw him grimace in pain and clutch his right side. That was where Tommy had been wounded, the family had told him.

"Are you all right?" Nilo asked.

"Yeah. Just a little sore. A beer will help."

"Your brother should not have hit you that way."

Tommy laughed. "He didn't hit me at all. He was pulling all his punches. If he had hit me all out, just once, he would've killed me. We were just putting on a show to impress those kids."

Nilo did not mention that he had been among those who were impressed.

A few blocks away from the Falcone apartment, Tommy led the way into a small, neat corner tavern. In Sicily, Nilo had never been in a tavern. He was too young, and besides, taverns were not common. Most Italians preferred to drink at home, and only occasionally did someone drink too much wine at an inn or a restaurant or social club. But Nilo had visited many with the other sailors when his cargo ship had stopped in port, and he had developed a liking for beer. Even though the weather was cold, a beer would taste good right now, he decided.

It was early in the day and the tavern was almost empty. The bartender was obviously a friend of the Falcones, because he greeted Tommy with a grinning "Hey, war hero." Then he said, "Now what are you boys doing here? You know you're not old enough to drink. You could fake it, Tommy, but he's not even close." He pointed toward Nilo.

"I won't tell if you don't," Tommy responded. "And besides, what are they going to do? Pull your license?"

"Ah, yes. Prohibition. The law of the land. It does embolden a man to break the law. Drink hearty, boys," he said as he poured them two beers from the spigot behind the bar.

"What is this Prohibition?" Nilo asked Tommy.

"A new law. In a few days, there will be no more taverns, no more places like this. No one will be allowed to manufacture or sell liquor."

"Not even wine?"

"No. No wine."

"In the whole country?" Nilo asked.

Tommy nodded.

"That is a stupid law," Nilo said. "In Sicily, such a law would just be ignored."

"A lot of laws are stupid. But here we obey them anyway. And a good thing, too. It's how I want to make my living someday."

"Explain, please."

"A lawyer. I want to become a lawyer."

"Good. You will be a very good lawyer," Nilo said. "Will you be a lawyer soon?"

"Whoa. Hold on there. It may be a long time. More likely never."

"Why?"

"Law school costs money. A lot of money. And I don't have any."

"Uncle Tony?"

Tommy shook his head. "He's just a cop. He's got no money. And if he did, he'd have to spend it on school for Justina."

"And so you . . . what . . . ?"

"I'll get a job, I guess. And if I can, I'll try to save enough money to get to law school."

Nilo scowled as he looked into the bottom of his empty beer glass. "Some things in America are very strange."

"What do you mean?"

"You showed me where that old brewery was where people were allowed to kill each other for years and years. But nobody will be allowed to use it to make wine. And you, you go off to fight in a war for them and you get shot and hurt, and now you are home and your country does not say, 'Tommy, we will send you to law school.' They are ungrateful." He hunched his shoulders in an exaggerated shrug, turning his hands palms up, as he had seen Maranzano do, as if imploring God to provide even a little bit of justice. "But what do you expect from a country whose people obey the laws even when they know they are stupid?"

Tommy signaled the bartender for two more beers. "But that's the way things are," he said, "and you've just got to learn to live with it."

"I will try," Nilo vowed. "I will try to be the best American there ever was. But I don't know if I can ever learn such stupidity." He saw the bartender coming and reached into his pocket for money, but Tommy was quicker. Then Tommy waited until the bartender had placed the fresh beers before them, before leaning close to his cousin and talking softly in his ear.

"Speaking of learning and stupid laws," he said. "You're doing well on learning to speak English, but you have to work very hard at it."

When Nilo looked at him quizzically, Tommy said, "Because you're in this country illegally, and the sooner you learn to look and sound like an American, the less chance you have of getting thrown out of the country."

"If I apply to become the citizen?"

"Maybe the government will let you in. And maybe it won't. You're best off not taking the chance. Just be here. Be an American. Be a member of the family. Whoever has to know different?"

Nilo smiled. "Your brother. I will be your brother. As Father Mario calls you, you may call me. If the world asks, I am Nilo, kid brother, great American."

Tommy Falcone pondered the idea for a moment, then put an affectionate arm around his cousin's shoulders.

"Brothers," he said. "Why not?"

Nilo took his knife from his pocket and with practiced hands snapped it open. Without hesitation, he pierced the tip of his index finger and then reached out for Tommy's hand. Tommy winced but let himself be cut. Then Nilo pressed their two bloody fingers together, even as he flipped the knife closed with one hand and put it back into his pocket.

"There," he said. "Now we are blood."

"Good enough," Tommy said. "But learn your English anyway. Papa's looking for a job for you, and it'd help if you could speak the language."

Nilo seemed not to be listening. "Brothers," he said again. "You and me. Until the end."

IT HAD BEEN A QUIET TOUR OF DUTY, but even though his detective partner, Tim O'Shaughnessy, had been looking longingly at the exit door for more than an hour, Tony Falcone would not leave the precinct until the exact moment their shift ended.

"If you are not the worst pain in the ass in the entire world, I'd hate to meet the one who is," O'Shaughnessy grumbled.

Tony stood up and put on his hat and coat. "Just being honest with the citizens who pay our salary," he said.

"Save it for Saint Peter. Let's get out of here."

The two men walked down the steps of the precinct, out into the cold January night. They were a study in contrasts. Falcone was medium height and, although he was muscular, he appeared almost frail next to O'Shaughnessy, who was a huge man, more than six feet five and weighing close to three hundred pounds. Falcone was dark and seemed always to be scowling—a look caused more by his nearsightedness and his vain refusal to wear eyeglasses than by any surliness of character. O'Shaughnessy was blotchy red-faced with the pre-alcoholic road map of capillaries crisscrossing his face, which was almost always set into a smile—a deceptive grin that masked a violent fury of a temper. They had been partners for ten years, ever since the Irishman had been assigned to the precinct.

They followed a well-worn path over to Broome Street, where Mike Mercer had run a tavern since before Falcone had joined the force almost a quarter of a century earlier.

Falcone was surprised that the streets were so quiet. Prohibition was about to become the law of the land; it was America's last legal drinking day, and he had thought that all the lushes in the city would be loading up one last time.

The previous day he had read a story in the newspaper, reporting on a speech made by the Rev. Billy Sunday in Norfolk, Virginia. Someone had held a mock funeral for John Barleycorn, and the Rev. Sunday said, "Goodbye, John. You were God's worst enemy. You were hell's best friend. The reign of tears is over."

Maybe Billy Sunday was right, Falcone thought, but only time would tell. He did not see how anyone, not even the Congress, could tell a whole country to stop drinking and expect them to do it.

When they walked into the tavern, Mike Mercer was behind the bar talking to another pair of off-duty detectives. He nodded to Falcone and O'Shaughnessy and, without bothering to ask, poured double shots of Irish whiskey and set them down in front of the cops, along with beer chasers.

"My turn," Falcone said, and began to reach into his pocket for money.

"Don't bother," Mercer said. "It's on the house tonight. My treat."

"It's only just a new year," O'Shaughnessy said. "Not the Second Coming of the Holy Ghost."

"My last night of business," Mercer said.

"This is a bad joke, right?" O'Shaughnessy said. There was a worried look on his face.

"No joke," Mercer said. "I know a lot of people are talking about ignoring it, but I'm going to obey Prohibition. I'm going to shut down for a couple of weeks and go to Florida. When I come back, this old joint will be totally redecorated."

"Redecorated for what?" Falcone asked.

"As a tearoom."

"A what?" O'Shaughnessy sputtered.

"A tearoom," Mercer said, almost defensively. "You know the kind. With all sorts of exotic blends for our regular customers. Blends from Scotland and Ireland and Tennessee and the Caribbean."

"Jumping Jesus," the big Irish cop answered. "And next thing you'll be telling us that there'll be women in here and we won't be able to spit on the floor and you'll not be serving liquor."

"Something like that," Mercer said.

O'Shaughnessy turned his back on the bartender and drained his whiskey. He told his partner, "Did you know, Tony, that in Ireland the Mercers are considered the scum of the earth? Lower than fish shit they are. Their word is worthless, and they would sell their children for an extra helping of English gruel, spilled on the floor for them to lap up. No self-respecting Irishman will have anything to do with anyone named Mercer."

"These last ten years here must have been a terrible burden on you then," Falcone said, winking at the bartender.

"I did it all for you. To keep you out of the clutches of this thieving tea peddler. Aaaah, I can't even bear to be looking at him. Let's get a table."

They brought refills of their drinks to a rear booth, where O'Shaughnessy insisted on clinking shot glasses in a toast.

"To Demon Rum?" Tony asked.

"To hell with Demon Rum. Let him get his own drink. I'm drinking to Tommy," he said. "How is he?"

"He's all right."

"So what's wrong?" When Falcone looked up, O'Shaughnessy said, "I've worked with you for ten years, Tony. I know when you don't like the new brand of tooth powder Anna buys. You think I don't know when something's bothering you?" He paused. In ten years they had saved each other's lives more than once. O'Shaughnessy had even run into a burning building and carried the unconscious Falcone out in his arms. They were as close friends as policemen could be, but here O'Shaughnessy knew he was getting into family business, and policemen were notoriously close-mouthed about family problems.

"Is it Tommy?" he asked. "He's healed, hasn't he?"

"His body has," Falcone said. He sipped slowly at his whiskey.

"Shell shock?" the Irishman ventured.

"That's the story he and Mario are peddling. I'm supposed to believe it. But it's not true."

"Then what?" The other policeman paused. "You don't mean those damn fool doctors got him hooked on drugs."

"That's what they did," Falcone said.

"Jesus H. Christ. How is he?"

"He looks fine. They had to do so much surgical work on his hip and stomach that they had him laying around that Frenchie hospital for a year. "

"I never did understand that."

"Apparently, there was some French surgeon who was the best in the world at this kind of stuff. So they wanted Tommy to stay nearby. No argument from me; physically, he's good as can be expected. But that's when they got him hooked, while he was laying around in pain between all those operations."

"So all this time they've been working on getting him off the drugs?"

"Morphine," Falcone said. "And he's been off it for six months now. We were supposed to think he was still in France, but Mario had him stashed in a convent upstate. He was working as a handyman to get his body back in shape and make sure that he didn't have any way to get any morphine. There sure isn't any in any convent. So now he's back, and maybe it was all for the best, except I'm not supposed to know anything. And I don't like it."

"So your pride is hurt," O'Shaughnessy said.

"What do you mean?"

"You're happy about your boy, but you're upset because your two sons—one of them a priest himself—think that they've pulled the wool over your eyes. Let's face it. You're just annoyed that Tommy and Mario dare to think they're smarter than you."

Falcone sipped at his beer. The Irishman had already finished both his whiskey and his beer and waved to the bartender for a refill.

"You're probably right."

"I'm definitely right. They were just trying to save you hurt. Tommy's healthy, so forget it. What's he going to do now?"

"I don't know. He's talking about going to college. Down with the Jew boys at CCNY, I suppose. I wish I had enough money to send him to a good school like Saint John's, but I don't. And then Justina is graduating from high school and she wants to be an opera singer, and I don't know where she'll get the money for voice lessons. I wish I had it, but I don't."

"Let 'em work for it like everybody else does."

"That's okay for Tommy, I guess. You can always be a lawyer. But Justina's different. You wait too long for voice lessons and by the time you take them, your voice is gone and you can't get it back. It's gonna break her heart if I get her a job in the coat factory."

Uncharacteristically, O'Shaughnessy reached across the table and put his hand atop his partner's. "Tony, there's always money to be made at our job. And with this new Prohibition thing coming in, there'll be fortunes to be made."

Falcone glared at him. "You know how I feel about that crap," he said. Then he recognized O'Shaughnessy's expression and began laughing. "You're just egging me on, you Irish son of a bitch," he said.

"Not me," his partner said. "I like being one of the only two honest cops in New York. Anyway, bring Tommy around some night. I'd like to see him. I remember him when."

"He's different now. Quieter. He's always got his nose in a book."

"He got shot up, for Christ's sake, to help the bloody goddamn Brits keep their goddamn empire," O'Shaughnessy said. "That'd change anybody." He took a deep breath, as if telling himself to change the subject and not mount his usual anti-British soapbox. "And what about this other kid? What's his name? Daniel or something?"

"Danilo. My sister's boy, and he calls himself Nilo now. He's doing okay. He and Tommy get along like brothers. I found him a little job, and he's after Justina to teach him how to read."

"To read, huh?" O'Shaughnessy laughed. "If he's like every other Sicilian I know, he's after her for more than reading lessons."

Falcone nodded. "That had occurred to me. And I wouldn't put it past him. Truth is, Tim, he's my family and all, but I don't like that kid. There's just something about him that sticks in my throat."

"Like what?"

"Like I don't know. He tries too hard, sort of. He's blood . . . but . . . I don't know. He always seems agreeable enough, but if you watch him and he doesn't know you're watching, he's always looking around, as if he's casing the place, trying to figure out where you hide your money. I've taken to locking my cash away in my bureau drawer."

"Hey, what do you want?" O'Shaughnessy said. "He's Italian."

"Go to hell, you big Irish moose."

JUSTINA FALCONE CLIMBED OUT of the claw-foot bathtub and quickly wrapped a large gray towel around her body. High up on the wall above the tub was a little window that was cracked near the top, letting in a constant stream of cold air that dropped to the floor and chilled the legs. Her father always promised to fix it, but he never seemed to get around to it. The truth was he hated doing any kind of maintenance work.

She vowed that one day she would be so rich that she would not ever have to worry about things like cracked windows.

She shivered slightly and found the sensation so pleasurable that she tried to make herself shiver again but could not. Justina crossed the floor and stood in front of the washbasin. There was a mirror-doored medicine cabinet above it and a small kerosene heater below. She felt the warmth from the heater and extended her foot toward it, reveling in the luxury of the heated air.

She realized that she was lucky. In fact, her whole family was lucky, and she crossed herself quickly and thanked Jesus for their blessings. Outside on this January day in

1920, it was cold—bitterly cold—but it was snug and warm here in the apartment while many of her friends lived in drafty cold-water flats and tried to keep warm by burning coal in the kitchen stove.

The Falcones' luck had not come, she knew, because they had much money. While her father was a police sergeant, he did not really make all that much. But just because he was a policeman, the building's owner had given them the best apartment in the building and charged them the going rent for a smaller apartment.

It was not because the landlord was a nice man. God, he was a greasy thing who always looked at Justina with lustful eyes. No, the landlord did it because he knew that having a policeman in his building would help prevent it from being damaged by vandals and would also help keep out the rougher tenants—the "gees," as the kids called gangsters. Her father had not wanted to accept the bargain rent—he wondered about its propriety—but Justina's mother had finally prevailed on him by explaining that he was providing a security service to the landlord and that he should be compensated for it.

Justina looked in the mirror at herself but could not see because of the steam that had condensed there from her hot bath. She hesitated a moment, then peeled the towel from around her body and wiped the mirror clear. She dropped the towel on the floor, studied herself, and decided, for perhaps the one hundredth time that week, that she was beautiful.

She thought with satisfaction that the Falcones might not be rich now, but she would be rich because she was beautiful, and in America, beautiful women always became rich

Her appreciation of her own beauty was not misguided vanity. It was just a simple fact, like the fact that she had black hair and dark green eyes. And not only did she have a good face, she thought, but she had a magnificent body. She turned this way and that, posing for herself in the mirror. She had a body like some of those old statues in the museum. Even better than the statues, she thought. Longer in the leg, slender in the hips and belly. Men liked that in a woman.

She watched herself closely as she ran her hands caressingly up her long legs, across her belly, and then stopped at her breasts, cradling each one in a cupped hand.

She loved to touch herself. She had never let anyone else touch her, but she had often thought about it. Justina had looked at boys and wished they would take her in their arms and crush her to them and run their rough hands all over her, touching her everywhere, even *there,* in front.

Without thinking, she let one hand travel down her belly and brush through her dark tangle and touch there. She smiled at her reflection in the mirror and thought of getting back into the still-warm bathwater and doing it again. She had only found out about how to do it at Christmastime, and she had not told anyone else about it yet, not any of the girls at Holy Mother Academy, where she went to high school—(they all called the school "Mama's")—and not even her best friend, Sofia Mangini.

Sofia was beautiful, too, Justina thought. Probably the most beautiful girl in her class except for Justina. Maybe Sofia had an even nicer face. But not as nice a body, she decided.

Justina had paid close attention to the other girls when they had to take showers. Sofia was not as tall as Tina, and her breasts, though beautifully shaped, were not quite so ripe. Still, they were beautiful, and she thought about her friend and about having boys' hands, many boys' hands, touching her, touching them both. She cupped her breasts again. She could feel her breath growing deeper and sharper. The room was getting warmer and she could see a flush coming into her cheeks and at the base of her throat. She fought hard to keep from making any sound.

There was a knock on the door.

"Hey, Tina," a voice called out.

Justina let out a little startled whoop and grabbed desperately for her towel, dropped it, and then grabbed her robe from a hook and tied it around her.

"Just a moment, please," she called back to her cousin, Nilo. He was very handsome, almost pretty, Nilo was, and if she had to pick someone to be the first to touch her, she might have picked him, even if he was a relative and only a little older than she and her fantasies generally revolved around older men. She had been fascinated by his looks the first night they met and had even flirted with him a little. But that was in the past. The sad fact was that Nilo was poor, an immigrant with no prospects, and she would marry only someone who could afford her.

She quickly pulled open the door and saw him standing there, blocking her way. He smiled at her with his beautiful smile.

Everything about him is beautiful, she thought.

"I'm sorry I took so long," she said. "I was daydreaming. Have you been home long?"

"Long enough."

"Oh." Justina blushed and pulled her robe more tightly around her.

"Where is everybody?" Nilo asked.

Justina stepped through the door and unconsciously backed away from her cousin.

"It's Wednesday night," she said. "Mama's at Novena,

and Papa's working on something down at the station. He won't be home till later."

"We're the only ones here?"

"Yes," she said, almost stammering on the word. She remembered her daydreams of just a few minutes before and blushed. But Nilo did not seem to notice.

"What about Tommy?" Nilo asked.

"He's over at the college, getting registered or whatever it is he has to do. I don't know when he'll be home."

Nilo nodded and said, "I won some money today at work. Would you like to go to Mangini's for supper with me?"

Mangini's was the restaurant owned by Sofia's father. It was directly across Crosby Street from the Falcones' building.

"I'd better not," Justina said. "Mama left supper for us, and I have homework to do. And I want to practice my singing."

Nilo shrugged and suddenly looked downhearted, like a badly disappointed small boy. "After supper, will you give me more lessons?"

Justina smiled. "After supper, I promise. We will practice our reading and our English."

WHEN THEY HAD EATEN, Nilo sat and watched as Justina washed and put away the dishes, then got out a small pile of books she had borrowed from the school library. They moved onto the living room couch, and she handed the books to him one by one to examine.

"What are these? Is this a joke?" he demanded, and tossed the books onto the floor.

When Justina laughed, Nilo's face clouded over. "I

have to read," he snapped. "I have to be able to learn so many things. I will not grow old, still a fool, locked in a prison of stupidity. And you bring me children's books."

"They are what you need," she said, even as she gathered the books up from the floor.

"You say I am not a man?" he asked softly. She noticed that his eyes were smoldering and his lower lip was trembling with barely suppressed anger. A shiver caught her body. Part of it was fear, part something else that she could not identify. She forced herself to smile again.

"I am sure you are a man," she said lightly. "In every way but reading. In reading, you are as a child, so these children's books are the way for you to begin."

Nilo slid closer to her on the sofa. "I am in no way a child," he said coldly. "I am a man who knows men, who knows women. I was home and I heard you making those sounds in the bathroom. I have heard those sounds many time but never by a woman alone. Always with someone. Always with me. So I look through the keyhole. Shall I tell you what I see?"

Justina's face flushed. She was unable to reply.

"I will tell you what I see," Nilo said. "I see one who was once a girl who is now a woman. I will make you a bargain, do you a favor. You treat me as a man. Teach me to read as a man. I will teach you to be a woman."

He reached over and pulled her close. His lips were on hers. Justina squirmed slightly, trying to move away, but before she could she felt his strong rough workman's hand move under her skirt.

A key rattled in the apartment door and Justina pulled herself free, managing to stand up just as her brother Tommy came into the parlor.

"Hi, Tina. Hey, Nilo. How's everything going? I was

thinking of you today. It's colder than a witch's heinie out there." Without waiting for an answer, he crossed the living room to his bedroom, which he had once shared with Mario and now shared with Nilo. "I hope Mama left something for me to eat."

Justina nodded and quickly went into the kitchen to heat Tommy's meal, aware all the time of Nilo's eyes following her.

When Tommy came out of the bedroom, he perched on the back of the sofa where Nilo sat.

"So, country cousin, how was the ditchdigging business today?" he asked. "You still happy Papa got you that job?"

Nilo shrugged. "It was very cold. The ground is so hard we do only emergency work. We work hard and fast. It helps to keep us warm."

Tommy smiled. "In this cold weather, that is the safest way of keeping warm. If you understand what I mean." To make his point clear, he glanced toward Tina in the kitchen, then cuffed Nilo lightly on the chin. Nilo did not answer. Tommy walked out into the kitchen to eat his supper. He was laughing and Nilo cursed softly under his breath.

Someday, no one will be present to rescue her, he thought. *Then she will learn who is man and who child.*

SOFIA MANGINI LAY in her darkened room, reading a book by the light of an electric sign outside her window, advertising her family's restaurant on the floor below her room. It was a book of poems by a girl poet not much older than herself who, right at this moment, Sofia knew, was living and working less than half a mile away.

She read the lines:

The soul can split the sky in two,
And let the face of God shine through.

She set the book down beside her on the bed, making no attempt to fight back the tears, not knowing whether it was the beauty of the words or something else entirely that had made her weep. After a while, she pulled a little notebook from its hiding place beneath her mattress and tried to write something. She used to be able to write lots of things, but lately the words just would not come. She did not know why. Perhaps she was changing. Perhaps she was coming to the end of her dreams.

Once, she had dreamed of many things. Of being a poet. Or an adventuress. Or a nun. She had often dreamed of running away from home and living in Greenwich Village and leading a life of dissipation, but now that Justina's brother Mario was the assistant pastor at Our Lady of Mount Carmel right in the Village, that did not seem like such a good idea.

Thinking of the Falcones made her feel bad again. Tina had everything. She had a father and mother who loved each other and who loved her. She had a nice apartment. She had two brothers—and now even a new cousin— to protect her. Sofia had none of those things.

It was nobody's fault, she told herself, and most certainly not hers. It was not her fault that after she was born the doctor had told her mother that she could never again have babies. It was not Sofia's fault that her mother kept trying and the pain and disappointments of the miscarriages and the stillborns kept mounting until her mother shut herself off from everybody and everything, going into perpetual mourning and becoming a small dumpy figure in black who did nothing other than sit at the cash register at the family restaurant, counting and recounting the money, with no time for her husband and not much more for her only daughter. Sometimes she caught her mother staring at her, and the look on the old woman's face was clearly one of accusation, as if Sofia had somehow been responsible for her mother's problems and her father's behavior.

Mr. Mangini's behavior—and everyone in the neighborhood knew about it—involved finding solace in other women's arms. Everyone pitied Mrs. Mangini for her husband's faithlessness, but they would have pitied her even more if they knew that Mangini would make his conquests and then regularly gloat about them to his wife.

And none of it was her fault, Sofia told herself, just as she bore no blame because her father—in order to put out of his mind his great sins and the nagging and carping of his wife—would drink himself into a near stupor almost every night and then beat his wife and terrorize his daughter.

Sofia got up and crossed to the window and looked out. It was not late yet, not even midnight. She stared across the street to the building where Tina lived. Lights were still on, making the apartment seem as warm and as hospitable as it usually was. Sofia wished she lived there. Then she would be able to see Tommy, Tina, all the Falcones, all the time. Even the new cousin, Nilo.

Tina often talked about who she would someday marry: how he would be both handsome and rich and absolutely devoted to her, and how they would stay in bed all the time, making babies.

Sofia had no such thoughts. It had always been a kind of joke between her and Tina that one day Sofia would marry Tommy, but she never dreamed of him in the way that Tina dreamed of her phantom lover. Perhaps she did not even love him, she thought. It might be that she loved the Falcone family and the warmth they all showed for each other. In her dreams, she always saw the family together, always saw Tina. But in her fantasies, she saw women poets, declaiming their verse in tantalizing little rhymes.

She tried often to make Tommy the subject of her dreams. He was kind and gentle and handsome and brave. Especially brave. He had been a big hero in the war, horribly wounded, and had suffered greatly. Tina said that he had all sorts of scars all over his body and, swearing her to secrecy, that Tommy's pain was so great that the army had made him a morphine addict to survive. Sofia tried to picture herself taking care of him whenever the pain came back—as Tina said it sometimes did, leaving him moaning in his sleep. But those dreams did not come easily.

She also tried to imagine herself with Nilo, the new Sicilian cousin, but that image was also hard to call up. Nilo was just too handsome; what would he want with her? And there was a hard edge to him, hidden but close to the surface, that she found distasteful. She had gone with Nilo to a carnival one night, along with Tommy and Justina, and Nilo had spent the evening clumsily brushing against Sofia's breasts, and she had spent the night pulling away from him. No, she thought, he would not be a good husband; he would not be like Tommy Falcone. Nilo was a pig. And maybe all men were.

She watched the Falcones' windows until the lights went off, and then she went back to bed. She was almost asleep when she heard the apartment door open and close. She was sorry now that she had stayed awake so late. Now she would have to listen to the inevitable arguing of her parents, followed by the inevitable screaming and shouting and then the beating. Sofia closed her eyes tightly and tried to make herself drop immediately off to sleep, but it did not work and moments later her father began shouting at her mother in Italian.

That was a bad sign. When he cursed in English, he seemed to put so much energy into picking the words that he did not have much left for the actual beating.

Sofia tried, but she could not really blame her father. No man should have to be married to a woman like her mother, a woman with no love in her heart, only greed for money, money, and more money, a woman who was hollow, a woman incapable of affection. But he should not beat her. Perhaps if Sofia asked him?

She got out of bed, put on her robe, and walked to the bedroom door, but there she hesitated. In the kitchen she could hear the sounds of an ongoing battle. For a moment, Sofia considered going back to bed, but then she decided she must have courage, must do what was right.

She opened the door and stepped into the other room. Her mother was backed into a corner, waving a heavy butcher's knife at her husband. She was bleeding slightly from the corner of her mouth.

Sofia let out a small gasp and her father turned toward her. He was a tall and handsome man, with wavy black hair that he kept oiled with scented pomade. His mustache was thin and well trimmed, and he showed his teeth, even and large and sparkling white, as he hissed to his daughter.

"Sofia, my baby, go to bed. This is none of your affair."

He looked as though he was going to say more, but just at that moment, with his attention diverted and his body half-turned away from her, Sofia's mother slashed out with her knife, slicing her husband's shirt.

He looked down with apparent surprise at the faint line of blood that suddenly appeared on his white shirt. Then, before Sofia's eyes, he seemed to change. What had gone before had been like a long worked-out ritual, more like war games than the real thing. But in that instant all was transformed. Matteo Mangini looked down at the blood coming from him and then at his wife, Rosalia. He slowly made a fist, and while his wife began crying he raised his big paw high and then with all his might smashed it backhanded into his wife's face. There was a loud noise and Rosalia's face exploded into a bloody pulp. She exhaled a slow, soft sigh and collapsed to the floor.

Sofia watched, unable to move. Matteo advanced on his wife and casually plucked the knife from her hand. He held it up in a muddle-headed way and seemed to be considering what to do with it.

"No, Papa," Sofia said. "Please don't. Please."

Matteo looked down at his wife and started to cry.

"I didn't mean to do it, Sofia. I didn't mean to hurt her."

"I know, Papa. I know."

Sofia moved closer to her mother. Rosalia was moaning now, crying softly.

"Help me take her into the bedroom," Sofia said.

Like some overgrown child, Matteo nodded vigorously. He lifted his wife in his arms and carried her into their bedroom, where he gently set her down. Sofia made him leave the room while she washed her mother's face. The nose was bloodied but did not appear broken. Sofia made her drink a tumbler full of red wine, then sat at her side, holding her hand until Rosalia was asleep.

When Sofia went back out into the kitchen, her father was seated at the table.

"Let me help you, Papa," she said.

Numbly, he let her take off his shirt and dress his wound. It was a long thin scratch across his ribs, which had produced more blood than real damage. When she was done bandaging it, she took him by the hand and led him into her bedroom.

"Sleep here tonight, Papa," she said. "I will sleep on the sofa."

Matteo said something incomprehensible and Sofia went to the door. But when he began crying, she hesitated.

"Sofia," he said. "Sofia, I'm so sorry. I'm no good. No damned good."

Sofia went back to him where he sat on the edge of her bed. She put her hand on top of his and stroked it gently like a baby's. He cried some more and she sat down beside him. She put her arm around him and he rested his head on her shoulder. She thought that he had suffered much and felt a great sense of forgiveness toward her father. Matteo Mangini could not help what he had become.

Sofia put her arms around him and patted him gently on the back. He was like an overgrown child who badly needed comforting, although this "child" was big and burly and reeked of red wine.

She kissed him gently on the forehead, and he looked up at her with grateful surprise. So she kissed his forehead again. Every person, she thought, deserves to have someone show him love and affection. It was life and it was poetry. It was beauty.

Suddenly Mangini stood, put his arms under her legs, and turned around to lower her onto the bed. Then his hands went to his suspenders and slipped them from his shoulders.

Sofia let out a gasp as her father began undressing. He stretched out beside her on the bed and clumsily reached inside her robe and cupped her naked breast.

Sofia told herself that it was not right. But the man had so much sorrow. And perhaps there could be love even in this house.

Slowly she put her arms around her father and pulled him toward her.

MARCH ADVERTISED ITS STUBBORN EXISTENCE with a wailing whistle of wind. Spring might be only a few weeks away, but down here, in the pit, there was only winter, cold, eternal, remorseless.

Nilo put down his pick and studied the dirt wall in front of him. It was a sticky gray clay, oozing water, but his only interest in it was that it was too damned hard to dig into. At the rate that the crew had been going, the job would take weeks to complete.

Nilo stepped back from the clay and wiped his face with the sleeve of his rough woolen peacoat. The sun did not penetrate down into the pit, and whenever he stopped working he began shivering. He could feel the sweat on his body turning cold and chilling him. Stay still long enough, he thought, and his sweat would turn to ice.

And so they rule you, he thought. *They work you like a beast of burden, and you have only two choices: to sweat until the fevers carry you off, or refuse the work and starve. Either way, long enough, you die and they bury you in the ditch that some poor fool exactly like you just dug.*

Nilo looked around at his world, the bottom of a twelve-foot-deep trench, barely wide enough for him to stand in sideways, covered with a foot-deep, ice-cold mud slurry on the bottom. Twenty yards away, another worker bent over his pick, his shovel leaning against one of the walls of the ditch. In the distance, Nilo could hear the sound of a ship's horn. They were working somewhere on the waterfront to do a job that had never been explained to any of them.

We are no longer humans, just beasts of burden. Is this the promise of America? Is this to be my reward for wanting to be a good citizen?

Nilo hated this. He had not liked the *tonnara,* but at least the weather had been good. He hated the weather in America. He hated his life. The only thing he loved right now was the thought of a cigarette. He looked around for the job's straw boss, a big hulking dumb Irishman, who had made it clear early on that he hated having to work with wops.

Not as much as we hate you, Nilo thought.

He was supposed to tell the boss whenever he left the ditch for any reason, but the man was not around and Nilo needed a smoke. At least American cigarettes were better than the ones back in Sicily. He climbed the ladder up to the pavement.

Topside, he could see the West Side docks, not far from where he had first come ashore nearly three months earlier. Up there, the sun shone with a mild warmth that took the chill from his bones.

He squatted down to give the wind a smaller target and lit a cigarette. He remembered that he was to have dinner tonight at the Falcones' apartment. He had lived with them for a few weeks after Tommy returned, but he had always seemed to be in somebody's way, so finally he rented a room in the apartment of an old Italian widow directly across the street from the Falcones, in the building where Sofia Mangini lived.

He still ate dinner with the Falcones three or four times a week; he had to, because he could not afford too many dinners on his skimpy pay and he resolutely refused to dip into the small stash of stolen funds he kept under his mattress. But except for meals, Nilo stayed away as much as he could. Tina was to blame for that. In his mind, she was just a tease, leading him on with her beauty and then going cute and coy and virginal at the last moment. He also feared that she might be saying bad things about him to Tommy.

It's because I saw her feeling herself up in the bathroom. People hate it when you find out their secrets.

"Hey, Sesta."

Nilo stood up and turned around. It was Chambers, the straw boss. Nilo slowly took a puff on his cigarette.

"What do you think you're doing?" Chambers said. "Taking a fucking vacation?" Nilo did not answer, and Chambers said, "Not on my shift, you dumb wop. I get paid to produce. Now get back to work."

Without even thinking of his reply, Nilo answered, "No."

The word surprised Chambers; it even surprised Nilo. Chambers looked at him for a moment, then turned away.

"Then get your ass the hell out of here," Chambers said. "I'll give you your chit, and you go back to the office and collect your stuff. You're through. Fired. Now beat it."

It was not fair, Nilo thought. *This is supposed to be America, where men are free. A man should not lose his job because he needs a cigarette. Who makes these rules?*

He could feel the rage boiling inside. There was a long-handled digging shovel on the ground, and he picked it up, ran after Chambers, and smashed the Irishman across the back with it, knocking him into the cold mud at the bottom of the ditch.

Nilo walked to the edge and looked down at Chambers writhing in pain, paused thoughtfully, and then dropped the shovel down on top of him. For good measure, he also flicked his cigarette butt down at the man.

After that, Nilo did not bother going around to collect

the half day's pay that was due him. Instead, he walked away from the site and kept on walking. Early afternoon found him in Midtown beginning to worry about how he was going to get along. His command of English still was not good, except for a fair number of obscenities he had mastered while on the job. All he knew was that he was never ever going to dig ditches again.

He walked up Broadway, surprised at how lively and warm New York City seemed up here. Down a side street he saw a modest-looking diner, and his stomach reminded him that he had left his lunch back at the work shack. He went into the restaurant, sat at the counter, and ordered apple pie and coffee.

He looked in his small money purse to check how much cash he had, and while he was fishing through it, he noticed for what must have been the hundredth time since he had put it there the card that Rocco had given him with the New York address of his benefactor, Don Salvatore Maranzano.

Nilo looked at the card, but figuring out the address was beyond him.

He asked a woman if she could tell him how to get to the address, but she shied away from him and walked quickly outside. Nilo had to admit that it seemed like a sensible thing to do since he looked and smelled like something that had just crawled out of a sewer.

After his meager lunch, he went back to the street and began to ask passersby if they would help him. One by one they ignored him and walked off, and finally a city policeman came up to him and told him to move along.

Nilo tried to explain in his halting English that he was looking for an address, and after a long few moments, finally succeeded in making himself understood.

The cop looked at the card. "Maranzano, huh? A friend of yours?"

Nilo nodded. "Sì. Yes," he said hopefully.

"That figures," the policeman said. "They're all as dumb as you." He handed back the card. "Keep walking up Broadway. You'll come to the number." He pointed to the number on the business card and then to a street sign on the corner.

Nilo nodded, fixed a big smile of thanks on his face, and walked off. But inside, he was seething. He knew the word "dumb." He had heard it enough from Chambers on the ditchdigging job.

And why did that policeman seem to know Don Salvatore? Perhaps the don is truly a big man in this city. And maybe he will have work for me.

A few minutes later, Nilo was standing outside a large brick building. A brass plaque on the front of the building announced:

MARANZANO
REAL ESTATE

Nilo could not decipher "real estate," but he was able to work out the letters for "Maranzano." He started for the large glass doors of the entrance but suddenly was brushed aside by two burly men who pushed their way out of the building.

They both wore crisp pin-striped suits, and their faces, under their snap-brimmed hats, were hard and suspicious.

At the curb they got into a parked car, and as one man clambered into the passenger seat Nilo saw a revolver in a shoulder holster under his jacket. The two men quickly drove off. Nilo watched them go, then turned back toward Maranzano's building.

This time he stopped short of the door.

Who am I trying to fool? Don Salvatore has a big business, and what do I know about business? Why would he hire me? To do what? To dig more ditches for one of his businesses?

In his mind, he weighed himself against the two men who had just driven away from the real estate office. Their suits . . . their strong faces . . . the gun he saw. Were these businessmen? he wondered. Did they work for Don Salvatore?

There are too many things I do not know. I speak of being a man, but I am truly not much more than a child. What use has Don Salvatore for a child whose only skill is digging ditches? I will dig ditches until I die. It is America's gift to Nilo Sesta.

He turned from the door and started the long walk back to Crosby Street. Softly, the rain began to fall.

TOMMY FALCONE PICKED UP the coffeepot from the stove, where it had been gently percolating itself into mud, and poured himself a thick steaming cupful and walked into the living room.

Outside, the day had changed from sunny and chill to a long, slow, cold drizzle. The weather fit his mood exactly, and he sank down into the sofa, kicked his shoes off, and stared out the window, studying the rain.

Tony Falcone came out of the bathroom rubbing his damp hair with a towel, looked over at his son, then went into the kitchen for his own cup of coffee. He sat down next to Tommy and said, "You look very serious. It must be all this philosophy that you are studying."

"Nothing so brilliant," Tommy said. "I was just trying to figure out which bank to rob."

His father grinned at him. "It might be easier to marry a rich widow," he said.

Tommy laughed. "I hadn't thought of that." After a pause, he said, "Do you think there's one around that old man Mangini doesn't have his paws on?"

The elder Falcone scowled. He did not like his neighbor from across the street and went into Mangini's Restaurant only when it was absolutely necessary. "The man gives philanderers a bad name," he finally said, then quickly dropped the subject, as if it annoyed him.

"Why this worrying about money all of a sudden?" he asked. "I thought between your army back pay and maybe working this summer, you wouldn't have any trouble with money for school."

"I won't," Tommy agreed. "So long as I don't go anywhere or do anything. Without cash . . . well, as far as girls are concerned, I might just as well have stayed up there with the Sisters of Quietude. . . ."

He stopped suddenly, realizing what he had said, aware that he had mentioned a part of his life that he had planned to keep secret forever.

"I mean . . ." he began.

Tony smiled softly. "I know what you mean," he said. "You don't have to say anything."

Tommy took a small sip of his coffee before turning toward his father.

"What do you know?" he finally asked.

Tony shrugged his shoulders.

"No," Tommy snapped. "You said you know. Now, what do you know?"

"I know most of it, Tommy. Look, it's not something you want to talk about. I don't want to talk about it, either."

"You know I was with the sisters?"

"Yes."

"How did you find out? Did Bigmouth Mario tell you?"

"Your brother is *Father* Mario," Tony snapped. "Don't forget it. And he didn't say a word. It was the postmark on your letters. I'm too good a cop to have missed that."

"What else do you know?"

Tony sighed. "Okay. I know about the morphine."

Tommy rose and walked to the window. "You let me come back home. Even after you found out?"

"Of course. Why not?"

"Your dope fiend son?" Tommy said.

"My son. Who was sick. And isn't anymore," his father replied.

Tommy came back to the couch and sat down again.

"We were talking about money," Tony said.

"I've been thinking about law school," Tommy said. "In a few years, after I finish at CCNY. But I want to go to a good one. Columbia's the one I want."

"You're right," Tony said. "You *will* need money for that. I hear it's pretty expensive."

Tommy nodded and Tony said abruptly, "I could probably get you a job somewhere."

"I had a different idea. Maybe I'll become a cop."

"No," his father answered sharply.

"Why not? I could learn a lot about how the law and the world really work. The money's not bad. They'd put me on late shifts and I'd be able to go to school days."

"No," his father said again.

"That's really not much of an explanation, Papa."

"All right, I'll give you a better one. You're too good to be a cop."

"It doesn't seem to have hurt you," Tommy said.

"Look, when the immigrants come, the first thing they think of is becoming a cop. And that's all right. But their kids . . . their kids have to do better. I didn't become a cop so you could become a cop. You've got to be better than me."

"I'm not talking about a career. I'm talking about a temporary job, while I get through school."

"There's another reason. For a long time now, the gangs have been dying out. We were winning. The criminals were losing. And now this stupid Prohibition."

"What do you mean?"

"The gangs are coming back and they're coming back worse than ever. There's a lot of money to be made in this illegal liquor, and if you get enough crooked money, criminals sprout like weeds. Every *gavone* who makes wine in his cellar is working overtime, peddling his stuff to criminals who sell it to taverns that are open illegally. They call it bootlegging now."

"What does that mean? Bootlegging?"

"I don't know. Maybe cowboys used to hide whiskey in a boot or something. Anyway, it's happening out there, Tommy. Every day it's getting worse. This place is going to be the Wild West before too long. You know they've started an Italian Squad in the department?"

"You didn't mention it."

"They asked me to take one of the top jobs. I turned them down."

"Why?"

"Because I don't want to be an 'Italian' cop. I want to be a cop. I don't want to think about there being so many Italian gangsters in this city that they need their own squad to deal with them. Our hope for the future is to be more American than Americans. How are we ever going to do that if we're separated from everybody else, behind a sign that says 'These are the Italian gangsters and these are the Italian cops who keep them in their cages.' I don't want to be an Italian. I want to be an American."

Tommy stared at him for a long moment. "I'll think about it, Papa."

"You are the most stubborn son a man could have."

"It must run in the family."

"All right. If you want to join, let me know. I'll help you walk the application through. And you don't have to worry about that stuff in the hospital. It was damned near impossible for me to run down and I worked hard at it. The department wouldn't have any reason to check that so thoroughly. You can waltz onto the force if you want to."

Tommy reached out and placed his hand on his father's shoulder. "I want to think about it some before I make a decision. But I don't want you worrying about it, and I sure don't want you worrying about money for me. You've got enough now, with Tina wanting singing lessons and a piano and God knows what else. So drop it. It's my problem."

They were interrupted by a loud knocking at the door. Tommy got up to answer it and Nilo came into the room, soaked to the skin.

"Hey, the stranger from across the street," Tommy said. "How are you doing, Nilo?"

"Hello, Uncle Tony," Nilo said, before answering Tommy. "I am fine," he said. "But I am freezing and I came over for a cup of coffee."

"Help yourself. It's on the stove."

As Nilo poured a cup, Tony called out from the parlor: "How's your new room?"

"Fine, Uncle Tony. The Widow Annacharico does not meddle or pry. She leaves me alone as long as I pay the rent on time. I like it that way."

"Speaking of rent," Tony said. "No work today?"

"I quit," Nilo said. He came back into the living room sipping at the steaming coffee, looking at his uncle over the rim of the cup.

God, he has eyes like a woman, Tony thought. *He is just too pretty.*

"Why'd you quit?" Tommy asked.

Nilo shrugged. "The boss, that Chambers. He insulted me."

"What did he say?"

"He called me a dumb guinea."

Tommy laughed. In New York City, anyone with an Italian name learned early on not to let such things bother him. But Nilo was not really a New Yorker . . . not yet.

"And?"

"And I hit him and left," Nilo said.

"Maybe I'll have a talk with that big mick," Tony said ominously.

"No, Uncle Tony. It was nice of you to get me that job, but I don't want you involved anymore. I have had enough of ditchdigging and will now find other work."

His two relatives looked at him silently, and Nilo knew what they were thinking.

Yes, it is true I am young and illiterate and do not yet know the ways of this city. But, in my brief life, I have already killed three men. I will find something to do in America besides carry a shovel.

There was another rapping on the door. When Tony answered it, a uniformed policeman stood outside the doorway. Tony walked into the hallway to talk to him, then came back and got his jacket from a coatrack.

"Damn," he said. "I was looking forward to hanging around this afternoon, but duty calls."

"What's happening?" Tommy asked.

"There's some gang trouble," his father answered. "One of Masseria's men got himself shot, and he had to pick our precinct to get himself killed in."

"Joe the Boss? Who'd shoot one of his men?"

"This is just the start," Tony said darkly. "There's a new guy in town and he's moving in on Joe's rackets. I think before too long we're going to see a big war between Masseria and this Maranzano. I'm glad I'm not working that Italian Squad."

"What is his name?" Nilo asked quickly. "This new man?"

"Salvatore Maranzano," Tony said as he struggled into his heavy raincoat. "Another fun-loving Sicilian." He walked to the door. The uniformed officer was still waiting in the hall.

Tony turned back. "Tell Mama I will try to sneak home for some dinner but not to wait for me."

"Take care of yourself, Papa," Tommy said, and Nilo nodded agreement. The policeman left without acknowledging the warning.

When he had gone, Nilo asked Tommy "Who is this Masseria?"

"Joe the Boss, they call him," Tommy said. "Mafia. He was some kind of a thug, but now he runs most of the rackets in town."

"He is very rich?"

Tommy laughed. "I never heard of a poor gangster," he said, adding glumly, "only cops are poor."

"And ditchdiggers," Nilo said. "Now this Salvatore Maranzano will challenge Joe the Boss?"

"He'll try to. If he lives long enough," Tommy said. "There are always challenges. And there are always people getting killed." He waved his hands, dismissing the whole matter as unimportant.

"But he has killed one of Masseria's men?" Nilo pressed.

"Well, no one's sure of that yet," Tommy said. "Papa is just going over to start the investigation now."

Nilo nodded. He thought of standing outside Maranzano's office and then seeing the two burly men in pinstriped suits brush by him. They had seemed as if they were in a hurry to get somewhere.

And maybe their appointment was with the henchman, now deceased, of Joe the Boss.

He smiled at Tommy. "Would you do me a favor?" he said.

"Hey, we're family. Of course," Tommy answered.

"Thank you. I wish to borrow your suit. For tomorrow. We are the same size and it should fit."

"Absolutely," Tommy said. "Do you have a big date?"

Nilo shook his head. "No. I am going to apply for a job and I want to look . . ." His English failed him and he looked at Tommy helplessly.

"Professional," Tommy offered.

Nilo nodded. "Professional. I want to look professional." He smiled. "I have my own shirt and tie."

WEARING TOMMY FALCONE'S DARK BLUE SUIT and his own Christmas-gift white shirt and tie—badly knotted because it was the first tie he had ever worn—Nilo Sesta walked bravely through the front doors of the Maranzano Real Estate Office at nine o'clock the next morning, squeezing the small sweat-stained business card tightly in his hand, as if it were the key to the exit door from hell.

He knew immediately that this was the kind of place he wanted to spend his life in. The walls and floors were of highly polished pink marble with real oil paintings, and sitting at the end of the reception room behind a big wooden desk was a beautiful young red-haired woman who wore a crimson dress with the top buttons open, and Nilo could see the crease where her breasts were pushed together.

She could not have been much older than he was, but she seemed cool and confident, and she smiled at him as he walked across the lobby toward her desk.

He was sweating already.

"Yes, sir. Can I help you?" the young woman said.

Awkwardly, Nilo stuck out his hand, holding Maranzano's business card. The woman took it, looked at it, and smiled again.

"Yes?" she said.

Nilo was confused for a moment. He had not expected that he would have to do a lot of talking.

"I would like to see Don Salvatore," he said.

The redhead nodded. Nilo found it hard not to look down into her cleavage. He was nervous about it, but he knew he must tell her that her dress had come undone.

"What is your name, please?" she asked.

"I am Nilo Sesta," he said. Without realizing he was doing it, he stuck a forefinger inside the collar of his shirt and pulled it from side to side, trying to loosen the stranglehold the shirt had on his throat. He quickly added, "I am from the don's home village in Sicily."

"Well, *Mr.* Maranzano is not in yet," she answered, stressing the "Mr." as if to let the yokel know that in New York men were called "Mr." and not "Don." "If you wish to wait, you could sit over there," she said, nodding to a row of chairs on the side of the room.

Nilo started to turn away, then looked back at the girl.

"Miss, I don't want to be . . ."—he struggled for the word—". . . rude. . . ."

"Yes?"

"Your dress . . . the buttons . . ." Nilo looked down helplessly at the woman's cleavage. So did she.

She nodded, then opened another button and spread wider the two halves of the top of her dress. Nilo's mouth dropped open; he beat a hasty retreat to the other side of the room, and he heard the young woman giggling derisively behind him. He sat and waited for Don Salvatore, casting occasional sideways glances at the young woman's bosom, trying not to be noticed.

He had not slept with any American women. Tina had seemed to lose interest in him, and there was something wrong with her best friend, Sofia, who, although she was very beautiful, was cold and unapproachable. In truth, Nilo stood a little in awe of American women. They seemed always to be well dressed and highly perfumed, and their hair was always carefully combed—even the girls he saw on the street down in Little Italy—all of them so different from the girls and women of the little towns of his native Sicily.

But this one, he thought, *is very different. She is a* puttana, *a whore, and if Don Salvatore favors me with a job I will climb between her legs and she will never again mock me. Unless of course, Don Salvatore himself is already crawling between her legs. In which case, of course, I will protect her virtue against all other assailants, as if she were the Blessed Virgin herself.*

The thought must have brought a smile to his face, because the young woman caught his eye and asked, "Something's funny?"

His months on a sailing ship had taught Nilo how to deal with whores. "Someday, when I think you're ready, I will show you," he said solemnly.

She smiled at him, a little more than was necessary.

The young man was really cute, she thought, all nervous and sweating, but despite that, pretty to look at, a big improvement from the goons who hung around most of the day, trying to make time with her. She was sure he was looking for a job, and she hoped Maranzano would hire him.

SALVATORE MARANZANO ARRIVED at 10:30 A.M. He moved into the lobby like an ocean liner flanked by two tugboats, they being the pin-striped men Nilo had seen the day before.

Nilo jumped to his feet and moved forward toward Maranzano, a smile set on his face, but one of the men blocked his way, and without even noticing Nilo, Maranzano walked quickly past him, the receptionist, and vanished through one of the rear office doors. The two men followed him in.

Nilo was confused, unhappy, and he looked toward the secretary, who said reassuringly, "In a minute or two, I'll let him know you're here." She looked down at the appointment pad on her desk. "It's Nilo Sesta?"

Nilo nodded, then added quickly, "Danilo. Maybe he remembers that name better."

It was a full ten minutes—ten painful minutes that seemed an eternity to Nilo—before the buzzer rang at the receptionist's desk. She stood, nodded toward Nilo, smoothed her dress out over her lush hips, moistened her lips with her tongue, and walked through the same door Maranzano had used.

Another ten minutes. Another eternity. *He will not remember me. He gives his business card to everyone he meets. I am just a peasant from the old country. Why should he care what happens to me? I will speak to him, and he will laugh in my face and throw me out into the street.*

He was on the verge of running away, walking out onto the sidewalk and never looking back, when the woman returned.

"Will you follow me, please?" she said politely, and smiled at him again.

Nilo followed her through Maranzano's office door, but it led just to another large office. It was simply furnished except for a large number of oil paintings on the wall. They all seemed to be landscapes or other pictures of places and things in America, and almost all of them seemed to be distorted, twisted. Nilo had never seen such paintings. At the end of the room, the two pinstripes, like bookends, sat on hard wooden chairs on either side of another doorway. They looked at Nilo as if he were a particularly uninviting bug that had wandered onto their dinner plates.

He followed the receptionist through the heavy oak door. Behind a gigantic wooden desk, pouring steaming tea from a delicate china pot, sat Salvatore Maranzano.

When Nilo entered, Maranzano rose, and with a large smile he came from behind the desk to greet the young man.

"My young friend. At last we meet again."

He embraced Nilo, startling him with his vigor, and said over the other man's shoulder, "That will be all, Betty. I'll ring if I want you."

"Yes, Mr. Maranzano," the secretary said. Behind him, Nilo heard the door close as she left the office.

Maranzano looked different from the last time Nilo had seen him, dressed in a black cassock, at the palazzo near Castellammare del Golfo. Now he wore a sleek silk suit and looked like a prosperous banker. His voice was still soft, sweetly resonant, but his eyes remained wary and cautious.

Clothing changes, Nilo thought. *But underneath, the man is always the same.*

When he finally released Nilo from his embrace, the young man bowed to him, formally from the waist, and Maranzano waited patiently, accepting it as his due, until Nilo met his eyes again.

"Don Salvatore, I have come looking for work."

Maranzano laughed. "Only in New York a few months and already you have learned the American lack of patience. No time for pleasantries. No time wasted on friendship."

Nilo blushed and murmured an apology.

"Oh, I joke. Come, sit here by the desk. Have tea. Tell me what you have been doing since last we met."

Maranzano poured tea for both of them. Nilo looked around for cream and sugar, saw none, and followed the older man's lead in sipping the tea straight, unsweetened, from the cup.

It tastes like horsepiss, he thought. *When I am rich, I will drink only cappuccino.*

He smiled at Maranzano.

"Do you like the tea?" Maranzano asked.

"Very much."

"I think it tastes like horse urine," Maranzano said. "But rich Americans drink it and therefore we must learn to tolerate it. To make one's way in a society, we must learn the ways of that society."

Nilo nodded.

"Tell me, Nilo. Have you learned to read yet?"

"I am trying, sir. But no, not yet. Not well."

"Good. I admire your honesty. A Roman virtue that seems lost in much of contemporary youth. What have you been doing?"

Glad for the opportunity to put down the teacup, Nilo told of his arrival in New York, his brief stay with his aunt and uncle, his job as a ditchdigger, and how he had quit when the foreman had insulted him. He thought it best, for the moment, not to tell Maranzano that his uncle Tony was a New York City police officer.

"A typical story," Maranzano said. "I have heard it many times before." He set down his own teacup. "And so now you want to work for me?"

Nilo nodded. "Yes, Don Salvatore."

"You must learn to read. If you are to work for me. If you are to be a success in life."

"I will do whatever you say, Don Salvatore."

The old man nodded. "Perhaps you wonder why I should give you a job. What do you have to offer me?"

He looked at Nilo and waited, as if expecting an answer, and finally Nilo said, "Loyalty. I have nothing else."

"You need nothing else," Maranzano said exuberantly. "America is a powerful and growing country. By providing services that people want, we can become powerful, too. But when one becomes powerful, he finds he has many enemies—even people he has never met. It is in times like those that loyalty is in great demand. Trust me, Nilo. In life, surround yourself with family. All wise men know that."

Nilo nodded, then said, "I am not of your family." He was surprised to see Maranzano reflect for a moment before smiling broadly.

"Time will tell," he said. "Do you have skills? Talents?"

Emboldened, Nilo said, "I am young and untrained." He paused. "I know how to kill, however."

"Ah, yes. Those evil fishermen. You have killed. And you think this interests me?" Maranzano said.

Nilo swallowed hard, then decided to risk it all. What had he to lose? He said crisply, "I had heard talk that an enemy of yours was killed yesterday. It happened soon after I saw those two men out there leave this office, carrying weapons."

"Very good, Nilo. You keep your eyes open. That is also a virtue. And I presume you keep your mouth closed as well?"

"See all, speak nothing," Nilo said. "My father taught me that."

"Your father," Maranzano repeated softly. "He has shown you the path to wisdom. And to long life." He rose from behind his desk.

"Danilo," he said, "I like you. You are just the kind of young man I want in this new organization. One day, you could even be its leader."

"You will lead forever, Don Salvatore," Nilo said.

"No man lives forever," was the sad answer, "except in memory." He came around the desk to stand in front of the young man. "As a fellow Castellammarese, are you willing to join with me?"

"I owe you my life. I will do anything my don wishes."

"Many say that, but few perform. Tonight. Perhaps you can do a small favor for me. And then, afterward, we shall consider your future."

IT WAS AFTER MIDNIGHT and Nilo was cold and scared. He stood in a darkened doorway, watching a tenement on the other side of White Street. The drizzle of the afternoon had turned into a sleety kind of rain, and Nilo pulled his big navy peacoat tighter around him. He felt the cold metallic touch against his thigh of the shotgun that was jammed down into his trouser leg. He had been here now for more than an hour, and in that time not one person had walked down the street. The weather was on his side, for often the streets teemed with people, even late at night. But it was too cold tonight for the Mediterranean blood. *We are not made for this weather,* Nilo thought.

He had felt elated after the morning's interview with Salvatore Maranzano and had gone back to the Falcones' apartment. Neither Tommy nor his father was there, but Mrs. Falcone had been cooking in the kitchen.

"Don't you look like a million dollars?" she said.

"Tommy's suit, Aunt Anna."

"Yes, he said he lent it to you. So did your job hunting go well?"

"I think so, Aunt Anna. I'll know more tomorrow."

After Nilo changed his clothes, his aunt insisted upon feeding him.

Then she seemed to want to talk. "Do you miss your family?" she asked.

Nilo shrugged. "In a new country, I have not really had much time to miss them." The truth was that Nilo hardly ever thought of his parents; America was bewildering enough to consume all his time.

Anna nodded agreement. "We cannot replace your family," she said. "But we are always here for you."

Nilo nodded, kept eating, and left quickly. He did not want to have to talk to Tommy or Uncle Tony about where he had been, what he had been told. Especially not Uncle Tony.

Now he was standing in the doorway in the cold and sleet. Time passed slowly, but finally all the lights in the basement—the place Nilo was watching—went out. Nilo waited another fifteen minutes, but no one came out of the building.

Good, he thought. *They've gone to bed the way they're supposed to.*

He crossed the street. Taking a small glass cutter from his pocket, he sliced a half circle of glass from the panel in the door above the lock, the way Maranzano had shown him, carefully opened the door, and stepped inside.

He instantly smelled the distinctive yeasty aroma of fermentation. In a bakery or in his mother's kitchen in Sicily, that aroma meant bread was baking; but here, in this basement, it meant that a still was busy cooking bootleg liquor—a still owned by the two Valenti brothers who had somehow offended Maranzano. Nilo guessed it meant that they were trying to cut in on his business.

Nilo's job was to destroy the still. He hesitated inside the hallway. He knew that he was now at a crossroads in his life and the path he took would irrevocably dictate his future. He had no illusions. Back home, Don Salvatore Maranzano might be as respected as a nobleman, but here in America, he was a criminal. A successful criminal but a criminal nonetheless. If Nilo continued with this mission tonight, he would be a criminal, too. He would have cast his lot with Maranzano and whatever future that might bring. Nilo had spoken boldly to Maranzano, but those were only words, the words of a bragging child. Now he was being called on for deeds—the deeds of a man.

Could he do it? Did he want to do it? He thought of Maranzano and his palazzo with the beautiful woman and his fancy offices with the sluttish secretary and men ready to murder at his bidding. Then he thought of the others in America whom he knew—the Falcones. Uncle Tony working his whole life and just barely able to support his family. Tina with no money for music lessons. Tommy with no money to go to law school, even though he had almost died in the service of the United States. They all obeyed the stupid laws, and what had it gotten them?

And me? Is my life to be one ditchdigger job after another? One foreman after another regarding me as a stupid wop? I cannot accept that as my future. I am made for better things. Perhaps the Falcones will settle for scraps, but not Nilo Sesta.

He walked softly down the hall. The smell was heaviest outside one door. He pushed it open and stepped inside. There, in the dim light from an outside window, he saw the overhead brass and copper tubing that carried the sour grain mix around until it distilled into alcohol for drinking.

It had been left to him to decide how to shut down the still, and now Nilo looked around the room for something that would burn. A fire would do the job nicely, he thought.

He found some old newspapers bundled in a corner and began spreading them around under the still. He guessed it would not take much of a fire to ignite the alcohol cooker. He also found some broken wood slats stacked in a corner, like a small lumber pile for a home workshop. Moving as quietly as he could, he spread those out in small pyramids over the piles of newspaper.

Then he lit a match and ignited the paper, first at one corner of the still, then at the other. In just a few moments, the paper was blazing and the long-dried wood had also caught fire.

Time to leave. This will burn like a bonfire.

Nilo turned to go but was caught up short when he saw an old lady standing in the open doorway of the room. She was all dressed in black and she seemed to be staring at him, as if trying to memorize his features so that she would be able to identify him later on.

Nilo felt panic rising. *This is a real mess now. No one told me about any woman. The Valentis I could handle, but this woman? She is probably their mother. And now what do I do with her?*

But he already knew the answer.

The woman began to open her mouth, but before she could speak or call out, Nilo ran to the doorway and clubbed her alongside the head with the stock of the shotgun. She fell heavily onto the floor.

He waited in the hallway until he was sure the fire was fully burning. Still unsure of the right thing to do, he turned toward the front door to leave.

"Hey!" A voice called from behind him.

"There's a fire." Another voice called.

He spun around and saw two burly men running down the stairs from an upstairs bedroom. These must be the Valenti brothers.

"Who the hell are you?" one called. Even as he shouted, he was raising a pistol he held in his hand.

Without thinking, without hesitating, without even lifting the shotgun to his shoulder, Nilo squeezed the triggers of the double-barrel from his waist.

The two brothers stopped on the stairs as if they had run face-first into an invisible wall, then both tumbled down into a pile at the bottom landing.

Nilo ran over to them, pulling the shells from the shotgun as he ran, stuffing in new shells. The face of one of the brothers had been blown away. He was gone. But the one with the pistol still groaned and tried to move. Nilo put a shotgun blast into the man's face at point-blank range.

He turned to leave, but as he passed the old lady and

looked down at her, her eyes opened, so he leaned over pulled the trigger, and watched her chest explode. For an instant, he felt regret and nausea. Without waiting for it to pass, he ran from the building, crossed the street, and stepped back into the doorway to make sure no one was following him. As he waited, he reloaded the gun again. No one followed.

It was then that he noted the tongue of flame curling up out of a basement window. In shock, he realized that there might be six more families asleep in the building. He thought of running back, trying to rouse them, but that was too dangerous.

The fire department. I can call the fire department.

It was too risky. He did not know how American police worked, but common sense said that if he called them he would be the first person they would suspect.

So he stood silently, watching the flames for a moment longer, feeling sorry for those about to die, then put his weapon back into his trouser leg and walked stiffly away.

He hoped Don Salvatore would be impressed with his new man.

• *The deaths of six people in the tenement fire Nilo set were big news that winter day in early 1920, but Salvatore Lucania was too busy to read about it in the papers.*

In the morning, he had been summoned to a meeting with Joe the Boss Masseria, and he had gone to the small restaurant on Mulberry Street with some trepidation because Masseria's reputation as a cold-blooded murderer was well known to him. Lucania had two of his associates, a pair of young thugs named Vito Genovese and Joseph

Doto, waiting outside the restaurant with orders to come in and get him out alive if they noticed anything wrong.

But the meeting with Masseria had been smooth as silk. "Don't be nervous," Joe the Boss had said. "I just want to do business." He went on to explain: "Every time I find a new whorehouse in town, I find out that you own it."

"I put up my own money for every one of them," Lucania said.

"Don't get hot," Masseria answered with a sour smile. "I don't want your whorehouses. I don't even want a cut. I just want you to sell liquor in them. And buy the booze from me."

Without hesitation, Lucania got to his feet, extended his hand, and said, "You got a deal." Then they ate lunch and played cards, and when Lucania left the restaurant two hours later he gave the thumbs-up sign to his two men who were waiting in a car parked two doors down from the restaurant.

- *In a Brooklyn courtroom that night, Maier Suchowljansky, the onetime tool and die apprentice, was fined another two dollars for disorderly conduct for his part in the beating of three of Joe Masseria's men who had tried to cut themselves in on the profits from a crap game Suchowljansky had been running. When he paid his fine and left the courtroom, Suchowljansky was surprised to be met by Salvatore Lucania, the man he had once hit on the head with a wrench. Moving up on the two men was Benjamin Siegel, still in his teens, but already Suchowljansky's bodyguard. He scowled at Lucania, who saw him coming and told*

Suchowljansky, "I don't want no trouble. I just want to talk to you."

"About what?"

"About how we get rich."

"Why are you so kind to me?" Suchowljansky asked.

"Because I been watching you and I think you're the only guy in this city besides me who's got any brains."

- With Siegel standing guard outside the door, the two young men met until 5:00 A.M. in Lucania's apartment at 365 East Tenth Street. Twice Lucania offered to have prostitutes sent over to entertain them, but both times Suchowljansky declined. "If a man can't control his pecker, he can control nothing," he said.

By the time the meeting was done, the two had worked out a plan to one day take over all mob activity in New York City. Lucania was twenty-two years old; Suchowljansky was seventeen. Benjamin Siegel, still waiting out in the hall, a gun in each of his jacket pockets, was not yet fifteen.

When the meeting ended, the two men shared a celebratory bottle of wine and made one final decision. They would both change their names, in order to seem more American. Maier Suchowljansky would henceforth be named Meyer Lansky. Salvatore Lucania took for himself the name Charlie Luciano.

As a good host, Charlie Luciano insisted on walking the two men downstairs to their parked car. No sooner had they driven away when Luciano saw a man running down the street toward him. He *turned to flee back into the apartment when the man called his name.*

"Alphonse," Luciano said, "what is it?"

"I didn't know you was home. I been waiting for you all night."

"What's the matter?"

"The cops is after me. A cop got beat up and died, and they want me for it. I got to get out of town."

Luciano said nothing.

"I could use some money," the other man said. "I didn't get no chance to go home."

Luciano reached into his pocket and pulled out a roll of bills that he knew contained almost a thousand dollars.

"Here, Al. You take this and get going before anybody sees you."

The other man grabbed the money. "Thanks," he said. "Someday I'll do you a big favor back."

"Where you gonna go?" Luciano asked.

"Chicago. My uncle will give me a job. I'll pay you back."

Suddenly the bigger man threw his arms around Luciano in a giant bear hug of gratitude. Then he turned and loped away down the silent street.

From the front stoop of his apartment, Luciano watched until Al Capone turned the corner and vanished onto West Street. He was glad to see him go. Capone was a hothead, bound to kill many people. Best to let him do it in Chicago, where he would not mess up Luciano's plans.

Then he went upstairs to go to bed. All in all, it had been a good day. A very good day.

CHAPTER 3

Summer 1920

Down Leroy to Seventh, left one block to Carmine, up Carmine to Bleecker, then right to Downing, and down that to Seventh again, and then the whole thing backward, over and over again, until it was time to go home.

It was enough, most nights, to make Tommy Falcone wish he had never become a cop. He could have dealt with danger, with excitement, but the insufferable dullness of walking a beat pushed him to the edge.

In the months since he had returned home, he had come to realize what a medical marvel had been performed on his right hip and leg to enable him to walk again. But the doctors had probably never counted on his walking a ten-hour beat, night after night, in a heavy, sweat-soaked police uniform. It was little comfort to realize that his father, before being promoted to sergeant, had done just the same kind of stultifyingly boring patrol work, just to be able to feed his family. He remembered being little and seeing his father coming home from work and soaking his feet in the big white-speckled blue pan in which Mama roasted holiday turkeys. And he remembered thinking at the time that his father must be old, very old.

He began whistling a melody from a Verdi opera. He could never remember its name—music was Tina's specialty, not his—but he had grown up hearing Caruso sing it over the family's treasured phonograph and the music was deeply imprinted on his brain. Up ahead, he saw the call box. The clock on a nearby bank read 1:30 A.M.

He opened the box with a key and reported in. The dispatcher cleared him for a thirty-minute supper break. For a moment, he considered crossing over to St. Luke's Place, finding a bench under a streetlight, and just spending the time reading. But he gave the idea up quickly. Every time he had gone over there, no matter how late it was, the benches were all taken up by ardent young lovers. Tommy was pretty sure they would not appreciate a cop sitting among them for a half hour, even if he was just reading.

Instead, he backtracked and crossed over to an all-night restaurant two doors up on Cornelia, so small an eatery that it had no name on its flyspecked front window.

A buxom blond waitress whom he had never seen before took his order and soon delivered Tommy a hamburger, a coffee, a slice of apple pie, and a smile that she seemed to have been saving up for years. By then, though, Tommy had already propped his copy of Dickens's *American Notes* up against the sugar container and was reading. The waitress shook his book from side to side to draw his attention to his food. Tommy thanked her mechanically and went back to reading.

Let us go on again; and . . . plunge into the Five Points. . . . This is the place: these narrow ways, diverging to the right and left, and reeking everywhere with dirt and filth. Such lives as are led here, bear the same fruits here as elsewhere. The coarse and bloated faces

at the doors, have counterparts at home, and all the
wide world over. Debauchery has made the very
houses prematurely old. See how the rotten beams
are tumbling down, and how the patched and broken
windows seem to scowl dimly, like eyes that have
been hurt in drunken frays . . . all that is loathsome,
drooping, and decayed is here.

While Tommy had been reading, he had been picking
absentmindedly at his food. Now he put the book away.
It was his neighborhood Dickens was writing about, the
way it had been when his father, Tony, had first come to
America.

As he sipped his coffee, he became vaguely aware of
two female shapes, one on either side of him, talking
back and forth over his head. He considered offering to
move but peevishly decided that there were enough
empty seats in the restaurant for them to find their own
without bothering him.

He heard one of the girls say something about his
being cute, and he wanted to tell her to go away and leave
him alone. He was annoyed at all the would-be Bohemi-
ans in Greenwich Village who thought it was their obligation to crawl into bed with everyone they met.

It was only when he felt one of the girls kiss him on
the cheek that he looked up, and it took him the briefest
split second to realize that the girl, strikingly pretty in a
Mediterranean sort of way, with piled-up black hair and
a figure that was just too voluptuous for her chic flapper
dress, was his sister, Tina.

When the other girl giggled, Tommy turned to her and
saw Sofia Mangini, done up in the same fashion, over–
made-up and overdressed.

"What are you two up to?" he said in a disgusted voice.

Tina giggled and Tommy saw that she was slightly drunk.

"Oh, Tommy, don't be a fuddy-duddy. We're just out having fun. That's all."

"At two o'clock in the morning? Do Mama and Papa know? You're supposed to be home in bed. What about school tomorrow?"

"Graduation tomorrow," Tina said. "Then we're done with that dumb old school forever. Right, Sofia?"

"Right," the other girl answered.

"And Mama and Papa don't know anything. We sneaked out, down the fire escape. Both of us. Then we went to a graduation party."

"You must have been a big hit. Both of you made up that way."

"Oh, we were," Tina said. "We met the cutest boys. Except one of them thought our bosoms were too big." Sofia giggled in embarrassment and Tommy realized she was drunk, too. Tina stood very straight, thrusting her bosom forward. "Do you think that, Tommy?"

"What I think is that you've had too much to drink. And now you're both going to come with me and walk this off, or I'll have to call the paddy wagon and have you hauled off to the drunk tank."

"That's not very nice," Sofia said with a pouty look. "Your brother's not very nice, Tina."

Tina seemed to be considering the statement. "No," she finally answered, "he's nice enough. It's just that he's a stuffed shirt."

"Get walking, girls," Tommy said.

He left some change on the counter for his meal, waved to the waitress, who had been clearly watching the whole episode with interest, stuck his book back in his jacket pocket, and took the two young women outside. He forced them to walk with him for one whole circuit of his patrol route. It was better, he thought, that they get home late than drunk. They would thank him in the morning.

It was a welcome break anyway from the dull, quiet routine of his late-night post, listening to the girls jabber.

"What are you going to do after graduation?" he asked Sofia.

"I don't know. Not much. Probably work at the restaurant until . . . I don't know, something else. Probably till I get married, I guess." She sighed.

"Have you found somebody yet?"

"No," Sofia said. "Nobody even knows I'm alive."

"Aw, that's not so. A lot of people know you're alive," Tommy said. "But isn't there something you'd really like to do?"

"I used to think I'd be a nun but . . ."

"But what?"

"I just can't do that anymore," Sofia said. Her voice seemed sad, as if recalling a tragedy.

"Why not?"

"I just can't."

Tina interrupted by announcing, "I'm never going to get married. I'm going to be a rich and famous opera singer and have scads and scads of rich, handsome lovers."

Tommy laughed softly. "Papa will kill you."

Tina looked crestfallen. "It's all a dream anyway. No money for lessons. No piano." She sniffed. "Oh, Tommy, I want that so much. I'm good. Really good. I know I am."

Tommy stopped at one of his call boxes and again checked his watch by the light of the streetlamp. It was nearly 3:00 A.M.

"I'm going to have the dispatcher send out a cab to take you two home." Eventually the taxi came, and just before it pulled away with the girls in back Tommy leaned inside and touched Tina's cheek. "I bought you your piano," he said. "They'll deliver it tomorrow. Happy graduation."

Justina squealed and leaned forward to hug her brother. When she let him go, she slumped back into the corner of the taxicab, sobbing. Tommy looked at her and then toward Sofia.

Tina's friend was looking at him with a curious expression, one that almost seemed tender.

"The Falcone family," she said.

"It's not much of a piano," Tommy said. "Used, out of tune, and with a broken leg at that."

Tina was still crying as Sofia wrapped her arms about her friend and said, "It really doesn't matter what kind of a piano it is. It's just what it means."

"I guess so," Tommy said dully. He was not good at these kinds of oblique, psychological conversations.

He watched the cab roll away. Since coming home six months ago, he had not paid much attention to Justina. Apart from warning Nilo to keep his distance, he had basically ignored her life.

He guessed he had assumed that Justina was still like she had been when he went into the Marines a couple of years earlier—a nice family girl whose ambitions teetered between singing opera and having a hundred children or becoming a nun. He had always thought that Sofia was exactly the same, but maybe not. Maybe they had changed more than he knew.

THE DAY AFTER HE TORCHED the house and liquor still of the brothers Valenti, shot them and their mother to death, and managed to kill, in the fire, three other innocents who happened to be trapped inside when the tenement went up like a Roman candle, Nilo had appeared at Maranzano's uptown office, expecting to see the don, hoping perhaps to get a word of congratulations for the fine night's work. But he was intercepted at the red-haired receptionist's desk by one of Maranzano's bodyguards, who gave him a ten-dollar bill and directions by train to an address in Brooklyn.

"Is something wrong?" he had asked. "Is the don angry?"

"The don wants you to go to this address," the other man answered gruffly.

The address in Brooklyn was a rather run-down real estate office near the corner of Saratoga and Livonia, right under the elevated train tracks. The office manager was frail and old with sweaty hands, and he nervously told Nilo that he had been expecting him and would personally train him to become a real estate agent.

"I don't want to be a real estate agent," Nilo said.

"Those are my instructions. If you don't like them, your argument is with someone else, not me."

Nilo grumbled but went to the desk the old man assigned to him. "Another thing," the man said. "We speak nothing but English in this office."

So Nilo had hunkered down, spending boring day after boring day looking at the pictures and trying to make out the words in *Il Progresso* and the *Daily News* and *The National Police Gazette,* copies of which were kept in the office for the convenience of customers. The first couple of days, he thought often of just getting up, walking out, and going to find a job on a merchant ship somewhere.

But on Friday, when the man handed him a small brown envelope containing five ten-dollar bills, Nilo decided he would wait this out and see what happened. He had never expected to be paid a fortune for sitting around.

Besides the old man, whose name was Mr. Ferrara, Nilo was the only employee in the office. Whenever customers came in, Ferrara took Nilo out with him as he showed houses to prospective buyers, and after the first month Ferrara let Nilo go out with customers by himself.

Despite his annoyance at what he regarded as a giant waste of his time, Nilo found that he was beginning to enjoy the selling of homes, especially when he was successful in peddling some run-down shack at a price far beyond its true value. He quickly got to be expert at steering people past the noisy pipes, the leaky toilets, the termite-infested basements, and convincing them that the house would be just perfect for their needs.

I am truly a criminal now, he thought. *I sell hovels to the unsuspecting.*

Almost without knowing it, he began to learn from Mr. Ferrara the rules of buying and selling and some of the laws that had to be obeyed in transferring real estate from one owner to the next. He developed a better-than-passing acquaintance with two local banks that financed most of the mortgages and whose clientele seemed to be almost totally Italian-speaking.

Mr. Ferrara was very old-country, Nilo figured out, and jealous of his prerogatives as manager of the office and dedicated to preserving his authority, so Nilo learned quickly to smile and yes-sir him to death, in return for which he was allowed to do exactly what he wanted to do.

The fifty dollars came regularly in the Friday envelope—more money than Nilo had ever thought he could earn at any one time—and he used his newfound wealth to buy himself new suits and shirts and shoes.

He toyed with the idea of renting an apartment, instead

of the furnished room at Mrs. Annacharico's, but he wasn't ready yet to leave the familiar confines of the Falcones' neighborhood. Besides, he never knew when this magical fifty-dollars-a-week nipple might dry up, and so he dutifully stashed at least twenty-five dollars every week under the mattress of his bed.

He saw the Falcones less frequently than he used to. He would have found it very hard to explain to them how he was making so much money—more than Tommy or even his father earned—while selling so few houses. Even though he had finally figured out the reason: the money he was paid each week had nothing to do with real estate; it was his reward for killing the Valentis and for keeping his mouth shut about it.

One night he bumped into Tommy on the street while walking home.

"Look at you," Tommy said, waving a hand toward Nilo's neat tan suit. "The real estate business must agree with you."

Nilo grinned. "I am selling every house in Brooklyn."

This is your blood brother, Nilo thought. *Talk to him. Tell him the truth. Maybe he knows something you should know. Maybe you could even help him.*

But he knew that was a foolish idea. How could he help Tommy? He could not even help himself. He was collecting his fifty dollars a week for doing little or no work, but what guarantee had he that one Friday the pay envelope would not be empty and someone would instead hand him a shovel and tell him to go back to digging ditches?

Maybe someday he could give Tommy advice, but not now. Instead, the two young men spent five minutes talking about houses, college, the weather, police work, and neighborhood characters until the conversation just grew old.

"Mario was asking about you. He says he hasn't seen you at Mass recently," Tommy said.

"Sunday is the big selling day for houses. I go to a church in Brooklyn when I get a chance." The truth was Nilo did still go to Mass when he could, but he could no longer take communion since he refused to go to confession first. He had never been able to figure out how he could explain away the deaths of six people in the tenement fire.

Tommy invited him home for dinner, but Nilo made an excuse to get away. *He is my blood brother and my friend, and his father too is my friend, but they are police. And police ask too many questions and I have no answers.*

So he kept his own company, went to work every day, and waited to hear from Salvatore Maranzano. But month turned into month and no message came.

Nilo took to eating his lunch at a run-down little diner and candy store down the block from the real estate office, where conversations were routinely disrupted every few minutes by the elevated subway roaring by on the tracks overhead.

He liked the luncheonette because it was constantly filled with young men his own age who behaved as if the place were their own social club. All of them seemed to be involved in crime somehow, and they were impressed when Nilo stretched the truth a little to say that he was "a friend" of Salvatore Maranzano's. Nilo said that primarily to gain acceptance into the circle. Mostly he talked little and listened a lot. He found out that criminals came cheap. One could be hired to kill a man for as little as three dollars.

Prohibition, he thought. *It has created too many crooks and there are not enough jobs. They have to work cheap.*

He often sat drinking coffee with another recent immigrant from Sicily. Nilo pitied the hulking man because his English was far worse than Nilo's had ever been.

The young man's name was Albert Anastasia and with his brother, Anthony, he had found a job right away on the nearby Brooklyn docks. But Albert Anastasia never seemed to work. Instead, he talked about beating people up when the union bosses told him to, of lending out money as a loan shark, of all the cargo he was able to steal and resell.

"You like it here?" Nilo said to him one day.

Anastasia smiled. "In Sicily, I nothing. Here, I be rich man. I be boss. Anybody tries to stop me, I kill."

Nilo grinned. "Maybe we'll go into business," he said. "You kill people and I'll sell their families plots in the cemetery."

"You all right, Nilo. Maybe we do that."

Nilo was surprised to realize that Anastasia was absolutely serious. But they had little chance to talk about it. A few weeks later, Anastasia was arrested for killing another longshoreman and soon after was sent to Sing Sing.

Nilo pitied him for the end of his criminal dreams. *Another dummy sent away to break rocks with a hammer. He should have stayed in Sicily.* And as summer rolled on, he often thought, *Maybe I should have, too.*

IN JULY, SUMMER CRASHED in on the city with full force and fury, stewing New York in its own juices for day after blistering day. Bad everywhere, it seemed worst in the rabbit warren of human existence that was the Lower East Side. There, tens upon tens of thousands of Italians and Jews and Chinese and Greeks and Slavs sweltered ceaselessly in airless factory lofts under a sun so relentless that it burned the sky white. As many as four thousand humans lived in a single block. At night, those same vast numbers fled from their tenement apartments, out onto the streets and sidewalks, waiting for a breeze to come and carry away the heat of the day, but for more than a week now that breeze had not come.

Just after midnight, Sofia Mangini stood at her open bedroom window, looking out to the street below. Downstairs, the family restaurant would normally be closing— but tonight it had been visited by some of those shrewd young men whom her father fawned over and who would sit in a private back room for hours on end, talking softly over whiskey and wine, which were illegal but which they seemed to have no difficulty acquiring.

She had worked in the restaurant earlier in the night and was surprised to see the man known as Joe the Boss Masseria come in. He ate in the back room where the young men were camped out, and when Sofia brought in a fresh bottle of wine Masseria had slipped his hand under her skirt and rubbed the back of her leg.

Later he had walked into the storage room to talk to her father, and she knew that meant her father had paid the Mafia boss protection money, pretending it was a gift made in friendship. Then, led by two bodyguards, Masseria had left. He had winked at her as he went out the door.

The young men in the back room were noisier than ever after he left. It seemed that each one was trying to talk at the same time. She brought in a large pot of espresso, and as she left it on the table she heard someone say with great disdain, "The Mustache Petes will have to go." She would have to ask Tina what the Mustache Petes were. Her friend always seemed to know such things.

Across the street, the lights were on in the Falcones' apartment. At least one light stayed on every night now, until Tommy came home from walking his police beat. Sometimes, if Sofia got out of bed early, she could look from the window and see him limping down the street toward his home.

She heard a truck driving down the street. It passed her building, then stopped at the corner; four workmen got out and began to lug into the truck the body of a dead horse, which had collapsed in the day's heat and been allowed to lie where it fell. Watching out the window, Sofia wrapped her arms around herself and, despite the heat, tried to make herself shiver. Sometimes she was able to do that and it made the heat less noticeable. But tonight the shiver would not come.

Twice more since that first winter night, her father had come into her bed. She had not minded the one time because she felt sorry for him, but the last time—three weeks earlier—he had forced himself on her. Both times she had hated the thought of what she was doing, had known it was sick and evil, but after it was over her father lay next to her, holding her in his arms.

Sofia's mind had told her to push her father away, to hate him, but her body wanted to be held, wanted to feel love. In some curious way, she blamed Tommy Falcone for her plight. Tina had been raised in a loving family, and as she grew up her thoughts had turned instantly, constantly to boys. Sofia's thoughts never had. Somehow she had just expected that Tommy Falcone was going to marry her, and since that had already been decided in her mind, she did not have to think about other young men.

But now it was clear that Tommy had decided to chart his own path through life and Sofia was no part of it. He had destroyed her last decent chance to feel honest affection, and now she was stuck with only her father. She loathed what they had done—were still doing—together, and, yes, she suspected that if she kept on living here it would continue to go on.

The thought made her shudder.

This isn't love, she thought, *sleeping with your own father. It isn't the way love is supposed to be. Love is warmth and sharing and friendship and poetry, and this is vile and sick.*

And it is all I have . . . all I have ever had.

She had wanted to tell someone. She had thought of confessing her sin to Father Mario, but it was too unwholesome for even the church to forgive. She had not even been able to tell Tina, her best friend from whom she had no other secrets, although she had wanted to day after day. But something always stopped her from speaking.

I will tell her and she will regard me as an animal, as something from a barnyard, and will no longer be my friend.

That was the explanation she gave herself. But there was another fear, too. If she told Tina, she and Tina would talk about it. Tina was still a virgin and she would want to know how Sofia did it and how it felt, and Sofia would eventually have to tell her the awful, frightening truth: that she hated it, but once it started sometimes her body took over from her mind and she wanted it never to stop.

She had become a wanton, an animal. What decent man would ever want to be with her? What woman? Anyone?

Since that night five weeks earlier when she and Tina had gone looking for him on his beat over in the Village, she had thought of Tommy often, tried to imagine them living Tina's dream of everybody living in the same house. She lay in bed at night, thinking of Tina and Tommy, and she touched herself, but her body would not respond to images of Tommy.

She had always assumed that she and Tommy would wed, and had never spent time thinking of other boys.

It was not as if she could not find someone else. Sofia was good-looking and she knew it, and she had for years understood the lustful gazes she drew while walking down the street. Every day she saw men who would race to jump into her bed.

Even Tommy's cousin, Nilo, still looked at her that way, and he now lived in the same apartment building with her, and his landlady was a dried-up old prune. Yet, while Nilo was undeniably good-looking and seemed to be working regularly, Sofia feared that down deep he was just another Sicilian peasant. But even Nilo would be better than what she had now, she thought sadly.

Perhaps if she met other men. Justina had a small part-time job in a nearby factory office—gotten for her by her policeman father—and for several hours every day when she wasn't home, practicing voice and piano, she met other people, people who weren't from the neighborhood, who weren't even Italian. Young men had even started calling for her at her house.

Sofia had wanted to get a job, too, maybe even in the place Tina worked so she could be close to her friend. It would have been easy for her father to get her such a job, he met so many people in the restaurant. But he had insisted that she stay in the restaurant and learn how to become his bookkeeper. She wasn't even a regular waitress, only being called on to serve tables when someone failed to show up for work or if they were very busy. A waitressing job might have been bearable. At least waitresses got a chance to meet and talk to other people. Most of the time, Sofia sat alone in the back room under a dim light, looking at bills and invoices and rows of numbers.

She would never meet anyone.

Tina had tried to help. She talked often of Sofia marrying Tommy, and while that idea did not terribly interest Sofia any longer, she liked being around Tina to hear her talk about weddings and marriage and love. The only problem with Tommy, Tina said, was that he was working all night as a policeman and going to school all day and there wasn't time for anything else. Tommy was planning to be a rich lawyer someday, and that took a lot of work and did not leave much energy left over.

"Not even for you," Tina had said. "But I'll work at him."

"Don't even think of it, Tina," Sofia had responded. "It doesn't matter. You and I will be friends forever."

Sofia walked away from the window and climbed into bed, kicking the covers away from her. She hesitated a moment, then said her nightly prayers, adding a quick Act of Contrition and begging Jesus to forgive her for what she had become, and stretched out. But sleep would not come.

Just a few blocks away, over in Greenwich Village, even this late at night, people were laughing, living, loving, she knew, and she was lying here like a bloated dying toad. She had dreamed of a life of freedom, of poetry . . . but none of the young lady poets of the Village, in all their works she had read, had anything to say that addressed how desolate and unhappy she had become.

She tried desperately to call up a poem, even a single line, that could tell her there was a bright side, but the only verse she heard in her head were lines and rhythms of death and despair.

Tears welled in Sofia's eyes. She could not think of Tommy Falcone; all that was in her mind was some broad

abstract idea of love. She forced herself to picture him
and she saw Tommy and Tina and Sofia, all together, as
one. Maybe Tommy could still be her way out of this trap.
She wiped her eyes with the back of her wrist, then
dreamily pulled up her thin nightgown and rested her fingers between her thighs and slowly began to move them.
Her breath started to come in little gasps. She could feel
the beginning of that special feeling start to take hold.
She worked her hand more quickly. Tommy's face was
gone now; all that was left in her mind was Tina. It was
happening. She could feel it almost there.

And then the outside door to the apartment slammed
open to a loud, rapid-fire burst of cursing and swearing.
The feeling ebbed. For a moment, Sofia tried to keep it
going, to get it back, but it was no use. She took her hand
away and tried to fight back her fears and frustration.
Outside her bedroom door, in the parlor beyond, the
battle between her parents raged, growing in intensity.

Sofia was surprised. Whatever result taking her father
to bed might have on her immortal soul, it had brought a
few months of peace in the family, the first that Sofia had
ever known. Not that things had greatly improved. Mrs.
Mangini had grown even more withdrawn and cold to her
husband than she had been before, and sometimes Sofia
felt the old woman had guessed what was happening
between her father and her.

But still, for a while, there had been no arguments or
shouting and, best of all, there were no more beatings.
Whatever else she had done, Sofia had brought her mother
personal safety.

Now that seemed to be over. Matteo Mangini was
cursing his wife with an unending stream of Italian invective. She pressed her fingertips into her ears, but she
could still hear them.

"Fatti i cazzi tuoi," her father shouted.

"Figlio di zoccola," her mother responded.

Sofia listened, afraid to do anything, afraid not to. Abruptly, the swearing stopped and she could hear her father's heavy footsteps lumbering across the wooden floor of the apartment toward her door. She heard his hand grab the doorknob.

Please, dear God, may he not come to me tonight. Please, may I not give in to him. Please, God, spare me this.

Then another stream of epithets erupted from her mother.

"Pisciasotto!" Sofia heard her call out. Matteo stopped with Sofia's door open just a crack. Then he closed the door. She could hear him walking away, heavily, deliberately.

Sofia was frightened. She got out of bed, pulled a robe around her, and tiptoed to the bedroom door. When she opened it a crack, she saw her mother backed against the far wall. Matteo had one hand over her face and was banging her head against the wall. With the other hand, he had a grip around his wife's neck and was trying to lift her off the floor.

Sofia watched in absolute horror for the space of two or three heartbeats. If she did not do something immediately, her mother would be dead. She threw open the door and ran into the living room, throwing herself on her father's back and clawing and hammering at him.

"Papa, stop! Papa, stop!"

At first, it did no good. It was as if he were a robot, made of steel, unable to be moved from his path. Then, slowly, he became aware of his daughter's attack. He dropped his wife into a heap on the floor, reached out and plucked Sofia off his back, and threw her onto the couch.

She started to get up and he slapped her down with a brutal combination of backhand and open-hand slaps. She slumped back, blood seeping from the corner of her mouth where his heavy ring had caught her.

Sofia saw his eyes were glassy from drinking too much. Her mother struggled to raise herself into a sitting position on the floor.

Matteo looked back at her, then at his daughter again. Slowly, elaborately, as if commanding his wife to bear witness, he pulled off his suspenders, opened his trouser fly, and slid his pants down his legs.

"Watch this, you dried-up old crone," he rasped bitterly.

He moved toward Sofia and extended a hand to touch her cheek. She stiffened. She could not stand it anymore, not anymore, not this way. She wished it had never started, but she vowed it would end here. As Matteo leaned over her, reaching inside his khaki-colored underwear, Sofia stretched backward, grasping for something, anything that would help. Her hand found a table lamp, closed around it, then, with strength she did not know she had, smashed it across the side of her father's head.

Matteo fell backward, away from his daughter, off the couch. He was down, moaning, but not unconscious. Sofia backed away from him, clambering over the edge of the couch and hurrying toward the apartment door. From the corner of her eye, she could see her mother slowly rising.

Wearing only her robe and nightgown, Sofia opened the door and ran out into the hall and toward the stairs. As she started down, the front door of the building opened and Nilo entered. He saw her above him, saw the blood on her face, and ran up the steps and put his arms around her.

"What happened? What's wrong?" he asked. His voice was thick and slurred, and Sofia smelled strong wine on his breath. Still, for a moment she thought of telling him, of even asking to spend the night safely in his room. But it would just be too scandalous.

"I'm all right," she said, and pulled away from him and ran down the steps and out the front door.

As Nilo came down to watch, he saw her clamber up the fire escape across the street and sneak up the two flights until she was outside Tina's bedroom, tapping on the window. He waited until he saw the window open and Sofia climb through before he went back inside.

He thought for a moment of going to the Manginis' apartment and seeing if things were all right, but then put the thought aside and stumbled up the steps toward his own furnished room. *I have my own problems. Let Sofia deal with hers. I can't take care of the world.*

THE NEXT MORNING, Sofia and Tina managed to leave the Falcone apartment without anyone seeing them. Sofia was wearing a dress of Tina's; she had applied a lot of powder to cover the bruise on her face.

On the street, Tina said, "I don't know if this is the right thing to do."

"Then you tell me what is," Sofia said.

"We could go over to Mount Carmel and talk to Mario," Tina said. "He's a priest. He knows how to take care of things. Or you could let my father go talk to your father and get it all straightened out."

Sofia shook her head. Despite their closeness, she had not told Tina what had actually happened, only that Mr. Mangini had beaten her and her mother up. Sofia decided that the rest of it must remain a secret.

"It's a family matter," she said. "I shouldn't even have come over to you last night. But I didn't have anyplace else to go."

"That's a fine thing to say," Tina snapped. "I'm your best friend, in case you've forgotten." She already knew there was something Sofia had not told her, and she had guessed what it was.

"Of course you are. But you're not family, Tina. Having anybody but family deal with this would disgrace my parents. What kind of Sicilian are you, anyway? You should know that."

"Don't you ever listen to my papa? This isn't Sicily and we're not Sicilians. We're Americans. You too."

"Just tell that to the English. Tell that to all those rich pigs who live uptown and look down on us. Or, worse yet, who want to help us with their settlement houses and their little youth programs to teach us to be just like them. But who won't give us any money, except what we grab from them with our hands and our brains."

Tina was surprised by her friend's ferocity. She did not answer and was silent for a long time before she asked, "How do you know he can help us? Or that he will want to?"

Sofia led the way across a busy street.

"Salvatore will help because he is family. My mother's cousin. And Sicilian too. Not like some Americans I can name."

"All right," Tina conceded. "Let's go and meet this cousin of yours. But I still think you should have talked to Mario first."

"These kinds of problems Mario can't help," Sofia said. "All he can do is pray, and my father needs more than prayers said over him."

"And Cousin Salvatore will do more than pray?"

"If he wants to," Sofia said. "Papa listens to him and is afraid of him. He is in the restaurant a lot, and he supplies Papa with all the illegal wine that he keeps for his regular customers."

"He's a bootlegger?" Tina asked.

Sofia snorted derisively, as if it were stupid to even ask such a question. "He's very tough," she said. "They say he's already killed two or three men. He works for Joe Masseria."

"That fat old man with the long mustache who walks around wearing a great big cape, like he's God or a movie star or something like that?"

"He is Mafia," Sofia said. At the corner of Kenmare and Mulberry, she pointed to an old two-story garage and warehouse. "That's where Salvatore works."

"In a warehouse?" Tina laughed. "I can see he's really an important man. Maybe he'll give us a free bottle of olive oil."

But she was pulled along by Sofia, who grabbed her sleeve and walked up to the door and knocked on it loudly. After a few seconds, it was opened by a good-looking very young man with sharp features and a highly creased suit that Tina thought was more whorehouse than warehouse.

"What do you want?" he asked, boldly appraising the two pretty young women.

"I'm Mr. Lucania's cousin," Sofia said. "I'd like to see him."

"If you were really his cousin, you'd know that his name isn't Lucania anymore. So why don't you go away?"

Sofia looked startled by the man's rudeness, but Tina snapped, "Just tell him that Sofia Mangini wants to see him. Do it quickly and we won't tell him what a rude baboon he has working for him."

Anger flashed across the young man's face. He swallowed hard, then nodded toward two hard chairs. "Sit down and wait," he said. "Maybe he'll talk to you. Maybe he won't."

He walked back into the dark confines of the warehouse, where Tina could see a half-dozen large trucks parked. They heard his footsteps clacking as he walked up metal steps to the second floor.

"Where'd you learn to talk like that?" Sofia whispered to Tina.

"Grow up in a house with two brothers and you learn fast. Jump on them before they jump on you. Besides, he's not even a man. He's a boy. He's younger than we are."

After only a few minutes, the handsome young man returned, followed by another man. He too was well dressed. He was stocky and olive-skinned, and his right eyelid drooped slightly so it looked as if he were winking. When he saw Sofia he brushed past the other man and hurried to them. Both girls stood up, and Tina saw that the man was also young, only a few years older than they were. And he was barely as tall as Tina herself

"Sofia," the man said. "I'm very sorry to keep you waiting. If I had known you were coming . . ."

"That's all right, Salvatore," Sofia said. "This is my friend, Tina Falcone. She lives across the street from me."

Lucania looked at Tina and smiled. "First of all, everybody calls me Charlie now. Charlie Luciano." His eyes were coldly appraising as he looked over Tina's face. "Falcone. You have a father who's a cop, haven't you?"

Tina was surprised that he would know that.

"Yes," she said. "And two brothers. Another policeman and a priest."

"A busy family," he said. "It's good to meet you." He

looked back to Sofia. "Now what can I do for you, little cousin?"

"I . . . I . . ." Sofia began, and then tears began to gush from her eyes. Tina put an arm around her and wiped her eyes with a handkerchief she took from her dress pocket.

"She is having family problems," Tina told Luciano, as Sofia sobbed in her arms. The swarthy young man nodded as if he had heard that story before.

"A lot of people still think they're in the old country," he said noncommittally. "Maybe we should go inside the office here."

He turned to lead them into a small office near the front door. As he did, the other young man who had been waiting about twenty feet away started forward, but Luciano waved him off with his hand.

"It's all right, Ben," he said. "A family matter."

The handsome youngster nodded and walked away.

"I guess Benny was rude to you when you arrived," Luciano said to the women as he escorted them to a threadbare sofa inside the sparsely furnished office.

"Did he tell you that?" Tina asked.

"No. But Benny is too young to have learned any manners yet, so he is rude to everyone."

Sofia had stopped crying, and when the man asked her again to explain her problem she told of the beatings and how her mother had once stabbed her father. She told him everything . . . except the part that she could not even bring herself to tell her friend, Tina.

"I'm scared," Sofia said. "I ran away last night . . . just across the street . . . but I'm afraid to go back. And I'm afraid to stay there. I know it's just a matter of time before somebody kills somebody else."

"And he did this to you?"

Luciano reached out and gently touched the girl's mouth where the small cut from Mangini's ring had already scabbed over. He let his fingers linger on her face.

Sofia looked up from the sofa and nodded. Tina noticed that Luciano had taken a position in front of them so that his crotch was right in line with their faces. She was sure that was not just an accident and thought to herself that this Charlie Luciano cousin of Sofia's was just another posing lowlife.

"Oh, Salvatore, I'm so scared."

She began crying again, and Luciano patted her shoulder but almost absentmindedly. His eyes remained on Tina.

"It's Charlie, please. And what would you have me do?" he finally asked, when Sofia's sobbing stopped.

"She doesn't need sympathy," Tina said sharply. "And if she listened to me, her father would be in a jail cell right now for what he's done."

"But you don't want that?" he asked Sofia.

"Maybe if you talk to him. I want you to stop him before he does something terrible. Before . . . before . . ."

Luciano helped Sofia raise herself from the couch, then put his arms around her.

"Don't worry," he said. "I'll take care of it." His words were meant to comfort, but Tina saw his face take on a sour, almost-nasty look. She knew he had figured out what had happened the night before, just as Tina herself had figured it out.

He said again, "I'll take care of everything," and Tina asked abruptly, "When?" fully expecting a "these-things-take-time" excuse from the man.

"Tonight," he said. "This will all be taken care of by tonight." As Sofia continued to sob in his arms, he looked past her shoulder at Tina. "Will that be quick enough for you?" he asked.

There was a smile on his face—as if the two of them shared a secret—but the smile never reached his intense dark eyes. He knew. Tina was sure. He knew.

*   *   *

"Sempre libera degg'io
Follegiare di gioia in gioia . . ."

Tommy laced his fingers behind his head and lay in bed, listening as Tina's light lyrical voice rang through the apartment. The sun was streaming through the window and made the room seem cheerful, almost gay, despite the nightstick and handcuffs dropped onto the seat of the easy chair in the corner.

He felt good, much better than he had ever hoped. A year ago, he would have thought that every single day would be a battlefield on which he had to fight back his addiction to morphine, but it had not worked that way. There had been no problem at all: no craving, no temptation. It was almost as if he had never been addicted at all. It seemed much too easy.

"Vissi d'arte, vissi d'amore, non feci mai
Male ad anima viva! . . ."

He translated the lyrics in his mind. *Love and music, that's what I live for, and have never harmed a living being.* Just like Tina herself, he thought.

Tina, he knew, really did have an exceptional voice, although whether or not it was as good as the sopranos he heard on the family's record player would have to be left to someone else's judgment. Tommy was pleased at how well she accompanied herself on the piano. When Tommy had bought her the old relic of a piano for her graduation, she played as if she had never seen such an instrument, but her playing now was certainly serviceable enough to accompany her voice.

Tommy began to itch, then started scratching his belly. It was the damned heat. He hated it. He hated sweating and always feeling damp.

Maybe he wasn't really a Sicilian, he thought idly. Maybe not even an Italian. Maybe his parents had found him in a basket on the street and just given him a home.

"And maybe I'm a teapot," he mumbled to himself, as he stretched and swung his feet over the side of the bed and sat up. He put on his robe and padded out into the living room.

"Morning," he said to his sister, who stopped playing and smiled at him.

"Sleep well?" she asked.

"Nahhh. There was this cat screeching out in the yard. Woke me up. At least, I think it was a cat."

Tina threw a music book at him. "You are vile," she said.

They both laughed, and Tina started playing again as Tommy went into the bathroom and took a bath as cold as he could stand. The precinct house where he worked was a cesspool, but it had a large bathroom with a pair of shower stalls, and Tommy often stopped in there after his tour, just to wash off the sweat and get comfortable. The Falcones' apartment had no such luxury as a shower. The only alternatives at home were to sit in the bathtub or to wash at the sink with a facecloth. Someday, Tommy thought, he would have his own home and it would have a shower. Definitely a shower.

As he dried himself he felt clean, but he was already sweating again as he went into the kitchen. Tina had poured coffee for him and was making him toast over the gas flame on the stove.

"You missed all the excitement last night," Tina said.

"Oh?"

"Sofia came running over in the middle of the night. Before you got home. She was pretty upset."

"Why?"

"Her father's been beating up her mother. Her too. Her mouth was even cut."

"Jesus Christ," Tommy snapped.

Tina shook her head as she was buttering the thick slices of Italian bread. "If you ask me, it might be even worse."

"How worse?"

"I think her father . . ." She hesitated as she put the toast in front of Tommy. She would not meet his eyes. "I think her father is trying to . . . you know . . . sleep with her."

Tommy put down his coffee cup. "I don't want to hear about this," he said. "Did she say that?"

Tina shook her head. "No. But I just get that feeling." She busied herself rinsing dishes at the sink. "I went with her this morning to see a cousin of hers. She asked him for help."

"What'd he say?"

"He said he'd help, but I don't believe him. He's just a dumb thug."

"Who is this cousin?"

"His name used to be Salvatore something, but now he calls himself Charlie Luciano."

"Never heard of him," Tommy said.

"He's one of the gees that hang around in Mr. Mangini's

restaurant," Tina said, using the neighborhood's slang term for gangsters.

"I don't want you hanging out with people like that."

"It wasn't exactly hanging out, Tommy. I just walked with her to this jerk's office."

"It's a good office to stay away from. What would Papa say?"

"Papa won't know. And you won't tell him," she said confidently. Now she turned to him and stared him down. Finally, reluctantly, Tommy nodded.

NILO WOKE UP COUGHING. His tongue felt thick and the back of his mouth was dry. He had spent much of the last night at the luncheonette in Brooklyn, drinking bad whiskey with the other young men, and he had trouble remembering how he got home.

I will not drink that much again, he promised himself. *Drunkenness is for the Irishers. I do not know what I will become, but it will not be a drunk.*

In the apartment outside his room, he heard his landlady bustling around, and he knew he could not put up this morning with her nosy questions about his work, his salary, even his love life, so he dressed quickly and sneaked downstairs.

Outside, he saw Tommy sitting on his front steps. He was looking away, down the block. Nilo followed his eyes and saw Sofia, carrying a market basket on her arm, walking rapidly away on her morning trip to the bakery. He remembered then meeting her in the hallway last night.

As Tommy got up to cross the street, Nilo intercepted him.

"Morning, brother," he said.

Tommy seemed startled for a moment, then nodded to him.

"Where are you going in such a hurry?" Nilo asked, walking along with him.

"I've got to talk to old man Mangini."

"About Sofia?"

Tommy stopped. "What about her?"

"I saw her last night. She was crying and her mouth was cut. Did her father do that?"

"Yeah."

"And what are you going to do?"

"Tell him to stop."

"I'll go with you," Nilo said.

"No need. It's no business of yours."

"Yours either," Nilo said.

"All right," Tommy said after a moment. "But stay out of it."

It was the first time Tommy had been in the restaurant since he returned from France. Tony had never liked Matteo Mangini, so Tommy didn't, either. The restaurant had not changed much. There was a linoleum floor and wallpaper imprinted with scenes of Italy. The tables were wood, covered with red-and-white-checked tablecloths.

It was still early, the Saturday lunch crowd had not yet arrived, and only a few of the tables were occupied, mostly by neighborhood people. Tommy nodded at the ones he knew. Mr. Mangini was seated behind the cash register at the back of the restaurant, and as Tommy walked up to him Nilo trailed behind.

"We have to talk," Tommy said.

Mangini looked at him with a quizzical smile.

"So talk."

"Let's go in the back room," Tommy said.

"Look. Now that you're a cop, if you're going to try to

squeeze me for money, forget it. I already pay off the important ones."

Tommy stood stone-still. "The back room," he said levelly. Even as he struggled to control his temper at the thought of this man beating Sofia, a part of him wondered why he was getting involved. He was not that close to Sofia and it was not any of his business. Still, he guessed, he was the closest thing she had to a big brother. It might have been something he learned from Mario.

The older man shrugged, then led the way into the back room. It was a large room with four tables that could be moved around to seat as many as twenty-five people. A small lamp burned on a table in a corner, throwing weird shadows across the textured tin walls.

Nilo followed them inside and closed the door, and when Mangini turned, Tommy said simply, "You've been beating your wife and daughter. You've got to stop."

"You been trying to do my daughter?" Mangini demanded.

"No," Tommy said.

"Then fuck you, you insolent snot."

"I hoped you'd say that," Tommy said.

"Yeah? Why's that?"

"So I won't regret slapping you silly."

Mangini snarled, drew back his right hand, and threw a straight punch at Tommy's face.

With the instinct learned from years of sparring with Mario, Tommy ducked. The punch slid past his hand, and Mangini's hand smashed into a tall brass hat rack with a loud crack.

"Owww," the man cried out, then doubled over, holding his right hand to his waist, his eyes wide and frightened. Then fear gave way to anger.

"You son of a bitch," Mangini shouted. "I've got friends. I'm gonna fix you good, get you thrown off the police. I'm gonna—"

Suddenly Nilo was on the man, his left hand around Mangini's throat, his right hand holding a knife point to the man's face.

"You're gonna do nothing," Nilo said softly. "Tommy will only beat you up, but I will cut your heart out and use it to feed rats." He pressed the point of the blade against Mangini's cheek. There was a sharp glint in his eyes that frightened Tommy, who said sharply, "Nilo, don't. That's enough."

Nilo let go of Mangini's throat but reached out and grabbed the man's injured hand. The knuckle on the index finger was already red and swollen. Nilo squeezed, and Mangini screamed sharp and short and pulled the hand away to cradle it to his chest.

"Don't make us come back," Nilo said.

Outside, Tommy told Nilo, "You're fun to have around."

"Some people cannot be talked to. With them, talk only results in more talk. He was talking too much, and I could not have him threaten your livelihood."

"Maybe so. But you're too quick with that knife."

"It is a souvenir of my days on the *tonnara* boats. I never want to forget where I came from."

"Be careful with it," Tommy said.

"These days, I use it only to clean my nails," Nilo said.

Tommy left to go to the college library to study. When Nilo walked down the street, he looked up and saw Tina sitting by the windowsill of the Falcones' apartment. She waved and Nilo merely nodded. He was thinking that he had nearly lost control back in the restaurant, almost had pushed his knife into Mangini's face. He would have to learn to manage his temper better. *A man who is out of control is only prey. But even worse is one who does nothing but talk.*

MANGINI'S RESTAURANT WAS EMPTY of customers except for the stay-late group in the private back room. Mrs. Mangini and Sofia had left, and Matteo Mangini was checking the night's receipts when Charlie Luciano came out of the back room.

He sat at one of the empty tables in the big dining room and gestured for Mangini to join him.

Mangini hurried over to him, and Luciano said, "Sit down." He nodded toward the bandage on Mangini's hand. "What happened to you?"

For a moment, Mangini was tempted to tell him, but some instinct caused him to hold his tongue.

"Accident. I broke a finger," he said instead.

Luciano nodded. He spoke softly, as if reciting a grocery list to himself. "I was going to break your hand myself, but I don't think I will do that now. You with two broken hands and where would we eat?"

"Break my hand? Why?" Mangini said.

"We will talk about it just this once and never again," Luciano said. "Your wife is a relative of my mother's. You have been putting hands to her and your daughter. You will not do it again."

Words of protest sprang to Mangini's lips. He thought of denying everything, of being outraged, of trying to look misunderstood. But as he saw Luciano's obsidian-chip eyes staring at him, he simply lowered his head and nodded.

"Good," Luciano said, rising. "Then we understand each other. Now please, more wine. The boys are thirsty."

ONE STEAMY DAY late in July, Mr. Ferrara closed the realty office to go to a funeral and Nilo rode an early train back to Manhattan. On a whim, he went uptown to Maranzano's office, arriving there shortly after five o'clock.

As he crossed the street toward the building, Betty, Maranzano's lush secretary, came out of the office and strolled toward the corner. Nilo hustled after her, catching up as she stopped to wait in a trolley stop.

Nilo touched her shoulder, and she turned around with the suspicious look that he thought characterized New York women. For a moment, she seemed angry; then her expression softened.

"Nilo," he said. "Do you remember me?"

"Sure I do," she said, and glanced down toward her bosom, now demurely clad in a dark jacket, and when she lifted her eyes again both she and Nilo laughed.

"How do you like it in Brooklyn?" she asked.

"It's too far away from you," he said.

"Oh, you're becoming an American very quickly," she said.

She seemed to want to patter on, but Nilo wanted to know how she knew he was working in Brooklyn. The young woman smiled. "Just another one of Mr. Maranzano's businesses. It doesn't really concern me."

"How'd you know I was there?"

"I see your name on the payroll list every week. I put the money in the pay envelopes."

"Good. Then you know I can afford to take you to dinner," Nilo said.

Betty had to beg off for that night, though. She explained that she lived with her parents and they had family members coming over for dinner. But Saturday, she would be free Saturday night.

"Saturday is so far away," he said.

She looked down the street. "It'll give you time to get ready," she said. "Here comes my ride."

Nilo took her arm to help her up onto the trolley's high steps.

"Tell me," he said before letting her go. "Does Don Salvatore ever speak of me?"

She smiled again. "You'll just have to wait till Saturday night to find out."

But the next day, Mr. Ferrara got a telephone call in the office that caused him to sit up straighter at his desk while he answered.

When he hung up the telephone, he nodded across the room to Nilo. "Tomorrow night," he said.

"Tomorrow night what?"

"You are to have dinner with Don Salvatore."

NILO WATCHED MARANZANO, then tried to imitate the older man, delicately cutting the beef on his plate into bite-size pieces. He failed. The fork would not hold the food still, and when he tried to use the knife it would slip and slide, making a screeching noise on his plate. Maranzano appeared not to notice.

He chewed a mouthful of food, swallowed, and told Nilo, "As Caesar said . . ." and then rattled off a long rapid statement that Nilo guessed was in Latin.

Helpless for something to say in response, Nilo picked up his wineglass and tried to sip, but his hand was shaking too badly. This was the first time he had seen Don Salvatore since March, and here he was, eating at the great man's table and disgracing himself with both his stupidity and his vile table manners. He could not drink. He set the wineglass back down, placed it squarely on yet another spoon that was on the table, and half the dark red wine spilled onto the brilliant white tablecloth before Nilo could grab it and set it right. *What is the need for so many spoons anyway?* Nilo wondered. *A man has one mouth; surely even Julius Caesar would understand that one mouth requires only one spoon.*

Maranzano leaned across the table, took Nilo's knife and fork, and cut the young man's thin slice of beef into a half-dozen smaller pieces. As he sat back, he said, "Let me translate Caesar for you: 'Sometimes, when the gods want to punish a man for his sins, they give him great prosperity so that he suffers even more when his fortunes change.' An interesting thought, don't you agree, Nilo?"

Nilo now had a mouth filled with food and could only nod. The truth was that Nilo thought nothing about Julius Caesar, but he wondered if there was a subtle message in those words for him. *Am I the one who has been given great prosperity? Is that what the fifty dollars each week means? I have been given prosperity so that I can suffer all the more? Was it my great sin to kill those people in the apartment house fire?*

Don Salvatore appeared to be waiting for an answer, and Nilo finally swallowed and said, "Yes, sir."

Maranzano smiled indulgently. "You are so very young, Nilo. Let me explain. I was just trying to reveal to you an important lesson we could all learn from Caesar."

Nilo nodded slowly. He did not have any idea of what Maranzano was getting at, but he was certain the man would eventually explain it. And explain it. And explain it.

Two young black serving girls came into the room, and Maranzano leaned back in his chair and waited for them to remove his and Nilo's dishes.

"Would you care for dessert?"

Nilo wanted dessert desperately, but the thought of having to maneuver his utensils one more time frightened him.

"No, thank you, Don Salvatore. I have already had too much to eat, thank you."

"A lemon gelato? Light and refreshing. Especially on a night as hot as this."

Nilo thought that perhaps every other place in New York City was stifling this night, but not Don Salvatore's apartment, which had handsome electric fans standing in every corner blowing breezes through the room.

"Thank you, no," Nilo said.

Maranzano nodded and stood up. "Very well, then. I appreciate a man who knows how to discipline his appetites. Too many in our business do not. Let's go into the next room for coffee. Or brandy."

"Coffee would be fine," Nilo said. Maranzano smiled.

"You are that rarest of young men. Moderate in all things," he said. They sat in the living room and Maranzano offered him a large cigar. Somehow, Nilo thought it would be offensive to decline and took the big stogie. But he had never smoked a cigar before and had no idea how it was done. He held the cigar in his fingers and watched as Maranzano bit the end off one, spat it into an ashtray, and then lit it. Nilo did the same, trying not to gag on the thick, rich smoke.

Maranzano said, "Never be ashamed, Nilo, to say you do not know something. It is only a fool who pretends to know everything. Ask. Learn. And then never forget."

The serving girls brought coffee, and after they left, Maranzano said, "Now, as I was saying about Caesar. This Joe Masseria has risen to power much too easily. You know who he is?"

"Yes, sir. They call him Joe the Boss of the Mafia."

"That is what he claims to be," Maranzano said, and there was an edge to his voice that Nilo had not ever heard before. "He has had much good fortune, but I do not believe his good fortune comes because he is favored by God. Instead, I believe it is because God plans his eventual destruction. Just as Caesar's words said. So he will suffer more later."

"I see, Don Salvatore," Nilo said. He took only the smallest puffs on the cigar, just enough to keep it lit, not enough to make him cough.

I hate cigars, their smell and their taste. I would rather lick a bull's ass than smoke these things.

"I also believe that this Masseria is merely serving to prepare the way for me." He looked hard at Nilo. "Does that surprise you?"

"No, sir. I have seen this Masseria walking around my neighborhood. He is a sloppy old man with dirty fingernails and stains on his shirt. I think you would be a far better boss of all the Mafia than he is."

"Thank you." Maranzano seemed content with the answer. He leaned back on his sofa, closed his eyes, and blew a large smoke ring toward the ceiling.

This man is vain, totally vain, Nilo thought. *There may come a time when I will have to remember that his weak point is his vanity.*

Suddenly Maranzano opened his eyes, sat up straight, and leaned forward across the couch toward Nilo.

"I have a plan and you are an important part of it," he said. "But we have some problems."

"Sir?"

"Stand up and walk across the room."

Self-consciously, Nilo did as he was told. On a signal

from Maranzano, he walked back and sat again in the soft stuffed chair.

"You move well," Maranzano said. "But you dress like a cheap gangster. And your table manners . . . well, they are those of a peasant."

Nilo felt his face flush.

"How long has it been since you came here?" the older man asked. "Six months? Seven?" He did not wait for an answer. "You speak English pretty well, better than any-body else I know in such a short time. But you have to get rid of that accent. Can you read yet?"

Nilo looked down at his two-toned wing-tip shoes but found no comfort there. He had once thought they were stylish; now, he realized, his mentor was right. They were cheap and gangsterish. Some of the men who hung around Maranzano might wear such shoes, but Don Salvatore himself never would.

"I read a little," he said. "I had started to take lessons from my cousin, but I moved out and she no longer has time for me."

"This would be Justina Falcone?" Maranzano said.

Nilo nodded. "She wishes to be an opera singer and spends all her time practicing." *How does he know about Tina? Does he know my uncle Tony and Tommy are police? I have never told him.* He quickly said, "She has no real money for lessons. My uncle Tony is only a policeman. Her brother too. They have no money."

Maranzano nodded, as if satisfied. "Is there anyone else who can teach you?"

Nilo thought. "There is a young girl in my building. Sofia Mangini. Her father owns the restaurant below."

"Is she a girlfriend?"

Nilo shook his head. "We say 'Good morning.' 'How

are you?' 'Hot today.' I don't think she likes me very much."

"Good," Maranzano said. "Then no personal business will interfere with your learning. I want you to hire her to teach you how to read and how to speak without an accent." Before Nilo could respond, he added, "Of course, I will pay for the lessons. There is more you must learn. You must learn to behave like a gentleman. How to eat, how to dress. I will pay for these things also. You must go to the museums and to concerts. And you will learn how to speak like an English. This Mangini girl can do that, too."

"Yes, Don Salvatore." Nilo's head was swimming.

Why does this man care about me, how I dress, how I speak? What does it matter to him?

It was as if Maranzano had read his mind. "I don't do this because I am a good man. I do it because I am a shrewd man."

"I think you are both."

"Very diplomatic, Nilo. I will tell you. There is much money to be made from this Prohibition. We are making it already. So is Masseria. He is large; we are still small. But he is a lowlife and spends his money, lighting cigars with hundred-dollar bills and buying fancy cars and fancy women, and the men under him act just the same way."

It did not sound at all bad to Nilo, but he merely nodded and tried to look sympathetic.

"That will be their downfall," Don Salvatore said. "This fool Prohibition will not last forever. If we are to survive and thrive, we must do something with all this money we will make. We shall have to find work for it. We shall have to buy friends among the English, especially among the rich ones. That is why we must speak their language. And I do not mean just in words. We must be like them. We must be able to eat at their tables without disgusting them. I dined last night with a judge. Next week, I have lunch with two congressmen. Cultivating such people is what we must do to survive. And we must have something else to talk about besides money. We must be able to laugh at their jokes. Most of us can't. We are still too dumb, too uneducated. But we can cure dumbness. We can cure a lack of education."

He sipped again at his brandy.

"You will be the first," he said. "After me."

Nilo sank back in his chair, overwhelmed by what Don Salvatore seemed to be saying, and wondered, *Why me? Why does he care about me?*

"I am not planning for today," Maranzano said. "I am looking at tomorrow. Who will lead us then? I have tested many of you young men. Some have been smart enough. Most have more education than you. But they had not the heart. Those who had the heart had not the brain."

Maranzano smiled. "You wondered why I left you in that real estate office for all these months."

"It did sometimes cross my mind," Nilo admitted, although he had come to believe that he had been banished until everyone was sure the police were not after him.

"It was a test of your loyalty. "

"I hope I passed your test."

"You did. Even though you did not know why you were there, you listened to Mr. Ferrara. You learned. You kept *faccia contenta*. A happy face. You were willing to wait because you believed your don wanted you to wait. You did yourself good by waiting. You are not now some thug, Nilo, who jumped ship and who scurries around the city like a rat, stealing bread crusts. You are a young man with a career in real estate. You have no criminal record. When the time is right, we will take care of your citizenship problem. You are a young man without blemish in the eyes of the law. That is what we must be in our next generation."

"Am I worthy of such an honor?"

"You will be. You are the future. But we cannot ignore the present and its dangers. I will take you into my confidence now. To prosper through this Prohibition stupidity, we will not only have to battle the police. That will not be difficult. We can buy them off. And the same for the government. We can buy the Democratic Party by buying the Tammany Hall organization, at least those that Masseria has not already bought, and that will give us friends in city hall. But the others we will have to fight will be worse than these. They will be ruthless men, perhaps like ourselves, perhaps worse. Masseria will be one of them, but he is only one. There will be more to follow him, many smarter, tougher than that old pepper.

"We must beat them off by being smarter and tougher at the top. That is true. But we must also beat them by out-organizing them. They call Joe Masseria the boss of the Mafia. Good enough, let them. The Mafia is a pack of thugs, and it is fitting that this thug be their boss. Our organization will be different. Long after the Mafia is gone and forgotten, long after I and even you are in our graves, our organization will live on."

Nilo felt as if he should say something, just to reaffirm to Maranzano that he was not some dumb clod, even though Maranzano seemed perfectly willing to go on telling his story in a vacuum.

The best Nilo could manage was a small question. "What is this organization? What will it be?"

"I need many, many men. But how to get them without

getting many, many traitors in the same barrel? Even great Caesar had his Brutus. But finally I have the solution. Next to his own family, the Sicilian trusts his neighbors. And that is what I will build my organization on. Many, many men from our village, from Castellammare del Golfo, have already come to this country, often with my help. It is from these Castellammarese like us that I will build my organization. It is a good idea, no?"

"It is like family without blood ties," Nilo ventured. "It will be a new Mafia."

Maranzano shook his head. "No more Mafia. The Mafia will shrivel up and die, but our organization will continue." He closed his eyes. "What shall we call it, this thing of ours?"

"Perhaps just that," Nilo said. " 'This thing of ours': *la cosa nostra.*"

After that, Maranzano was silent for a long time. It seemed to Nilo as if the air had finally drained from the older man. He sat nursing his brandy and his cigar, both luxuries that Nilo had barely touched. His mind was reeling. A new crime organization.

And suddenly he knew his destiny, knew it as surely as if an angel had come and whispered in his ear. *Someday, with God's help, I will run this Cosa Nostra. I am as smart as this old windbag. Thank God, who sent me Don Salvatore. Thank God and his angels, who sent me here. Thank Fredo and the two Selvini brothers, whose evil work brought me here, too. Thus out of evil comes forth good. I am glad now I did not piss on their bodies.*

"That is enough for one night," Maranzano said in a dull voice without looking up. "We will talk much in the future. Nilo, I will make you a leader of men."

"It is an honor I will never deserve," Nilo said.

"Only time will tell. And now to lighter things. Get

this Sofia Mangini to tutor you. Do you ever eat in the family's restaurant?"

Nilo nodded. "It is a place where Masseria's men hang out."

"Exactly. You are young and, at least for now, it is safe. Just keep your eyes and ears open. There is a man named Salvatore Lucania who frequents the restaurant. Do you know him?"

"I don't think so."

"He may try to get close to you. Allow it."

"As you wish, Don Salvatore."

"It will no longer be necessary for you to go back to the real estate company in Brooklyn. From now on, report to my office in the morning."

Nilo nodded.

"I understand you are going to take my secretary out to dinner," Maranzano said.

Nilo was startled for a moment. *Am I stepping on the old man's toes by taking his secretary to dinner? Is this a problem I have made for myself?* Nervously, he nodded.

"She is a beautiful girl," Maranzano said, and smiled lewdly. "Enjoy her charms. You will not be the first. But do not imagine you are falling in love with her. And let her know that. Treat her badly. That way, she can fall in love with you while never believing that you love her in return. Capisce?"

"I do. And thank you for the advice."

The older man stood; so did Nilo. The two young black maids reentered the room. Maranzano put his arm around the youth. "Now go. I think I shall help my two serving girls put things in their proper place."

Nilo felt the man's body shake as he chuckled to himself. Maranzano led him to the door of the apartment. Before he opened it, he said, "Do not underestimate this

Lucania. Be careful with him. He is young, too, but he is very shrewd. He has whatever brains may exist in Masseria's operation, and someday he may be useful to us."

"I will be on my guard." Nilo smiled. "At least his name, Salvatore, being your name, too, will not be hard to remember."

"I hear he has changed his name to something more American."

"Oh?"

"Yes. He now calls himself Charlie. Charlie Luciano."

NILO HAD ARRANGED TO MEET Betty on Saturday evening, just outside Maranzano's office building on Broadway. He arrived there without any real idea of where they would go or what they would do. Betty arrived, a fashionable half hour late, and Nilo was angry at having to wait so long, but he cooled off quickly when he saw her.

Betty had tightly curled her long red hair and packed it under a beaded turban. She wore white satin shoes and a harem outfit, which was a very short skirt over gauzy pantaloons that flashed her legs as she moved. Her top was beaded, too, matching her turban, and, defying the latest flat-chest fashion, it was cut low and her breasts seemed ready to pop out of it.

Nilo had never seen anyone so beautiful.

"Sorry I was late," she said as she leaned forward and kissed his cheek. "It took me a while to get dressed."

"It was worth the wait," he said. He began to tell her that he had no idea of where they should go for dinner when Betty told him she had already made reservations for them at the Silver Slipper, a Forty-fourth Street speakeasy whose owner was close to Maranzano.

He was immediately annoyed again. *It is not right that*

a woman makes these decisions. A man should make such choices, he thought.

"Of course," Betty said, "if you'd rather go somewhere else . . ."

"No. If you have your heart set on this Silver Slipper, the Silver Slipper it will be."

It was Nilo's first time in a speakeasy. They were admitted through a locked door after a guard had checked them out through a peephole and Betty had mentioned Maranzano's name.

There was a floor show downstairs with pretty dancing girls and tap dancers and a comedian, none of whose jokes Nilo understood, and after the show a small orchestra played for dancing. Betty dragged him out onto the dance floor, and while Nilo did not know how to do any of the fashionable dances, Betty clearly did not mind, because she treated each song as a showcase for her solo talents.

Nilo, by this time, did not mind much, either, because in addition to their dinners they had a constant supply of wine at the table and he had drunk too much. Finally, he tired of Betty showing off her dancing by herself and walked back to the table, where he sat when the speakeasy owner came up and introduced himself.

"Is everything all right?" he asked Nilo.

"Everything is fine."

"Food okay? You have enough to drink?"

"Everything is fine," Nilo said, although in truth, his stomach was not feeling too fine.

"Good. Well, enjoy yourself. The check's on me. Give my regards to Don Salvatore when you see him."

"I will," Nilo said, "and I will be sure to tell him of your hospitality to his friends."

The owner beamed and walked away. The band stopped

playing in a few minutes, and Betty, who seemed not to have noticed Nilo's departure, returned to the table.

"You like to dance alone?" he asked.

"Sometimes." She slurred the word; she was drunk, too.

"Do you like to do everything alone?"

"There are some things you can't do alone," Betty said, and giggled.

"Let's get out of here."

Out on the street, Nilo realized that he had no place to take the girl. She had already told him she lived in her family's apartment. That was out. So was the ratty furnished room in Little Italy where he spent his nights.

Before he could decide what to do, Betty had stepped onto the curb and hailed a cab. While Nilo was still thinking, he heard Betty tell the cabdriver, "The Princess Hotel. And hurry."

He sank into the backseat with her, and she took his hand and slid it under her beaded top. Nilo caressed her breast and he felt her squirm on the seat. He hoped the cab ride would last a long time, but the Princess Hotel was only a few blocks away. He insisted on paying the cabdriver and tipped him a dollar, too.

He was walking better now; the alcohol seemed to be wearing off, and he followed Betty into the lobby of the small hotel. She ignored the clerk, who looked up at their entrance, and instead led Nilo by the hand to the stairway.

The room was up one flight, at the end of the hall.

"How did you get this room?" Nilo asked.

"Mr. Maranzano keeps it all the time, for people who come to town to visit him. I made sure nobody would be using it tonight." She showed him the key, then unlocked the door and went inside. Nilo followed her and felt her body against his in the dark.

"I do not know that I like you making every decision for me, as if I am a child."

"Are you angry?" Betty asked.

"I think so."

"Then you will punish me?"

"Yes," he said.

"I have been bad. I will do anything you wish," Betty said, and Nilo felt her hands begin to unbuckle his belt.

Some months before, when he had first met her, Nilo had promised himself he would teach the girl some sexual manners. He tried. But there was nothing he could do to her body that offended her. Everything he did she liked and wanted more of.

Later, naked in the bed, he closed his eyes and tried to sleep but found himself awakened by the young woman, naked too, washing his body with a soapy cloth she had taken from the bathroom. Then she washed his face. Somewhere, she had found ice cubes, and now she rubbed them on Nilo's bare chest, and he could feel himself being aroused, and then she climbed on top of him again.

Betty above him, squirming over his body, was the most lascivious sight Nilo had ever seen. He reached up to cup her breasts in his hands and smiled at her, happy to let her do all the work.

"Do you know why I'm so nice to you?" the young woman asked.

"Why?"

"Because Mr. Maranzano loves you," she said.

"He has spoken to me once in four months," Nilo said.

"Still, he loves you. Every day, he gets a report on you. Every day, he makes sure that you are well. Every week, he asks me the same thing." She tried to mimic Maranzano's deep voice. "'Betty, did you make sure that Nilo was paid today?' Oh, yes. He loves you."

"It is nice of you to tell me that," Nilo said.

"It is true."

"I told Don Salvatore that we were going out to dinner."

"So did I," Betty said.

"Did he give you advice?"

"He told me to be nice to you," she said. "Did he give you advice?"

"Yes."

"What was it?"

"He told me to treat you badly. He said that will make you love me."

"I don't want to love you," she said.

"But I do want to treat you badly," he said.

"Then why don't you?"

"It's still early," Nilo said, pulling the girl to him, even as he thought, *I am surely one of God's chosen creatures. And life will only get better. America is full of opportunities, if one is wise.* He just felt bad that the Falcones were too stupid ever to have figured that out.

AS THE TWO GIRLS LEFT Mass at Our Lady of Mount Carmel, the skies had darkened, and they ran all the way back to the Falcone apartment, arriving just moments before the rain started. No one else was home and Tina brewed tea, and like two dowager queens, she and Sofia sat by the apartment's front window, watching the sudden cold September rain, driven by gale winds, crashing against their window. Thunder echoed through the canyons of the streets and lightning danced among the clouds.

"I love it when it's like this," Sofia said. "It makes me feel so small and insignificant. It makes all my problems seem unimportant. I can almost feel God right here with me."

"Mmmmm," Tina mumbled, not looking at her friend.

"You're not paying any attention to me," Sofia said.

"Yes, I am. You feel insignificant and God's with you, right?"

Sofia blushed. What had seemed like an insight a moment ago now was only a childish outburst.

"Oh, never mind," she said in mock irascibility, and they both sat in companionable silence for a few minutes.

"Where's Tommy been today?" Sofia finally asked.

"He has some woman somewhere," Tina said airily. "A waitress."

"Are you telling me the truth?"

"Yes. I heard Papa telling Mama about it. He didn't know I heard. It is some waitress in that diner where we met Tommy that night."

"That big blonde?" Sofia asked.

"I guess so. I don't really remember seeing her."

"And Tommy's there now?"

"I guess so," Tina said again.

"Do you think that they're—"

"That they're doing it? Probably right now. All sweaty and sliding all over each other. At least, I don't think they're trading recipes," Tina said. "Would your insignificant self like more tea?" she asked with a smile. "Since God's with you, ask him if he'd like some, too."

"Sacrilege," Sofia said. "You'll have to confess that to Mario."

"Some other priest," Tina said, picking up both tea-cups. "I don't go to Mario anymore."

Sofia followed her into the kitchen. "Oh, it's like that, is it?" she said. "Your sins are too great to tell your brother about?"

Tina laughed. "Not yet. But I'm afraid that someday they will be, and I want to have a priest who doesn't know me . . . just in case."

They sat at the kitchen table, waiting for more water to boil on the stove. "How is your cousin?" Tina asked.

"Charlie? He's fine. I can't get over how things have changed at home ever since I went to see him. Why do you ask?"

"Just wondering."

"You like him," Sofia said.

Tina laughed. "He's a clown, a little man in a good suit, acting tough. The only things nice about him are his hands. Real long fingers. You know what they say long fingers are a sign of?"

"No. You want to tell me?"

"Wait till you grow up," Tina said.

There was another long silence while the building shook with the crash of three thunderclaps in rapid succession.

"Do you ever think about that?" Tina asked.

"About what?"

"Oh, having babies. And, you know, the part that comes before."

Tina walked away and busied herself at the stove with the tea.

"Well, do you?" she asked again.

"I don't know. It just all seems so awful and messy," Sofia said. "Why don't we just run off together, you and me. Go live in the woods and eat berries."

"I hate berries," Tina said.

She carried the two cups of tea back into the parlor. As she set them on the windowsill, Sofia asked from behind her, "I suppose you'd like to do it with him?"

"Do what with whom?"

"You know. With my cousin."

Tina hesitated. "Papa would die of apoplexy and I would die of shame. Your cousin is a lowlife."

"Tina?"

"What?"

"Have you ever done it with anybody?"

"No. I try not to think about it," Tina said. "I don't have time. I'm going to be an opera singer. Doing those things wastes your energy so you can't sing as well."

"You could always sing flat," Sofia said, and both girls laughed loudly.

"Tina?"

"Yes?"

"You have a lot of boys come over now from where you work. Have you ever let a boy touch you?"

"Yes," Tina said slowly. "A couple of times. Only up here, though." She touched her bosom.

"Boys from work?"

"Sometimes," Tina said.

"Nilo too?"

"No," Tina said. "He's my cousin. That's almost illegal. Why? Has he tried anything with you?"

"No," Sofia said. "But he wants to. You know, he's moving out of Mrs. Annacharico's. He's going to take an apartment of his own somewhere. If we wanted to do it, we would even have a place to do it."

Again both girls grew silent.

"You know," Sofia said after a moment, "maybe if I loved somebody, really loved somebody. Otherwise I don't think I want to do it with anybody. No man, anyway."

"What do you mean, 'no man'?" What else is there?" Tina asked.

Sofia was silent and Tina said, "Nilo's very handsome. And you're always with him when you're teaching him." She poured more tea. "You were lucky to get that job. I tried to teach him to read, but he didn't have any money then and I was just doing it for free. Now that he's a big real estate salesman, I guess he's got lots of money for lessons."

"I don't think he's selling real estate anymore."

"Maybe not," Tina said. "One night I heard Papa telling Tommy that Nilo is working for Salvatore Maranzano."

"Who's he?"

"He's another gangster. Like your cousin."

Sofia said, "It's all too much for me. And I don't know anything about gangsters. Everybody's always talking gangster this and gangster that, but I don't know. Sure, Cousin Charlie sells Papa illegal wine to serve in his restaurant. But so what? Everybody does that. I heard that uptown, they are even starting places, like restaurants, that sell liquor right out in the open. They call them talk-easies or something. Prohibition is stupid. No one pays attention to it."

"Speakeasies," Tina said. "I've heard Papa talk about them. But it's not just selling liquor, you know. The gangsters do other things, too."

"Like what?" Sofia asked disbelievingly.

"Oh, gambling, murder, they even sell women."

"I hear those things, too," Sofia said, "but I don't know what I believe. I think you hang around with too many policemen."

Outside, the rain was letting up. Sofia said, "How do those women do it? You know, let strange men put their hands all over them."

"Better strange men than no men," Tina said flippantly.

"Oh, you talk a good game," Sofia said. She looked out the window again. "Maybe in this world, I love only you," she said, and then suddenly embarrassed by her own honesty, she added quickly, "Do you wish you knew what would happen in the future?"

"I do know. I'm going to be a big star. You're going to be happily married to Nilo, who is going to be the richest man in the world, and you'll have lots of little children, and I will be their godmother."

"And life won't be dull or dirty?" Sofia asked.

"No," Tina said, looking out the window, too. "Life won't be dull." Both girls giggled. "Dirty maybe, but not dull."

- *New York City was awash in liquor. Speakeasies were sprouting like weeds, beginning to operate around the clock, and they had a big thirst. Traditionally, many Italian families had made their own wines, and now their products were snapped up by the gangs for resale. Stills were set up in almost every barn and deserted factory building in the city. Across the river in New Jersey, plants—operating under the guise of cereal manufacturers—were pouring out thousands of barrels of beer every week. European liquor was being shipped into Canada and Mexico and then smuggled across the borders or in by boat for sale in the United States. Outnumbered Coast Guard and alcohol enforcement agents worked around the clock to halt the shipments but with little success. And still, New York wanted more . . . more . . . more.*

- *There was such a demand for liquor that some bootleg gangs began to rob the booze shipments of other bootleg gangs, and as the era of generalized lawlessness spread, a new criminal name was heard in the city: "Kid Trouble." Hardly a week passed without Kid Trouble hijacking one of Joe Masseria's liquor shipments, and a ten-thousand-dollar bounty was instantly put on his head by an angry Masseria. No one knew Kid Trouble's identity, but, fanned by a growing string of tabloid newspaper stories, his exploits quickly began to take on the aspect of a Robin Hood legend. Working with only a small group, Kid Trouble was fearless and, when necessary, brutal. Bootleg drivers who offered any resistance to a hijacking were killed without warning. By the end of 1921, Masseria had increased the bounty on Kid Trouble's head to twenty-five thousand dollars.*

- *Jack and Charlie's 21 Club opened, eventually becoming the most famous gin mill in the city. A night on the town now meant dinner at the Little Restaurant, later renamed Sardi's, then a Broadway show, and finally a trip to the nearest speakeasy for a night of carousing.*

- *Soon after his late-night meeting with Luciano, Meyer Lansky had begun to pay less attention to his penny-ante gambling rackets. Working with his underaged but deadly partner, Ben "Bug" Siegel, Lansky branched out into stealing cars and*

*making them available to different gangs. Slowly
they developed a stable of Jewish toughs who
thought nothing of killing, and when he thought they
were ready Luciano convinced Joe Masseria that
the Bug and Meyer gang could do a good job of
protecting Masseria's liquor shipments from being
hijacked on the streets of New York, and, if they
ran into him, ridding the city of Kid Trouble in the
bargain. Masseria complained about the price but
finally went along. It was easy to go along with the
persuasive Luciano.*

*Meanwhile, Lansky and Siegel had made it their
mission to protect Luciano from murder at the
hands of any other mobster. They needed him; they
planned to go a long way together.*

- *On a summer evening in 1921, Luciano met
another young man named Frank Costello in a
speakeasy on Forty-fourth Street at Eighth Avenue.
Annoyed because the dapper and older soft-spoken
Costello seemed to be a favorite of Masseria's,
Luciano argued with him and then pulled a knife.
Cooler heads prevailed and later Luciano apolo-
gized. Costello, he had found out, was close to
Arnold Rothstein, the Broadway gambler who had
fixed the 1919 World Series and who had provided
a lot of the seed money for new crime organizations. Luciano considered this a good contact to
have, and soon he convinced Masseria to put
Costello in charge of all the bribes being paid by
Joe the Boss to city hall and to the courts.*

*"Costello," Luciano said, "is a man who
knows how to keep his mouth shut."*

- *Margaret Gorman, sixteen, measuring 30-25-32,
won the first Miss America contest in Atlantic City.*

- *Eddie Cantor was a Broadway star, singing "Ma! (He's Making Eyes at Me)."*
- *Enrico Caruso died. The world mourned. New York City got drunk and everybody sang America's favorite song: "Ain't We Got Fun?"*

CHAPTER 4

February 1922

Nilo had started out as an errand boy, hanging around Maranzano's office, delivering envelopes to city hall and to lawyers' offices, collecting envelopes from dingy betting parlors, frustrated because he knew big things were being done and he had nothing to do with them, but he did his job anyway.

His regular sexual interludes with Betty—and then with an endless string of other willing girls, available in Maranzano's speakeasies—helped, but he still champed at the bit, waiting to be given work that he thought was worthy of him. He was impatient, but he knew he had some curious hold on Maranzano. *When I am ready, he will call on me. I am young. I can wait.*

Still, there were too many people around. Too many people who came into the office every day and gossiped among themselves about what they had done the night before—Masseria bookies they had robbed, Masseria trucks they had hijacked. Finally, Nilo lost his patience and reminded everyone how he was Don Salvatore's favorite boy and wanted to know everything—where they were going, what they were doing—and he slowly insinuated himself into every piece of Maranzano's operation.

He did not try to lead. He was content to follow until he learned how it was all done—about the gambling, the prostitutes, the speakeasies, the merchant shakedowns—and then slowly, without anyone's clear approval, he put his hand in more and more.

The gangs of toughs who hung around Maranzano's real estate offices, the other thugs who worked in garages and stills and whorehouses and gambling parlors, all soon came to realize that Nilo was someone especially close to Don Salvatore, and after a while they knew that he had Maranzano's ear and felt that his word could be accepted as Don Salvatore's word.

For himself, Don Salvatore had not given Nilo approval for what he was doing, but neither had he told him to stop. And, in the tightly knit organization, there was no doubt that he knew what Nilo was up to. So in the absence of orders to the contrary, Nilo decided he would keep on until told otherwise.

Instead of criticism, though, within a year he had been promoted officially. It became Nilo's responsibility every Tuesday to make the rounds of all the speakeasies in the city that bought liquor and beer from Maranzano and to collect for the previous week's shipments. This was considered one of the most sought-after jobs because record keeping was careless and a man with sticky fingers could make an awful lot of money.

But Nilo was meticulous in his duties. He kept careful records of who owed and who paid, and he delivered the cash to Maranzano each Tuesday evening, and even though the collections regularly totaled well over one hundred thousand dollars, never a penny was missing.

Maranzano was very pleased with his protégé's performance. When he had put Nilo in charge of all bootlegging, he had worried that the young man would run into trouble with other gang members who resented his promotion over other, older men. But Nilo had never reported any trouble, and the operation was working more smoothly than it ever had before. Early in the period of Prohibition, speakeasy owners had been known to complain because Maranzano's strong-arm men were more efficient than his liquor suppliers, and often the gin mills could not get all the liquor they needed. But since Nilo's promotion, those complaints had died out.

Having enough sources of supply was a continuing problem, and until it was solved it would always hinder the growth of the Maranzano crime family. In the number of speakeasies that bought liquor from him, Don Salvatore was still Number Two in the city behind Masseria's gang, but he was a closer Number Two now. Nilo had done well and Maranzano was satisfied. And while he knew about Nilo's liking for the violent life, he chose to look the other way. He expected that Nilo would grow up one day. In the meantime, his loyalty was unquestionable.

So Maranzano would have been surprised to know that on a cold February Tuesday, Nilo had left his office and instantly turned over the job of making collections to another young member of the gang. Then Nilo had gone downtown to an abandoned commercial garage on the edge of Chinatown, where three other young men waited for him.

Nilo had specially recruited these three. They were all Castellammarese, all lived in New Jersey, where they had relatives, and all were unknown to the New York mob. Around Nilo's age, they were, like him, unafraid of violence. He paid them well, probably better than he had to, but Nilo thought it a wise investment because if anyone were to reveal that Nilo was Kid Trouble his life would not be worth a nickel.

"Any word?" Nilo asked, as he entered the shabby garage.

"We just got it," one of the young men said. "My sister's boyfriend was told to get ready to bring in a big shipment tonight. Two trucks. All imported Scotch whisky sent down from Canada. He'll take over the driving when it gets to Jersey."

"Where's it going?"

"To the Masseria warehouse over near Twelfth Avenue," the young man said.

"That's where we'll hit the shipment then," Nilo said.

One of the other men looked surprised. "You don't want to take it in Jersey?"

Nilo shook his head. "No. Let Masseria go to all the trouble of driving it through Jersey, past the cops, get it over the river. He can do the work and take the risks. Then we'll just nail the two trucks and bring them over here." He looked back at the first young man. "Good work," Nilo said, then smiled. "How close is your sister to this truck driver?"

"He's a roll in the hay, is all."

"No wedding plans?"

The man shook his head. "Good," Nilo said. "I wouldn't want to be making her a widow before her time. There's a thousand dollars in it for her. Tell her to give him a little nookie and spend the day with him. Find out when and where he picks up the truck. Then we'll be ready. Any questions?"

No one spoke.

"All right," Nilo said. "Hang around. Go to a movie or something. We'll meet back here at five o'clock. And—"

The three men laughed at once. "We know, Kid. Keep our mouths shut."

TOMMY HAD WOUND UP in the bed of Mabel Fay because of his simple good manners. One of his call boxes was on the corner near the all-night diner on Cornelia Street, and one evening in 1920 he had been reporting in to the precinct when he saw the waitress leave the restaurant at the end of her shift.

Tommy called out, then walked along with her to make sure she got home safely to her apartment, which was near the river, only a block away from his regular patrol path. He had not made a pass at the tall, buxom blonde, and when he left he politely wished her good night and thought no more of it. It soon became a habit for Tommy to walk her home. The walk was a pleasant respite from the normal lonely monotony of his job.

They talked about his college work and the long path to law school that was still ahead of him. For her part, Mabel occasionally talked about her unhappy life in Atlantic City, where she'd met her husband, who seemed to have devoted the years before their divorce to unwanted rape and undeserved assault. But what Mabel Fay really liked to talk about was the movies. Apparently, she never missed seeing one, and she confided in Tommy on one walk home that she was saving her money to go to Hollywood.

"Where's Hollywood?" Tommy asked.

"In California."

"Why go to California?"

"To be in the movies," she said. "I seen all those movies, and I don't want to be blowing my own horn, but those girls don't have any more than I got."

"I thought they made movies over in Jersey."

"They do. I still go over to Fort Lee and watch them.

A couple of times they let me be in a crowd scene. But the weather is better in California. They don't even have a winter there, I hear."

"That must make it tough to make movies about Eskimos," Tommy said.

"Oh, Tommy, you're such a joker."

"Well, I'm not joking now," he said. "You go to California and you're going to be a big star."

"You think so?"

"You can't miss," said Tommy, who rarely went to the movies because he spent all his free time studying his college work.

Mabel's apartment building was just up ahead. He stopped with her in front of the flight of steps leading to the main entrance of the three-story walk-up and squeezed her hand, in a brotherly fashion, as he did every night.

This time she had a key in her hand and she transferred it to his.

"What's this?"

"That's my key. Why don't you come up when you're done?" Mabel said. "Two-B. Second floor, on the right."

Without waiting for an answer, Mabel walked up the steps into her house. Tommy slipped the key into his trouser pocket and went back to his regular patrol rounds.

When his tour ended at 5:00 A.M., he walked back to Mabel's apartment. He planned to tell her that she owed him nothing for walking her home and then he would have a cup of coffee and leave. Feeling very noble, he used the key to let himself into Mabel's apartment.

It was dark inside when he closed the door behind him, and he softly called, "Mabel?"

"In here," she answered. A dim light came on down at the other end of the railroad rooms. He picked his way through an amazing clutter of furniture and found himself at the open door of her bedroom.

A small lamp burned on an end table. Mabel lay on the bed naked, the covers clustered in a lump at the foot of the mattress. Two kerosene heaters glowing cherry red in the room made it summer warm. Mabel's body glistened in the faint light, as if she had oiled her skin. Her breasts were even larger than he had imagined them to be. Tommy gulped and Mabel said, "I've been waiting for you. I hoped you'd come."

Still on her back, she extended her arms toward him. "Come here, Tommy," she said in a throaty voice. "And get out of those clothes." A minute later, Tommy was in her bed.

Tommy's sexual experience had consisted of a couple of visits to French whorehouses while he was overseas. He had always assumed that being with Parisian prostitutes had made him a man of the world, but in the hands and other parts of the experienced Mabel Fay he quickly found out how wrong he was. Mabel did things to him that Tommy had only heard of in barracks and locker rooms.

When they were done, he rolled onto his back and lay there breathing heavily. Mabel instantly reached for a cigarette on the night table, casually lit one, and smoked quietly in the semidark room.

Tommy felt he should say something, but when he tried to speak she shushed him by putting an index finger across his lips and pursed her own lips.

He lay in the dark, vaguely annoyed, somehow convinced that some words should follow their act. She did not have to say that she loved him; he was not going to say he loved her. But he felt they should say something, just to prove that they were there together.

Her silence left him with a curious sense of dissatisfaction and just reignited the confusion he had always felt when trying to understand women's ways.

It was still dark outside when Tommy got up to go; Mabel did not protest; she did not ask him to stay, and when he went out Tommy left the apartment key she had given him on the kitchen table near the front door.

That was the first time with Mabel. He did not see her again until the following week, when she told him that the boss had just changed her hours at the restaurant. She now worked late each Tuesday night, getting off just around Tommy's quitting time of 5:00 A.M.

"Walk me home?" she asked.

"Sure," Tommy answered, and wound up in her bed again. And so for almost two years, it had been a regular Tuesday event for Tommy, spending a few hours after work rolling around on the sheets with Mabel.

She still did not talk much after they made love, but Tommy came to accept that. It was enough that on that one night a week they needed each other and they had each other. If it made the rest of the week better for both of them, who could complain about that? Except for his brother, Mario, and what he did not know wouldn't hurt him.

One thing Tommy learned was that he was able to talk to women much more easily now than he had before. The great tongue-tying mystery of sex was not such a puzzle anymore, and with the mystery gone, the awe had gone, too.

It was deep into the early morning hours near Washington's Birthday in 1922 when Tommy left Mabel's apartment. He was outside only a few minutes before he shivered and cursed. He should have stayed with her; it was just too damned cold to be outside on a night like this. The thermometer had been in the single digits for seventy-two straight hours and everything was frozen. Underfoot, the snow was so cold that it squeaked and moaned as he walked on it, and in the moonless pitch of the night he felt as if he were walking through a graveyard.

All he wanted to do was to get home quickly, and he turned off the main street and into a long commercial alley that ran for two blocks between banks of small factories and warehouses.

The wind whipped through the alley as if it were a mountaintop. There was not even a welcoming doorway to step into to get out of the wind. He walked faster. He never should have had that good-night cup of coffee with Mabel ten minutes earlier. It had tasted good, warmed his insides, but he had not reckoned on the consequences. Everything that went in had to come out, and in cold weather it seemed to have to come out that much faster.

He hesitated at just urinating in the broad alley. He was no longer a rookie policeman, but he still took the job seriously enough to worry that if someone drove through the alley he would not be setting a very good example by being seen urinating against a wall. He had arrested people for things like that.

He saw to his right another half alley leading back between two old brick warehouses. He walked down there, then could not wait anymore, and, turning his back to the main alley and the wind, partly from modesty, partly to keep from spattering himself, he let loose a long steaming torrent. He sighed with relief, rebuttoned his pants, and turned to go back to the main street.

Then he stopped to listen. The cold night air carried

sounds that at other times might have been lost. Some sound was coming from farther back in the small alley.

His first thought was that a burglary was taking place, and he cursed under his breath. All he wanted to do was to go home and get warm.

He considered walking away, for only a split second, then unholstered his revolver and moved over toward the darker side of the alley and slowly began moving forward, trying to be silent, all senses alert for trouble.

As his eyes grew more accustomed to the deeper darkness back here, he noticed a dogleg turn in the alley, a turn that had been invisible until he was right up on it.

The indistinct sounds grew louder, clearer. Tommy took a deep breath and stepped cautiously around the corner, and the sounds, no longer muffled by the wind and the walls of the buildings, became instantly clear. Ahead, he could hear the sound of two different motors running. The sound clearly came from two dark splotches in the night. He could hear the sound of scurrying feet but could not tell how many people they belonged to. He stopped for a moment, trying to will his heart to stop pounding so loudly, to stop making so much noise. It did not work. He could hear voices, voices talking softly in Italian. He understood the language well enough to know they were cursing good-humoredly, cajoling each other to work faster.

Tommy stepped back against a building wall and tried to think clearly. Whatever was happening was nothing small. Not with two trucks involved. This had the smell of being a professional job of some sort. Probably bootleggers, and that meant big trouble because bootleggers always went on jobs carrying enough weapons for a small army. The sensible thing to do was to get the hell out of the alley, find the nearest call box, and call up reinforcements.

That was what he would do, Tommy decided. There were too many of them for him to handle by himself. He would get out of here and call for help.

Then he heard another sound. It was a moaning wail. He had heard that sound before, heard it in Belleau Wood, and he would never forget it. It was the sound of a wounded, perhaps a dying, man.

Tommy cocked the hammer on his service revolver and started toward the spot where the two trucks were parked.

Suddenly a flashlight flicked on from close by, its beam striking him in the eyes with the force of a quick left jab. He hesitated for only a split second, but it was too much.

"Don't move," another voice said from behind him in Italian. "Put the gun down." He felt the cold barrel of a gun against the back of his neck.

"Jesus Christ," came the voice from the man who was somewhere in front of him holding the flashlight. "It's a goddamn cop. Shoot the bastard."

The flashlight beam wavered for just a split second, and as it did, Tommy made an instantaneous decision. He dropped to one knee and fired a round at a spot directly above the light. Then he lunged backward against the legs of the man behind him, trying to turn his body as he moved so he could fire another shot.

He heard a man curse in pain and then the metallic clatter of the flashlight rolling across the graveled deck of the parking lot. He tried to free his gun hand to take out his other attacker, but somebody had a death grip on his hand.

And then he felt another body crunch down onto his and another pistol was poked roughly into his neck.

"Stand up," said the voice behind him. "And let go of that gun."

Tommy did as he was ordered.

"Move," the voice ordered.

He hesitated and somebody kicked him, sending him sprawling forward, and then he saw a starburst as he was cracked across the back of the head and dropped to the ground. He lay there in a crouched position, struggling to maintain consciousness, but he could see nothing and all the sounds seemed distant and echoing.

"What's this?" another voice called out in Italian.

"A cop. He shot Vinnie." This came in English from somewhere behind Tommy. He wanted to turn his head to see who was speaking, but he could not move.

The voice spoke rapidly, and Tommy could not make out all the words, but the ones he understood said: "Then kill him and let's get out of here before anybody else comes. Shoot him and get it over with."

"I'll only do it if the Kid says to."

There was a moment of palpable crackling tension and Tommy thought that death was at hand. He wondered if Mario would conduct the funeral Mass. It seemed such a waste to have survived the war and beaten morphine, only to die like this. He thought about his family, all of them he would never see again, and he kept his eyes tightly closed.

No bullet came. He tried to open his eyes and felt himself bathed in light. Someone behind him was shining a flashlight on him. He heard another voice, almost familiar, speak softly in Italian. It too sounded far away.

"What the hell's going on here?"

"We're loaded, ready to go, and this cop wanders in here and shoots Vinnie. We was just waiting for you."

"I'll take care of him. The rest of you get the hell out of here. And take Vinnie with you. Get him fixed up."

"You going to kill him, Kid?" another voice asked. It belonged to the man who earlier wanted to shoot Tommy.

"That's none of your damned business, Rico. Just get that truck out of here. I'll take care of this."

"If you want him killed, I'll kill the bastard."

"You just move your ass," snapped the one they called Kid.

Tommy listened with a sort of detached fascination. It was as if they were not arguing about killing him but were talking about someone else. The flashlight's beam stayed fixed on Tommy, and he was afraid to try to turn his face from the wall.

He heard people running and then the sound of doors slamming and the two trucks grinding into gear. They crunched over the gravel as they pulled from the lot. He saw their headlights slash across the walls as they drove away. The silence of the night closed in around him. He wondered if everyone had gone. Maybe he could flee. If only he could get to his feet.

He heard footsteps approaching him from behind. Involuntarily, his shoulders tensed as he expected the loud crack of the bullet.

Instead, he heard a voice close by his ear. It spoke in English this time, and while it was muffled and soft, he thought he recognized the voice.

Before he could react, the voice said, "Sorry," and even as he heard it, he felt another thud against the side of his head. His face smashed forward against the brick wall and he sensed himself losing consciousness. The last thing he heard before he settled onto the icy gravel was the sound of footsteps running away.

He mumbled to himself. "Nilo." And then he lay still.

TOMMY CAME TO, cradled in the arms of a uniformed policeman who squatted down on the frozen gravel next to him.

"Easy, Tommy." Tommy recognized one of the precinct sergeants, Artie Tracey. Tommy was surprised at the officer's apparent concern; he could not remember Tracey ever speaking to him in the station house, except to give him an order.

"How you feeling?"

"I'm okay," Tommy said. "I think so anyway."

He did not know how long he had been unconscious.

He sat up slowly. There were four other policemen wandering around the now-empty parking lot.

"How'd you find me?" he asked.

"Somebody phoned the station house, said we'd find you here. Good thing, too. You could've frozen to death out here."

"You know who it was?"

Sergeant Tracey shook his head. "He didn't give no name. But he was one of your goombahs. He talked with an accent. You got any idea who it was?"

Tommy hesitated, then shook his head. He tried to get to his feet, but Tracey would not let him.

"You stay put," he said. "An ambulance'll be here any minute."

He stood, took off his heavy overcoat, and wrapped it around Tommy's shoulders, then squatted next to him again. "What went on here? Can you tell me?"

"I was on my way home and I heard noises in the alley. When I looked, it was some guys in two trucks. I guess they were heisting stuff from one of these warehouses. A couple of them jumped me and then they bopped me and got out of here."

"Get a look at any of them?"

"No. They had a flashlight in my eyes. But before I went down, I think I shot one of them. I heard them call him Vinnie."

"That might be. We found your gun over there," Cole said. "One bullet was fired. I hope you killed the son of a bitch, whoever he is. You hear any other names?"

"Just Vinnie. And there was somebody named Rico."

"There always is," Tracey said drily.

A siren neared then silenced abruptly, and Tommy heard its tires crunching over the gravel as it came down the alleyway.

"What is this place anyway?" Tommy asked.

"Well, it's supposed to be a warehouse, but it's actually one of Joe Masseria's stills. From what you say, somebody heisted two truckloads of his booze. They busted some watchman's skull."

That was the moaning he had heard, Tommy realized.

"He all right?" he asked.

"He's not complaining about anything. One of the trucks rolled over him on the way out of here. He's dead."

It was murder, Tommy thought. And Nilo was part of it.

DESPITE TOMMY'S ANNOYANCE, the doctors at St. Luke's insisted on admitting him so they could monitor his progress for at least a few hours.

"I'm telling you I'm fine. I'm getting out of here."

"And I'm telling you you may have sustained a concussion, and if I release you too soon, you may keel over in the street and derail a trolley car, and then there'll be hell to pay." The speaker was a courtly old doctor with a thin pencil-line mustache and rimless glasses that perched on the end of his nose. He smiled at the young patrolman, who sat in a hospital bed, propped up by pillows behind his back. Outside, a cold winter sun bounced its light off the rooftops of other smaller hospital buildings into the room.

"Now you can just cooperate or I can call the chief's office and have you ordered into this hospital. And then you'll stay for three days, minimum, because they'll want to protect themselves from criticism. I'll leave it to you."

"All right," Tommy grumbled. "Can I call my family and tell them I'm okay?"

"Your father's outside, waiting to see you."

A few moments after he left, Tony Falcone entered the room. With him was his partner, the hulking Detective Tim O'Shaughnessy.

When he saw Tommy, O'Shaughnessy boomed, "Will you be looking at this goldbricker? Some'll be doing anything to get some time off work."

Tony came over to the bed. "How you doing, son?"

"I'm fine. They're making me stay here for no reason at all."

His father reached out and touched Tommy's face. Even the delicate soft touch made the younger man wince.

"You look like hell," his father said. "I guess you left some of your face on that brick wall."

Until then, Tommy had not realized that his face had been injured at all. He reached up and found three different bandages on his face.

"The doctor says you'll be fine, though. Not even a scar," Tony said.

"There. You see. So get me out of here."

"In a while. What happened down there?"

O'Shaughnessy brought up a chair and sat next to the bed, and Tommy began relating the night's events.

"So it was about six and you were on your way home? Why so late?" his father interrupted.

"I stopped in at a friend's house."

"Mabel Fay?" his father said. Tommy was startled. He saw a grin crease O'Shaughnessy's florid face.

"What do you know about Mabel?" Tommy asked.

His father pulled his gold badge from his pocket. "That says 'detective sergeant.' Detective. It's my business to know things."

"And here I thought I was being discreet."

"You be as discreet as you want. I'll still know everything you do."

"Okay, Papa. So I was with Mabel and—"

"She tell you to go or you go on your own?"

"I went when I felt like going. Why?"

"'Cause I just want to make sure you weren't set up tonight by someone who was gunning for you."

"No, Papa, it wasn't like that. I took a shortcut home because it was so cold. Then I had to take a pee and I went into that alley. It was just bad luck. I shot one of the guys. Did they tell you that?"

"Yeah."

"Somebody named Vinnie. And there was another one named Rico."

"Think hard, Tommy. You hear anybody called Kid? Or something like that?"

Until that moment, Tommy had been planning to tell his father the whole unvarnished story, but now he found that he could not. Perhaps it was O'Shaughnessy's presence. While the big cop was like a family member, the fact was that he was not a family member. Nilo was. And this was a family thing.

Too, his father was in this room not just as his father, but as a policeman. He was investigating the case, and if Tommy told him about Nilo, Tony would, without a moment's hesitation, go and arrest him.

But Nilo had saved his life when everybody else back in that alley wanted to shoot him. Would it be fair to incriminate him now? The doctor was right, Tommy thought: he needed time to rest and to think.

"I don't think so," Tommy said. "But I was slugged and kind of not thinking real well. Why?"

"This has the look of a Kid Trouble operation," Tony said. "And I've got some ideas of my own about him. And I guess I'm just wondering why they didn't shoot you."

"I don't know why they didn't shoot me, either," Tommy said. He looked out the window at the bristling sun on the roofs. "I heard some of them talking about it, but I guess, I don't know, maybe they figured shooting a cop might be more trouble than they needed."

"Yeah, maybe that was it," Tony said in a grudging tone. "Cop-killing gets all kinds of people's backs up. How many men were in this gang all together?"

"It was dark, so I couldn't really see. And I had that damned flashlight in my eyes most of the time. I don't know. Maybe four."

"It's usually four," Tony said. "And you didn't hear any other names? Didn't recognize anybody else?"

"No," Tommy answered stolidly. "The man who was killed. Was he a . . . you know, innocent bystander?"

"Don't worry about that," O'Shaughnessy said. "He was just another one of Masseria's punks. He had a gun in his hand, so he was probably asking for it. Somebody else killed him, it saves us a bullet."

Tommy tried to change the subject. He asked, "Mama's not coming down here, is she?"

"Try to stop her," Tony answered.

"If she sees me like this . . ." Tommy touched his bandages. "She's going to be wailing and weeping. They'll have to send out for extra mops."

"She's been wailing and weeping since they came to the house to tell us. Look. You wind up in trouble, you're going to have to put up with Mama's hysterics. That's how it goes. I do. Mario does. Tina does. You do." He turned suddenly to his partner and said, "Tim, would you go down and see if anybody here knows what they're doing?" He nodded toward the door.

O'Shaughnessy stood, towering over the bed, and grinned at Tommy. "I'm glad you're okay, kid."

"Thanks for coming down," Tommy said.

"Somebody had to keep him from shooting up the neighborhood," O'Shaughnessy said, nodding toward Tony. After the door had closed behind him, Tony sat on the edge of the bed.

"So. Is there anything else you want to tell me?"

"No, Papa. That's all of it."

"You're sure?"

Tommy nodded. His father stared at him for a long time, his eyes as cold as glass, then stood up. "All right. Mama will be here soon."

"Try to get this doctor to let me out of here," Tommy said.

"You go when he says you go."

"Yes, Papa."

After Tony left the room, Tommy felt fatigue grip his body. His father had known he was lying about something. But he could not tell him about Nilo. Tony would have arrested him and Tommy did not want on his hands the blood of someone who had probably saved his life.

He closed his eyes. It was bad enough that he had not told his father the whole truth. But even worse was his realization that it was the first time since he had become a policeman that he had gone against the book. His duty had been to tell all of what happened, but instead he covered up a crime because it was personal and close to home. It had been Tommy's first test and he had failed.

MAMA AND TINA HAD BEEN GONE a couple of hours—Mama surprisingly all full of brisk efficiency when Tommy had expected a torrent of tears—when the doctor came by and told him that it was all right for Tommy to go home.

"My head's okay?" Tommy asked.

"As much as any policeman's head can be," the doctor said. "But if anything was going to go wrong, it would have happened by now. So you're a free man."

Tommy rapidly started dressing in his heavy blue uniform before the doctor had a chance to come back and change his mind.

He was standing, his foot up on the small cabinet next to his bed, lacing up his ankle-high leather shoes, when he heard the door swing open. Before Tommy could even turn around, he felt an arm come across his shoulder and heard Nilo and knew, for sure, that it was the same voice he had heard in the alley.

"I came as soon as I heard you were here. How are you feeling?"

Tommy was surprised at how well Nilo was speaking English. He had not really had a conversation with him in several months, and almost all trace of his Sicilian accent was gone. The lessons Sofia had been giving him obviously had been successful. Tommy squeezed his eyes shut for a moment and wondered idly if Nilo and Sofia were lovers.

He sat back on the bed to finish lacing his shoes. He was a little confused. He had wondered what he would say to Nilo when they met again. "I'm okay," Tommy said.

"How'd it happen?" Nilo asked.

Tommy looked up, the shoelace still in his hands. "What?"

"The accident. How'd it happen?"

"Nilo, there's nobody else here but us. What the hell are you talking about?"

"Tommy, my brother, are you sure it's all right for you to go home? Did the doctors say you could leave?"

"This is stupid," Tommy said. "Look, Nilo, I didn't tell anybody that you were there. Nobody but you and me knows what happened, and I'm willing to let it stay that way."

Nilo smiled his sly happy-child's smile. "You did not tell the other police this fable of yours?"

"I thought I owed you one for saving my life," Tommy said.

Nilo stepped forward and took Tommy's hands in his. "Tommy, if you want me to, I will take credit for saving your life. I would be proud of that."

Tommy looked into Nilo's limpid dark eyes, silent, unsure of what to say.

"I have a car outside. Do you want a ride home?"

"No, I don't think so," Tommy said.

"Any reason?"

"None in particular."

"As you will." Nilo stepped forward and they rather formally shook hands. Tommy sensed that it might be more than just a handshake, that it might be a ceremonial ending to their relationship.

But no words were spoken and Nilo turned to leave the room.

When he reached the door, Tommy called out.

"Hey, Kid."

Nilo turned at the familiar nickname, then smiled almost sheepishly.

Tommy said, "Take care of yourself. The streets can be dangerous."

AS NILO DROVE DOWNTOWN, he thought over Tommy's last words. Was it a hint that the identity of Kid Trouble might soon no longer be a secret? Tommy, he had come to believe, was dumb and would be no problem. But his father was a different case. If Tony knew who Nilo was, he would be after him like a bulldog.

No matter. *It is time to retire Kid Trouble and his gang anyway.*

Tommy had clearly tried to pay him back for sparing Tommy's life, first by saying nothing to the other police and then by passing a warning to Nilo. It was so like Tommy, he thought. *Good-hearted and weak. Like he was the day we went to see old man Mangini at the restaurant.*

He wished Tommy had more spine. Nilo could have found a good spot for him in Maranzano's business, but Tommy would always prefer the other path of being a policeman, then a lawyer. *My blood brother is a good man, but he has no nerve. I suppose it's in his blood.*

As he always did, Nilo parked a block away from the warehouse and walked to it, just so he could make sure there were no suspicious—and dangerous—people hanging around the area.

When he was satisfied that everything was still secure, he went inside, where Rico and the other young man, whose name was Angelo, were waiting.

"How's Vinnie?" Nilo asked.

Angelo said sadly, "He didn't make it, Kid. He bled to death before we could get him to the doc."

"I'm sorry," Nilo said. "He was a good guy." *And so, now Tommy has killed, too. Too bad he will never know it.* Nilo nodded once, ending that conversation, then waved at the two liquor trucks. "Masseria must be going nuts. A quarter of a million in booze swiped right out from under his nose."

The two men grinned. Nilo said, "After dark, I'll have small trucks coming up here. You help load everything out of these, and we'll move it up to our warehouse in the Bronx. Then dump these trucks somewhere. And be careful. Masseria's probably got men looking all over for them. So don't take chances."

As he turned to leave, Angelo said, "When's our next job, Kid?"

"I'll let you know," Nilo answered. "But in the meantime, if you'd like to go away on vacation for a while and get some sun, make plans. I'll be back to pay you later."

Driving away, Nilo thought long and hard. Kid Trouble had had a good run, but it was over. And now, any remnant of that operation could bring him nothing but trouble. *It is the way it goes,* he thought. *This is a tough business, and it is always a good idea to work with people no one will miss.*

After midnight, when the last of the imported Scotch had been transferred to a small panel truck, Nilo returned to the warehouse. He was there only a few minutes. When he left, Angelo and Rico lay dead with bullets in their heads. When their bodies were found next to the hijacked

Masseria trucks, everyone would think they had been found and killed by Joe the Boss's men.

And so, Kid Trouble is no more, Nilo thought, driving away. *But there will be many more adventures.*

TOMMY WENT TO OUR LADY of Mount Carmel Church in Greenwich Village to talk to Mario, but his brother was busy hearing confessions, so Tommy stood last in line, waiting his turn to enter the small booth on the side of the church.

"Forgive me, Father, for I have sinned."

"Tommy?"

"Yes, Peppino, it's me." Tommy spoke softly, his face close to the thin screen that separated him from his brother, Mario, on the other side of the confessional booth.

"Is this business or pleasure?" Mario asked.

"I've come to confess. Do you grill all your parishioners this way?"

"Only the ones who haven't been around for a few weeks. I like to know if they still belong to the church or if they're spies for the devil."

"Ever since you people terrorized poor Galileo, you've been insufferable."

"All right, then get to it. You can skip missing Mass. What else is on your excuse for a mind?"

"It's Papa. I think I've lied to him and I don't know what to do."

"You only *think* you've lied?"

For the first time since it had happened a month before, Tommy told the full story of what had happened in the alley that February night. And how, since that time, it seemed that his every waking hour was filled with guilt and recriminations aimed at himself.

"I thought the newspapers said that this Kid Trouble was found dead."

"Papers get things wrong," Tommy said.

"Nilo says he wasn't in that alley?"

"He didn't say he was, he didn't say he wasn't."

"But you're sure he was there?" Mario asked.

"Yes."

"One hundred percent positive?"

"I don't know, I'm just sure he was there. And I should have told Papa."

"Ah, see, you're not one hundred percent sure. So you don't *know* anything for sure; you only think. And if you had told Papa, what would he do?"

"Pick Nilo up for questioning, I guess."

"And maybe arrest him and maybe have him deported. All because of something that you are not sure of. Would you destroy his life on just the possibility that he did something wrong?"

Tommy was silent for a moment. Put that way, it made sense. He was not sure. Why cause problems when he wasn't sure? When juries weren't sure, they were supposed to acquit. As a policeman, could he hold himself to any other standard?

"Maybe you're right," he said. "Are you sure you're not a Jesuit?"

"It's not a matter for the church or this confessional," Mario said. "Whatever you decide to do will be the right thing."

It was very like Mario, Tommy thought, to steer him in a direction and then let him think that he had chosen that path himself. He had always done that. Maybe that's what big brothers were supposed to do. Maybe, he thought sadly, he should have been that kind of big brother to Nilo, to help him choose his life's path more wisely. But who was he to give anyone advice?

He moved on the hard wooden seat, ready to get up.

"Thanks, Mouse," he said.

"Not so fast," Mario said through the curtain. "As long as you're here, let's try confession. And don't leave anything out. Not even the waitress."

"Does everybody know all my secrets? You people are like spies."

"Papa knows. And because Papa knows, Mama knows. And anything Mama knows, she spends all her time worrying about. She thinks this divorced woman is going to trick you into marriage. Is she?"

"She's single and I'm single. I plan to stay that way."

"Just fornicating your little heart out. Let's hear it all."

As he had when he was a child, going to confession with other parish priests, Tommy thought the penance was too much. Six Hail Marys and six Our Fathers and a meaningless promise to go and sin no more. But he knelt dutifully in the back of the church, reciting the prayers it seemed he had known all his life, then went out into the sunshine, feeling curiously refreshed and relieved.

Mario came to the steps of the church in his black cassock and watched him walk away down the street. He wondered if Tommy's story had something to do with Nilo's visit to Mario just a week earlier.

Nilo had visited him in the rectory and given him an envelope.

"What's in here?" Mario asked.

"There's two hundred dollars. I thought maybe you could buy some equipment for your boxers—gloves and stuff."

When Mario asked him why he wanted to make the donation, Nilo had said, "Because God has been good to me."

Mario had already heard his father's complaints over and over about Nilo being the bad seed of the family, only twenty-one years old and already a full-fledged mobster, so he left the envelope lying on his desk, untouched. "God would be even better to you if you would come to Mass on occasion," he said.

"Mario, I won't lie to you. I hang around with some rough people. Once in a while I do something maybe that you can't wash away with Our Fathers and Hail Marys. When I get the chance, I go to a church where they don't know me, where they don't ask any questions. In the meantime, that little donation might score me a point or two in heaven, if I need it." Nilo flashed his most seductive smile, and in the end, Mario took the money and thanked him for it, but after his cousin had left, Mario wondered if he had done right. The thing that bothered Mario most was that he seemed to be on his way to becoming a politician—able, on request, to find two sides to every question.

It had always been his weakness, always being able to empathize with someone else's position, even in the boxing ring. He had had a chance to move up in the professional ranks, but it never happened, largely because Mario lacked the killer instinct. He knew when he had another fighter beaten, but instead of ending it swiftly as he should have, he would carry beaten fighters for the full four or six rounds of the fight, rather than inflict unnecessary shame or punishment upon them. A couple of times, he had lost the decisions in fights in which he had just been coasting, letting an opponent finish the bout on his feet instead of on his back.

He had won more fights than he had lost, but he was workmanlike rather than exciting, finding little pleasure in the sport of beating someone else to death. Toward the end, he had begun to question the sport itself—and when his manager told him one day he was having trouble booking Mario's next fight Mario said, "Don't bother. I'm quitting the ring."

He was in the seminary three months later.

AFTER MORE THAN A YEAR of tutoring him, Sofia had begun to consider Nilo as a possible solution to her problems.

She knew she could do worse. Nilo was handsome—no, actually he was pretty—and seemed wellmannered, and even though everyone now knew he was one of Salvatore Maranzano's gangsters, he clearly was prospering, enough to support a wife.

As this interest in Nilo was kindling itself, Sofia tried to make lists of the pros and cons of being with Nilo, but after not too long she tore the list up and threw it away. First of all, there was something in Nilo's eyes that frightened her. Silky long lashes or no, his were the eyes of someone who viewed all other people as things to be used, to be moved around for his own advantage. Anybody who got in his way would be treated as an impediment, nothing more. She also guessed from his eyes that Nilo really did not care for women, that he believed them worthless, useful perhaps for only one thing. That made them even, she realized; she did not care for men and regarded them all as rapists waiting to strike.

Even if she did try to encourage Nilo, she knew that she was absolutely ignorant of any practical way to do it. She had none of the coquettish charms of Tina Falcone, who seemed to know just when to smile, when to look down demurely, when to chatter gaily, when to act seductive. Tina's talents had probably come from growing up with older brothers and having to find ways to get them to do what she wanted. Sofia had no such experience, and although she knew in her heart she was as beautiful as Tina, she had no confidence in her ability to entice men, but deep in her heart she knew that enticing men was not going to be high on her list of things to do.

She saw Nilo often now. He had taken to eating dinner frequently at Mangini's Restaurant and she met with him every week to study language and speech. And in all that time of being thrown together with him, she doubted if they had devoted as much as one hour to pleasant small talk.

He spent more time than that talking with her cousin, Charlie. It struck her as odd that Nilo, who worked for Maranzano, should have so cordial a relationship with Luciano, who was known to be Joe Masseria's top man.

She had been bold enough one evening, three months earlier, to mention that fact when talking to Charlie before he left the restaurant. Luciano had looked at her as if she were a bug.

For a long frightening moment, she thought her cousin would strike her, but instead, finally, he smiled and said, "So how can I talk to the employee of my enemy? Is that what you wish to know?"

"Something like that. Yes."

"I will tell you. Not because it is any of your business but because you are family and young and your life will be better if you are wiser. A wise man once said, 'Keep your friends close by, and your enemies even closer.' Do you not think it might help for me to know what Nilo's people are up to?"

"I see. It was presumptuous of me to ask," Sofia said.

Luciano shook his head. "No. You're not presumptuous. You're merely young. Young . . ." He snaked his hand across the table and rested it on hers. "Young and beautiful." She made no effort to move her hand, nor to take his. "Young and beautiful," he repeated. "And family." He released her hand and brought his back to lift his espresso cup. "So how are things with you?"

She looked around. The restaurant had only a half-dozen diners in it. Her mother was busy in the kitchen, and her father had gone to an organizational meeting of the newly formed Sons of Italy.

"I know I never thanked you properly for helping me that time," she said. "With my father."

Luciano raised a hand. "I did nothing," he said.

"To you, nothing. To us, everything. Since that night, he has not laid a hand on my mother or me. That is a very big thing indeed."

Or dragged you into his bed, Luciano thought. He smiled his acknowledgment. In truth, the girl had thanked him before and he had accepted the thanks as his due, even though he had done nothing except talk to Mangini after his hand had already been broken. Later, he found out from Mangini's wife—his mother's cousin—that it was the young policeman across the street, Tommy Falcone, who had straightened out Sofia's father. And the girl never knew. Perhaps best just to let it stay that way. Let her think whatever she wants to think. It is not bad to be owed favors by beautiful young women, especially ones who might be enticed to spread their legs.

He wondered, though, why this Sofia did not know that the young cop had been the one to help her, especially since her best friend was that cop's beautiful sister, Tina. There were no family secrets in Little Italy, but maybe he had stumbled onto one: maybe the Falcone girl was on the outs, somehow, with her family, not privy to their secrets or their actions.

He filed that away in his mind. The truth was that even though he now managed a large stable of prostitutes and call girls, who were always available to him, he thought often of the breathtaking Tina Falcone.

I have plans for her. Someday . . .

Meanwhile, he would stay in touch with this nosy, meddling Sofia to find out from her what was happening with the Falcones, even if it meant pretending to tolerate her insolent questions about his relationship with Nilo Sesta.

Luciano had told Sofia nothing that night in the restaurant, but she had noticed that he did not deny spending time with Nilo, and shrewdly she decided that he was doing it on Joe the Boss's orders, as just a way to get a pipeline into the Maranzano operation. Of course, she did not mention that.

And she never mentioned it to Nilo, either, when he came for his weekly English lesson. If he had been a closer friend, she might have warned him that Luciano was using him. But Nilo and she were not close; he would have to learn on his own.

She had moved back into her family's apartment because, despite the money she made at the restaurant and the weekly five dollars she got for tutoring Nilo, she did not have enough money to get an apartment of her own. She simply could not stay forever with the Falcones. And now, just last night, she had seen her father looking at her in the restaurant and she had recognized the look in his eyes for the lust that it was, and she knew she had to get away.

When Nilo came for his regular lesson, Sofia had him

read aloud from various newspapers and books. During a break, she brewed tea.

"You must be very busy," she said.

"I am. I haven't even seen the Falcones in months. How are they?"

"Everyone seems fine."

"And Tina? She is still working at that factory?" Nilo asked.

"Yes. Still saving for her singing lessons. I guess they're very expensive."

"And Uncle Tony can't help?"

"They don't have that kind of money, Nilo. You know that."

"No. Honest policemen never get rich, do they? I've often thought of offering to lend them money but . . ." He raised his hands in despair.

Sofia just shook her head.

"Maybe if I sent the money directly to Tina."

"Her father would find out and make her pay it back," Sofia said.

Nilo sighed. "Ahh, the pride of the Sicilian. It'll be the death of all of us yet."

They returned to their lessons, and as the clock struck the end of the second hour Sofia took the magazine away and said, "I can't do any more with you. Your accent is gone. You read well. You know as much Latin as I do. You no longer need me."

Nilo smiled, a flash of almost satin-looking teeth.

"One always needs a beautiful woman."

She wanted to respond but could think of nothing to say, and after a moment Nilo said, "You should be a teacher."

She laughed bitterly. "Or a poet. Or a nun. Or a lot

of things, perhaps, but I think I will learn to run a restaurant."

"Have lots of babies?"

Sofia shrugged.

"With Tommy?"

"Tommy has his own life," she said sharply.

"That's his loss. Who is your young man?"

"I don't like talking about my personal life," she said.

"You brought it up."

Sofia managed a smile. "I guess I did. There isn't any young man. If there ever is, he will probably be fat and dumb and useful only for making babies. That will be my life."

"Only if you want it to be. You control your own fate."

"Everyone says that, but only men believe it," she said. She began to gather up the magazines. Usually Nilo, at lesson's end, jumped to his feet, handed her an envelope containing a five-dollar bill, and left immediately. But today he seemed to be lingering.

"Nilo," she said. "This is none of my business, but . . ."

He stepped closer to her. "Yes?"

"I see you with my cousin, Charlie. Do you consider him a friend?"

"Why?"

"He knows you work against Joe Masseria. I think he is your enemy."

Nilo laughed. "I *know* he is my enemy," he said. "Thank you for worrying. But let others worry. You have done me a great service by being my teacher. Some night I would like to repay you by taking you to dinner."

She swallowed hard and finally was able to blurt out, "I would like that." She felt herself blush.

Nilo took two envelopes from his jacket pocket. "This

is your fee," he said. "And this other . . . There is the carnival tonight at Mount Carmel. Some friends of mine are running a place to eat there. I have tickets for you. Tickets for two. Maybe you would take Tina and cheer her up."

"That's very nice," Sofia said.

"There are two tickets in there for free meals and ten raffle tickets. Cash prizes." He smiled. "Give half of them to Tina."

TONY SAT AT HIS KITCHEN TABLE, drinking a glass of wine and reading the newspaper, when Tina and Sofia came into the room.

"Mama should be home from church any minute," Tina said. "You sure you don't want me to fix you something?"

"I'm growing a potbelly like an icebox," Falcone said. "I can wait a little while for a meal. Where are you two beauties going?"

"The carnival at Mario's church. We'll get something to eat over there while we're examining this season's crop of boys," Tina said with a smile.

Sofia noted that Tony did not smile back. This was uncharacteristic behavior, because he doted on Tina, spoiling her totally, and she had always been able to lead him around by the nose.

"Well, don't waste any money gambling. All the games are fixed. And be careful. There's a lot of dangerous characters out on the streets these days."

"I'll just tell them we are protected by the great Sergeant Falcone. No one will bother us," Tina said.

Totally without humor, Falcone said, "They'd better not."

On the street outside, Sofia said, "Your father seemed worried about something."

Tina shrugged it off. "He spends all his time chasing Italian criminals. I heard him talking to Mama about it. First he's got Joe the Boss to worry about. Now he's got somebody named Maranzano to worry about. Joe the Boss was moving illegal liquor into the city. Now it seems this Maranzano is illegally stealing this illegal liquor from Joe the Boss, and my father worries that they are going to start illegally killing each other. I told him I thought it would be a good idea. Let them all kill each other and we'll be done with it. He said that wouldn't be so bad except some civilians would be sure to get hurt. Anyway, this is making him so crazy that now he thinks everybody is a criminal. Your cousin Charlie is on the list. Most nights Papa sits around the apartment wearing his gun. Really. You heard him. He even thinks the carnival games are crooked."

"Should we have told him Nilo gave us free tickets?" Sofia asked.

Tina stopped on the street, looked around conspiratorially, and gave a big overdramatic shush of her lips. "Nilo's name is not mentioned in our home anymore. To hear my father tell it, he is the worst bandit since Jesse James."

Sofia laughed at her friend's charade and said, "Our Nilo?"

"Yes. Do you believe that? Because Nilo's real estate company is apparently owned by this Maranzano. That makes Nilo a criminal, too. A murderer even. Have you ever heard of anything so silly?"

As they continued strolling down the street in the direction of Greenwich Village, Sofia did not answer. But she was thinking that her friend Tina was very naive. She lived with policemen but never listened to what they were saying. Sofia, meanwhile, worked only in a restaurant and yet knew, firsthand, that there *were* criminals out there and that, without a doubt, Nilo Sesta was one of them. His life had nothing to do with selling real estate.

THE RESTAURANT TO WHICH Sofia had been given tickets by Nilo was filled with customers when they arrived, and they expected to be told there was a long wait, until the proprietor looked at their free meal tickets.

"These are your tickets?"

"Given to us by a friend," Sofia said, almost defensively, wondering if Nilo had perhaps stolen them and they had been reported to the police.

"You have very fine friends," the proprietor said, and somehow, magically, he was able to find them a table right in the front of the room. At last, for a little while, they were free of the horde of young men who had been following them ever since they arrived at the carnival on the street in front of the church.

The proprietor's largesse did not end with table selection. Without their having ordered, suddenly their table was heaped with entrées of all sorts, veal and beef and chicken and pasta and salads and vegetables and seafood. Tina protested to the proprietor, "Both our families together couldn't eat all this food."

He simply smiled and answered, "I would have it no other way for friends of Don Salvatore."

Tina nodded majestically, but when the man had left she asked Sofia, "Who's Don Salvatore?"

"It must be this Maranzano crook. Nilo gave me the tickets."

"God," Tina said in mock astonishment. "We're guests

of the Mafia. Do you think they'll sell us to the White Slavers if we eat too much?"

"You just wish," Sofia said, and giggled.

After stuffing themselves with food, they sneaked out a side exit and found that the admiring herd of boys that had been following them had dispersed, probably because the carnival site was now packed with people and there were other, perhaps more-willing partners for their zealous lust.

After a few moments of strolling, Tina and Sofia were suddenly pushed aside by a large mass of people. Around them, they heard the sound level drop, as if people were suddenly afraid to talk. The two young women stood on tiptoe and saw a roundish looking man wearing a cape and a white hat, strolling down the center of the walkway, waving almost papally at the other carnival-goers. He was eating fried peppers from a grease-soaked paper bag.

"That's Joe Masseria," Sofia told Tina in hushed terms. "He comes into our restaurant once in a while. He's a pig."

"He acts like he's the King of Sheba."

"Around here, I guess he is," Sofia said. When the crowd surrounding Masseria had moved on, Tina and Sofia wandered off in the other direction, Tina flirting shamelessly with everyone who looked at her. For a while, they amused themselves playing bingo and the spinning wheels, on which Tina won a stuffed elephant toy. Later in the evening, they bumped into Sofia's cousin. He was dressed nattily in a white suit and was standing alongside a game-of-chance booth. He smiled when he saw the two young women. Tina nodded curtly, and Sofia said, "Hello, Charlie."

Nearby Tina saw two of the young men who always

seemed to be hovering around Luciano. One of them was the very young one Luciano called Benny, the one she had heard beat up prostitutes. He was baby-faced and handsome, Tina thought, and he still seemed too young to have such a reputation. The other was older, Luciano's age, and handsome too in a darker Mediterranean way.

"Do you girls need anything? Money, tickets for anything?" Luciano asked.

Sofia hesitated, and Tina answered quickly, "No, Mr. Luciano, we're fine. Except maybe some information."

"Charlie. Please. I told you, Charlie."

"Charlie," Tina said.

"And this information?" he asked warily.

"Some people we talked to tonight told us this place is filled with gangsters."

Sofia looked shocked. "Tina," she said sharply.

"No, go ahead, girl," Luciano said.

"I was just wondering why gangsters would care about a neighborhood carnival."

"Well, I don't know anything about that personally," Luciano began.

"Of course," Tina said with clear, if muted, sarcasm.

"But some of the proceeds from the carnival go to Mount Carmel Church. And there are different factions of . . . businessmen . . . who want to make sure that the people in the parish regard them highly. So they see that their own people come here and spread their names around and spend lots of money."

"You're talking about Masseria and Maranzano," Tina said. Sofia stood silently to the side, aghast at the turn the conversation was taking.

"Ah, you have been listening while your father speaks," Luciano said, with a patronizing smile on his face.

"And so tonight, this peacock contest of criminals, will there be a winner?"

"At the end each one hopes that the church will say the followers of so-and-so or the followers of so-and-so-other were the biggest supporters of our carnival. This will let the parishioners know they can deal with this man as a man of respect. The one who does not win will lose respect."

"Who will win?" Tina pressed.

"For that you should have asked your other brother, the priest who is not a policeman, because that is the wonderful part of it," Luciano said. "It is always the same. Neither of them wins. Your brother and the other good fathers at Mount Carmel wish to offend no one, so they always say it was a tie. That both won. There was no loser. I tell you, the church knows something about playing politics." He paused. "But you would know that, I guess. Wouldn't you, Miss Falcone?"

Before Tina could answer, Sofia said, "We have to be going. See you later, Cousin."

Luciano nodded.

"Bye-bye, Mr. Luciano," Tina said with a smile, and let Sofia lead her away. Luciano watched as the two young women sauntered off. The young boy, Benny, came to his side and looked appreciatively at the two beauties.

"Good-lookers, Charlie," he said.

"Yeah, Benny, they are," Luciano said softly. "And that Tina Falcone thinks she is very smart."

"A lot of them think that way until they're on their backs," Benny said.

"That time will come."

They both watched the girls walk away for a few moments longer, and Benny said, "I want seconds."

"WHY DID YOU TALK to Salvatore that way?" Sofia asked her friend. "You were taunting him."

" 'Charlie. Please.' He likes to be called Charlie," Tina said mockingly. "And he started it. What does he think, we're little girls and he can impress us by giving us lollipops?"

"He was just trying to be nice."

"Come on, Fia, think. Do you really believe that these gees are around because they want to give a lot of money to the church? Did you watch your cousin's eyes? He was watching the gambling game that was going on. Papa was right. These thugs run all these games, and first they steal the public's money and then they give a little tiny piece of it back to the church and pretend they're holy."

A few minutes later, they passed a raffle booth that advertised with a large hand-painted sign: 50-50. TICKETS, 25 CENTS.

"Oh, look," Sofia said. "We've got some tickets on the fifty-fifty." She reached into her purse and brought out ten little tickets. "We should turn them in." She separated them and let Tina pick out five of them.

They went to the long counter in the front of the booth, and the operator, a sweating hairy man wearing a peasant's cap pulled down over his ears, carefully made them sign the back of each small ticket with their name and address.

He took the tickets from them, glanced at the names, then said, "Why don't you hang around, girls? We'll be drawing the winner in five minutes."

Tina seemed reluctant, but Sofia convinced her. "Five minutes, Tina. Maybe we'll be lucky."

"It'll be the first time ever," Tina said sourly.

But they waited, and the crowd started to swell around them as the game's operator put on a loud phonograph record of Italian music and began to shout loudly that the 50-50 drawing was ready to begin.

There was no skill to the drawing, of course. A 50-50 simply meant that the proprietors added up all the money that had been spent on tickets, picked a winning number out of a barrel, and the holder of that ticket won 50 percent of the money that had been collected. The other 50 percent went to those who ran the game, in this case, to Mount Carmel Parish.

Finally, after suffering through three badly scratched records of Neapolitan music, the crowd surged forward as the proprietor of the game, standing on a small platform at the back of his booth, stirred and shook a small beer keg that was filled with tickets. He called a little girl, not more than five years old, forward from the crowd, opened the top of the barrel, and told her to reach in and draw a ticket. He held on to her hand as she leaned over and reached into the barrel and he was still holding her hand when she withdrew it, with a ticket held between her thumb and index finger.

"Thank you, little girl," the man said, taking the ticket from her. He reached into his pocket with the hand that held the ticket and brought out a fresh one-dollar bill. "This is for being my helper."

He turned back to the crowd. "And now the big moment," he said. "I can tell you, this is going to be the biggest cash prize in our history. Are you ready?"

The crowd roared.

"Let's go," somebody shouted.

"All right." The man looked down at the ticket in his hands, stretching the moment out as long as he could. When the crowd started to grumble, he shouted aloud,

"And the winner is . . . Justina Falcone . . . of Crosby Street. Is Miss Falcone here?"

The crowd groaned when each member realized he or she hadn't won. But Sofia was jumping up and down.

"Tina, you won. You won!"

Tina shook her head. She was numb with shock.

"Here," Sofia screamed. "Here's the winner!"

All around them, people backed away and turned toward them to get a look at the lucky girl. Sofia grabbed a still-stunned Tina by the arm and pulled her forward to the concession stand.

"And you're Miss Falcone?" the operator said.

Tina nodded dumbly.

"You've just won"—he looked at a paper in his hand—"five hundred and forty dollars." The crowd cheered. A male voice called out, "Will you marry me?"

Tina turned to Sofia. "I've just won my future," she said softly. Tears glistened in her eyes.

Neither of the girls noticed the proprietor glance off to the side of the booth. Standing there in the shadows was Nilo Sesta. He nodded once to the proprietor and walked away.

AS HE HAD TOLD HER to be, Maranzano's secretary, Betty, was waiting for Nilo in the room at the Princess Hotel. She wore a blood-red dressing gown and she was lounging on a sofa in the barely lit room, listening to a phonograph record of a dance band.

When he closed the door behind him, he said, "Take that off."

"The record?"

"What you're wearing."

"Go fly a kite." She turned her face away, toward the window that overlooked the street.

Nilo strode across the room. He reached down, grabbed the top of her robe, and yanked it down off her body, then pulled her into the bedroom of the suite.

Later, Betty lay alongside him in the bed, her head on his chest, idly running her long nails up and down his smooth skin. It was hard for her sometimes to reconcile his almost-delicate good looks with his growing reputation as one of Maranzano's deadliest soldiers.

In a rare moment of introspection, she thought that it was possibly that same reputation that made her find him so attractive. She often thought that, if Maranzano ordered him to, Nilo would kill her without even a second thought. There was something very sexy about danger.

"Does the moth like the flame?" she asked aloud.

"What kind of question is that?"

"A simple one. Does the moth like the flame? Why does it come so close that it gets burned?"

"Because moths are stupid. They do not know that the flame burns. So they die. Are you a moth?"

"No," she said after a moment's hesitation. "Because I'm not stupid. But you *are* a flame."

"You, I promise not to burn," Nilo said. "Tonight I am a flame who is very satisfied with himself."

"Why?"

"I arranged for a girl who needed it to get money for her education."

"Some little tramp you're sleeping with, I bet."

"No."

"Then why did you help her?"

"Because her brother could have caused me trouble a few months ago and he did not. I wanted to do something to repay that debt."

"Are these those Falcones, those relatives of yours?"

"Yes."

"You gave the priest money to buy toys for the kids. When do you stop paying them back?"

"I'm done now. I never want to owe anybody anything. If somebody does you a favor and you don't pay it back, it is a way that people can control you. I will not be controlled."

"You are a flame, Nilo," she said.

He pulled her atop him. "I am a flame."

TINA FALCONE HAD PROMISED herself she would not be nervous, so she blamed her perspiration on the weather, even though the day was cool for July and lacking the chronic high humidity that made New York unbearable in midsummer. But she could feel the sweat leaking through her very best dress.

Being nervous only caused problems with her singing. Her teacher, Carlo Crivelli, had told her that nervousness made her voice breathy and, every now and then, shrill. That could not be allowed to happen, not today of all days. She told herself over and over not to be nervous. The reminder just made her nerves worse.

She took a deep breath and started up the stairs of the brownstone. The brass nameplate read: UTA SCHATTE. Tina rang the doorbell, and while she waited she looked across the street at the park, closed in by a wrought-iron fence. She recognized one of the buildings across the way as the Players Club, a private club started long ago in the home of the great actor Edwin Booth.

She had never before seen a private park, for rich people only, and she vowed that when she was herself rich and famous she would come back to Gramercy Park and buy one of these brownstones, and then she would invite all the poor kids she could find to come up and play in the park.

She heard the door open. A young black woman, dressed in a simple maid's uniform, stood there, and she was one of the most exquisitely beautiful creatures Tina had ever seen: tall and lithe with café-au-lait skin and a wide generous mouth with perfect teeth; she had long delicate fingers and almond-shaped eyes.

"I can help you?" she said in a curious accent that Tina did not recognize.

"I am to see Frau Schatte," Tina said. "I have an appointment. My name is Justina Falcone."

The maid seemed to study her for a moment and then smiled, as if having found her worthy of this visit.

"She is expecting you," she said, and stepped aside to let Tina through the doorway. She felt as if she were entering another world, a fantasy world. The house was a marvel. The furnishings were not new, but they were elegant, and Tina could see ahead into a large drawing room that seemed filled with brightness and air.

She followed the maid through half a dozen rooms and up a grand rear staircase before being shown into a large room, where a very blond woman, whose hair was cut as short as a man's and marcelled into tight waves, sat at a piano at the far end. The maid walked away and left Tina there.

For an instant Tina felt as if she should curtsy, but that passed. She stopped momentarily at the door, took a deep breath, remembered to hold her head up high, and started forward. Frau Schatte waited for her to get more than halfway across the room before she arose.

She was taller than Tina, nearly Amazonian in height. Her skin was pure alabaster and her eyes were icy blue.

In her early forties, she was breathtakingly beautiful in a regal sort of way.

Tina thought despondently that, of the three women in the house, she was the homeliest of the bunch. She had not expected her day to start that way.

Frau Schatte held out her hand and smiled, and all Tina's thoughts that the woman was an ice queen disappeared because her smile was warm and friendly.

"And so you're Justina Falcone. You are really quite beautiful, my dear. Come closer. Now turn around. I must see what you look like. Yes, yes. Fine. Every inch the prima donna. All we have to do is get rid of those dreadful rags you're wearing. That is, *if* you can sing."

Tina felt flustered. "Thank you," she said, stammering slightly.

"And how is my old friend, Carlo?" Frau Schatte asked.

"Signor Crivelli is fine, ma'am," Tina said. "He said to send you his best regards."

Frau Schatte laughed, a soft deep rumble that sounded like a cat purring.

"He wrote me that you have a very fine voice," Frau Schatte said.

Tina made embarrassed sounds.

"Tell me, dear, how old are you?"

"Nineteen. Almost twenty."

"I remember that age. So long ago. Tell me, has Carlo made love to you?"

Tina reddened. "No, ma'am," she said.

Frau Schatte laughed. "He *is* old, isn't he? He was my first. At least that's what I told him. Men are such fools. They are always easy to trick. Well, come now, sing for me. What would you like to do?"

"I brought two pieces of music. 'Tacea la notte placida' and 'Vissi d'arte.'"

"Verdi and Puccini?" the other woman said, raising an eyebrow. "Very ambitious.'"

"I grew up with them," Tina said. "I mean, on the phonograph."

"Ahh, the charm of the Italian family. Surrounded by music. Very well, I will accompany you. Begin."

Tina made two false starts before settling down enough to sing. And then it was all so easy, easier than it had ever been with Signor Crivelli, who lived in the neighborhood, seemed to be one hundred years old, and had started giving her voice lessons as a favor to her father.

"He was once a fine musician," her father had said. "He played at the Met."

"Papa, he's so old."

"And so is opera. His ears still work. He can help you."

There was no arguing with her father, and she had gone to Crivelli each Saturday for a few months, but he was very old and even his ears did not work very well anymore. Finally, he told her that she needed more instruction than he was able to give. From him came the name of Frau Schatte.

"She is a queer one," he told Tina. "But she knows music. You have a voice. It will take someone stronger than me to make it grow."

And now here she was, in Frau Schatte's music room, singing, and it seemed to be just as it should be. There was no straining, no effort at all. It was as if the music wasn't really coming from her but was emanating from somewhere else and her throat just happened to be the medium for presenting it. Then it was over.

Frau Schatte sat silently for a long time, looking over the sheet music on her piano. Then she smiled at Tina. "Very nice," she said. "You will move in tomorrow. You will be staying here with me. Ordinarily, I have as many as three girls here, but as of right now, you will be the only one. You can have one afternoon off a week for personal business."

Tina was flabbergasted. She tried to think of something appropriate to say, but the only thing that would come out was, "How much will it cost?"

Frau Schatte stared at her for a moment. "Spoken like a true prima donna. Never forget the money. It is the most important thing in a career. It will cost you a hundred dollars a month, and you must stay a minimum of one year."

"A hundred dollars a month!" Tina exclaimed. She had not expected to be moving into Frau Schatte's home as a lodger. After forcing a very reluctant Sofia to take one hundred dollars as her share of Tina's winning raffle ticket, she still had four hundred dollars. She had thought this would be enough to finance a full year of lessons with Frau Schatte. Now she saw that her windfall was only a pittance; it would cover only four months of the teacher's fees.

To Frau Schatte's puzzled look, Tina said, "I had not thought it would be so much. Or that I would be moving in here. Couldn't I just come in for regular lessons?"

"No," the other woman answered bluntly, then softened her tone. "Dear Justina, you need more than just singing lessons. And yes, the money is a lot, but don't be dismayed. It will cost me far more than that to take care of you. You must have food and new clothes and scores. You will need maid service and you will need money for your amusements and to pay for your abortions—all my girls have those. It is very expensive learning to be a prima donna. You must become accustomed to the very best. And of course you will need other lessons. What languages do you speak?"

"English and Italian."

"No, my dear, you do not speak Italian. You speak Sicilian, a very different thing entirely. You sang those arias beautifully but your pronunciation was atrocious. You sound like a fishmonger. Then you must learn French and German. And your walk. You even have to learn to walk. When you crossed the floor in this room, you looked like a duck trying to imitate a turkey. That will never do, my dear. It will simply not do."

Tina fought hard to hold back the tears. "I have only enough money for a few months," she said.

"We have to have at least a year's commitment. Otherwise I am not able to plan. What about your father? What does he do?"

"He's a policeman."

"Then money should be no problem. All police officers are rich now that we have this Prohibition."

Tina bridled at the remark. "My father takes nothing he doesn't earn. He is not rich."

Frau Schatte sighed. "Well, think it over. Perhaps your father has some savings nobody knows about. Or maybe you can get a loan. Talk it over with your family and let me know. Within a week."

She turned away, indicating that the interview and audition were over, and the brusqueness of her manner annoyed Tina, who said sharply, "I may be able to do it, but it will take more than a week."

"Oh?"

"Yes. I have obligations that I would have to take care of first," Tina said, although the only obligation she could think of was giving two weeks' notice at the dismal, depressing office in which she worked. "I will have to see when I might become free. I will let you know, either way, as soon as I can."

Now that she had established who would be employer and who employee, Tina picked up her music and walked away, trying to remember not to meander like a duck imitating a turkey. At the door, she turned back and was surprised to see Frau Schatte smiling at her.

"A prima donna," the older woman said admiringly. "You will be a real prima donna."

NILO STOOD BEFORE one of the antique mirrors in the outer office. Instead of his usual suit and silk tie, he was wearing tennis whites with a sweater tied in a careless fashion, which had taken him a full minute to get just right. He thought he looked perfect—like the spoiled youngest son from a wealthy family.

And if not that, at least a far cry from the wharf rat who sneaked ashore in this country nearly three years ago.

When he was satisfied with his appearance, he glanced at Betty, who smiled her approval, then walked toward the door to Maranzano's inner sanctum. The regular pair of bodyguards nodded to him and then went back to reading their papers. Nilo walked into Maranzano's office without knocking.

"Good morning, Don Salvatore," he said. Maranzano glanced up from papers on his desk and grunted absentmindedly. He gestured with his head for Nilo to sit, and for five minutes Nilo watched the older man shuffle papers, occasionally scrawling his initials on a page. Finally, he shoved all the papers into a pile, as if formally done with them.

"I'm sorry to keep you waiting that way," he said, "but the bigger one's empire becomes, the more paper one has to handle. Someday, Nilo, we will own a paper company and a printing plant and there will be jobs for everyone and everybody will need us and we will be rich."

"Everybody needs us now," Nilo said. *And you're already richer than a hundred men. And I am richer than I ever thought I would be, if not as rich as I someday will be.*

"Because of the stupid Prohibition, yes? For now. But sooner or later, America will see that this is foolishness and they will call an end to this 'noble experiment' of theirs. And when that happens, what will you do?"

Nilo looked at Maranzano in a way he had perfected: it was a shy sidewise glance as if the speaker were battling his modesty. "I will do whatever my don tells me to do."

"Oh, Nilo, you are already an American politician. You belong in Tammany Hall, except they are all thieves and scoundrels there and I would not expose anyone I care for to those influences. We will keep doing what we are doing, Nilo. We will take the money from the liquor, from the gambling, from the other vices, and we will use it to move into honest businesses. And when, one day, this government in Washington says we must put all these bad people behind bars, we will say, what bad people? We are just honest businessmen trying to earn a dollar. Not like that stupid *gavone*, Masseria, with his expensive cigars and his horse-blanket suits, who will never know what hit him."

Nilo nodded. He had heard the speech before. *He's right. It's just common sense to plan for the future. Still we live in the present. We should not forget to act here and now. That is really what puts bread and wine on today's table, not plans for tomorrow.*

"You look like a college boy," Maranzano said. "Which reminds me. How are your lessons?"

"Sofia says she can teach me no more."

"Your speech is excellent. You no longer sound as if you just got off the boat. And your reading?"

"I can read anything, Don Salvatore. Latin too."

"Good. Read, read, read. You are still an uneducated street rodent. I will give you books. You read them, you learn things."

"Yes, sir."

"I heard you arranged for the Falcone girl to win the Mount Carmel prize drawing."

Nilo nodded and tried to show no emotion. He had wondered how much Betty told Maranzano. Now he had his answer. She told him everything. "She needed the money for music lessons, and I felt I owed something to Tommy—he's the young policeman—for not mentioning me to the police."

"I have no problem with your generosity. After all, someone had to win. But did you let the family know the money came from you?"

"I couldn't. My uncle, Sergeant Falcone, is a very hard man and does not approve of me. He would not have let her keep it."

"Well, generosity has its place, but you should not give without the receiver knowing the gift was from you. Someday you may need a favor and it is good to have others indebted. Wait too long and no one will believe it was your gift. Always regard a gift as an investment in the future."

Nilo's brow wrinkled. "But how do I do that without involving Tina Falcone's father?"

Maranzano smiled. "First, wait until she spends the money. She is a pretty girl?"

"Most beautiful, Don Salvatore."

"Fine. Beautiful girls spend money as if it came out

of a faucet; she will spend it soon enough. As soon as she does, then let word trickle out that it was a gift from you. Do not say it directly to her; that would be crude and impolite. Instead, have someone you know tell someone close to her. The story will get back. By the time it does, the money will be gone and it will be too late for this policeman father to do anything about it. Then, like it or not, he will owe you. And he will respect you for not having spoken yourself about your generosity."

Nilo nodded. "As ever, you know the way."

"Enough of your flattery. You think I am my secretary and you can work your will on me?"

Nilo blushed and Maranzano smiled, then stood behind his desk.

"And so. Now, we spend this beautiful day on a drive into Long Island? Is that your plan?"

"It is, Don Salvatore."

"And will we come back richer than we left?"

"Not only richer but tanner," Nilo said confidently. Maranzano laughed heartily, clapped an arm around the young man's shoulders, and led him from the office.

Three hours later, they were driving east, along the narrow main road that traversed the south shore of Long Island. They had passed through look-alike town after look-alike town, and once, when the road passed right at the ocean's edge, Nilo ordered the driver to pull over and he took Maranzano out onto a high sand dune that looked over the narrow beach.

Nilo pointed toward the east, where far out, almost at the end of eyesight, a long string of boats of all sizes bobbed up and down in the water. "Have you seen this before?" he asked Maranzano.

"This is what they call 'Rum Row'?" Maranzano said. He had never been out here before to see it in person.

"Yes," Nilo said. "Hundreds and hundreds of boats, all out there at the three-mile mark, all of them carrying European liquor that is legal in Canada to be smuggled into America."

"Some of that liquor is ours," Maranzano said.

"Yes. And small boats will pick it all up, and some will get past the Coast Guard and deliver it to shore. But half of it will be seized and dumped in the ocean. And our costs go up and our profit goes down."

"You're managing to ruin a beautiful day," Maranzano said. As they walked back to the car, parked at the roadside, Nilo thought Maranzano did indeed look relaxed.

Maranzano's new driver was leaning on the front fender, watching them. He was a coarse, thick-looking thug who insisted on wearing black leather gloves, even on the hottest days. Nilo thought there was something familiar about his face, but when he could not place it he decided it was his imagination.

Riding again with Nilo in the backseat of the car, Maranzano grew expansive.

"You are still too busy with our activities," he said.

"I'm sorry. I don't understand."

"I've told you that I want you to be a businessman for our organization. Instead, they tell me that there is not a liquor shipment that comes in or out, not an interception of Masseria's shipments, that you are not personally involved in."

"I blame myself if things go wrong. I want to be there to make sure they don't."

Maranzano continued as if he had not heard Nilo. "People who are too visible get too well known. And then they are in danger. Think of that poor hijacker that was called Kid Trouble. Killed in a garage with a bullet in the head."

Nilo looked sharply at Maranzano and knew immediately that the don knew that he had been running the Kid Trouble operation.

"A person first winds up in the newspapers and then winds up in jail or dead," Maranzano said.

"I see," Nilo answered. *Don Salvatore may talk too much, but often there is wisdom. There are angles and angles and he seems to see them all. It must be in his blood.* "I will have no nicknames," he said. "I will be Nilo Sesta."

Maranzano held up a hand. "In years to come, you will be one of those who deals for us with the outside world. An American name will be a good thing to have. With us Italians, Sicilians, there is already so much prejudice. Everybody with an Italian name is thought to be part of a gang. You can escape that. I have given this a lot of thought and I think a good name for you would be Danny Neill."

"Danny Neill," Nilo repeated. He grinned. "I am truly an American now."

"When we get back, go to our bank and start a small account in the name of Danny Neill. Use that name when you rent your apartment, when you pay your bills, when you have your clothes cleaned. On the street, with our people, you can remain Nilo. But for the Americans, you will become Danny Neill."

"Yes, sir." *And someday Danny Neill will run everything.*

Less than twenty minutes later, the big car rolled into the small town of Amagansett and Nilo gave the driver instructions on getting down to the waterfront.

Maranzano was looking about through the car windows. "Are all these towns so ugly?" he asked.

"Every one of them," Nilo said.

"Who would ever want to live here?"

"Well, fortunately for your real estate business, many people do," Nilo said. "That is how I came onto this place. And we are here."

The car parked on the dirt road in front of a large frame house whose back opened onto the beach. While the driver waited again at the car, Nilo took Maranzano behind the house. There, a man-made jetty reached far out into the water. At its end, facing out toward the sea, was a large boathouse. The beach, on both sides of the house, was deserted for half a mile in each direction.

Nilo led Maranzano up onto the stone and concrete jetty.

"Far out there," Nilo said, pointing, "are all those boats waiting to unload. And between them and the shore are the Coast Guard and the federal alcohol agents."

"You showed me that before."

Nilo opened the wide wooden doors of the boathouse. Inside was as big as a three-car garage.

"Your idea, Nilo," Maranzano said impatiently.

"We no longer send boats out to unload bottles from boats. Instead, inside this garage, we install a giant reel. We load it with three miles of hose. We bring in our liquor ships at night, without lights. They stay outside the three-mile limit. We run the hose out to the boat and we pump the liquor back into a truck that parks in this garage. Then drive it back into the city and bottle it ourselves. The whole unloading thing can be done at dark, without lights. There are no rumrunner boats for the Coast Guard to intercept, and by daylight, our hose is rolled up, back into the boathouse, and we are long gone."

"This will work?"

"Yes, Don Salvatore. I've thought about it for a long time. It worked when I was a child when we brought water onto the *tonnara* boats. All we need out there is a boat with a pump and a hose connection. We bring the liquor in in bulk, so we have the added expense of bottling it ourselves. But we more than make up for that by not losing any to the Prohibition cops."

"It's an interesting idea," Maranzano said.

"Right now, Don Salvatore, the big difference between your business and Masseria's is that he has better sources of supply. He gets more liquor into the city, so he has more speakeasies under his control. But his liquor is sewer water. With this, you would overtake his business in six months."

Maranzano rubbed his clean-shaven face. "Who owns this house?" he asked.

Nilo grinned. "You do. Or, at least, your secretary does. Betty's name is on the purchase papers."

"Betty? Is that wise?"

"Her name is on the papers, but I signed it," Nilo said. "She knows nothing."

"It seems you think of everything," Maranzano said.

"Somebody taught me to be a real estate man."

They walked back to the car, and Maranzano said, "Not a word of this to anyone. Not even my driver. His face is still too new and I do not trust him yet. And the fewer who know, the safer we are."

"Yes, Don Salvatore."

As they got back into the car, Don Salvatore said loudly, "Nilo, it's too far out for a house for me. And it's just not big enough." He winked at Nilo, who responded, "I'm sorry. I thought you might like it. But at least the day was sunny and the drive pleasant."

"A very pleasant day," Maranzano agreed.

When the driver left the car to get cigarettes, Maranzano told Nilo, "Yesterday, one of our collectors in

Midtown was set upon and beaten by one of Masseria's thugs and our money was stolen. This *gavone* was . . . let me think . . . a Joseph Doto. I think Mr. Doto needs a lesson in manners."

"How big a lesson?" Nilo asked.

"A medium lesson with a promise of more lessons to come if he is a slow learner." He looked over to Nilo. "Get people to do it. Do you have a problem with this? Should I give this assignment to someone else?"

"No, sir. It's just that I know this Doto. They call him Joe Adonis. He is one of Luciano's men, and I see him often at Mangini's Restaurant."

"Somehow I don't believe that Luciano gave permission for such renegade outlaw activities," Maranzano said.

Nilo just nodded.

"If Mr. Doto is rolling around on his own, without direction, I think Luciano would not complain if somebody were to muzzle him. But don't make it more complicated than it is. And I don't want you personally involved. You're done with that. Stay out of sight. Get a couple of our men that you trust, and have them administer this lesson. Kid Trouble is no more, and you are finished with this kind of work."

"It is as good as done," Nilo said.

When the car parked in front of Maranzano's office, the old don and Nilo got out and walked off to the side of the entrance to talk undisturbed. Maranzano's bodyguards had come out of the office and were standing nearby, out of earshot but still watching the passersby.

"Go ahead with your plans for the house at Amagansett," Maranzano said. "But report only to me. You did good work on that."

"I want only to justify your faith in me," Nilo said.

"You thought well to use Betty's name for the property. But don't tell her anything. She is a woman and women are not to be trusted."

Nilo nodded.

"And remember to open those accounts as Danny Neill. That will be your new working name."

"Yes, sir."

"You're American as apple pie."

"Yes, sir."

"But I still want you to give a good wop beating to this thickheaded Joe Doto."

WHEN SHE WAS TEN YEARS OLD, Sofia Mangini had once gone to Coney Island with the family of an aunt and had seen a white rat in a cage, running endlessly around an exercise wheel, while people stood there gawking. Every once in a while, the wheel would stop and the rat would be given a kernel of corn. And then it would run some more, until it was time for the next corn kernel.

The crowd around the cage had seemed to think this was high, good fun, but Sofia wondered if any creature, even one as useless as a rat, should lead such a life. Wasn't it cruel, she wondered, to always run and to get nowhere? What kind of life was it that could be measured in one kernel of corn after another kernel of corn, never any more, never a dream—if rats dreamed—of any more?

And because her aunt was a generous, warm-bosomed woman who was always Sofia's favorite, she had asked her, "Isn't that cruel?"

"Cruel? What is this cruel?"

"To the rat."

"Fia, you can't be cruel to a rat. Rats don't have any feelings to be cruel about. They're just rats. You put this one in a cage and you feed him corn, and at least he's not hiding in your walls, eating holes under your sink. Corn's gotta taste better than your walls. Rats got no complaint."

Rats got no complaint. Rats got no complaint. No complaint.

Sofia cleaned the dirty dishes off one of the tables and looked up at the clock over the front door of Mangini's Restaurant. Not yet nine o'clock. The night had hours to go. *She* had hours to go, nights to go, years to go, a lifetime to go, running around her exercise wheel in this restaurant, receiving an occasional kernel of corn, but never being free to leave. Of everyone she knew, she was the only one totally trapped.

Nilo had spoken once of inviting her out for dinner, and she thought of that often. Nilo, she knew, was not as smart as he thought he was. If she let him have his way and then got pregnant, she might be able to marry her way out of this trap. It might not be love, but it was better than she had now, and she had no other options. Tommy was shacked up with a waitress, and soon he would be in law school. And Tina someday would be on stage, singing in opera houses all over the world, and Sofia would not be with her but would still be wiping off tables after sloppy diners.

Rats got no complaint.

She carried the dishes into the kitchen, stacked them on the new stainless-steel sink, and then winced with pain. She leaned against the kitchen wall to catch her breath. She was nauseated and tired and wanted to cry. It was like this always, every month, when her time was coming.

She tried to will the pain out of her mind but could not. The summertime heat, the humidity of the kitchen, the pungent smells made everything worse. She felt herself sweating and shivering at the same time. All she wanted to do was go someplace dark and lie down. Sofia closed her eyes and let out a little gasp. When she opened them again, her mother stood there.

"Is it the curse?" she asked her daughter.

"Yes, Mama. It's coming on."

"Ah. This is no place for you tonight. You'll scare away the customers with your sour, pained face. Go, go upstairs and lie down. Sleep. We can do without you here tonight."

Sofia managed a smile. "Thank you, Mama."

She took off her apron and hung it up. In a corner there, her father was seated at a desk, looking over the books. Sofia did not know why he bothered; he didn't understand them anyway. It had always been Mrs. Mangini who had taken care of the bookkeeping, and now the job was slowly being passed to Sofia.

For which, she thought, she would get kernels of corn, handed out grudgingly, one a day for the million years remaining in her life.

She walked past her father to the stairs that led up to the apartment hallway, and as she did, Matteo grumbled, "What's the matter with you?"

"I don't feel good. Mama told me to rest."

Matteo grunted something and went back to his records.

In her room, Sofia lay on the bed fully clothed but began to twist and turn. It was just too hot. The clothing bound too much. She slipped off her dress and her slip, then lay back down.

On a small table in the corner, she could see the half-dozen books of poetry she had bought when Tina insisted that she take some of the prize money from the carnival raffle. Sofia had protested but finally gave in and accepted one hundred dollars. She spent almost twenty dollars on books and hid the rest under her mattress.

She had not opened one of the books since buying them. Once she had lived for such books, lived for the chance to read of the freedom of the young poets who were making lives for themselves in Greenwich Village, just a few blocks away. Now it could just as well have been happening on the moon. Rats got no complaint and rats don't read poetry.

She fell asleep.

It seemed like only a few minutes later when she woke up. Somebody was opening the door. For an instant Sofia was afraid; then she realized her mother was probably worried and just looking in on her.

"Papa," she said, startled.

He closed the bedroom door softly behind him. "I have missed you."

"No, Papa. No more. I don't want to. You said you never would again."

"To who I say this? To that snotty little policeman friend of yours who comes here to threaten me? Or his rat friend?"

She did not know what he was talking about. She said, "To cousin Charlie. You told him."

Her father smiled. "But he will never know."

She tried to get up, but he pushed her back on the bed. She fought him as hard as she could, but he was on top of her. She fought harder and he kept ramming himself at her. She cried out.

And then she stopped fighting.

Is there any other love I will ever know?

She heard singing far away and she thought of Tina Falcone. She would not scream.

Rats got no complaint, she thought.

———

IN THEIR APARTMENT across the street, the Falcones were holding a meeting around the kitchen table. It had started as a family dinner, brought about by the fact that both Falcone policemen were off duty that night and Father Mario also had the night off.

After dinner, everyone had gathered in the parlor and Tina sat at the piano, singing Sicilian folk songs, in which everyone joined loudly and often off-key. But during one difficult aria, while the rest were just listening to her silently, Tina had suddenly stopped singing, and then, with a sob, dropped her face down, slumped, her chin resting on her chest.

"What's the matter, Tina?" Mario asked, and Tina looked at him with the sad, scared eyes of a lost child, and suddenly the whole story of Frau Schatte's impossible teaching fees gushed out.

When she was done, Tina was in tears, and the tears of an Italian woman under the age of thirty were a fact that had to be discussed. As Mrs. Falcone rushed to bring in a fresh pot of espresso, Mario and Tommy tried to sort out Tina's problem. Tony listened and sipped from a water tumbler of red wine that was made legally by one of their downstairs neighbors.

"How much money do you have?" Mario asked.

"I have four hundred and sixty-three dollars," Tina said. "I've been saving."

"And you need how much more?"

"Probably another eight hundred dollars. That will train me for a year. After that, I should be able to start getting singing work."

"Your little job at the button factory? Can you save anything from there?"

"Of course she can't," Tommy told his brother. "She barely makes enough to keep herself in clothes."

"Silence, soldier boy. I was asking Tina."

Tina shrugged. "Eight hundred dollars. Maybe in three or four years I could save that much."

"Well, you would still be young," Mario said.

"But my voice would be old. Without good training now, I will start to lose what I have. In a year or two, it will be lost forever."

"But—"

"Oh, I'll be able to sing. I'll be the best soprano in your congregation, Mario. But opera?" She shook her head. "It will be too late."

"And this German woman? She can teach you?" Tommy asked.

"Tommy, she sang at Covent Garden. That's one of the great opera houses of the world. She says I can get there, too."

"Well, then we need eight hundred dollars," Tommy said.

Mario looked sheepish. "I've got forty," he said. "Maybe forty-five."

"Ohhh," Tommy groaned in mock sorrow. "Stealing from the poor box again. You should be ashamed."

"What about you?" Mario asked.

"I don't have any savings. I use it all for schoolbooks and trolley fare. But I can get it."

Tina looked at him, her face brightened. "The whole eight hundred? How?"

"I can get it," Tommy said lightly. "When you're working, you can pay it back."

"Who'd lend you eight hundred dollars?" Mario scoffed.

"I don't spend all my time hiding in a church basement,

teaching delinquents to beat each other up," Tommy told the priest. "I've got friends."

"All your friends rolled up together wouldn't be worth eight hundred cents," Mario said.

"You laugh all you want. But I have friends and they are not all poor church mice like you, Mario. Tina, you go tell this Frau Schatte that you'll have the money. But be shrewd. Maybe you can negotiate her price down. Never pay the first price they ask," Tommy said. He nodded to his sister. "Okay? Settled?"

Tina looked at him and Mario in bewilderment, then turned toward her father, who was still quietly sipping his wine.

"Papa?" she said.

"I'm glad somebody finally thought of me," Tony said. "I was beginning to feel neglected."

"What do you think, Papa?"

"I think, Justina, that we have wasted all the time we should on this petty problem of yours. I think we should talk about me. I think we should all raise a glass of wine to congratulate me, because I am being promoted to lieutenant."

He looked around the room at his wife and children. Tina seemed bewildered at her father's response.

"And," Tony went on, "it just so happens that my promotion carries with it a large pay increase . . . say, in the neighborhood of eight hundred dollars. So while I think it's very nice that your brother wants to imitate J. P. Morgan, I will provide the missing eight hundred dollars for this German yodeler of yours. And, by God, she'd better be a good teacher."

"Papa . . ." Tommy started, but Tony silenced him by raising his open hand before his face.

"I am the father and it is my decision. And *now* it is

settled. So? Will you please resume singing, Tina? And Mama, get out the rest of the wineglasses. We are celebrating my promotion."

All three of his children came over and hugged Tony. Then Tina returned to the piano, and the apartment rang with the sound of happy music, sung by happy voices, punctuated by the clink of wineglasses.

Later, after Mario had returned to his parish and the two women had gone to bed, Tommy and his father sat alone in the kitchen.

"You're going to lecture me, Tommy, but don't do it," his father said.

"I really could have borrowed the money."

"You know and I know there's only one person you could borrow that kind of money from." Tommy looked down at his hands on the table, holding the wineglass between them.

"You borrow from Nilo, Tommy, and while it is a loan, they own you. Never again are you a free man."

"It's only Nilo," Tommy said defensively. "He's family, for heaven's sake."

Tony shook his head. "Not anymore. He's gone their way, not ours, and he's walked away from this family. Borrowing from Kid Trouble would bring you more trouble than you could imagine. I know these people, Tommy. It's in their blood."

" 'Kid Trouble'?"

"That was Nilo's name. The stories that said Kid Trouble was dead, they all got the wrong guy. And if you borrowed from him, it would be a payoff to you for not saying he was in that alley the night of the hijacking."

"You're sure he was there?" Tommy asked.

"As sure as I can be. Nothing happens without somebody knowing about it and somebody talking about it."

"I never really saw him," Tommy said defensively. "I heard somebody call somebody else 'Kid' and then I thought I heard his voice. But I never saw him."

"You don't have to explain," his father said.

"I asked Nilo about it at the hospital. He wouldn't admit anything."

His father shrugged. "Switch places with him. What would you have done?"

Tommy thought for a long moment. "I should have told you, though."

"You conducted your own investigation," Tony said gently. "It didn't pan out, so you didn't spread any rumors about who was or wasn't in that alley."

Tommy looked down at his cup of espresso coffee, now cool. "It was Nilo," he said dully, "and he saved my life."

"Stop worrying. He's not in jail, even if he does belong there."

"You let him go? Because he saved me?"

"No," Tony said, "because if I did that, I'd be no better than the rest of them. I asked him where he was that night, and he said he spent the night with some floozy secretary and she'd swear to it. So that was that. It didn't check out."

It didn't check out, Tommy thought, because his father had let up on the case. Because Nilo had saved Tommy's life, Tony had let him go. Tommy was stunned by the realization. The first time his father had ever played outside the rules, and it was Tommy's fault.

"Never again, Papa," he mumbled.

His father put his big hand over Tommy's on the table. "You've got a long life ahead of you, Tommy. And you're the only one who gets to decide what that life will be like. You can do it your own way, be your own man.

Or you can sell off little pieces of yourself to the highest bidder. A lot of cops do. A lot more lawyers do. But once you start that, you're bought and paid for. Someday, when you least expect it, someone will walk up to you and say, 'I own you,' and he'll be right. I don't want that to happen."

"It won't," Tommy said. "I may be slow, but I do learn."

"Good enough. Now I'm going to bed."

As the senior Falcone rose from the table, Tommy said, "This promotion."

"Yeah?"

"It's the Italian Squad, isn't it?"

"It doesn't have to be so bad. Hell, maybe I can even educate some of those Irishers," Tony said, and walked toward his bedroom in the back of the apartment.

AS TONY WAS RETIRING, Nilo arrived at Mangini's Restaurant across the street. He had already eaten dinner, so he ordered just a cup of cappuccino from Mrs. Mangini, who seemed to be the only person working in the place. Nilo was glad he did not have to see old man Mangini. Since Nilo had put a knife to his face, there had not been even a pretense of friendship between them.

He sipped at his coffee, as a burly man with a thick swatch of jet-black hair and sharp features came from the back room, carrying a snap-brimmed fedora. He paused in the doorway, saw Nilo and nodded casually to him, then tossed his hat onto an empty table and went to the men's room in the far corner.

Joe Doto, better known as "Joe Adonis," was one of Luciano's most-feared men. Whenever Joe the Boss Masseria came into the neighborhood, it was to Doto that Luciano assigned the protection of the Mafia boss. Doto was known to be a man who would kill first and ask questions later.

And someday I will surround myself with men just like that. Only crazy men are good bodyguards, because only crazy men will give up their own lives for someone else's.

Doto came out of the men's room and started for the front door.

"Joe," Nilo called.

The bigger man turned. The expression on his face was always one of surly suspicion. Nilo knew that Doto was now staking out much of Midtown for himself, supplying speakeasies with Masseria's liquor, and cutting himself in as part owner of many of the illegal nightspots.

America is wonderful, Nilo thought. *Even a dumb thug like this one can climb high. There is no limit to how high I can reach.*

"You forgot your hat," Nilo said, pointing.

Doto nodded, grabbed the hat, and left the restaurant, without even a word to Mrs. Mangini, who was at the front desk, separating the night's receipts into neat little piles.

Nilo walked up to her and said, "Mrs. Mangini, I need to use your telephone. I'll pay for the call."

She nodded and pointed to the instrument at the end of the desk.

Nilo picked it up. This was one of the new telephones that had its own dial and that you no longer needed to talk to an operator on. He carefully dialed a number. He let the phone ring precisely three times before he hung up.

"Nobody answered," he told Mrs. Mangini. He smiled.

"No charge," she said dourly, without looking up.

When he turned, Luciano was walking toward his table and sat down as Nilo came back.

"Nilo," Luciano said with a nod. "Late to be making telephone calls." He spoke in Sicilian dialect.

"Damned *puta* of a girlfriend," Nilo answered in the same tongue, his face twisting into a scowl. "She likes to go out when I'm not around." He sat and grinned at Luciano. "I think I might have to explain some things to her."

"Women, like dogs, need training or they will crap all over you," Luciano said, his dark hooded eyes impassive. "I saw you at Mount Carmel," he said.

"And I you," Nilo answered. "I was just watching our raffle stand," Nilo said. "Did you buy any tickets?"

"For a fixed game?" Luciano smiled; it was not a pleasant smile. "I leave that foolishness to those rich enough to throw away money."

"Just as well," Nilo said. "I thought it would be a nice gift for Sofia and the Falcone girl to win some money."

"It was well done," Luciano said. "And of course it is a good thing to do favors for policemen's families. You never know when a policeman might do you a favor."

"The Falcones are family to me and have done me many favors. So a little favor to them now and then. But of course I can tell no one. The Falcones are proud; they would not accept such a gift."

"Especially not the sergeant," said Luciano.

"Especially not Uncle Tony," Nilo agreed.

It is done, he thought. *He will pass this story around and it will get to the Falcones. But by the time it does, Tina will already have spent the money and they will have no way to pay it back. The Falcones will owe me a large debt. Maranzano was correct.*

"Perhaps someday Tina will repay your kindness," Luciano said, with just the trace of a leer washing across his face.

Nilo grinned. "I never turn down a repayment," he said. "I—"

He stopped as the front door of the restaurant flew open. Joe Doto stood in the doorway, his clothing ripped, blood streaming down his face.

Seeing Luciano, he called out, "Charlie. They . . ."

And then he stumbled forward onto his knees. Luciano and Nilo ran to his side. Luciano shouted and other men poured out of the back room to help. Nilo noticed that the young one, the one some called "Bugsy," held a gun in his hand and was looking wildly about the room for someone to shoot.

Nilo grabbed a napkin from a table and squatted on the floor next to Doto. He blotted the blood from his head, then looked up and said, "I think somebody should take him to a doctor." He kept wiping Doto's face. The man's blood spilled onto Nilo's suit, but he pretended not to mind.

Is anything better than this? Nilo wondered. *To set the trap, to snare the victim, and then to pretend to know nothing about it? Joe Adonis will think twice before robbing one of our men again. Life is sweet indeed.*

And then he noticed that Luciano was staring at him.

SOFIA LEFT HER FATHER sleeping naked in her bed. She washed and dressed and went down to the street with no idea of where she planned to go, and bumped into Nilo as he was leaving the restaurant.

"Hello, Nilo," she said. Then: "Are you all right? Is that blood on your suit?"

"Yes. But not mine. Joe Adonis got his ass kicked and bled all over me."

"If you don't get that blood out right away, that suit will be ruined."

Nilo shrugged. "It's just a suit. I've got a lot of suits."

"But this is my favorite. I always like you in this suit."

"Well, then, I guess I ought to get home and wash it out."

"I'll do it for you," Sofia said. "There's a way to do it."

Nilo looked at her sharply. "Come on," he said, and led her to a car parked on the corner.

"I didn't know you had a car," she said.

"It belongs to my boss. He's got a lot of cars."

She tried clumsily to make small talk as they drove uptown to Nilo's apartment in the West Sixties.

"You said once you would take me to dinner. I kept waiting," she said.

"I got busy. At my place, I'll make you a sandwich. Will that count?"

"Why not?" she said.

"Yeah. Why not?" he answered.

His apartment was up five flights in a brownstone building whose street-level door was kept locked. The apartment was big but sparsely furnished, and clothes were strewn everywhere.

"You need a wife," she said, looking around.

"Or a maid."

"Now get out of those clothes."

"Usually I'm the one that says that," Nilo answered. As Sofia blushed, Nilo smiled and took off his jacket and trousers, standing in the middle of the room in his white dress shirt and underwear. In the bathroom, Sofia scrubbed the bloodstains from his suit, then hung it up on a hook behind the door.

Outside, Nilo was still in his shirt and underwear, sitting on the sofa, drinking a glass of wine.

"Won't your folks worry about you?" he asked.

"No one cares about me," she said. "What about that sandwich you promised me?"

He pointed toward the kitchen. "Help yourself. Everything's in the icebox."

"Maybe I'll just have a glass of wine instead."

"Sure. It's over there."

She poured herself a glass from a large jug and sat next to him on the couch. After an awkward silence, she said, "So, how do you like your job?"

"What do you know about my job?"

"Nothing, just talk."

"What kind of talk?"

"That you're Maranzano's favorite gangster," she answered.

Nilo laughed. "It's true. I came to this country to be a good American. And all America had for me was ditchdigging and being called a dumb wop. The only one who cared for me was Don Salvatore. I was a boy and he made me a man. So, okay, now I'm a gangster. I kill people. I steal things. Every day I try to figure out new ways to break the law." She looked over, but his face was stolid, humorless. "And someday I will run everything."

"If they don't shoot you first."

"Everything has risks. You took a risk in coming here tonight," Nilo said.

"I'm not afraid of you."

He put down his wineglass. "You ought to be." He leaned forward and kissed her, then slipped his hand under her blouse and cupped her breast. His fingers were soft, his skin smooth, unlike her father's hands, which were coarse and rough. He breathed in her ear, "I want to make love to you. I always wanted to make love to you." He guided her hands to touch his body, then pulled her to her feet and led her into the barely lit bedroom.

Sofia was afraid but told herself there was no turning back. Nilo would not let her undress herself but insisted on taking her clothing off. When she was naked and embarrassed by her nudity, he looked at her for a long time. "You're very beautiful," he said, then took off his own clothing.

"You are, too," she said.

His lovemaking was as brief, coarse, and brutish as her father's. Despite that, when he rolled off her, she put her head on his shoulder and said, "That was wonderful."

"I never get any complaints," he said.

"I love you, Nilo."

"I've got no time for love."

"Do you think . . . maybe . . . you and me . . ."

"What do you mean?" he asked.

"Maybe we could be . . . together?" she said haltingly.

"You weren't a virgin," he said. "When I get serious, it's going to be with a virgin."

"Why?"

"Because she's going to be just mine and nobody else's. Who was it? Tommy? No. Tommy's too dopey. I bet it was Charlie Luciano. He's a pimp and he's always trying out new women. Charlie, right?"

She put a hand over her face as if to shut out his voice.

"Was he as good as me?" Nilo asked. When she did not answer, he said, "What about Tina? Is she getting it, too? I bet you two are always talking about getting it, aren't you? Who gets it the most? Why don't you bring her up sometime and I'll give it to both of you."

"Oh, Nilo. It's not like that," she said softly.

"It's always like that," he said. "Except, maybe, I guess

when you want to get married or something. But my wife's got to be a virgin. Nobody else's leftovers is gonna get knocked up and trick me into a wedding."

Sofia rose from the bed and began slowly to put on her clothes.

Tina had been living and studying in Uta Schatte's house for two months. With no other students in residence, the blond German woman was able to give her undivided attention to Tina, and she managed to fill Tina's days with music and work.

From wake-up time until bedtime, Tina sang scales, endless scales in every key. She practiced her piano-playing. When her voice was tired and her fingers were sore, she listened to recordings of great opera singers. And then she sang and played some more.

Hour after hour, day after day. And it was working. Tina knew it was working. Her voice felt more powerful and she knew she had better control of it. She had still sung nothing but scales and exercises, but she understood that when it was time for the arias her voice would be ready.

Frau Schatte would see to that. Frau Schatte saw to everything.

Despite the intensity of the work, the two months flew by at whirlwind speed, and then it was a special Sunday, and for the first time in sixty days, Tina had gone home to visit her family for dinner.

Her parents and Mario and Tommy had greeted her as if she had just returned from a lifetime spent in another land, and for a little while, it was warm and loving, the way it had always been when she was around her family.

But after just a little while, it began to pall on her. She seemed to feel that she should be back at Frau Schatte's, practicing her scales, practicing her piano.

The conversation was of the neighborhood, of old friends, of aunts and cousins and nieces, and Tina began to realize that she was not of this neighborhood anymore. She lived elsewhere, not just in body, but in spirit too. Nevertheless, she had tried to smile and joke and take part in the conversation, but as soon as it was seemly, she took her leave, explaining that she had to get back, since her lessons continued, even on Sundays.

Frau Schatte had been in the parlor; she might even have been waiting for Tina, and when Tina came in, the older woman asked how her visit had gone, and Tina had slipped to her knees next to Frau Schatte's chair and began to cry.

The blond woman patted her gently on the head. Tina had offered no explanation and the woman had not asked for one. But, knowingly, she said, "I've seen it before. You are becoming a woman, Tina, and you are making your way in your own world. Not a world that your family created for you, but one you are creating for yourself. And when you go into that world, you will go alone."

Tina had lifted her tear-streaked face.

"You will go with me, won't you?" she sobbed.

"For a while. For as long as I can."

Tina had gone to her room to wash up, and later, Frau Schatte had knocked on the door and announced, "You have worked hard enough. Tonight we will go out together and we will experience life."

She laid out Tina's clothes, her finest dressiest dress, and then the three women—Flora, the maid, had come as well—got into a carriage and rode in style to Delahanty's, down on MacDougal Street.

Tina was nervous. Delahanty's was a speakeasy, and even though it was against the law, it seemed to be operating wide open, in full view of the street, and she wondered how it would look if she, the daughter of a policeman, was arrested and wound up in jail. But her nervousness passed as they walked inside. Tina knew they had made a great entrance. From the moment they walked in, all conversation had stopped, until the waiter had seated them at a table. Only then did people resume talking.

On a small stage at one end of the room, someone was reciting poetry that he had written. Then somebody else began reading from an original story. They were fine, sensitive-looking American boys. And all the time that they read, a bunch of loudmouths standing at the bar and looking like dockworkers had catcalled and hectored them.

After a while, a couple of the rowdies came over to their table and talked and laughed with Frau Schatte, and she explained to Tina that they were painters and expected to be boors.

"It is a part of their artistry," she said.

The men objected strenuously, drunkenly, and invited themselves to stay to plead their case, and after a while Frau Schatte went away with one of them, asking beforehand if Tina thought that she could find her way home alone.

A little later, Flora got up onto the little stage and began to half-speak, half-chant something that could have been a hymn or a pagan prayer or a poem. After each stanza, she sipped from a glassful of whiskey and opened another button on the bodice of her high-necked dress.

When she reached the end of her performance, her dress was opened almost to the waist and Tina could see the swelling sides of her large chocolate bosom.

Flora came back and sat down, smiling at Tina.

"Don't be embarrassed," she said in her delicate accent. "This is Greenwich Village. It is expected." Only minutes later, she got up to dance with one of the painters, and then, when Tina went to the ladies' room, Flora disappeared. Tina was all alone and a little bit scared, but that soon passed. The last painter continued to fill her glass with cheap gin, and people were singing and laughing and dancing, and she had given up worrying about where she was.

During the middle of the night, she was surprised to wake up in a dirty bed with a stranger next to her, horrified to realize that she was no longer a virgin. She hurriedly dressed and sneaked out before he could awaken and say anything. She ran all the way home to Frau Schatte's. Neither of the other women had returned, and she went to bed, crying for the passing of her innocence.

- *As Joe the Boss Masseria continued to squeeze the small gangs for a bigger and bigger cut of their take, rumblings began to be heard and Luciano warned the old man to be careful. Masseria chuckled and told Luciano he was losing his nerve. Until . . .*

- *On the morning of August 9, 1922, Masseria left his fortified and guarded apartment at 65 Second Avenue. Out on the street, two men opened fire on him. Masseria dodged into a man's hat shop. The gunners followed, blasting away. They hit mirrors, windows, and even put two bullets through Masseria's straw hat. Masseria cowered on the floor as another half-dozen shots were fired at him. They all missed and he walked away. Two hours*

*later, Luciano told him the assassination had been
ordered by Umberto Valenti, head of a small rival
gang.*

- *A young whore named Polly Adler, using money
  advanced to her by Luciano, opened a brothel at
  Fifty-fifth Street and Madison Avenue. Luciano
  told her to use only the prettiest showgirls as
  prostitutes. His own personal stable of whores
  would soon number five thousand women, hustling
  every night for prices that ranged from one
  hundred dollars a night to two dollars for a half
  hour. He took 50 percent of their gross.*

- *Ford's Model T sold more than every other car
  combined. It cost $319.*

- *On a cold winter night in 1922, Luciano arranged
  a conference between Masseria and Umberto
  Valenti. They ate spaghetti in a restaurant on East
  Twelfth Street and shook hands in a peace pact,
  which Valenti said wasn't really necessary since
  he had nothing to do with the earlier attempt on
  Masseria's life. Outside, the three men walked
  down the street to hail a cab for Valenti. When
  Masseria stopped to light a cigar, Vito Genovese
  and Joe Adonis stepped from an alley and began
  pumping bullets into Valenti. As he fell, Luciano put
  a final bullet into his head. By the end of the next
  week, Luciano had taken over Valenti's operations,
  including a small but growing narcotics business.*

- *Between Christmas and New Year's, 1922, waitress
  Mabel Fay left New York to find fame and fortune
  in Hollywood. Tommy Falcone never heard from
  her again.*

- *Construction began on the Holland Tunnel,
  linking Manhattan and New Jersey. One of the*

    first vehicles to drive through was a truck carrying
    bootleg beer.

- *The hot new slang phrase was "You slaughter me."*
- *On June 5, 1923, Luciano was arrested for selling two ounces of morphine to a federal informer. Frank Costello, the mob's bribe-master, went immediately to work. Soon after, Luciano told the feds where they could find a large stash of illegal narcotics, and all charges were dropped.*
- *The best-selling nonfiction book of 1923 was* Emily Post's Etiquette: The Blue Book of Social Usage.
- *In Washington, a young Justice Department lawyer named John Hoover was named to head the scandal-ridden Bureau of Investigation. One of his first major decisions was to begin calling himself J. Edgar Hoover.*

CHAPTER 5

Summer 1924

Although, as deputy commander of the police department's Italian Squad, Tony Falcone was entitled to wear civilian clothes, once a month he wore his lieutenant's dress uniform to work, making it a point to walk the streets of the city's Italian neighborhoods. The idea was to let himself be seen.

When Tony first broached the idea, his boss, Captain Milo Cochran, loudly labeled Tony's pedestrian jaunts as just the waste of a working day.

"So? So these guineas are going to see an Italian cop. That's gonna make them stop shooting each other over a stolen tomato?"

"No, Captain," Tony explained patiently. "I don't expect it'll have much effect on the stolen-tomato murder rate. But what it will do is show these people that we're *their* police department, too. That it's not all—pardon the expression—thickheaded Irish cops who wouldn't recognize an idea if it sneaked into their whiskey glass."

"We're the police department of the city of New York. We represent everyone," Cochran said with mock unction.

Tony said, "Humor me on this one, Captain. It's good for the people to see a ranking Italian officer around. The kids like the uniform, and maybe someday we'll start to see a lot of them thinking about going into law enforcement."

"If they're not all in jail already for stealing tomatoes from each other."

"And the old Italians, they don't speak English and they're confused and scared in this city, but they hear things, and it's good for them to know, too, that there's somebody out there who can talk to them in their own language."

"Like you?"

Tony shrugged. "Someday when I uncover a big plot to assassinate all the Irishmen in the department, you'll thank your lucky stars."

"You'll be leading the pack of brigands pounding on the doors of the precinct," Cochran said. "Get out of here. Be gone with you and your whole nefarious tribe."

After almost two years, the Italian Squad had turned out to be not so bad as Tony had feared it would be. Credit for most of that rested with Cochran, a small, compulsively tidy man who affected the attitude of an Irish racist know-nothing, but who was, in truth, a dedicated cop who wanted, like Tony, to put the bad guys in jail. His anti-Italian bantering with Tony was just that— bantering—and he understood very clearly the need to get good information from the streets.

They had discussed that the day Tony got his lieutenant's bars and first reported for his new position.

"From what I hear, you're not terribly happy about being here," Cochran had told Tony.

"That's basically true, Captain," Tony had said.

"Mind telling me why?"

"Because I think this whole idea of an Italian Squad is a kind of racism that stamps my people as subhuman.

When the Plug Uglies were running around, and the Potato Peelers and all the rest of those Irish gangs, nobody ever thought of having an 'Irish Squad' to deal with them. So I think having an Italian Squad is an insult to my people."

"I agree," Cochran said.

"Excuse me?"

"I agree with you. But our problem is this: the brass has decided they're going to have an Italian Squad, so we're stuck with it. Maybe it's best that they put two smart young men like us in charge of it. That way, we can do our jobs, clean this all up, disband the Italian Squad, and I can go on to become chief of police and you can retire and go start a Mafia gang of your own."

Tony looked up sharply at the comment, but Cochran was grinning. "Hey, Tony," he had said. "Have a sense of humor. It helps when the crap gets too deep."

It had been good advice and Tony had tried to take it. He had also found Cochran honest and fair and just as frustrated as Tony was when they had made a really solid arrest of some gangster, only to see him freed because the political fix was put in with the prosecutors and judges.

So it was that Tony Falcone was walking slowly down First Avenue, through the heart of Italian Harlem, on a bright Thursday in July. The next day would start the three-day-long festival of Holy Rosary Church, the gaudiest celebration of the year in Uptown Manhattan, and it was his job to make sure nothing went wrong.

Harlem was separated from Little Italy by little more than eight miles of streets. Down there, where Tony lived and had raised his family, all the Italians and Sicilians, no matter where in the old country they came from, were pretty much mixed together with no one hometown or region predominating in any area. But at the northern tip of Manhattan, in Italian Harlem, it was different. There, each neighborhood, sometimes each street, was settled by immigrants from some individual town or village or region back in the old country.

That meant there were whole blocks peopled primarily by Sicilians from Castellammare del Golfo or Villalba or Palermo, and by Italians from Rome or Naples or Calabria. For recent arrivals in America, it provided an easy way of fitting in to the New World. But it also brought over intact many of the rivalries, feuds, and vendettas between factions.

Shakespeare got famous writing Romeo and Juliet *about Italians,* Tony thought. *But up here, that story happens every day. If you want to know about feuds, ask an Italian. We invented them.*

Cochran and he had decided that keeping a tight rein on these feuds was the second most important job of the Italian Squad, outranked in importance only by the goal of curbing the Mafia.

Usually, Tony thought, the squad did not do too good a job on either. Especially now, because of what was happening in Italy. Normally, immigration to the United States was a gradual thing, with people arriving in manageable numbers and with good, ambitious reasons for searching out America.

But now Italy had a new ruler, somebody named Mussolini, and while Tony thought he looked like a clown, all dressed up in military uniforms he had done nothing to earn, Mussolini had not been clownish in dealing with the Mafia. He had sent his troopers into Sicily, ordering them to shut down all criminal organizations, and already thousands had fled that little island, trying to get to the United States ahead of Mussolini's hangmen and firing squads.

The new arrivals, not ready for immigration, without even a clue about American life, were putting a strain on New York City and its ability to manage the newcomers. They had to learn, and quickly, that this was not a place where arguments were settled with the stiletto or the *lupara* shotgun, and that jail awaited anyone—Mafioso or not—who broke the laws.

Making sure everyone knew that was another of the reasons Tony liked to walk the streets in uniform, and today he was pretty pleased. Everybody seemed to be working smoothly on getting the festival site prepared. Tony had spent weeks in painstaking negotiations, arranging truces among the various local and regional factions. In the end, he had wound up dividing the festival sites among the groups himself. This had apparently wound up displeasing every single one of them, because Tony had received a half-dozen complaints, demanding a conference.

He had called such a meeting inside a school classroom, unused on the weekend, and the two dozen petty warlords who had attended grumbled and growled for two straight hours about the smallest of details until, finally, in frustration, Tony had silenced them by thumping on the small teacher's desk with his clenched fist.

"Shut up," he shouted, and pointed around the room. "You don't like it? And you don't like it? And you don't like it? Fine. Next year, all of you come back here without me and you work it out so that everybody's happy. But this year, you're doing it my way. It will be peaceful and it will be a time for great community pride and happiness. All over the city, people who are convinced that you, we, all of us are a pack of guineas, little better than animals, those people, even those Anglos, will look at this festival and see, not a bunch of thugs battling with each other over the right to rob honest folks, but they will see the representatives of a proud people, people who represent the glory of the Roman Empire. That is what I want. Next year, do it your way. But this year, we will do it my way and we will make every one of us proud that in our veins runs the blood of the Caesars."

It was the longest speech he had ever made in his life, and he stopped abruptly and stared around the school-room at the men sitting there. There were all kinds: old men with mustaches and beards and heavy wool suits, side by side with young, clean-shaven men with silk shirts and expensive shoes, united only by their distaste for each other. After Tony's outburst, the room was painfully silent. Then one old man in the back began to applaud, softly. He continued for two seconds, five, ten seconds, and then others joined in, until finally everyone in the room was on his feet, giving Tony a standing ovation.

Tony silenced them by raising his hands. "We will work together; we will be worthy of each other's trust," he said softly. He left unsaid the clear promise that any-one who did not cooperate would answer to him, and then he adjourned the meeting.

He knew that if he left immediately, he would hardly be out the door before the tribal chiefs in the room would start arguing about inconsequential details, and this frag-ile truce would degenerate into bloody, savage argument. He could not have that, so he hung around, making sure he was the last to leave.

He had gone from that meeting to another set of nego-tiations, which he was equally proud of, even though his superiors would prefer to pretend that it had not occurred.

There was no sense in being naive. There would be liquor and wines on sale at the festival. Some of it would be vaguely legal, brewed or distilled in private homes for personal use, and no one cared much about that. But there would be other liquor that would come from the bootlegger mobs.

At first, Captain Cochran had looked on this as an opportunity to crack down on the hordes of illegal liquor dealers, but Tony had talked him out of it.

"Captain, you'll have everybody mad as hornets up there."

"Why? Liquor's illegal, in case all you Eye-talians hadn't noticed."

"Yeah, we noticed," Tony said with a grin. "We also noticed that before Prohibition started four years ago, there were fifteen thousand saloons in the city. Now there are twenty-five thousand speakeasies, filled with Irish drunks. We can't do anything about that, but, by God, we can crack down on some religious festival honoring the Holy Mother. Shame on you, Captain. Three Hail Marys and four Our Fathers."

"Oh, do whatever you want," Cochran said. "All you peppers are just too devious for my dull Irish mind. I just don't want Harlem awash in blood because one botcha-galoop wino doesn't like some other botchagaloop wino. You take care of it."

Tony had taken that as permission to do the final thing he wanted, which was to get an agreement between Masseria and Maranzano. Doing that might be a little sticky, though, he thought. He did not want to meet either of the men face-to-face. It would be too easy later for lying witnesses to claim that he had taken bribes, and that would be the end of his career. Normally sending word through the grapevine would have been enough, but he could not count on such gossip reaching either man accurately, without sounding like an insult that might start the very battle he was trying to prevent.

In the end, Tony went to see the priests in whose parishes the two Mafia bosses attended Mass.

His official status as deputy commander of the Italian Squad and his personal credentials as the father of a priest himself got him a respectful hearing. His message, he said, was simple:

The police would not, during the Holy Rosary Festival, do anything out of the ordinary. Both priests, in separate meetings, asked the same immediate question:

"Does that mean no arrests?"

"I can't promise that," Tony had said. "But we're not going to make a big deal out of things. We want peace and we don't want armed mobsters all over the place. We don't want anybody knocking off somebody else's entertainment booth. We don't want any innocent bystanders shot. For this weekend, we want peace. After that, we go back to normal. I go back to trying to get them all arrested, put on a ship, and sent back where they came from. But peace this weekend—that is our goal. We know that your esteemed parishioner can certainly guarantee the peaceful intentions of his followers."

Both priests had listened to Tony's explanation and then agreed. One said he would get word to Joe the Boss Masseria through Charlie Luciano. The other said he would tell Nilo, who would get the message to Don Maranzano.

"Nilo?"

"Nilo Sesta," the priest had said. "He handles Mr. Maranzano's business affairs. Do you know him? A very nice young man."

"I've seen him around," Tony said.

The festival would start the next night, and already many of the people were in a holiday mood, and it showed in their greetings. He felt a curious satisfaction in knowing that he was respected by the people on the street.

It was just another of the wondrous gifts that life had given him. He had a wife who loved him. His son Mario could have ended up in one of the gangs or, worse yet, a pug-ugly brain-damaged boxer, but had instead become a priest. Tommy had defended his country, almost with his life, and had been rewarded with morphine addiction. But he had fought his way back, had now graduated from college, and this fall he would begin his law-school studies while continuing to work as a policeman. He felt secure that both his sons had their feet on the ground, aimed in the right direction for life.

He worried occasionally about Tina. She had a beautiful voice, a rare talent, but so far there had not seemed to be any payoff in it. Instead of singing at the Metropolitan Opera House—even a role in the chorus would be a start—Tina instead seemed to be earning a precarious living singing private concerts, earning her keep while living with Uta Schatte.

"The opera's just not hiring, Papa, and this is a good way to keep my voice in shape. And I'm also learning all kinds of new pieces. Listen." And she shattered the stillness of the Falcones' small apartment with a beautiful coloratura trill.

"Very nice," Tony would grumble. "When do you sing it at the Metropolitan?"

"Papa, I'm still learning. There will be operas enough for all of us one day."

"And in the meantime, you are happy?" Tony asked, because he thought that he saw just a hint of weariness on Justina's exquisite, sculptured face.

"I'm fine. Uta . . . Frau Schatte . . . and I are great friends. It's not really like she's my boss. And every note I sing is under her supervision."

It was hard for him not to be excited by her exuberance

and to be happy for her, but he sometimes wished he had money, real money. If he had, he would insist that Justina stop this no-future singing and start going to auditions at the Metropolitan until they hired her.

If it came to it, he thought, he could probably pull a string or two to get her hired somehow at the Met. Even opera houses had police problems, and someone, somewhere in the department was owed a favor that could be called in.

It did not occur to him as odd that while his sturdy rules of conduct would never allow him to ask a favor for himself, he would not give a second thought to the propriety of asking for one for his daughter.

Instead, he just reflected that Tina would be fine until she got her break. That was more than he could say for Nilo. Even though Nilo was not his child, he was the son of Tony's sister and that made him family, but somehow he had gone bad. Tony had prided himself that his children had escaped the corroding touch of the gangs, of the criminals who ran wild through Little Italy and much of the rest of New York City. But Nilo had been seduced, and now, to hear that priest tell it, Nilo handled business affairs for Maranzano, whose Castellammarese crime family had become rich and powerful.

Maybe Maranzano had more connection with him back in Sicily than I know about, Tony thought. *Or maybe Nilo just sprang from a bad, twisted seed.*

AS BETTY STOOD at the ornamental desk pouring the tea, she managed to rub her knee against Nilo's thigh, out of the line of sight of Maranzano, who sat waiting politely. With a smile at Nilo as she turned, she left the tea tray on the desk and went back outside.

"She cannot keep her hands off you, can she?" Maranzano said with a chuckle, after she had left the office.

"It must be my charm," Nilo answered lightly. So much had changed, he thought, since the first time he had been in this office, frightened and nervous, wearing a borrowed suit and expecting to be thrown out into the street. *Now I am the don's right-hand man and all know my name. God bless God who has showered me with such gifts.*

"Oh, to be young again," Maranzano said.

"You are young in heart and mind, where it counts," Nilo said, pleased with himself that he had learned the give-and-take of glib conversation. It meant nothing, but he had decided that people who succeeded in life were able to say nothing and make it sound interesting. It was one of Don Salvatore's great gifts. *Blowhards will conquer the world, and if that is what it takes, I will be the biggest blowhard of all,* he thought.

"Have you told your uncle that we will abide by his peace agreement at the Holy Rosary Festival?" Maranzano asked.

"I sent word to him through my cousin, Mario, the priest," Nilo answered. "I don't think Uncle Tony would appreciate hearing directly from me about such business."

Maranzano nodded approval.

"You told me once to always cause as little discomfort as possible when dealing with others. This way I speak for you, but if he wishes, Lieutenant Falcone can still regard me as Nilo, his nephew."

Maranzano nodded. "And all else is well?" he asked.

"Every day it gets better. Three new clubs opened last week in Midtown with our liquor. I think we have as many now as Masseria does."

"We should have. We have better merchandise. They

are selling rotgut and we sell whisky from Scotland, thanks to your wonderful idea to pipe it in from offshore."

Nilo lit a cigarette and basked in the older man's approval.

"We are ready to take a new step now," Maranzano said. "From now on, you are out of the day-to-day operations." When Nilo seemed about to protest, Maranzano held up his hand. "No. No more. We want heads busted from now on, somebody else will do it. You have disobeyed me over and over again. I have told you to stay off the streets, and yet you run with the young gunmen every chance you get."

Nilo would have protested if he had not noticed a note of pride in Maranzano's remarks. The old man said, "You are going to be the next generation of businessman for us. I want you to meet with our lawyers and form Danny Neill Enterprises. I have already given them orders."

"And what will I do with this Danny Neill Enterprises?" Nilo asked.

"The lawyers will handle it. Danny Neill Enterprises will start buying legal businesses. It is not enough to hide money under mattresses or in safety deposit boxes. We must invest it for the future."

"And the liquor business?"

"We will continue to supply bootleg as long as this stupid Prohibition remains in place, but it will not last forever. Someday, America will forget the whole business. When that happens, I want us to own factories, stores, theaters, trucklines, even legal breweries—all kinds of businesses. Not in my lifetime, but in yours, all these illegal things that we have done will be just a memory. We will be respectable businessmen. And we will own much of New York."

"And you want me to run this operation?"

"With my help, of course. Remember, you have no po-lice record. You are a real estate broker. I made it that way so you can carry the fortunes of this family forward."

Nilo stubbed out his cigarette and leaned forward in the chair, looking earnest. "I am overwhelmed, Don Salvatore."

"We just keep moving forward," the Mafia boss said. "And now, get out of here. I have business to take care of that no longer concerns you."

Nilo stood, then impulsively walked around the desk, took the don's hand in his, and kissed his ring. "Be gone," the old man said.

Walking through Maranzano's outer office, Nilo found it hard to restrain himself from shouting exultantly. He was on his way. The future fortunes of Maranzano's whole operation would depend on him. He would be rich and he would be respected. In his heart, he knew he would miss the excitement of running with Maranzano's mob, the thrill of hijacking Masseria's liquor trucks, of robbing the receipts of some of his gambling operations, the thrill of wearing a gun under his jacket and always being ready to use it.

But those were the games of a child. I am a child no more. I am the leader to be. I will put away my gun, never to wear it again.

Betty was at her desk when he stopped in the outside office. She smiled at him and said, "I was hoping we might go out tomorrow night."

"Don't you have something to get in the supply closet?" Nilo said, in a stern voice. She looked at him with a puz-zled expression, and Nilo took her wrist and led her across the room to a door that opened into a large closet, filled with filing cabinets and office supplies.

He flipped on the light switch and locked the door

behind them. She stretched up to kiss him, but he turned her around and pushed her forward against a shelf. Then he lifted her dress and pressed himself into her.

"You're an animal," she said softly.

"And you love it," he said, reaching around her body and squeezing her fiercely. *And I will be don.*

When he was finished, he went out and sat at her desk, where he found a long list of names, all Sicilian sounding, with addresses in New York.

These must be the new immigrants, the ones Mussolini has frightened away. All come here looking for jobs from Don Salvatore.

Idly he scanned the list of names, then glanced up to see Betty come out of the closet and approach the desk. Her face was flushed.

"So what about tomorrow night?" she asked.

"I'll be busy tomorrow night," Nilo said offhandedly, continuing to read the names.

And then one burned into his vision, as if it had been written in blood.

Enzo Selvini.

The bottom seemed to fall from Nilo's stomach. Enzo Selvini was one of the three who had raped him back on the *tonnara,* one of the three he had killed back there in Sicily.

"He did not die," Nilo said softly. "The bastard lives."

"Excuse me?" Betty said. Nilo did not answer. He crumpled the list of names and stuck it into his jacket pocket and moved quickly toward the front door.

WHEN NILO REACHED Selvini's apartment house, which was only three blocks from Holy Rosary Parish in Italian Harlem, he noticed that a lot of workmen were around the streets putting up booths for a street fair. Kids flocked in the traffic-free streets, and neighbors milled around, doing their daily business. Pushcarts lined both curbs. Watching the crowd steadily grow in number, Nilo smiled. *This city will be mine and I should know what goes on. It is good to see so many people out today. Many people, and none will see me or remember my face.*

He reached inside his jacket and made sure the safety was off the pistol he carried. Despite knowing that violence was to be kept to a minimum during the festival, Nilo knew better than to travel anywhere unarmed. And he had other plans for that day.

He walked up the steps of the apartment building and knocked on the door of Selvini's apartment. He had planned no fancy ritual, no elaborate execution. When Selvini answered, he would just shoot the bastard dead.

But Selvini did not answer. Nilo waited, gun in hand, for a while, then gave up. In the basement, he told the building superintendent he was a friend of Selvini's, but the super seemed suspicious, and only on the transfer of a five-dollar bill would he admit that Selvini was out looking for work.

Nilo thanked him and went outside to wait. He paused at the mailboxes. None of them had Selvini's name. He pried open one of the boxes at random, took out a letter, then ripped the flap from the back of the envelope. He walked back upstairs and at Selvini's apartment he pasted a small piece of the envelope paper across a top corner of the door. It would be very hard to see unless someone was looking for it. But anyone opening the apartment door would tear or dislodge the paper. He looked inside the letter to see if there was a check or cash, but there was not, so he crumpled the letter and threw it into a corner of the hallway.

Nilo went out, found a quiet restaurant three blocks away that handled Maranzano's liquor, and tried to eat lunch. But his stomach was too unsettled and instead he sat alone, quietly consuming a bottle of red wine.

After a couple of hours, he went back to Selvini's apartment building. Pulling his hat down low over his face, he walked up the steps. At Selvini's apartment, the small piece of paper was still glued to the top of the door-frame. No one had entered since Nilo had left.

He had barely gotten across the street, lounging in a doorway, casually smoking a cigarette, when he saw Selvini walking down the opposite sidewalk, whistling quietly to himself. The man was dressed in peasant style and seemed to have put on weight. Not that he was fat, but he no longer had the gaunt, starved look of the im-poverished Sicilian fisherman he had been. It took Nilo a moment to recognize him, and by the time he did it was almost too late.

It was dinnertime now and the street was no longer crowded. Earlier, children had been playing stickball and the stoops had been filled with men in undershirts and women in black dresses that looked as if they weighed ten pounds each. But now people were inside eating, it was growing dark, and only a few kids lingered on the street.

Nilo felt in his pocket again for his gun. Its cold weight in his hand was comforting. He had not realized until he touched it that he needed comforting, but Selvini, he remembered, had survived an up-close shotgun blast. He should not have, unless he was under the protection of some especially powerful demon.

Nilo began to walk across the street, angling so he could meet Selvini at the steps to his apartment build-ing. For a moment, Nilo thought he should get away, not make this effort now.

Nilo called out his name: "Enzo."

Selvini turned toward the street, looking for a familiar face, smiling. The smile lingered for just a fraction of a second, and then Selvini seemed to recognize him. A fearful, hunted look appeared in his eyes. Nilo slowly pulled the pistol from his pocket and raised it to fire at Selvini.

The other man moved more quickly than Nilo expected. Just as Nilo was ready to pull the trigger, a young boy strolled past and Selvini grabbed him and yanked him toward him as a shield. He snatched a pistol from his own jacket pocket.

Don't shoot! Don't shoot! Nilo's mind screamed the warning, but was it too late? His finger was already tightening on the trigger, but to avoid hitting the child, he tried to turn the gun toward the sky. There was the loud report of his pistol and then return fire from Selvini.

Nilo dove into the street, rolling to avoid the gunshots from the other man. He got to one knee and tried again to aim at Selvini, but the child was still in the way. Nilo heard another shot, found himself squeezing the trigger. Just as he did, Selvini pushed the boy toward Nilo as both men fired. Nilo felt the weight of the child as his body slammed forward into Nilo and carried him to the pavement. Behind him, he heard a shout. He scrambled to his feet and looked down at the boy. He was dead. Nilo knew it. He had seen death before.

He heard more shouts and fled down the street, running after Selvini.

There are others there. They will care for that child. But I think there is no hope. No hope for Selvini, no hope for my immortal soul. A child is dead.

He did not know if he was being chased, but after several blocks Nilo cut through an alley, came out on another street, and was quietly alone in this foreign world.

It would be dark soon. Nilo wandered around, not knowing for certain where he was going, hoping against hope that somehow he would come across Selvini's trail again. The man would not return to his apartment anytime soon, and when he did, it would be with friends to protect him.

Nilo walked the streets for an hour without success. What had happened was terrible, but at least no one had seen him, no one could recognize him. Night came and he gave up. It was the end of everything. There was no way he would ever be able to get that close to Selvini again.

Maybe I'm wrong and maybe the child will live. What kind of animal is it, anyway, who would hide from his fate behind a child?

He found a small speakeasy and went inside. He sat in a corner, nursing yet another bottle of wine, feeling lonely and morose. He said a prayer that the child would be all right, then another and another. Then he said a prayer asking God to forgive him. He had begun a gunfight, and a child had died. He wondered how much money he should send the parents to compensate for their child's death. Finally, he paid his bill and left.

He stepped out on the sidewalk. He was only a few blocks from where Selvini lived. He looked left and right, searching for a cab to take him back downtown.

I will have to tell Don Salvatore about it, about the dead child, about everything. And it is best to do it now and get it over with.

He still had the gun in his pocket and wished he did not have it with him. The damned thing had done him no good. Don Salvatore had told him to put his gun away, but he had insisted on using it one more time. He walked to the gutter and dropped the gun into a sewer.

When he turned, incredibly he saw Enzo Selvini leaving a restaurant only a few doors away and walking down the block.

Nilo darted into a doorway and waited until Selvini was almost a half block ahead of him before he began walking slowly after him.

The other man seemed to be strolling through the streets, but finally, after fifteen minutes, he turned a corner, then went into a movie theater. Nilo quickly bought a ticket and followed him in.

Selvini took a seat in the last row, scrunched down in it, and within moments was sound asleep.

Nilo took a seat on the opposite side of the movie house. Now, seeing that his prey was asleep—Nilo could hear the snores, as he had heard snores years before on the *tonnara* fishing boat—he got to his feet and walked around the back aisle of the theater, wishing he had not thrown away the gun.

He came up to the chest-high wall that bordered the last row of seats. Selvini was now in front of him, just a few feet away. No one else was in the row and Tony thought for a moment that maybe he could strangle the other man.

He rejected the idea. *It might take too long. Selvini may be too strong. Surely, people will see me. Some might even try to stop me.*

He backed away for a moment to think; then he saw what he needed. A three-foot-long fire ax was mounted inside a glass case on the wall. Nilo opened the box, removed the ax, and carried it back to the last row of the theater.

He came around the wall and stood next to Selvini. In the bright light reflected from the movie screen, he could see the man's eyes were closed; a dribble of spittle ran down his chin. He was snoring softly.

Nilo leaned close to him and said, "Enzo. Guess who's here?"

Selvini opened his eyes and instantly recognized Nilo. He saw the ax. He opened his mouth to scream.

Too late. Nilo swung the ax and its blade bit deeply into the center of Selvini's face.

The man uttered not a sound. Nilo stood back and admired his handiwork. The ax was embedded into the other man's head, and Nilo just removed his hands from it and the ax stayed in place a moment before slowly sagging toward the floor.

Suddenly someone in the audience saw what had happened and shouted. A woman screamed. Nilo took his handkerchief and wiped his fingerprints from the ax handle.

Then, while people were screaming and shouting, he casually walked out of the theater.

AT 115TH STREET, Tony Falcone, sweating, now unaccustomed to the weight of his heavy blue uniform, turned east toward the river and Holy Rosary Church, the center for the next three days' activities. Earlier, he had heard sounds like fireworks and then police sirens, but they were too far away for him to concern himself with. Instead, he kept meeting, as he had planned, with each of the merchants who would be providing food for the festival. None reported any trouble, and Tony was beginning to think that maybe everyone would live up to their agreements and this festival could go on without serious trouble.

As he neared one corner, he passed a movie theater and stopped to study the posters outside. They advertised an Italian film, some blood-and-thunder-spectacle of the days when the Italian city-states dominated the culture and commerce of the civilized world. Tony smiled to himself. Despite what he had told the group of festival organizers at their conference, he did not give a damn about ancient Rome, and as far as he was concerned, too many immigrants spent too much time mooning over the Old World.

If Italy was so damned great, he thought, why didn't they stay there? Why bother coming to America?

He was about to walk away when the doors of the theater burst open. A straggling crowd started to pour out, some shouting, some women crying. At first, Tony thought it might be a fire, and then he heard the shouts, "Murder! Murder!"

He pushed through the crowd to get inside. People bumped into him. The crowd started to thin. He pushed his way into the lobby, then turned toward the entrance doors, where he thought he saw somebody he recognized. He could only see the back of the man's head. The man pulled his hat down lower over his eyes and went quickly from the theater.

Nilo? Was it Nilo? Tony went inside and found Selvini's body.

WHEN NILO WENT TO DON SALVATORE'S APARTMENT to tell him what had happened, Maranzano had to struggle to control his anger. "You have jeopardized all my plans for you," he snapped.

"I could not let Selvini live," Nilo protested.

"And we have people who can take care of things like that. Why must you get your hands dirty? Must you always be a street hoodlum?"

"I am sorry, Don Salvatore."

It was agreed that Nilo would go into hiding until it was determined whether or not he was suspected of the killings. Nilo found a place to hide, but he could not get the murdered child out of his mind.

WHEN HE HEARD THE RECTORY housekeeper at the door of the dining room, Father Mario spread out the copy of *Progress,* the Italian-language newspaper, on the table in front of him. But as soon as the woman had left, he put the paper to the side and began to read the *Daily News,* which he had hidden underneath it.

The headline was the same as it had been since last week:

POLICE SEEK BABY-FACED AX KILLER

And inside the paper, one story wondered whether the "Dago of Death" would ever be found or if he had sneaked back to Italy in the dead of night.

A BULLET FOR A KID; AN AX FOR A REFUGEE read another headline, recounting how the killer had murdered a young boy in cold blood with a pistol while trying to shoot Selvini and then tracked Selvini into a movie theater and buried an ax in his face. It described Selvini as a recent immigrant from Castellammare del Golfo in Sicily. No one apparently had seen the killer's face, except one old woman with bad eyes who thought that "he looked young," which was enough for the press to call him "baby-faced."

Mario sighed and picked at his breakfast. He was tired and felt far older than his thirty-one years. He had never wanted to help people solve their problems, either with earth or with heaven. He had never been good at that. The only contact with people that he had ever been good at was contact with his boxing gloves.

He knew he should have been a monk, away from the world and its people. Sometimes he wished that there were someplace he could go for just a few hours, where no one would know that he was a priest, where no one would know that he was a man of God, where he could just be Mario Falcone, surprisingly devout ex-pug. But the priesthood had been his choice.

Every day, people had choices. His father had one when he thought he saw Nilo Sesta leaving that theater, and his father's choice was to tell the department, but only as much as he had to. He went to his commander and said he thought he had a line on who the killer was. But if it was announced, he said, the killer would vanish from the country.

"Keep it quiet," Tony had told his boss, "and I'll bring the guy in."

Captain Cochran had looked at Tony silently for a long few seconds. "Do I get the idea there's something personal in all this?" he asked.

"Captain, I think the guy who's involved in these killings is somebody I know. Now if I was playing it cute, there wouldn't be anything easier for me than not tell you anything, not anything at all. Remember, I didn't have to tell you that I thought I had a lead on this case. It's not really our jurisdiction. But I did, because I want to bring this guy in. I think I deserve the benefit of the doubt and a chance to do it my own way."

"Fair enough," Cochran said. "Just so long as you know that if there's any backlash over this, I'll hand you up in a flash. Put all the blame on you."

"Okay," Tony said.

"And what about the Holy Rosary Festival?"

"Let it go on," Tony said. "This dead guy, Selvini, wasn't part of any gang, so I don't think this has anything to do with the gees. The truce should hold, and maybe the festival will calm people down."

Cochran agreed and they finished their conversation in light, joking phrases, but the truth had been told in jest. It was up to Tony to get the Dago of Death. If it was learned that the man escaped before Falcone ran him down, Tony's neck would be in the noose.

Mario knew about this because his father had told him the previous evening while they were sitting on the front steps of the family's apartment building.

"Why not just give them Nilo's name?" Mario had asked.

"Because maybe, just maybe, he was just going to a movie and didn't have anything to do with the killings. I don't think so, but I think he merits that much of a chance." His voice sounded tired and unconvinced. "If I've done wrong, I'll admit it at confession."

Nilo had also had a choice, Mario thought. He had not been compelled to go after this Enzo Selvini to kill him. If he had not made that choice, two other people would have been alive and Nilo would not now be a fugitive, being hunted down by his own family.

Another choice. Was it always that simple to make the right one?

When he had left Tony and returned to the rectory, there was a message, with no name attached, which read merely that a parishioner was in deep trouble and needed help. An hour later, a man showed up to bring Mario to that parishioner. Mario had gone, even though the man refused to tell him who he would be visiting.

He skipped his dinner to go.

The meeting place turned out to be an old warehouse over on the fringes of Little Italy, in a neighborhood Mario did not know well. Loiterers, many with liquor bottles hidden inside paper bags, dotted the nearby street. A guard at the warehouse door had patted Mario down and searched his valise before letting him in. Another man took him upstairs and pointed him to an office, where he found Nilo sitting behind a desk.

"Hello, Mario," he said politely.

"Morning, Nilo. The message was from you?"

"Yes."

"I had half-expected to find someone dead or dying."

"Disappointed that I'm not?"

"Of course not. I'm not your enemy, Nilo."

Nilo had a petulant look of disbelief on his face, almost like a spoiled young boy, and Mario realized that no matter how much Nilo had grown up in his handful of years in this country, he was still not much more than a boy.

"I don't approve of how you live your life. You know that. And you knew that before you called me here. Now if you have something to say, I'm here to listen and to help, if I can."

Nilo stared at him a long time and then went over to lock the office door. When he spoke, the words came slowly, his voice threatening to crack.

"Father, forgive me, for I have sinned." Nilo dropped to his knees in front of Mario. "That little kid is dead and I had something to do with it. It's the first time I've ever been sorry for anything I've done. The first time. I've tried to ignore it, but I can't. I've done something really, awfully wrong. I have killed before, Father, but it was the right thing to do and I have never regretted it. But this . . . it's driving me crazy. I need to know what to do."

Mario helped Nilo to his feet, and the two men sat in chairs facing each other. "Tell me about it," Mario said softly. "Did you kill that boy?"

Nilo hesitated. He covered his eyes. It took almost a minute before he spoke again.

"No. But I caused it . . . and it wasn't right. It wasn't supposed to be that way."

"You will be forgiven," Mario said firmly.

Nilo's face seemed relieved, then darkened over. "But there's a penance, isn't there?"

"The penance is to go to the child's parents and ask their forgiveness, to seek to help them in Christ's name."

"I didn't shoot the kid," Nilo protested.

"It doesn't matter. You know your own responsibility. Get the parents' forgiveness."

"I can't do that."

"Why not?"

"Why not?" Nilo fairly shouted. "I'll tell you why not. They'll kill me. That's why not. Even you must know the rules of vendetta. They'll kill me. Or the cops'll kill me. I can't take the chance."

"Then there can be no forgiveness," Mario said.

Nilo glared at him.

"Get out of here, you goddamned eunuch," Nilo shouted. "Go on back to your incense and candles and all the rest of that crap. I know people who have studied for the priesthood, too. I'll get their advice. They will take care of this."

"Thank you," Mario said with a faint smile.

"For what?"

"For showing me that I really am a priest. Because if I weren't, I would kick you all around this building till you never walked again."

Mario walked slowly back to the rectory. In the end, he knew he could say nothing of his meeting with Nilo, not even to his father. It had been done under the seal of the confessional. In the end, the drama would have to play itself out.

Mario finished his breakfast, put the newspapers in the trash, and walked over to his small parish office, where he found Sofia Mangini waiting for him. The bright and beautiful and vibrant young woman he had known was gone. He had not seen her for more than a year, and it took him a moment to recognize her. She was pale and haggard and looked burdened with anguish.

"Mario," she said, and stopped. "Father," and stopped again. "Oh, I don't even know what to call you." She began crying and Mario patted her gently on the back.

"Call me Mario," he said. "It doesn't make me any less a priest. And we were friends before I ever put on this collar."

It was not exactly true, since Sofia was not yet even a teenager when Mario had found his calling. But the statement put her at ease.

Sofia sniffled a time or two, then made a game effort to smile.

"Everything's so wrong," she said. "Everything."

"Explain it to me very slowly," Mario said.

"It's about Nilo. I was reading the newspapers. Is Nilo the one the police are looking for? For killing that man, the one from Castellammare del Golfo?"

"Why do you ask?" Mario asked cautiously. Sofia's eyes searched his face.

"Because . . . because it's Nilo, and he's one of us."

"It's a police matter. I don't know anything about what the police are doing. And Nilo's hardly ever been one of us."

"I thought . . . I thought with Tommy and your father, you might have heard."

"They don't involve me in their business," Mario said. "I'm afraid I can't help you."

Sofia rose from her chair. She no longer seemed so mousy or frightened. "You're right," she said. "I shouldn't have come." Without waiting, she left the office. Sitting at his desk, Mario had the curious feeling that he had just been used for something, but he could not tell what.

Sofia walked down to the Battery and sat on a park bench, looking out over New York Harbor.

There was no one to help her, no one to love her, no one who cared if she lived or died. She was alone and would always be alone. No man was her friend and only one woman, and she too had turned away from Sofia. And now she did not care. She was in this alone and only for herself. That was the hand she had been dealt, and that was the hand she would play.

Sofia took a trolley uptown to the Broadway real estate office of Salvatore Maranzano. She presented herself to the redheaded receptionist and asked to see Mr. Maranzano.

"Do you have an appointment?"

"No," Sofia said. "My name is Sofia Mangini. I am a friend of Nilo Sesta's."

The secretary nodded and said, "I'll talk to Mr. Maranzano. Please wait."

As the receptionist walked away, Sofia looked her over. The young woman was beautiful, and Sofia had no doubt that she had been sleeping with Nilo. There had been a brief glint in her eyes when Sofia mentioned his name. Just another of the many young women Nilo had bragged about having. Sofia thought, for a fleeting moment, that her idea was stupid and she should just flee, but, despite her nervousness, she forced herself to wait in the office.

A moment later, the receptionist returned and said in a chilly voice, "Follow me, please."

Maranzano rose to greet Sofia when she entered his office. He escorted her to a chair and poured her tea from a large carafe on his desk.

"Miss Mangini. I've heard a great deal about you."

"Oh?"

"Yes. You've done a wonderful job in tutoring Nilo."

"Thank you."

Maranzano returned to his seat, then said, "Now what can I do for you?"

Sofia swallowed hard. "I know the police are looking for Nilo in connection with those two killings."

"Oh? And how do you know this?"

"I've heard it," Sofia said. "I thought I could help Nilo."

"And how would you do that?"

"I could say that I was with him that entire day. That I spent the day in his apartment. That we made love."

"Why?" Maranzano asked.

The teacup was shaking in her hand, and Sofia put it back on the wooden coffee table. "Because I want to marry Nilo. I love him. And I want to show just how much."

Maranzano shook his head. "On the day those two people died, you will say you were with Nilo. But someone will surely come forward and say, no, you weren't, because they saw you here or there or somewhere else."

"No," Sofia said. "In the morning, I took a train to Coney Island. I was there by myself. I saw no one. I came back alone at night. No one can ever say I was not with Nilo."

"We could probably find someone else who would say they were with Nilo," Maranzano said.

"But someone from his neighborhood? A childhood

sweetheart? Trained by the nuns and of impeccable reputation?"

"This will be very difficult for you. It will be your word against Lieutenant Falcone's. He is an old friend of your family, I believe."

"I am not afraid," Sofia said.

"You truly love Nilo."

"I do."

Maranzano rose. "I will have one of my drivers take you home. You will hear from me."

"Do you look with favor on my proposal?" Sofia asked.

Maranzano nodded. "You are a brave and beautiful woman. You will make a very fine witness. And wife."

TONY FALCONE HAD BEEN STANDING across the street for more than two hours watching the front door of Nilo's apartment building, and twice a local beat cop had tried to roust him. In this uptown American neighborhood, the people grew suspicious when olive-skinned men, who just might be those dreaded foreigners, stood around too long, no matter how well dressed they were.

Tony took a long, final drag on his cigarette, ground it out on the sidewalk, then crossed the street and entered the apartment building. Fortunately, there was no one on duty in the lobby. Tony did not want to see anyone or be seen, so instead of waiting for an elevator, he climbed the five flights of stairs to Nilo's apartment.

Tony knocked on Nilo's door, three measured, middle-of-the-road knocks that could come from a neighbor or a custodian. He put his ear to the door but heard no sound inside. When another knock received no response, he took a ring of keys from his pocket and methodically began trying one after another in Nilo's door.

The third key worked, and Tony stepped inside and closed and locked the door behind him.

It had been a full week since the two killings up in Harlem, but the frenzy created by the press had every cop in the city on the lookout for the "Dago Baby-Killer" as he was now being called in the tabloids. So far, nobody had been able to put a name to the killer's face, but that hadn't stopped the vast majority of New York police from keeping an extra-tight lookout for whomever he might have been. Nor had it kept the family of the dead child from swearing to deliver a slow and terrible death to the one who had killed a mere baby. Tony wanted his nephew, Nilo, in custody before the young man was killed out on the street.

He was not quite sure what he was looking for, except for some clue on where Nilo was, but he began methodically to search through the apartment. In the kitchen, he eventually found a new, shiny revolver wrapped in an oily rag and kept in a bread box. In the back of a small built-in pantry was a hidden shotgun, its barrel cut down to only eighteen inches long.

We Sicilians never change, Tony thought. *We love the* lupara.

He left both guns on the kitchen table, then moved into the bedroom. A closet there revealed nothing but enough clothes to dress three ordinary men, but that was all. The dresser too held only clothing.

Tony went back into the living room, sat down at a small desk in the corner, and began going through it drawer by drawer.

"Is that legal?"

Tony looked up. "Charlie Luciano. What brings Joe Masseria's chief punk into a high-class neighborhood like this?"

Luciano seemed not to take offense; he just smiled.

"Just running an errand for a friend," he said.

"I didn't know you had any friends," Tony said. He casually unbuttoned his jacket to make it easier to reach the pistol in his hip holster.

"I have all kinds of friends," Luciano replied, and there was something oily and mean about the answer. Tony felt, but could not understand how, Luciano was taunting him.

Sure, Tony thought, *whores and dope fiends and other pimps. But why is Masseria's boy in an apartment that belongs to one of Maranzano's men? Especially when he must have let himself in with a key?*

Tony said nothing. He often found that being silent was a very valuable tool in getting information from people. Quiet seemed to unnerve many, and by holding his tongue he had found that sooner or later they would start to talk and maybe spill more than they had planned to.

After a moment, Luciano said, "I was asked to bring you to meet a friend of your nephew's."

"How did you know I was here?"

"You were seen hanging around," Luciano said.

"And why would anyone send you to get me?"

"Maybe they know how far we go back."

"How far is that?"

"You arrested me when I was a kid. You smacked me around."

"Sorry. I tossed around so much garbage that I don't remember."

Luciano smiled. "I remember, though. I've always remembered. Tough Tony Falcone. The honest cop."

"This friend who wants to meet me. Would he know where Nilo is?"

"He might," Luciano said as he sat on a sofa on the

far side of the room and began looking through a copy of an Italian newspaper.

"Don't strain your brain," Tony said. He picked up the telephone on the table, dialed a number, and said, "This is Lieutenant Falcone. I'll call in later. I'm with Charlie Luciano."

When he hung up, he saw that Luciano was smiling.

"That wasn't necessary," he said. "I wouldn't hurt you."

"Just humor me," Tony answered. "I'm the cautious type."

He put the two guns he left in the kitchen inside a brown paper sack he found in the cupboard, wrapped it tight, then followed Luciano out of the apartment and down in the elevator.

As they reached the curb, a sedan pulled up and Tony climbed into the backseat after Luciano. The driver was darkly handsome and Tony recognized him as Joe Adonis. He was no ordinary driver but instead one of Luciano's top guns and the man in charge of delivering Masseria's booze all through Midtown Manhattan.

"Where are we going?" Tony asked.

"To Maranzano's office."

Tony held the bag of guns on his lap. "Since when are you doing favors for Maranzano? Everybody knows Masseria and Maranzano don't get along."

"Just between us in the car here?" Luciano said.

Tony nodded.

"Fighting between our group and their group is not going to help anybody." He smiled. "Except maybe your group. The police. I'm trying to build bridges of understanding. And in case you're wondering, Joe Masseria knows what I'm doing."

"Quite a diplomat," Tony said. "It must come from negotiating labor contracts with your whores."

"No need to be nasty," Luciano said.

"You make it so easy, though."

The rest of the ride passed in silence. Adonis stopped the car at the curb in front of Maranzano's Broadway office, and Tony, clutching the paper bag with the guns, got out.

Luciano said, through the open rear window, "Now, don't do anything I wouldn't do."

"And just what is it a pimp wouldn't do?" Tony answered. Luciano's face clouded over, and the car pulled away from the curb into the busy traffic.

When they were a few blocks away, Luciano said, "He's going to take a fall someday."

"It's not good to hit a cop, Charlie. It gets everybody agitated."

"I'm not going to hit him. I'm going to break him," the other man said.

"Just because he arrested you once when you was a kid?"

"Because he treated me like dirt then. Because he still treats me like dirt," Luciano said. His lips were pressed tight over his teeth. He made an effort to relax. He lit a cigarette and put it into a thin ivory holder. "Anyway, we done good work today."

"I'm gonna have to take your word for it because I don't know *what* we did today."

Luciano stifled a sigh. Sometimes, he thought, Adonis was too stupid to be allowed loose on the street. He spoke slowly as if lecturing a backward student: "First we let Maranzano know that we know Sesta is this 'Dago of Death' the papers are talking about, but that we aren't going to do anything about it. It keeps our hand in with him pretty good. Then we brought Falcone up here for him to talk to. Who knows? Maybe he can talk Falcone out of testifying against the little bastard."

"I don't like the idea of Sesta maybe getting off. I don't forget that night you said he set me up for that beating."

"Don't worry; he's not getting off. Once we find out where he's hiding, then he gets shot by the cops or else he's gonna fry. Either way, Sesta is dead meat. But we stay Maranzano's good friends. You never know what day the shooting's going to start around here between these two Mustache Petes, and I don't want us to be in front of anybody's guns. Not until we're ready, Joey."

"How do we know that the cops want Sesta anyway? That Falcone spotted him as the killer?"

"Because somebody always talks, and we've got a guy on the inside with Maranzano."

"You're real smart, Charlie. I just want to look in the bastard's eyes when he dies," Adonis said.

"Enough that Sesta dies," Luciano answered. "We can't afford to do anything that'll mess us up with *Mr.* Maranzano."

"Don Salvatore," Adonis said mockingly.

"His turn will come, too. Meanwhile, life goes on."

"Yeah," Adonis agreed cheerfully. "Life goes on. Until it's over."

WALKING INTO MARANZANO'S real estate office, Tony felt dirty. Meeting Luciano always made him feel as if he needed a bath, because there was something corrosively sinister about the sneering droopy-eyed gangster. He was, Tony knew, not even thirty years old yet, but slowly and carefully, he was pulling all of New York City's crime together in a network under his control. And when he had done that, he would be more fearful, more dangerous than all the old-time Mafia bosses had ever dreamed of being, because like a spider, he would sit in the middle of the web, pulling strings, and no one would be able to reach him.

The receptionist announced him. Tony thought this must have been the girl whom Nilo was ready to use for an alibi that February night two years earlier when Tommy was slugged. He wondered if Nilo would try to use her again.

After a few moments, a large, well-dressed man came through the door. He smiled, and before Tony could respond he pumped the policeman's hand in a warm gesture of welcome.

"Lieutenant Falcone, I'm Salvatore Maranzano. I appreciate your coming. Come inside, please. Can I take your bag?" He nodded toward the paper bag of guns Tony was still holding in his left arm.

"I'll hang on to it, thanks," Tony said. Maranzano nodded and led Tony back through an anteroom into his large private office. He waited until Tony had seated himself on one of the leather chairs in front of the desk, before walking around to sit behind it.

It was the first time Tony had ever met Maranzano face-to-face. The man, whose challenge to Masseria's position as head of New York City's Mafia was growing more serious each day, seemed hardly the type to be a crime boss. Masseria was old-style, a crude, foul-mouthed man, usually wearing a dirty wrinkled suit. Maranzano was impeccably dressed in well-tailored silk. His nails were trimmed neatly and polished. His voice was soft and his Italian was courtly, rather than coarse. He looked like a college-trained bank president.

Tony knew that among the younger men in the mob

people like Masseria and Maranzano who were not born in America were derided as "Mustache Petes." He thought that description fit Masseria quite well, but anyone trying to apply it to Maranzano, thus underestimating him, might be in for a surprise.

Maranzano bridged his fingers in front of him. Tony noticed that he wore no rings, another sign of his difference from the crowd, where gold and diamond rings of all sorts were a kind of badge attesting to the owner's success in this world.

Maranzano spoke calmly. "I know you're a busy man, Lieutenant Falcone, and I will get right to the point. You and I have a mutual problem. Your nephew, Nilo Sesta."

Tony nodded. "I think he has a bigger problem than either of us," he said.

"I will not waste your time by beating around the bush. You want Nilo for killing that man in the motion-picture theater. I will say now he did not do it. But if he had, he would have been fully justified. If I had been a mere boy and raped by that animal and other animals like him, I would also be after my revenge."

"Raped?" Tony said.

"You did not know."

Tony did not answer.

"It is true enough. I blame myself for the whole sad affair. We get so many people here, new arrivals from Sicily, looking for work, and this rapist Selvini was one of them, but I did not know it. I should have. Instead, Nilo found the man's name. As I say, I blame myself."

Tony remained silent, wondering to himself where this conversation was going.

"Lawyers, and we have many, tell me that many people will attest to the fact that Nilo was otherwise engaged at the time these two tragedies occurred."

"Alibi witnesses have been known to lie."

Maranzano dismissed that thought with a wave of his hand. "Trust me, Lieutenant, one way or another, we—and I am speaking for Nilo—would win the case. But how much damage would be done to our Italian community if we should have to go through a long, complicated, noisy trial." He made a spitting gesture toward the floor. "Already, the press is filled with stories of dago baby-killers. It could only get worse. All our efforts to help Italians fit into the life of this new land could be set back for years."

"Maybe we ought to think about things like that before we start shooting down people at random."

"The hotheadedness of youth. Someone wise once said that it is a shame that youth is wasted on the young. How very true. But too late an insight to resolve our problem."

"Just what is 'our' problem?" Tony asked.

"Selvini is dead and deserves to be. He was killed in a theater by person or persons unknown. The child was killed, probably by yet another person. It would seem—"

"Persons unknown?" Tony interrupted. "I saw Nilo leaving that theater."

"And you are the only person who connects him to any crime. I must ask you to ask yourself, Lieutenant: Are you certain that you saw Nilo at the theater? Are you absolutely certain? Because if you were to realize that it was not really Nilo you saw leaving that theater, then there would be no case against him. Many witnesses would testify as to his presence elsewhere at the time of the slaying."

"You can call in witnesses until hell freezes over," Tony said in a soft level voice. "I will testify to the truth. I saw Nilo leaving that theater. I am certain of it. Nothing will change that truth."

"Look at it this way, Lieutenant. Nothing is going to bring that child back to life. That tragedy cannot be repaired. It was probably a tragic accident. Should all our people be punished for such a mishap? If you were to realize that it might not have been Nilo leaving that theater, then there will be no need for a trial. Everyone, our entire community, would owe you a great deal of thanks."

Tony got slowly to his feet. In even, measured tones, he said, "You can put all the fancy words around it all you want, but it doesn't change anything. You sit here like some octopus, and every time you talk about that dead kid, you say the same thing—'a tragic accident,' a 'tragedy'—as if somehow saying that makes it different. It all happened because you couldn't control one of your thug gunmen, whether he is my nephew or not. Calling it a tragedy doesn't wash your hands of it. It just puts a label on it so you can deal with the label, without thinking of the dead boy that's under that label. He is dead with a bullet in his chest. His guts were spattered all over the street. You call it a tragedy all you want, but it was a fucking savage, senseless murder, and that blood is on your hands. It stays on your hands. Blowing Sicilian wind at it doesn't get rid of the stench."

Tony felt his body shuddering in his anger. Through his outburst, Maranzano simply sat in his chair, waiting for the anger to subside. When Tony had finished, Maranzano smiled at him.

"I know how terribly upset you are and how mightily you work to bring law to all our people. Nilo's prosecution will not help that cause; it will hurt it. And it will hurt many people around you."

"Why, Mr. Maranzano, do you care so much about what happens to Nilo? He is my blood kin, not yours, and yet . . ." His voice tailed off.

"There is blood and blood," Maranzano said cryptically. He paused. "Things will change in this city," he said. "It could help a police officer to have powerful friends. And no one needs powerful enemies."

Tony rose to his feet. "Don't threaten me, Maranzano," he said. "As a lieutenant of the New York City Police Department, I am now asking you formally: do you know where the suspect, Nilo Sesta, is?"

"No," Maranzano said. "I hear from him from time to time by telephone. That is, assuming he is still in this country. If I hear from him, I can deliver a message to him."

"No message," Tony said.

SOFIA STOPPED NEAR the family's restaurant, then went instead across the street to the Falcones' apartment and, when nobody answered her soft knock on the door, let herself in with the key she knew the family kept hidden atop the doorframe.

She walked into Tina's room and sat on the bed, trying not to cry but failing and weeping softly. There were still some clothes of hers in Tina's closet, left there a long time before when she had moved back across the street to her own family's apartment. Woodenly, she began to gather the clothes into a neat pile on the bed.

She might as well move all her belongings away, she thought. The Falcones would have no use for her after she went into a courtroom to lie for Nilo.

The whole thing was ugly, she knew, but it was her only chance to escape the sorry trap that her life had become. She would trade the chance of love to have a chance to escape.

She found a long white peignoir she had bought for

herself while on a little shopping spree with Tina after Tina had won the Mount Carmel Church raffle. Sofia had not wanted to buy it, but Tina had insisted.

"For your wedding day," she had whispered into Sofia's ear.

She looked at it now as the bitter joke it was, then took the garment off the hanger and began to remove her clothing. Naked, she examined herself in the mirror. She was beautiful. She had always known that she was and she was especially glad about that now. Her beauty might help her in whatever her life would be from now on. It just would not be a special gift for anyone.

She held the peignoir in front of herself. White in color. Virginal. Or the color of mourning for the Chinese, she remembered reading in one of her poems. She put it on, wiped away her tears, and smiled at her reflection.

It was a travesty, she thought. She was here, playing dress-up, pretending to be a blushing bride. But instead, she was a slut who was her father's mistress, who was soon to lie about fornicating, like a whore, with some common criminal in the desperate hope that another criminal might convince him to marry her. She thought bitterly that she should take the garment over to a neighbor so she could use it to wash the pigs she kept in her backyard.

She raised her hands to her shoulders, to grab the straps, to pull the nightdress off, then stopped. *No. I am a slut. This is the way a slut should dress.*

She took a little vial of lip paint from Tina's dresser and painted a garish wide red mouth over her already-full lips. She opened the front of the peignoir and took a bottle of scent and splashed it liberally between her breasts. With her fingertip, she rubbed some on her nipples, which hardened instantly. It was not perfume, only toilet water, but it smelled of lilacs. Still, somehow, it was no longer a clean scent. It smelled of decaying flowers to her.

She put some of the scent in her hand and dabbed it on her legs, between her thighs, on her shoulders and arms.

This whore will wrap you in the scent of her own corruption, she told herself. *Come on, boys, only a dime, only a dime.*

"Only a dime!"

She would have sworn she was speaking quietly to herself, but then the door to the bedroom burst open and Tommy stood in the doorway.

"Oh, my God!" he exclaimed.

She turned slowly to face him. Her hands held the peignoir closed in front of her.

"I . . . I . . ." he stammered.

"It's all right," she said.

"I was sleeping inside and I heard shouting. I thought there was something wrong," Tommy explained. He seemed to be having difficulty swallowing.

"There's nothing wrong," Sofia said.

"O-okay," he stammered. "I just—" He turned to leave and Sofia crossed the room in two strides and caught his forearm. He turned back.

"I was just wondering," she said. "Do you like this perfume?"

He took a deep breath.

"It's nice."

"I put it on just for you."

She moved closer to him and laid her head on his shoulder.

Tommy did not answer. He tilted her head back and wiped her face dry with his shirtsleeve.

"What's the matter?" The words seemed to fight their way from his throat.

"I was just thinking. I will miss you all very much," she managed to sniffle.

"Why? Are you going somewhere?" he asked. As he did, he wiped her face again, this time with his handkerchief. He looked like a little boy, intently mopping up spilled milk, she thought. He had always looked boyish.

"Everybody goes somewhere," she said.

"There," he said. "As good as new."

It would never be as good as new, she thought. Nothing ever would be.

"It's nice of you to say that," she said, and slowly moved forward into his arms, pressing her body against his. She pulled his face to her and kissed him, and as their lips touched he took her hands and pushed them down to her sides. He held them there as he backed away. The fabric of her gown separated. She felt her body naked.

"I've always wondered what you'd be like," he said thickly.

"I'm here now," she said. She pulled him into the room, closed the door behind them, and pushed him onto the bed. When he reached for his shirt buttons, she slapped his hand playfully away.

"Let me," she said.

She undressed him, and as she did an urgency overcame her, a need to be with him, to have him.

For a moment, she wanted to tease him, to show he had no effect on her, by carefully folding and placing his clothes on a chair. But when she saw his war wounds on his side, his hip, his legs, the wounds she had dreamed of nursing, she felt a longing that could not wait and she tossed his clothes aside, pushed him back on the bed, and climbed atop him, hugging and rubbing, kissing and bit-ing. He laughed at her insistence, then pulled her to him.

She did not love him. She never really had. But for a few moments, she could pretend to, because this was like real lovemaking, gentle, tender, warm with passion, and she screamed instantly in delight.

They stayed together for a long time afterward, hold-ing each other, not speaking.

"It could have been nice, Tommy," she said.

"It *was* nice."

"Try to remember this day," she said.

"How could I ever forget it?"

But he would try to forget, she thought bitterly. Every time he thought of what she had become, he would wish this day had never happened.

And then the glow was gone and she got up from the bed and said, "Your family will be home soon. Go. I have to get dressed and leave."

Confused at his sudden dismissal, Tommy left the bed-room. When he had, Sofia cried softly, then removed the peignoir, cut it in two with a pair of scissors, balled the pieces, and tossed them into the wastebasket.

LUCIANO WAS DRESSING to go out for the night when he was telephoned by Joe Adonis.

"Charlie, I think I found Sesta."

"Where?"

"An old warehouse Maranzano owns down near Five Points. Some rumdum who hangs out around there saw a priest going into the place earlier. From what he said, it sounded like that Father Falcone. I figure he might just have been going to see Sesta. They're related, right?"

"Yeah." As Luciano wrote down the warehouse address, Adonis asked, "You want me to send some boys over to take care of this?"

"No, no, no," Luciano said quickly. "Just leave it to me."

"I don't want Sesta to get away," Adonis said. "I owe him."

"He won't get away. None of them will."

A few minutes later, as Tony Falcone was cleaning up his desk at the Italian Squad to go home for dinner, his telephone rang.

In thick Sicilian, a voice told him: "I know where to find the man you're looking for." Before Tony could ask any questions, the voice said, "I heard him say that tonight he's going to be at a liquor club on One Hundred and Seventeenth Street." The man gave the name of the club.

"When's he going to be there?" Tony asked.

"Sometime tonight. I don't know. Maybe early. Maybe late. Just tonight."

"Who is this? Why are you telling me this?"

"I hate the bastard and I want you to get him." The line went dead.

Tony sat at his desk for a few moments, then put on his jacket and walked from the squad room. On the way out he told the duty sergeant, "Call my wife. Tell her I won't be home for dinner."

As Tony drove away from police headquarters, a man in a dry-cleaning shop across the street dialed a telephone number.

"He just left," the man said.

"Thanks," said Luciano.

TWO HOURS LATER, the telephone rang in the Falcone apartment, where Mario and Tommy had just finished dinner with their mother. When Tommy answered it, a voice said in a hard New York accent, "Listen, Falcone. I got news about your cousin."

"Yeah?" Tommy said suspiciously.

"He's getting ready to skip the country. Right now he's in a warehouse down near the Five Points. But in about an hour, he's gonna be leaving. He's there alone now, and if you want him, you can get him."

The guttural voice gave an address on Worth Street and hung up before Tommy could ask any questions.

"Problems?" Mario said as he came into the room and saw Tommy holding the phone near his waist before hanging it up.

"I don't know. Does anybody know where Papa is?"

Mario shook his head. "The desk sergeant called and said he went out but didn't tell anybody where. They can't reach him. What's the matter?"

"Some guy just called. He told me where Nilo is."

"Oh?"

"He said a warehouse on Worth Street. He's only gonna be there a little while. You think it's a crank call?"

Mario remembered his visit to the warehouse to see Nilo. "What if I told you it was true, that Nilo is there?"

"I'd wonder how you knew. But Papa wants him picked up. I'd go and get him."

"*We'll* go and get him," Mario said.

Tommy thought of protesting for a moment, then shrugged his shoulders. There was no point in arguing with Mario when he had his mind made up. "Not a word to Mama," Tommy said softly, then went into his bedroom to get his gun.

———

Luciano, accompanied by Meyer Lansky and Bugsy Siegel, was having a quiet catered dinner with Arnold Rothstein in a private suite at the Plaza Hotel across from Central Park.

For the last year, Rothstein, the gambler and fixer, had taken Luciano under his wing, acting as the younger man's mentor. Rothstein knew talent and he could see that Luciano was a rising star in the crime world. In a few years, when the old-line Mafia chieftains were out of business, Luciano would be running things. This was Rothstein's belief and he had always made it a habit to bet big on his beliefs.

One of his projects had been to get Luciano to drop the cheap gangster image he had, like so many others, to cultivate and adopt a quieter manner of dress and speech. So he was pleased to see Luciano show up wearing a quiet, well-tailored dark suit that would have been at home in a Wall Street boardroom.

Luciano had immediately poured himself a large Scotch and then raised a toast in the air.

"To a wonderful night," he said.

"You seem pretty happy," Rothstein said. "What's the occasion?" He was a tall lean man with slicked back hair that he constantly pressed into place with his fingers.

"Tonight I start squaring accounts with some pests who've been on my mind a long time," Luciano said. "It's a night for a party."

Siegel laughed.

"What's so funny, Benny?" Luciano asked.

"Here you are, a Sicilian celebrating, and all you got with you are us three Jews."

"You three and me?" Luciano said. "I'll take my chances on us. We're the future."

TOMMY LEANED FORWARD and told the cabdriver, "Third streetlight down on the right. Pull over there and park. We're going to walk to that warehouse down the block. You wait for us for just thirty minutes. If we're not back or if you hear some kind of disturbance, go get some cops quick and bring them back here. Got it?"

The driver nodded. He had seen Tommy's badge and had his five-dollar bill in his pocket. He could afford to wait a half hour.

Tommy and Mario got out of the cab and moved quickly down the block. Tommy reached into his jacket and touched his service revolver.

"Nervous?" he asked his brother.

Mario shook his head.

"No. Scared. And maybe most scared about what Papa's going to say."

"Me too, Mario. But I've got to do this. Otherwise . . ."

Mario grunted.

"There's still time for you to back out," Tommy said.

"What are brothers for?"

Brothers. The word made Tommy think. *Nilo once said that he and I were brothers, too.*

"Well, if we're afraid," Tommy said, "pity poor Nilo. He must be really scared at all this."

"Which means that he won't worry about shooting us," Mario said.

"Can't nothing happen to me," Tommy said. "I brought my priest."

They were in the shadows across the street from the warehouse door. The light over the door was out. There were no signs of light inside the building, and up and down the block there were only a few parked cars. All of them looked empty. There were no pedestrians.

The two brothers went down a long alley separating the warehouse from a low factory building on the next lot, looking for a back way inside the building. They found one, but the door was bolted and padlocked.

Tommy cursed, but Mario whistled softly. "There," he said, pointing at a window.

The window was large and metal framed, but its base began only three feet above the ground. A rectangle cut from an old box covered one of the panes and Tommy used a penknife to cut a hole in the cardboard. He peered inside and turned back to Mario.

"All dark. He might not even be here," he whispered.

"Still worth a try."

"Just don't trip over your own feet, you big elephant. I'm too young and beautiful to be shot."

Trying to work without sound, Tommy pried the taped piece of cardboard loose from the broken shards of glass still left inside the window frame. He was able then to snake his arm through the hole and unlock the inside latch.

Carefully, so he did not rip himself on the glass, he pulled his arm back out.

"I'll try to open this," he said. "If it squeaks or sounds an alarm, run like the devil himself is after you," Tommy said.

Tommy held his breath, but the window, hinged on pins at its center, swung open quietly, and both men had room to clamber inside the warehouse. It was still dark.

"There are stairs over there," Mario said, pointing. "There's rooms upstairs."

"How do you know that?" Tommy asked.

"Don't ask."

Tommy flicked on a small pocket flashlight, just long

enough to make sure there was nothing on the floor between them and the stairs, which were barely visible in some reflected moonlight from outside. It was a little better now; his eyes were becoming accustomed to the dark.

When he reached the steps, Mario started to go up first, but Tommy brushed him back and led the way himself. The top of the stairs opened into a large area, big enough for a meeting hall, with doors on the far side that apparently led to rooms. Here it was lighter. The moonlight shone through the windows, which had not been painted over as they had been on the ground floor.

From under one of the doors across the way, a thin strip of light was visible.

"There," Tommy said.

He started toward the door, unsure how he would enter the room. He had been a policeman for more years than he had wanted to be, but nothing in his experience had prepared him for this.

He could not just knock because then somebody might say, "Who's there?" and what would he reply? Nor could he just grab the door and yank it open. There might be somebody on the other side with a gun, ready to shoot at anything that moved.

He had no chance to figure out a strategy, because a voice suddenly snapped out in the dark.

"Hold it. Don't move."

Tommy turned toward the sound of the voice, trying to move his body between the sound and Mario behind him. But he couldn't sense where Mario was.

"Who are you? What do you want?" the voice demanded.

"Nilo?" Tommy said.

"Tommy, what are you doing here?"

"I've come to bring you in."

Still invisible, hidden in the darkness, in a corner somewhere, the other man groaned.

"Oh, no, it's not going to be that way."

"You come with me peaceably now or there'll be a gang of cops here, and you know they want to bring you in feetfirst."

It felt curious, Tommy thought, to be talking into the dark, as if the dark had an identity, had a soul of its own.

"Dammit, nobody's supposed to bring me in. The whole thing is being taken care of. Why do you have to be sticking your nose in here for anyway?"

"Because it's my job. Because they want to talk to you about two killings."

There was a long silence. Tommy thought he should reach for his gun, and then the chilling thought came to him that if he did, Nilo—if he was armed—might fire without warning.

Of course he was armed. Nilo was a killer and had nothing more to lose.

"I'm sorry, Tommy. I won't go with you."

"There's only one way to stop me."

"Then that'll have to be the way."

For a moment, there was only silence in the loft, and then Tommy heard a grunt. He heard the sound of a pistol dropping to the floor. And then a voice.

"Come on, lump, you going to help me or not?"

Mario!

Tommy ran across the floor and saw a pileup of bodies on the floor. He flicked on his flashlight and found Mario sitting astride Nilo's back. The gun was a few feet away and Nilo was trying to stretch to reach it.

Tommy picked it up and stuck it into his pocket. Then he came behind Nilo and, with Mario's help, handcuffed the suspect's hands behind his back.

"Sorry, Nilo, but it has to be this way," Tommy said. "Get up."

"Damn you," Nilo snarled. "You two. All you Falcones. Damn all your souls to hell."

Tommy pulled Nilo to his feet, grabbed the handcuffs, and pushed him toward the stairs.

On the first floor, Tommy walked toward the front door.

"Shouldn't we go back out the window?" Mario asked.

"No need. Nobody's here. Let's just get our cab and beat it."

Tommy looked up and down the street. The cab was still in the next block; he could hear its motor running. But something was different. Not wrong exactly, but different.

It took a moment to figure out what it was. Before, most of the parking places had been vacant; now, many more were filled with cars.

"Let's go," Tommy barked.

Mario and Nilo stepped out into the street. Tommy kept between the two of them and the curb. Something felt very wrong. He saw a worried look on Nilo's face as the young man looked up and down the street.

He sees it, too. Something's going to happen.

His hand tightened around the gun in his pocket; then he caught a glimpse of some movement out of the corner of his eye.

"Hey, baby-killer," somebody shouted.

"Run," Tommy called.

Mario started to pull Nilo along; the prisoner hesitated for just a second and then the night exploded into blinding whiteness. The world stopped for a second. Tommy tried to blink the purple and orange spots out of his eyes. They had almost gone when another white light burst in the night and then a second and a third and a fourth. After that, Tommy lost count. He heard the sound of men running. Photographers: the exploding lights were flash-bulbs.

Somebody's gone and told the damned press where we were going to be. They had the place staked out.

A pack of reporters surrounded them, baying questions, acting like a pack of wolves trying to down a wounded deer.

"Keep moving," Tommy said to Mario and Nilo, and turned back to keep the crowd from them. Something new had been added; he was not sure what, but it was bad. Newsmen began making way for someone else, parting like a sea. Tommy glanced ahead at Nilo and Mario and saw them go down in a heap, Mario's foot sweeping Nilo's legs out from under him and then Mario jumping on top of him.

When Tommy glanced back at the reporters, two simul-taneous explosions went off in front of him and to one side. These were different from flashbulbs. Behind him, Tommy could hear a metal hailstorm on the wall of a building. Somebody was blasting them with shotguns. By dragging Nilo to the ground, Mario had probably saved his life.

Tommy did not even try to get his gun out of his pocket. He twisted the jacket up and fired right through the cloth. One, two, three, four times.

His shots missed, but he saw two men turn and run from the scene. The sawed-off shotguns they had been carrying clattered onto the pavement.

Tommy waited a moment to make sure they had gone, that there were no more of them, then turned to hustle Mario and Nilo back toward the taxicab. Already flash-bulbs were lighting the night again.

Inside the cab, Nilo vowed softly, "You're dead. You two . . . every one of you Falcones. I will dance on your graves."

———

- *When the young immigrant thug named Albert Anastasia was released from Sing Sing after a short term for murdering another longshoreman, he went back to the seedy little Brooklyn candy store, just down the block from the real estate office, and set up a loan-sharking operation. He was disappointed that Nilo Sesta, whom he had liked, no longer came around. But he made new friends. Eventually the store changed ownership and became known as Midnight Rose's. Anastasia's gang, with the encouragement and help of Meyer Lansky, would also change their name. They would call themselves Murder Incorporated. Anastasia's idol was Charlie Luciano.*

- *In Chicago, Al Capone was cheered by the crowd when he showed up for a baseball game at Cubs Park, later named Wrigley Field. He told reporters, "I only give people what they want." Then he went back to his fortress apartment and decided he had had enough of Dion O'Banion, who headed the city's Irish mob.*

- *On November 10, Frankie Yale, Albert Anselmi, and John Scalise entered O'Banion's flower shop on North State Street, across from the cathedral where O'Banion had once been an altar boy, and when Yale shook O'Banion's hand the other men shot him, twice in the chest, twice through the throat, then in the right side of the face and again in the left side of the face. Al Capone sent a wreath to the funeral.*

- *In New York, Luciano showed the story of O'Banion's murder to his latest girlfriend, Russian showgirl Gay Orlova.* "Capone is an asshole," *he said.* "He just can't learn to get along."

- *Luciano was prophetic. In Chicago, the Irish mob declared war on Capone. Five hundred gangsters would die in the next four years. Capone retreated behind a phalanx of bodyguards and stayed away from Cubs Park.*

- *In New York, Luciano went to Mass at Mount Carmel Church and heard Father Mario Falcone deliver the homily on how in this new land of America all people of all backgrounds were now Americans and had to learn to live and work together. When he was finished preaching in English, he repeated the sermon in Italian.*

- *At the Manhattan courthouse, as it did before every election, Tammany Hall had arranged for the mass swearing-in of thousands of new naturalized citizens. They stood by the hundreds in drafty courtrooms, raised their hands, and were pronounced by a judge to be citizens of the United States. Hidden on the list of names was that of Danilo Sesta, late of Castellammare del Golfo, Sicily. The citizenship papers were dated three months earlier. Nilo was in The Tombs, awaiting trial for murder, and did not attend the happy ceremony.*

- *King Tut was America's newest fad. No girl considered herself fully dressed unless she was wearing a scarab ring or a turquoise Tut bracelet. The hot new dresses had hieroglyphics printed on them. Newborn children were named Tutter or Tuttie.*

- *George Gershwin's* Rhapsody in Blue *debuted at New York's Aeolian Hall. The critics were lukewarm.*

PART TWO

Tommy

CHAPTER 6

Fall and Winter 1924–1925

Wretchedly sick, Sofia Mangini bent over the toilet bowl and vomited her breakfast. Then she sat down on the floor and held her stomach.

It'll pass. In a few hours, I'll feel fine.

But then . . . tomorrow morning . . . all over again.

"Sofia, Sofia, where are you? Are you all right?"

"In here, Mama. In the bathroom."

She had been living at home. If she had ever entertained any idea of living again with the Falcones, that had become impossible when she said that she had spent the day of the child's murder with Nilo, in bed with him in his apartment.

They were all on different sides now. Tommy and his father were policemen, with the law. And she, Sofia . . .

I am now one of the criminal class. Ready to perjure myself to save a murderer from punishment.

And why? Because there is no one in this world to love me but me, and I will take care of myself, whatever it takes.

Father Mario had been another reason she lived at home. Alone, among everyone involved, he knew the truth. She had told him under the seal of the confessional about the mob's threats to tell about her and her father, and while she trusted that Mario would never break that confidence, having him close by while she was living out the lie would have been intolerable.

Maranzano sent a lawyer to accompany Sofia to the precinct building on the chilly September morning she was to give police her statement that she had been with Nilo all day on the day of the twin murders.

As she came out of her apartment building and walked toward the waiting car, Tommy came quickly across the street, his face set in a scowl.

"You don't have to do this, you know," he said.

"Do what?"

"Don't play games with me, Sofia. I know you weren't with Nilo that day. He was off somewhere else killing people." His tone was sharp and hectoring.

It is so easy for you to be moral, she thought. *You have never lived with a pervert and been a partner in his perversions. You, Mario, Tina, have all been raised with love, with people who love you, and I have been loved by no one. At least now people will know my name. And some will respect me and I will use them. And that is how it should be because only I care about me.*

She snapped back at him. "You know nothing. Less than nothing. I was with Nilo and I will tell the truth. Does his life mean so little to you?"

"Not as much as yours," Tommy said. "I thought . . ."

He thinks what? That because we had sex once it would mean something in this vile thing I call my life? Tommy, you are a child. . . .

"You thought wrong," she answered angrily.

"I guess I did. But if you ever need a friend . . ."

The lawyer got out of the backseat of Maranzano's car and walked up to them.

"Sofia," he asked, "is everything all right?"

She smiled at Tommy. "You see, I have all the friends I need," she said, and walked with the lawyer to the car.

The police interview with a young lieutenant and a lawyer from the district attorney's office lasted only fifteen minutes. In a dull voice she stated that she and Nilo had spent the day in his apartment, often in bed together. She cooked dinner for him, veal parmigiana, which was one of his favorite dishes. They ate together, and she had not left him until nine o'clock that evening.

"At that same time," the district attorney said, "Lieutenant Falcone reports he saw Mr. Sesta leaving the theater where Enzo Selvini was killed. What do you say to that?"

"Lieutenant Falcone is mistaken," Sofia answered. Then her lawyer told the two investigators that they had her statement and she would answer no more questions.

An hour after leaving her apartment, Sofia was back home, where she went into the bathroom and threw up.

"WHY WOULD SHE DO IT? Why would she tell that obvious lie?"

Tony looked around the Falcones' dinner table for an answer.

Tommy shrugged. "She told me it was the truth," he said.

"But it's not the truth. Dammit, I saw him myself."

"Tony, please," his wife said as she placed a platter of food onto the table. "Don't get upset."

"I'm not upset."

"Maybe she's in love with him," Tommy suggested, and Mario nodded. Sofia had told him just that, but it was a private conversation and he did not feel comfortable repeating it to his family, especially since he was not sure that she had been telling him the truth.

"She is going to ruin her life," Tony said.

"It's her life," Tommy answered. "Has anyone asked Tina? She would know."

Tony sniffed. "Who can ask her anything when we never see her?"

"Mama, sit down. Let's say grace," Mario said. "For Nilo too."

Tony glared at his son, then stubbornly folded his arms across his chest. "Forget Nilo. He made his bed. Let him lie in it."

Mario said the prayer anyway.

FOR A MONTH AFTER giving her statement to the police, Sofia confined herself to the family apartment. The story of what she had done was all over the neighborhood now, and she knew if she worked downstairs in the restaurant she would be the object of scorn. Or, even worse, of pity.

The whole matter had clearly affected her nerves, too. She found herself throwing up most mornings, and early in November she was sitting on the floor in front of the toilet when Rosalia Mangini came into the bathroom, wet a washcloth, and began to wipe her daughter's face.

"I don't know why I'm so sick," Sofia said.

"I think you can guess." When Sofia did not answer, the woman said, "You are pregnant. Whose baby is it?"

"It is . . . Nilo's, of course."

"Does he know?"

Sofia shook her head. "We have not talked since they arrested him."

"He will have to be told," her mother said, then added

almost as an afterthought, "Mr. Maranzano is downstairs. He wants to talk to you."

"Maranzano?" Sofia had not spoken to the man since she had gone to his office and offered to be Nilo's alibi. "I don't want to see him, looking like this," she said.

"Nevertheless, he is waiting."

"Let me put on clean clothes, at least, and then I will come. These are all covered with vomit."

"I will tell him."

Sofia hurried to get herself ready. She wondered what this man would have to say to her. Probably he wanted to coach her how to lie in court about being with Nilo.

When Maranzano rose from the table in the private back room to greet her, Sofia was again impressed at how different he seemed from the other gangsters she saw, most of them in the family restaurant. He was impeccably dressed; his long hair groomed and oiled, his fingernails clean and polished. Maranzano looked first at Sofia, then at her parents, who also sat at the table.

"Nilo Sesta is like a son to me," he said. "I want only what is best for him. I know that, as friends of his, you wish that, too."

Sofia nodded dutifully, even though she knew that Maranzano did not give a damn about Nilo.

Maranzano reached across the table and patted Sofia's hand. "You were very brave in coming forward to try to help Nilo. But now there is a problem."

"What?" Sofia asked.

"Someone has reached into his pocket and bribed several men to lie. They will swear they saw Nilo shoot the child and kill Selvini in the theater."

In the pit of her stomach, Sofia felt a sinking feeling of despair. Did this mean she was going to go to jail, too?

Something bad is going to come of this. This is going to be a very bad day in my life.

"I have thought this through carefully," Maranzano said. "It seems to me to be best that Sofia and Nilo are married, as soon as possible."

This suggestion took Sofia's father by surprise. "Why, Don Salvatore?" he sputtered.

"There are a number of reasons. First of all, Sofia—in bravely telling the truth about being with Nilo that fateful day—has given him an alibi for the tragic killing of that poor child. The police will try to break down Sofia's story. But if she is Nilo's wife, unable to testify against him in his trial, they will leave her alone. So I am looking out here for her best interests, as well as Nilo's. Two, Signor Mangini, it will be useful in preserving your family's honor. It is not right for a young girl to be known as sleeping with a man who is not her husband. This will right that situation."

Sofia looked at Maranzano while he was talking and felt only contempt. Then loathing.

You are a filthy hypocrite, she wanted to scream at the Mafia boss. *You talk about protecting my honor from a belief that I was sleeping around like a wanton. But you know that I only lied in order to protect Nilo, even if it meant sacrificing my honor. Honor: you know not the meaning of the word.*

She felt Maranzano's eyes on her, and when she met them, she wondered if he was thinking about trying to take her to bed himself. She could not read it in his eyes, and usually she could see it in all men's eyes.

I hate it and I hate men. I hate sex. It is not worth it, not for a woman. For a few minutes pleasure, we hostage our futures. Give yourself to a man and there is no longer trust or hope or love. There is only sex. The only use of sex for a woman is as a weapon. Thank you, Don Maranzano. You have taught me something important today.

Maranzano was still speaking. She struggled to catch up with what he was saying.

"Of course, you're pregnant, aren't you?"

Sofia almost laughed aloud at the look of shock on her father's face. It was shock; then it was outrage.

This from the pervert who had made his own daughter's bedroom a brothel.

"Yes, of course I am," she said quickly. "And I'll be very happy to marry Nilo."

As soon as she said those words, she knew her life had just been changed forever. The dreams of childhood were gone; so were the fantasies of youth. What was left now was the raw, dirty reality of day-to-day existence.

I will not just survive. I will win. Nilo will give my baby a name and save the child from shame and ignominy. And I think Don Salvatore can be used to get me out of this rathole. For that, for the love of my child yet to be, I need only give my own life away to others.

In my whole life, has it ever been different? she wondered.

"But Nilo is already in jail," Sofia said. "How can we be married?"

Maranzano smiled. "It can be arranged," he said.

Her father was still staring at Sofia, in shock at her pregnancy but clearly afraid to speak in Maranzano's presence. The Mafia don reached out his manicured hand to pat Sofia's hand in a warm gesture of avuncular reassurance.

"My dear," Maranzano said, "you are a beautiful child and you will be a beautiful bride. I will make arrangements for you to be cared for. I have every hope that Nilo will be freed of these unfortunate charges. But it may be a long, time-consuming process. If during that time, you need any help while your brave young husband is away, I will be nearby. I will be your padrone."

I hate them. I hate them all.

NILO WOKE SLOWLY, yawned, and stretched, before remembering that he was in The Tombs, the castlelike main New York City jail. But a few short minutes before, while he still slept, he had been back in Castellammare del Golfo, a young boy again, playing hide-and-seek among the turrets and terraces of the old Moorish castle that jutted out into the bay.

Nilo slowly sat up, his bare feet chilly on the cold stone floor. He felt dirty, and laughed silently to himself. He had not been so fastidious for all that long. A few years ago, he seldom bathed from one week to the next. Now, if he could not bathe and change his underwear every day, he felt dirty and contaminated. He wondered how much longer feeling clean would seem important to him.

Then Nilo remembered what day this was. It was to be his wedding day, a big important step along the path that would set him free. It would help show the public that he was a fine, upstanding, responsible young man— not the kind of "Dago of Death" who would shoot down an innocent child in the street.

At least, that was what Koehler, the lawyer Maranzano had hired for him, had told Nilo. And it would also make it impossible for the prosecution to call Sofia to testify. There was no way they could paint her as a liar and trace that lie back to him. He hated the whole idea, but he would do what he had to to get out of this place.

He stood at the door to his cell as the guard brought

him breakfast, the usual strong black coffee and two doughnuts. He was barely done eating when the guard returned.

"Come on, wop."

"Where to?"

"We've got to get you shaved. Make you look pretty so that the newspapers say we take good care of you bums down here. Now let's get a move on."

An hour later, shaved, bathed, and wearing one of his own suits, which had been delivered to the jail, Nilo was led into the warden's office.

Sofia was already there with her parents, standing awkwardly on one side of the room. On the other were the warden, Koehler the lawyer, and a priest wearing a scruffy-looking robe. Nilo was not surprised that the prison chaplain would be performing the ceremony. In better times, he might have hoped that Father Mario would do the wedding, but all that had changed in the last couple of months. The Falcones were no longer his family. They were his enemies.

It is because of them that I am here in jail. First Uncle Tony telling the police that he saw me at that theater. Then Tommy and Mario coming to arrest me.

Looking around the room at the solemn faces, Nilo said, "Cheer up. It's not a funeral." He crossed the floor to stand by Sofia's side. She was wearing a long white dress, not quite a bridal gown but a close facsimile, and carrying flowers. She avoided his eyes, and when he touched her arm, she seemed to cringe, to move away from him.

"Mr. Sesta."

Nilo turned to the lawyer.

"Would you come with me for a moment?" Koehler said.

Nilo shrugged and followed Koehler into a small conference room.

"First of all, Don Salvatore wanted me to tell you his thoughts are with you today. But you can understand . . . showing up here . . ."

"I know," Nilo said. "I'm not offended. Thank him for his concern."

"All right. I'm afraid I have some bad news," the lawyer said.

Nilo tensed.

"I've been talking to the district attorney. It looks like he's got some witnesses who have recently come forward to identify you. Not just for the theater killing; for the kid too."

"What do you mean?" Nilo demanded.

"It's that damned Masseria gang. They figure if they get you, it might cripple Don Salvatore. So they've bought and paid for a couple of people who will identify you and say they saw you shoot the boy."

"Doesn't the DA smell a rat?" Nilo asked.

"That's irrelevant. He's on Masseria's payroll, too."

Nilo sat heavily on one of the hard-back wooden chairs.

"So what does it all mean?"

"Before this, I would have thought you had a fifty-fifty chance of getting off on the kid's killing. Now I'd say you're almost sure to be convicted and sentenced to the chair."

Nilo's heart pounded; his knees seemed jellied.

"And that's the end of it?" he asked, struggling to keep his voice calm.

"No. That's just the beginning of it. You'll get convicted, but we'll get you off on appeal. See, Masseria bought the DA and the local courts. But Mr. Maranzano's smart. He bought the appeals courts. They can throw out anything the lower courts decide."

"Then I don't want to get married."

"Fine," the lawyer said, dragging out the word until sarcasm seemed to ooze from it.

"What's your point?" Nilo asked.

"That part hasn't changed. If you don't get married, the DA will call up Sofia at the trial and ask her about your alibi. She's already told the cops she spent the day with you. But if she says that on the stand, and they've got other witnesses who all swear to the opposite, then they're going to get her on perjury. If they threaten her with prison, she might just admit that she lied when she said she was with you. And if that happens, the appeals court won't dare to set you free."

"And if I do marry her?"

"Then she can't be forced to testify."

"So I'm stuck with this bitch."

"It could be worse. She could be fat and ugly. Instead she's a beauty."

"You marry her," Nilo said.

"If I were looking at the chair, I would."

"Answer me a question. Why'd we get her in the first place? Wasn't there somebody else we could use as an alibi?"

"Sure, a lot of people," Koehler said. "But their backgrounds might not stand close checking."

"Don Salvatore's secretary? Betty? What about her?"

"Mr. Maranzano thought about her first. It turns out she's already married."

"Married?"

"Yes. To some penny-ante drug fiend. What she makes—and steals from Mr. Maranzano, as it turns out—pays for his addiction. No. Sofia Mangini was the right choice. She is as pure as the driven snow."

"It wasn't a snowstorm that knocked her up," Nilo said sharply.

"I beg your pardon?" Koehler said.

"Start whistling," Nilo said.

"What?"

" 'Here Comes the Bride.' Let's get this over with."

He got up and walked through to the other room. The service was speedy, the vows perfunctory. After the priest pronounced them man and wife, everyone seemed to freeze, and Nilo realized he was supposed to kiss the bride. He leaned his face over to hers and she turned away.

Nilo touched his lips to her ear and whispered.

"So you got what you want. Even if you had to make me knock you up. A real slut trick."

She spun her face around to him, trying to disguise the hatred she felt. For the eyes of the others in the room, she forced herself to smile as she put her face close to his.

"And what makes you think the baby's yours?" she asked softly.

He looked at her in shock, then in anger. He touched his lips to her ear. "Whose bastard is it then?"

"Some dirty bum I picked up on the street. He reminded me of you, dear husband."

TINA FALCONE THOUGHT that there was a certain touch of poetry in the present situation. She had grown up with Sofia, sharing school and family and hopes and dreams. And now they were sharing pregnancy.

Since that first night in Greenwich Village when she had awakened next to a paint-smeared artist whose name she did not know, there had been more trips and more men, all of it encouraged by Frau Schatte, who told Tina that she must be sophisticated and worldly "because art feeds on life and life feeds on experience."

Tina had not expected that her experience would so quickly include pregnancy. And now she had to think about an abortion because she could think of no way in which she could ever let her father know about her condition.

She stayed in her room at the townhouse that morning, lying on her bed, worrying, and finally she knew who could help.

Sofia's cousin, Charlie Luciano. She had heard all the stories about how he ran a string of prostitutes. Even if only some of the stories were true, she thought, he would still have connections.

Girls like that, she thought, must be needing abortions all the time. He might even have his own doctor under contract, somebody who knew what he was doing and not one of those back-alley butchers she had always heard about.

But would Luciano help her? Tina began getting dressed. She remembered the way Luciano had looked at her the last time they'd met at that street fair. He would help her. And of all the people she could think of, he would be the least likely to spill anything to her father.

And if I have to be nice to him in return for the favor . . . well, it's not like it's the first time. God. The first time. It seems so very long ago.

Luciano had sounded surprised and, Tina thought, pleased when she finally found him by telephone and invited him to come to the Village so she could buy him a drink. Of course, he would not come. While he didn't give any reason, Tina had heard that he was a very careful man now because he had collected many enemies over the years.

"You think I'm going to shoot you?"

"Maybe not you," he said carefully. "But I've got a better idea."

He invited Tina to a small club in the Broadway theater district. She was disappointed by the looks of the so-called club. It was a little hole in the wall, with no signs outside, and only one small heavy metal door.

Tina knocked on the door and only after a full thirty seconds of knocking, one of Luciano's men—the young one called Benny—swung open the door for her.

"Tina Falcone," she said. "For Mr. Luciano."

Benny looked her up and down, frankly and openly appreciative.

"I know who you are," he said.

"Oh?"

"Yeah. Charlie and I talked about you once." There was a smile on the young man's face, but it was an unpleasant smile, the kind that accompanied a nasty bad joke. "He's inside. I'll take you."

Tina smiled and touched a gloved fingertip to her lips and then touched Benny on the nose with it. Despite his tough-guy act, he blushed slightly. It was a technique she had learned from a girl she met at a party down in Greenwich Village. A cheap trick maybe, but it never failed to draw a reaction from a man—whether he was a gangster or an artist, a banker or a shopkeeper.

The club had looked small from the outside, but inside the main room things were clearly changing. Carpenters and electricians were tearing down walls and installing lights, and the place was a beehive of noisy activity.

Luciano was at a table, talking to a well-dressed, good-looking man who had a quality that Tina decided was a kind of quiet dignity. She doubted very much if he was a gangster, too.

She nodded to Benny, then stood there waiting. She did not speak; she would wait for Luciano to notice her. She knew he would; all men did.

Finally, he looked up. It took perhaps thirty seconds longer than it should have and Tina knew he had been aware of her long before that. He was just making sure that she knew who was the boss here.

Men are so transparent. Even this one who's supposed to be such a tough guy. I'll twist him like a strand of pasta.

Luciano rose from his seat. "Tina, you look beautiful."

"Thank you."

"This is my friend, Frank Costello. This young lady is Tina Falcone."

The quiet man rose also. "Pleased to meet you, Miss Falcone," he said. "You bring a touch of beauty to this madhouse."

"And are you in the restaurant business?" she asked.

Costello smiled. "No," he said. "I'm sort of in government."

Luciano laughed and Tina smiled as Costello excused himself. When he left, Luciano waved his hand and immediately a half-dozen people who had been hovering nearby scurried away.

"In case you're wondering why I laughed, it's what Frank said about being in government."

"Isn't he?"

"He spreads money around to government, to people who do us favors."

"Bribes?" Tina asked.

"Now would we do that?" Luciano asked. "Political contributions. All perfectly legal." He paused. "So, it's nice to see you again. How's your family? And your voice lessons?"

"You always surprise me with how much you know about me," she said.

"I like to keep track of things," he said with a slight smile. Then as if overcome by her beauty, he reached out and took her hands in his, raising them as if she were a display piece. "You're magnificent. You've really blossomed."

"I'm about to blossom a lot more," she said.

"You're pregnant?"

She nodded.

"How far along?"

"Two, three months. No more than that."

"Hmmm, that's not too bad." He looked at her searchingly for a moment, and Tina thought she understood what a prize cow might feel on sale in an auction ring. "Why did you come to me?"

"I thought you might know someone. I thought—"

"I can imagine what you thought," he said. "And?"

"And I wanted to talk to somebody who wouldn't talk to my father."

Luciano chuckled. "Your father and I are hardly on speaking terms. This could be expensive. Can you afford it?"

"No."

"What about the baby's father?"

"I don't know who it is," Tina said in what she hoped was a frivolous voice.

Luciano's dark eyes narrowed. "You've been a busy young lady. Have you been having a good time?"

Tina flashed her best smile and reached over to touch him lightly on the knee. She knew the effect it had on other men; could this self-important clown be any different?

"The best of times," she said airily. "Living and singing. What else is there? About the cost . . . I was hoping that you and I could come to . . . er, a sort of understanding."

"What did you have in mind?"

"I was going to leave that to you," Tina said.

"We'll think of something," Luciano answered.

THE TRIAL OF THE STATE of New York versus Danilo Sesta lasted only three days. Tony testified that he had seen Nilo leaving the theater where Enzo Selvini had been murdered with a fire ax. Four other people in the theater at the time identified Nilo in the courtroom as the man they had seen walking away from Selvini's body. Tommy testified that he had arrested Nilo in a warehouse, where he had been hiding out. Glumly, he admitted under direct examination that Nilo had resisted arrest.

Then two men Nilo had never seen testified that they had seen him shoot young Eugenio Roggerio on the street, when the boy got between Nilo and Selvini. Under cross-examination by Koehler, they denied having been paid to testify. The attorney tried to ask if they knew Joe Masseria, but the question was ruled irrelevant by the judge.

On the third day, Nilo testified. He said that when the boy was shot he was with his wife at the other end of the city. He denied ever being in the theater. On cross-examination, the prosecutor forced him to admit that he had known Selvini back in Castellammare del Golfo, and that they had in fact worked on a fishing boat together.

"Were you friends?"

"No. We were never friends." Nilo was determined that he would say nothing about having been raped by the three fishermen, but the question never came up. The prosecutor seemed to feel that it was enough to show that Nilo had known Selvini back in the old country.

So did the jury. They took only ninety minutes to pronounce him guilty of both murders. Immediately after the verdict was returned, the judge sentenced him to death in the electric chair.

The new Mrs. Sofia Sesta never testified.

A HEAVY SNOW HAD STARTED to fall just as the train left New York City, and by the time it had reached the little upstate town of Ossining, the whole town was buried under a blue-white blanket.

A forlorn-looking Christmas wreath hung over the main door of the train depot as the train pulled slowly into the station.

"Looks like a white Christmas for sure," the policeman on Nilo's left said, and the other cop leaned across Nilo to look out the window.

"What about the prison?" Nilo asked sarcastically. "Is that decorated, too?"

"Sure. The electric chair has a big red ribbon. With your name printed on it."

The warden's office was in a separate building inside the gate, just a few steps away from the guardhouse reception area. Nilo's escort knocked timidly on the door, then led him inside. To Nilo's eye, it looked like a pretty normal office area, not especially pleasant but not terribly oppressive-seeming as he had expected.

The assistant warden who met him was a thin, rabbity-looking man with a heavy mustache and a severe case of prison pallor. He was leaning back in his chair, flipping through a brown covered folder.

"Not much here that I don't know, Sesta," he said. "I

read about you in the papers. Killed a kid and then a guy in a movie house. Hmmm." He looked up. "Now's the time when I always ask the condemned man if he actually did it."

Nilo stared at the warden. There was something about the man he did not like, so he did not answer.

"I asked you a question, Sesta. Now answer it. Did you kill those two? Are you really the Dago of Death, the way I heard you called?"

What's he going to do? Nilo thought. *Kill me?*

The warden was waiting for an answer, and Nilo said suddenly, "No, no, I didn't do it. I was framed. Those three hundred witnesses lied."

Nilo saw a smile on the face of the guard who stood near the warden watching, but clearly the assistant warden had no sense of humor. He said solemnly, "I kind of figured you'd say that. Almost all you condemned men say the same thing." He picked up Nilo's file again.

"Says here your wife is expecting. Due in April." He laughed. "I wouldn't worry about it if I were you. You won't still be here by then."

"We'll see," Nilo said.

The assistant warden glared at him. "If there is one thing I can't stand, it's a smart aleck."

"I'll try to remember that," Nilo said. This time he had meant no disrespect, but the warden reacted as if generations of his family had just been insulted. He came around his desk and stood in front of Nilo, then began to raise his hand as if to strike the prisoner.

"Don't," Nilo said. He spoke softly. "I have a large family. They might not appreciate you treating me that way."

The warden hesitated, his hand suspended motionless in the air. He stared into Nilo's eyes, then dropped his hand and turned to the guard. "You can take the dago baby-killer out of here. You know where to put him."

Nilo preceded the guard down a long whitewashed corridor that led into the heart of the prison. At the end was a heavy steel door with a barred viewport in its top half. The viewport swung open at the guard's knock, and a moment later the door itself opened and Nilo and his escort went inside.

Directly across from them was a green steel door. Despite himself, Nilo felt a shiver of fear chase through his body. This was the door leading to the electric chair. On either side of the green door were three cells. Directly opposite those cells, flanking the door they had just come through, were six more cells.

The inside guard opened one of the cells closest to the green door and beckoned for Nilo to enter. "This will be yours," he said.

The cell was more comfortable-looking than Nilo had imagined it would be. There was a wooden-slat bed with a thick mattress, blankets, cotton sheets, and a feather pillow. In the corner was a washbasin and toilet. Toward the front of the cell was a writing desk with a small seat in front of it. Nilo looked around. In here, he thought, a man really felt as if he were buried alive under tons of rock. And the tomblike feeling was magnified by the deadly silence.

It doesn't matter. Soon enough, I'll be really buried.

"Is it always like this in here?" he asked the guard through the bars.

"Like what?"

"So quiet."

The guard shook his head.

"Just on the nights they're going to burn somebody."

"You mean . . ." Nilo started to say, but he could not

finish the sentence. Of course he knew that people came here to be executed, but he had not expected to come face-to-face with it so quickly.

"Yeah. Billy. That one over there," the guard said, pointing to a cell holding a sandy-haired sweet-faced young man, who looked no older than Nilo.

"Oh." Nilo went to his bunk and tried to read a book from his pack but could not concentrate. Within an hour, he saw a priest enter the condemned man's cell. The priest looked barely old enough to have been ordained.

Nilo went to the bars and looked across the small cellblock. A guard waited outside the other prisoner's cell, watching the meeting between the convict and the priest.

"God bless you, my son," Nilo heard the priest say. "I've come to let you set your soul right with God before you die, to absolve you of your sins, and give you your last Communion."

The priest spoke the words solemnly, as if they were a ritual in themselves. The prisoner laughed aloud at him.

"Get the hell out of here."

The priest mumbled prayers anyway, then gestured to the guard and left.

Two hours later, six guards came into the cellblock from outside and moved quickly from one cell to the other, pulling the shades that covered the cells. Nilo squeezed into a corner of his little enclosure and managed to find a large enough crack in his shade that he could watch what was going to be his own fate.

The guards opened the door to the man's cell. He backed away into a far corner and began crying. He held his hands out in front of him, seeming to want to fight them off but not having the physical strength to do anything. Four of the guards grabbed the prisoner and held him tight. He began to sag at the knees, but the guards kept him upright. The other two guards slit his trouser legs open from his knees on down, then began moving him toward the door.

Billy stopped. He grabbed the metal bars on either side of the door and jammed his feet into the corners. He stood spread-eagle, not moving.

"Oh, God," he cried. "Please don't let this happen to me."

Two of the guards rushed him from behind, jarring him loose and knocking him out into the corridor, where he collapsed on the floor, crying.

Half-lifting, half-shoving, the six guards gradually moved him the twenty feet, past Nilo, to the green door and then shoved him through it.

The door clanged shut heavily behind them.

In a few minutes, a low droning sound came from the death chamber, but it was almost a half hour later before the green door opened again and the six guards came back out onto death row. They moved quickly from cell to cell, and with a snap and a clatter raised the shades that covered the cells. A subtle smell of burned meat filled the air.

Nilo was still standing where he had been when the other prisoner was dragged out, but now he went across the cell and lay on his bed.

And what will I be like when my time comes? he asked himself. *Please, God, let me die bravely at least.*

It wasn't until two days later, Christmas Eve, that the burning smell was completely gone.

TOMMY REMEMBERED THE FIRST YEAR he had been allowed to help his father carry the Christmas tree home.

He was only eight years old, but how big he had felt holding the small end on his shoulder while his father up ahead of him carried the thick end—and almost all the weight—of the tree.

Some impoverished families in Little Italy tried to celebrate Christmas the American way by making do with ersatz trees, fashioned of a broomstick stuck into a bucket of rocks and festooned with coat hangers, from which they hung paper decorations. Most other families bought their tree on Christmas Eve from a corner vendor, hoping for rock-bottom prices. But Tony Falcone bought early and bought big. This year he started shopping for the tree several days before the holiday.

This is like being a kid again, Tommy thought as he walked with his father in search of a tree peddler whose wares seemed to meet Tony's high specifications. At least, that was the reason the older man gave for passing up some of the nearby tree lots, but Tommy knew it was not the real reason.

The truth was that Tony was too well known in his neighborhood and so well respected that none of the tree merchants in the area would quibble with him over the price. They all knew him; they knew that his reputation was one of the things that helped make the streets safe enough for them to do business, and if he offered two dollars, they said "sold," and if he offered one dollar, they said "sold," and every year Tony wound up going farther and farther afield to find a merchant who didn't know him, who didn't want to do the neighborhood cop a favor, and who would argue the price of a tree down to the last penny.

They found such a peddler almost a half mile from their apartment. He did not know Tony and clearly did not want to. He immediately rejected any offer that was

not up to his stated price. It took thirty minutes of con-
certed haggling, laced with Sicilian invective, dire threats
against each other's family, and vague entreaties to a God
cruel enough to put such bandits on his own good earth,
before the deal was struck. Meanwhile, Tommy stood
nearby, smoking cigarettes, warming his hands over a
wood fire the peddler kept burning in an old oil drum.
He finally heard his father say, "Okay. Deal. Tie it up."

"Tie it yourself, you thief," the peddler said. Tommy
laughed and took the rope from the man and began to
tie the branches flat against the trunk so the tree would
be easier to carry.

Tony helped him and mumbled, "A dollar and a quarter
is all it cost. The man's a fool. This is the best tree ever."

"He probably thinks it's worth taking a loss just to get
rid of you, Papa."

"He's never going to get rich chasing away good
customers," Tony answered with a grunt.

They lugged the tree home together. It did not seem
nearly as heavy as it had when Tommy was eight years
old, but it still presented serious logistical difficulties nav-
igating the narrow apartment steps, and both men were
sweat soaked when they finally got their precious cargo
onto the living room floor. Tony decided that a glass of
wine was called for to celebrate the occasion.

They sat at the kitchen table, drinking homemade red
out of water glasses, and Tommy asked, "Did you ever
read Dickens's *Christmas Carol*?"

"Of course I have," his father answered. "Just because
you're a college boy, do you think I'm an uneducated
clod?"

Which meant, Tommy knew, that his father had not
read it, had probably never even heard of Dickens, but
was embarrassed to admit it.

"Sorry," he said. "But I was just thinking about Scrooge in that story. When he finally gets the Christmas spirit, Dickens says he really knew how to keep Christmas, and I was thinking that you're like that, Papa. You really know how to keep Christmas."

"I'm like Scrooz. I like celebrating Christmas. Especially now, with Mario busy at the church and Tina maybe off someplace on her career and you someday probably getting ready to leave us, it's even more important to celebrate right." He sipped his wine. "Tradition maybe is the ribbon that ties us to our memories."

Tommy considered the thought for a moment and said, "That's very beautiful, Papa."

"You're making fun of me."

"Not me. Not ever," Tommy answered truthfully. He sipped his wine, then refilled their glasses. "I wish sometimes that Nilo could be with us." He saw his father's face cloud over.

"It was in his blood. He went bad and brought it on himself."

Tommy shrugged. "I know that. It's just . . . well, I think there's something wrong that he was convicted because of perjured testimony."

His father said, "Maybe those witnesses were not at the scene. But what they said was true. Nilo killed that child. He deserves to rot in hell for that crime."

"Only if he's rightly convicted," Tommy said. "Liars should not be allowed to send men to the electric chair."

His father stared into the bottom of his wineglass for a long time before speaking. "What do you expect me to say? That that's the difference between a lawyer and a cop?"

Tommy shook his head, but Tony shrugged him off. "In the real world, things don't run according to neat theories.

You have to balance things. How many gees did I arrest who got off because the fix was in? This time, the result was right. Nilo chose to run with the criminals in this city. They didn't call him Kid Trouble for nothing. He was one of Maranzano's killers and he killed that boy and the electric chair is where he should be. That's reality."

It was his turn now to refill the wineglasses. "This is a great country, Tommy, and it'll be a great country for all the Italians who move here. But it won't be so great if we come over here and we bring our Mafia and our vendettas and our blood feuds with us. Did you see how easy it was for the newspapers to call Nilo the Dago of Death? That's what we're becoming in the eyes of the people—a race of criminals. And it just shouldn't be. We're the newcomers. We should be more American than the Americans. I don't care about criminals. There are always criminals. There are always cops. They commit a crime, we lock them up. What's wrong here is that these criminals are giving an entire race a bad name. And Nilo, flesh of my flesh, blood of my blood, was one of them. I never liked the boy, that's true. But I never expected him to become one of them."

They had never talked about it before, and until that moment Tommy had not realized how deeply his father had been hurt by Nilo's entrance into gangster life.

"It was him, Papa, but it could have been me. It could have been Mario that joined the mobs. What if it had been us?"

"Then I would have put you in jail, too," Tony answered instantly. "I believe in justice, Tommy. I would have wept for your soul, but I would have put you away."

"Would you? Would you really?"

His father waited a long time before answering. "I don't know," he said. "I just don't know."

"Everybody can't make his own laws, Papa. There has to be one law and the courts have to apply it. And it has to be fair for everybody. For you, for me, even for Nilo."

"You're right. I hope someday we live in a world like that." He grinned. "Now shut up. You college boys are too smart, and arguing with you always gives me a headache." He stood up and drained his wineglass.

"Come on. We've got a tree to put up." He turned toward the living room and threw open his arms in a large theatrical gesture, and Tommy saw that he was more than a little bit intoxicated. "Make way, world," Tony called. "Here comes Scrooz."

"Scrooge."

"And his son, Little Scrooz."

WHEN SHE HAD LEFT LUCIANO'S CLUB, Tina had almost vomited in the street, because, despite all her brittle, worldly, sophisticated talk, she was frightened to death of facing an abortion.

A few days later, Luciano had called and told her he had made an appointment for her under the name of Miss Ross with a doctor up on Park Avenue. The doctor's offices were elegant, and the procedure itself was quick, professional, and relatively painless. But when she had asked the doctor for his fee, he smiled at her in a superior way and said, "It's a favor for Mr. Luciano, Miss Ross."

"I'd rather pay," Tina had answered.

"And he'd rather you didn't," the doctor said. "Please work out your settlement with him." He had looked down at the sheaf of papers he was carrying, signaling her that the discussion was at an end.

She had recuperated in her room for a few days but had

delayed calling Luciano, knowing he would be calling her very soon.

And I will do what he wants me to do because a deal is a deal, she thought.

But Luciano had not called, and as the days stretched into weeks, then into months, she began to feel more and more like an ingrate who had been done a great favor and who had failed to acknowledge it even with a simple thank-you.

Twice she had gone uptown to Luciano's speakeasy but both times had failed to muster the nerve to go inside and speak to him. Maybe, she thought, she had been mistaken and Luciano had no interest in her. *Maybe I was just another slut from the neighborhood that he did a favor for.*

Meanwhile, Tina's mind was taken up with other problems.

In the last two months, Uta Schatte had taken on two new students, who had also moved into the big house with them, and since that time she had seemed to have little time for Tina.

Of course she still got her twice-daily lessons—now, it seemed, with even greater intensity than they had had before—but when there were recitals to give, Tina was no longer asked to go. Instead, the two new girls would accompany Uta and Flora, the maid, on the trips, while Tina was left behind to rattle around the big house by herself. And Frau Schatte had suddenly become cold to her. It was the feeling of being left out that bothered Tina. She certainly did not mind passing up the recitals because, in truth, she had begun to question just how legitimate all of them were. They were generally held in hotel suites or in large private homes, and the audiences were usually only a handful of men. Frau Schatte showed up with Tina and Flora, and a handful of pretty, overdressed girls Tina had never seen before. Even with Frau Schatte accompanying on the piano, the music was rather perfunctory and seemed merely to be a prelude to a kind of cocktail party, which led to a lot of drinking and carousing and finally the young women pairing off with men and heading off toward other private rooms.

Tina's biggest problem was that during the past year she had not been charged tuition because Uta explained that the fees from her work at the recitals more than covered her training, room, and board. But if she no longer sang at the recitals, she feared Uta would again ask her to pay for lessons, and Tina simply had no money for that.

Voices had been singing downstairs, and when they stopped, Tina went into the large living room, where Uta was alone, arranging stacks of music.

The tall blond woman looked at her icily and acknowledged her presence simply by speaking her name.

"Tina."

"I hope you have a moment to talk," Tina said.

"Of course. What's on your mind?"

"I'm wondering why I no longer go with you to the out-of-town recitals."

Tina was sure she saw a shadow of anger momentarily darken the other woman's features, but Uta simply answered, "All right. That's one question. Have you any others?"

"I also wonder . . . perhaps this is foolish . . . but if you are angry with me. You have seemed to be cold and distant since—"

"Since you had your abortion?"

Tina thought it sounded vile and vaguely obscene when Schatte referred to it in that cold mechanical way. She merely nodded.

"Those are your questions?"

She wants to be cold. I can be cold, too.

"Yes," Tina answered crisply. "And I'd like some answers, if you don't mind."

"Very well. First. I am not taking you out of town with me because the other young ladies here need the experience."

"And I need the money," Tina said. "To pay for my lessons."

"Have I asked you for any money?" Schatte said.

"No."

"Then that is not an issue, is it?" Before Tina could speak, she went on. "The second reason is that I believe you have made great strides, so much so that I am planning a private concert for you here in New York in the spring. I am trying to book Carnegie Hall. I want you to save your strength, to practice well, and to sing all the time. I want you to be ready."

Tina was stunned. "Oh, Frau Schatte. A concert? Carnegie Hall?"

"Yes," the woman answered, but she did not smile, and her face showed no expression. Her voice still had the cold, impersonal tone of a city hall clerk.

Tina wanted to shout her happiness, to hug the woman, to shower her with thanks. She looked at the woman, hoping for some hint of encouragement, but Schatte merely looked back down at her music and said, "Now if you'll forgive me, I have to prepare my next lesson."

Tina turned and fled from the parlor. Back in her own room, she sat on the bed, crying softly. She looked up as her door opened and Flora, the maid, bustled in with an armful of clean linen. She seemed surprised to see Tina.

"I'm sorry, Tina. I knocked on the door a few minutes ago and I thought you were out. Is everything all right, honey?"

"I don't know. I just don't know what's happening."

Flora put the fresh linens on a chair, closed the door behind her, and came over to sit on the bed alongside Tina.

"Can I help?" she asked in her light singsong accent. She put her arm around Tina and drew the younger woman closer to her. Unrestrained now, Tina began to weep and, through her sobs, told Flora of her fears and her worries.

"What is it?" she finally asked. "What have I done wrong?"

"Have you asked your boyfriend?"

"Boyfriend? What boyfriend?"

"That Mr. Luciano," Flora said.

"He's not my boyfriend. He never has been."

Flora put her arms on Tina's shoulders and moved her back so she could see her face. "Oh, God, child, you really don't know, do you?"

"Know what? Oh, Flora, please."

"You have to promise me you won't say anything to Uta."

"I promise, I promise."

"A couple of months ago, one night while you were out, I think at your family's, this Luciano fellow came to the house to talk to Uta. She didn't know I was there, but I was in the next room and I heard everything."

Tina nodded in anticipation.

"He told Uta that you were in trouble and that it was her fault. And then he started on her. He told her that as far as he was concerned, she was nothing but a pimp and a whore, providing girls while she was pretending to provide music. He told her he wasn't going to do anything about it, but that you weren't going to be part of it anymore."

Tina felt the color drain from her face.

"He got real nasty. He told her she was supposed to be some kind of singing teacher, that she better—I remember just what he said—he said, 'You'd better get your fancy ass working to get Tina some real singing work or else.' Well, Uta got real mad. She said, 'Who do you think you are, coming here, threatening me?' And he said, 'I'm your landlord, lady. I own this building. I bought it last week. And I'm also a guy with a lot of friends. If you want, I'll send twenty or thirty of them over here some night and we'll see how much you like lying on your back with your legs in the air, getting humped all night long. For nothing.' I was peeking through the slats on the door then, and I saw Uta's face go all white. I never saw her afraid before. So he stands up and he unbuttons his fly and he says, 'I ought to take this out right now and show you what I think of you.' But then he buttons it back up and says, 'You're too old. I wouldn't even use you in one of my houses. But if you make any more mistakes with Tina, you might get your chance, lady. Take my word for it. You won't like it. Just you teach like you're supposed to teach. If you've got bills, send them to me.' So then he says something like 'I hope I don't ever have to talk to you again; the next time won't be so pleasant,' and then he leaves. Later I came back into the room from the other door, and Uta was sitting at the piano, just staring, and I asked her who the man was who just left, and she said, 'That was Tina's boyfriend. He's a well-known gangster. We were talking about her career.'" The black woman stopped and stared at Tina's face. "You don't know anything about this, do you?"

Tina shook her head. "He's not my boyfriend. We don't talk. We've never even gone out with each other."

"Did he arrange for the baby doctor?"

"Yes. But I thought he was just doing me a favor. We're from the same neighborhood. I haven't talked to him since before then."

"Well, girl, be careful 'cause someday he's going to hand you a bill for everything. And I wouldn't want to be around when it happens."

"So that's why Frau Schatte is arranging a concert for me."

"I guess so," Flora said. "I know I would if it was me. I saw that man's eyes, and I wouldn't want him mad at me." She rose from the bed. "Remember now, you can't say anything about this to Uta, or I'll really be in trouble."

"I won't say anything."

"All right. I'll come back later and do your bed," Flora said, walking to the door.

"Flora?" When the black woman turned, Tina said, "What did he mean that Uta was a pimp, arranging girls for clients?"

"What do you think Uta gets paid big money for? It's not for singing. We go somewhere, Uta and you or somebody else does some music, and then we have a party, and sooner or later everybody goes to bed with somebody. That's why Uta got those two new girls. They can't sing much, but, well, they'll do other things. But you just put that all out of your mind. Girl, you're going to be a singer. You're going to have a concert." And with a big warm smile, Flora left the room.

Tina touched the dry salt from her tears and thought, with astonishment, that she had been working for a pimp and never even knew it. She washed her face, then went downstairs to make a telephone call. From outside, she heard nearby church bells ringing carols, calling true believers to Christmas Eve worship.

I should go to church, she thought, while waiting for

her number to connect. *I'm a believer. I believe in anything.*

SOFIA SESTA—GOD, how she hated that new last name, hated it even more than her twisted father's name—leaned back in her new easy chair, folded her hands softly across her swelling belly, and cried.

Outside, she could hear the church bells calling people to midnight Mass, but she had decided earlier that she would not go. God simply did not care about her, and so she no longer cared about him. He had never done anything for her. Instead, he had sent her suffering and misery and pain. He was no God of love, no God of goodness. He was a bringer of evil.

The baby kicked, kicked so hard she winced. She smiled to herself and thought it strange that she should love this little bastard in her womb so much. The child kicked again. Sofia rubbed the spot on her belly lovingly and began softly crooning an old lullaby to her unborn child. She was sure it was a boy.

At least that way, as a boy, he will have a chance in this world.

She felt the tears roll down her face but could not question them. She knew why. She was crying because she was just so damned lonely, so totally alone in the world with nobody who really cared that much about her one way or the other.

The church bells still rang, but they were not part of her life anymore. It had been a long time since she was a little girl, and the sound of the bells was a call to enter the body of the church, to share in its mysteries, to dream one day of being a nun, holy, dedicated, consecrated in spiritual marriage as a bride of Christ.

Later, older, she had fallen in love with poetry and dreamed of herself as one of the new voices who, sad, alone, and unrewarded, would yet devote her life to bringing happiness to the rest of the world.

A nun? A poet? Sofia laughed bitterly. *I will be a breeder of bastards. At least that way I will be part of this world. Poetry is powerless in the face of evil and God. . . .*

The apartment was still and she looked it over with appreciative eyes. A week after she and Nilo had been married in the prison, a driver had come to bring her to the uptown offices of Salvatore Maranzano.

She had been impressed by the splendor of the place, by the beauty of the young red-haired secretary who sat inside the door, by the courtliness of Maranzano himself. A few years ago, she had often heard Maranzano referred to in contemptuous terms by the gees who frequented her father's restaurant as a silly, useless pretender to the throne of Joe the Boss, but clearly, despite their dire forecasts, the man had prospered.

There was almost a regal nature to Maranzano himself when he brought her into his office and poured tea for her. He greeted her with quiet dignity, inquired after her health, thanked her for having stood by his young friend, Nilo.

"Of course," he said, "you will be needing a place of your own."

"I hadn't thought of that," Sofia answered.

"You have someone to stay with you? A sister, perhaps, a girlfriend?"

She had shaken her head no, and Maranzano smiled a fatherly smile.

"Suetonius quotes Caesar," he said. " 'Meo tam suspicione quam, e crimine iudico carere oportere.' Which is usually—"

"Which is usually incorrectly translated as 'Caesar's wife must be above all suspicion,'" Sofia said. "Yes, I know of what you are speaking."

Maranzano should have sounded like a pompous ass, Sofia thought, spouting Latin at her like that, but somehow he hadn't. Somehow it all seemed of a piece with what she knew of the man.

"Ah, you know the language of our ancestors?"

"School and church, many years," Sofia said.

Maranzano seemed pleased. "Then you will understand the importance for your proper behavior. Quite aside from the matter of morality, of course. I expect Nilo will be coming out of prison before long, and when he does, it is imperative that he return to an unsullied home." There was an edge to Maranzano's voice. "For a woman as beautiful and as young as you, there will be many temptations, many opportunities to disgrace yourself and your family. That must not happen. A young lady who knows Latin must surely understand."

He phrased the last sentence almost as a question, but the implication of it, and the expression on Maranzano's face, was so blankly chilling that Sofia recognized it instantly as a threat.

She had said she understood.

The next day, she had stayed upstairs in her family's apartment as she had every day since the trial ended, unwilling to go downstairs to work in the restaurant, unwilling to be gawked at by strangers as the bride of the Dago of Death. Late in the afternoon, an envelope had come to her containing four crisp new fifty-dollar bills and a pair of keys. The messenger said that he would be bringing the same amount of money the first of every month as long as it was necessary. The keys, he explained, were to her new apartment. She was to live there as long as Nilo was away. Without her participation, a moving truck came later that same day to transport her pitifully few belongings to the new place, which was just north of Fourteenth Street, closer to Midtown Manhattan but still only a long walk away from Little Italy.

That had all happened three months ago and Sofia had since seen her mother only once, when the woman had taken some time off from her work at the restaurant and had come to her daughter's new place, only to sit quietly and stare at the newness and expense of it all. Sofia had not seen her father at all, and she lived in the fear that he might show up one night, uninvited, and try to force himself on her.

So when her mother, just before leaving, asked, "Who is paying for this apartment?" Sofia answered, "Nilo's employer. Mr. Maranzano."

Her mother nodded without comment, and Sofia added, "He has told me that if anyone tries to hurt me, he will kill them."

Her mother nodded again.

"You might tell that to Papa," Sofia said.

Her mother nodded and left.

If Matteo Mangini did show up some night, she promised herself, she had Maranzano's phone number. She would make that phone call and her father would never bother her again.

In Sofia's early weeks at the apartment, Tina had stopped over several times. It turned out to be a rather pathetic attempt to try being old girl chums again, but it had not worked. Or rather it had not been given a chance to work.

Tina had seemed distracted and dissatisfied with something involving her singing teacher, the German woman she always called Frau Schatte. Sofia wanted to talk about her pregnancy but was stunned into silence when Tina glibly admitted having had an abortion and that she had not even the faintest of inklings whom the father might have been.

"I have been with so many men," Tina said.

"Do you think that's good?"

A harsh laugh erupted from Tina. "Sure. One of them gave me that nice little gift I had in my belly. At least you know your baby is Nilo's."

Sofia was silent. They had changed so much, she thought, that they no longer had anything to talk about, and the visit quickly ended. Still, a week later, in another desperate attempt at frivolity, Tina had invited Sofia to accompany her on a visit to some of her new haunts in Greenwich Village.

The excursion promised to take Sofia to the places she had always dreamed of being, the dens of poets and writers, the hangouts of artists and freethinkers, but instead she found just a lot of drunks who seemed only to want to paw her and Tina.

She had left early, and not an hour after returning home there was a knock on the door. She opened it to Salvatore Maranzano, who said that he had just stopped in to see if she was comfortable in her new apartment or if she needed anything.

"I have everything I want, Mr. Maranzano," she said.

"That is good. Because I have heard stories that you've been seen in places where young wives should not be without their husbands. I knew such stories could not be true."

He had said no more than that, but it was enough. His voice had not changed, nor had his ever-present smile, but deep in the back of his eyes Sofia saw something that sent cold shivers through her.

After he left, she realized that Maranzano had somebody watching her—probably the apartment doorman to start with—and the next time Tina asked her to go out to a party, she declined and said she had no interest in such things.

TINA HAD NOT CALLED AGAIN, until this night, this Christmas Eve, when she arrived and asked Sofia if she wanted to go to Mass with her, a Mass that Mario was celebrating at his church in the Village.

"Then we could go over to my parents' house to celebrate," she said brightly.

But both of them knew somehow that Sofia would not go, and so there was a sense of sadness and futility to Tina's whole visit. Still Tina tried to put the best face on it. She talked of the old neighborhood and fondly recalled their close friendship when growing up together. The memories, so long forgotten since Sofia had tried to block all happiness from her heart, charmed and warmed her, and after they recalled one story of an escapade of theirs from parochial school, Sofia blurted out honestly, "Oh, Tina, I loved being your friend. I guess I always loved you most in the world. It just all seems so long ago."

"That's because you don't try to remember the happy times, the fun we had," Tina said. She talked of their visit one day to see her cousin, now known as Charlie Luciano, when Sofia had been having trouble with her father.

But just a little way into the story, Sofia realized that Tina was really trying to drag information out of her about Charlie. *When was the last time you saw him? Did you have a chance to talk to him? I wonder if he would remember us. I wonder if he would remember me.*

Sofia thought, *She has something going on in her head with Charlie, and I don't know what it is.*

Bluntly, she asked, "Has Charlie been your lover?"

Tina laughed merrily. "Oh, no. I bumped into him once and we chatted, but he never even called me. From what I understand, he has lots of women."

"He has a Russian woman," Sofia said.

"Oh?"

"Yes, a showgirl of some kind. She would come into the restaurant with him once in a while, and people would always treat her with respect, even though she wore as much makeup as a circus clown. It was clear she was Charlie's girlfriend." She could not resist adding: "She probably still is. He seemed very much taken with her."

"Is she very beautiful?" Tina asked.

"Barely as beautiful as you," Sofia said with a smile, "and not nearly so lovely as I am." She stood up and held out her belly with both hands, and both girls laughed.

Sofia collapsed back onto her chair, looked at Tina, and said, "Do you remember that once you promised me our lives would never be dull?"

"Yes," Tina said. "But I made no promises about their not being dirty."

The two young women sat quietly for a long time, and the evening grew long and tedious. Sofia tired early and wanted to go to sleep. Finally, she was forced to yawn and Tina said, "I can take a hint. I'll let you get some rest."

When she was gone, the church bells rang again. It was almost midnight.

She sat in the chair near the window. A light snow was falling and it seemed brighter on the streets outside than it did here inside her apartment. She looked at her new clock. It was already Christmas morning, way past time to go to bed. When she got up to turn off the lights, there was a light knock at the door.

She walked to the door and talked softly through the wood.

"Who's there?"

"Tommy."

Sofia stood very still. She could feel her heart pounding inside her chest.

"What do you want, Tommy? It's very late."

"I saw the light in your window. I want to talk to you. Please open the door."

"Go away, Tommy."

"Please."

She wondered if he was drunk. He did not sound it. She opened the lock on the door but kept the security chain closed, then peeked her head around to talk to Tommy through the opening. Her body was hidden by the rest of the door. He was wearing his police uniform and a heavy overcoat.

"What do you want, Tommy?"

"I'm going to try to free Nilo," he said, and then seemed at a loss for words.

"You arrested him. How are you going to free him?"

"I'm going to try," Tommy said. "Can I come in? I walked up here, off my post."

"No. It's too late."

Tommy leaned closer to the door.

"Sofia, I . . ." His words seemed to stick in his throat.

Sofia caught her breath and felt faint. But some things were best left in the past.

"Please, Sofia," Tommy said.

"Why? You got hot pants since your waitress left town?"

"Please."

"Go away; I'm married."

"I want to help you, Sofia."

Suddenly the macabre reason for Tommy's visit became clear. He wanted to free Nilo so that she and Nilo could live happily ever after.

Poor dumb Tommy. I don't care if Nilo lives or dies. I hate him, just as I hate you, Tommy. I hate everyone. Especially myself.

"Do what you want. I'm going to bed. Merry Christmas."

She closed the door and locked it again. Still standing there, she began crying.

This world is just a practical joke, and God, if there is a God, plays with our lives.

She turned out the lights and stood there for a long time waiting for Tommy to leave. Finally, she heard his footsteps going down the hall.

THE DINER WAS ONE OF A STRING of anonymous all-night places, set down in the shadows of the big ocean liners that used the Hudson River docks. It had been constructed from an old railroad car, and in a doomed, desperate attempt to give it a holiday atmosphere, some-one had hung a small green wreath on the front sliding door. But now with Christmas gone, and the new year of 1925 already a week old, the needles had fallen off the wreath and it was just a mass of twigs that looked like a bird's nest in training.

The diner was on the fringe of Tommy's beat, and he had stopped in occasionally for a meal. As far as he knew, he was the only cop to set foot in the place, whose usual clientele consisted of tough-talking dockworkers and an occasional sailor.

As he came inside out of the sleet and snow that was blowing across the Hudson, Tommy saw the man he was looking for and went up to his booth and stood beside it. He waited for what seemed like a long time before clearing his throat to draw the other's attention.

When the other man did not respond, Tommy said, "Mr. Kinnair?"

The other man turned to look at him. John F. X. Kinnair was younger than Tommy had imagined—youthful, almost baby-faced. He had light sand-colored hair, pale blue eyes, and a face filled with freckles. He held out his hand.

"Tommy Falcone, I presume." They shook hands and Kinnair nodded to the bench across the table. "Sit down. Have some coffee. You can call me Zave. That's short for Xavier. Most people do." He spoke in a rapid series of short bursts of words. "I'm glad you came. These people are giving me the evil eye and I started to worry about getting out alive."

"You're safe now," Tommy said with a grin.

"I thought me dear old uncle Timothy would be with you," Kinnair said in a thick, fake Irish brogue.

Tommy shook his head. This was a job where he needed another policeman he could trust. His father would have wanted no part of it, so he had called on Tony's old precinct partner, Detective Tim O'Shaughnessy.

"He's at the place already," Tommy said. "Just in case."

The waitress brought over a fresh cup and a pot of coffee and poured. The two men cradled their cups in their hands, as if to protect themselves from the cold outside. Tommy was surprised to realize he was a little nervous. He had never really talked to a newspaperman before and he did not trust them much.

Apparently, Kinnair could see that. "Okay," he said.

"Tim has told me what you're up to and that you wanted to meet with me, but why don't you just go through it in your own words."

"Why?"

"Because I want you to," Kinnair said. He smiled like a kid playing poker and holding aces in the hole. But when Tommy looked at the wall clock over the diner counter, Kinnair softened. "I want to hear it from you so that I know it's all for real," he said. "And so I can find out if I should trust you."

I've been a damned fool to come here, Tommy thought. *Papa was right. You can't trust a reporter.*

He stood up abruptly. "Maybe this is all a mistake," he said.

"Will you sit down and calm down?" Kinnair said. "Look, you came to see me because you didn't know of a lot of cops you could trust. At least, that's what me sainted uncle Timothy said. Is that true, or is it that you just don't trust anybody at all, including me? If that's so, you're going to lead a lonely life. But you might ask around. You won't find a cop who'll tell you I ever lied to him or tried to harm him. Who have you got but me?"

Tommy sat down, and the counterman, who had been watching them, seemed to relax and lean back against the wall near the big coffee urn.

"What do you want to know?" Tommy said.

"From the beginning. And I'll take notes."

Tommy moistened his lips. "Okay. You know I'm the one who brought in Nilo Sesta, the Dago of Death, the papers called him."

"Not my paper and I don't take to that," Kinnair said. "We called him Kid Trouble."

"That was his gang name."

"I know. I took the trouble to find out," Kinnair said.

"Nilo's a cousin of mine from the old country," Tommy went on. "I think I know him pretty well and I don't like him all that much, but he's family. You know what family is to us Italians. Okay, now I can believe that Nilo would have killed that guy in the theater, maybe did that ax job. But I don't think he did that kid. He's too smart and too careful for that."

He stopped to sip some coffee.

"So I was surprised when they came up with these two guys to testify so definitely that they saw him shoot the kid. And I keep hearing this story around that these witnesses that put him at the scene of the kid's killing were a put-up job. They were paid by Masseria because Nilo worked for Maranzano. You know all about that stuff, right?"

Kinnair nodded his head.

"So I started checking around, and I find out that these two witnesses, Pasquale Cierli and Alberto Numia, help run one of Masseria's stills. And they were working at the still at the same time they were supposed to be up-town seeing Nilo kill this kid."

"How did you find out? You Italians aren't supposed to talk."

Tommy held out his hands. "Among ourselves we do. We just aren't big on talking to the law. Or to the press."

Kinnair grinned.

"Anyway, I tracked down the still. It's in an old building on the waterfront. The two so-called witnesses *were* there that day and evening. And there were two other people working with them."

"Who are they?"

"Their name's Randisi. Two brothers."

"But they won't say anything, right?"

"They might. They used to work for Joe the Boss. These days, they have a different employer."

"Maranzano?"

"You said it, not me," Tommy replied.

"I don't know," Kinnair said. "You've got two Italians who maybe lied, and now you got two other Italians who are going to say that, and I don't know if anybody's really going to believe either of them. It's not much."

"There's more," Tommy said. "Whoever it was who called and told me where Nilo was didn't want him arrested. He wanted him killed. That's why those gunmen were waiting outside for us."

"Maybe they just wanted to kill *you*," Kinnair said.

Tommy shrugged and grinned. "I don't know. You're talking to a man without an enemy in the world. Anyway, I think after trying to have Nilo killed didn't work, then whoever's behind this bribed the witnesses to get him convicted and executed."

"I got to admit. You sound like you might be on to something. So what do you want me to do?"

"Nilo's scheduled to die in another ten days." Tommy searched Kinnair's face. It had seemed expressionless, but he noticed deep back inside the man's eyes something that looked like a gleam, a predatory gleam.

"So, you want me to do a story and get done through publicity what maybe you can't get done through the law. Is that it?"

Tommy nodded and Kinnair laughed aloud. "I love it," he said. "I love all this corruption shit. It's great ink. Just one question."

"Yeah?"

"What's in it for you?" Kinnair asked. "First you locked this Sesta up and now you're trying to free him. Why?"

"Do I sound like a jerk if I say I think he deserved a fair trial?"

"Not a jerk," Kinnair said. "But definitely odd."

Tommy shrugged. "Then I'm odd." He looked at the wall clock again. "I've kind of set up these two phony witnesses, this Cierli and Numia. I had one of the Randisis call them and say that they have to meet tonight to talk about something. Randisi is going to demand money to keep his mouth shut. When he does, you can be there taking it all down. You were supposed to have a photographer with you. Where is he?"

Kinnair motioned with his head. "In the car. He had a rough night and he's trying to sleep some of it off."

"Drunk? How the hell will he be able to work?"

"I've never known him to work sober," Kinnair said. "He'll do just fine. What do you want us to do? Get some pictures of these two guys coming out of the Randisis' place? Is that it?"

"You're the newsman, but I would think so," Tommy answered.

"And where will you be?" Kinnair asked.

"Your uncle and I will be outside," Tommy said. "We'll be ready to come in and arrest them if they try any rough stuff. If not, we get them outside when they leave the building."

THE RANDISIS LIVED in a semiabandoned building not far from the docks, a couple of blocks away from the usual accepted boundary of Little Italy. Their private still was in the basement, Tommy had explained, but its yeasty fumes hung out over the street, even on a night as cold as this one.

Tommy could smell it through the open car window

as Kinnair parked his sedan across the street. The photographer was slouched in the backseat, snoring occasionally. "I thought you said that my uncle Tim was out here keeping watch," Kinnair said.

"He's supposed to be. Maybe he ducked around the corner to take a leak. Let's wait a couple of minutes."

They waited awhile and Tommy took out his pocket watch and studied it. "We've still got fifteen minutes before Cierli and Numia are due."

"What if they came early?" Kinnair asked.

The same thought had just occurred to Tommy and he was already opening the car door. "Then we've got trouble," he said. "I'm going upstairs to check. You two better wait here."

Tommy slammed the car door shut against the wind. It seemed to have gotten colder and stronger. There was no sleet now; it was all snow and it was coming down in blinding quantities. Crossing the ice-slicked street was perilous by itself. He got to the entry to the Randisis' building, unholstered his pistol, and looked back. Behind him he could see the bigger shape of the photographer skidding along in his tracks. Kinnair had decided not to wait.

The stairway was lit by three bright bulbs suspended on cords with reflecting metal shields around them. Part of the moonshiners' early warning system, Tommy supposed. He felt totally naked as he walked upstairs. Each step creaked as he put his foot down. That too was part of the warning system. He remembered something his father had said to him years before, when he was just a child: *If you walk on the edges, the stairs don't squeak. They squeak most in the middle.*

Tommy moved his body to the side near the banister and went up foot over foot, almost crablike. The steps stopped their groaning under his weight. From the top of the stairs came the sound of a phonograph turned up to full volume. It was playing some tinny-sounding popular dance tune.

That did not seem right somehow. Tommy went upstairs faster. When he got to the top, he inched toward the door of the sole apartment on the floor and put his ear up against it. Except for the music, he could hear no other sound. That too did not seem right. He tried the doorknob gently. It was locked.

He was about to knock when he heard a strangled sound from inside the apartment, followed by a shout and the sound of dull heavy blows.

Tommy positioned himself in front of the door, brought his gun up into firing position, raised his foot, and slammed his heel into the door. The frame gave way and the door pivoted into the room.

Tommy lunged forward two steps into the apartment before he could stop. He dropped to one knee. Off to his side, he saw some people and glanced there to see a fat Italian woman sheltering two young children with her own body. He swung his head around in the other direction, and as he did he heard a buzzing zip past his ear. It stopped with a squishy plop somewhere behind him in the hallway. It was followed by a howl of pain and a curse. He raised his gun to fire, then stopped.

Two men were facing in his direction. He recognized them as Cierli and Numia. Cierli was standing at the open living room window, a window facing out on a brick wall and an air shaft. He had his knee on the middle of something that was sprawled across the windowsill and was leaning down on it with his left hand and arm while holding a gun in Tommy's direction with his right. It took Tommy a split second to make out that the something in the windowsill was a man—Randisi—bent over double backward, his head and shoulders hanging in space, his feet desperately scrabbling for a hold on the floor. Cierli was smiling. In the corner, bent up on the floor was Tim O'Shaughnessy, and Numia was squatted over him, his gun aimed at the cop's left ear.

"Stop, copper," Cierli said.

Tommy froze.

"Drop your gun."

Tommy hesitated and Numia shouted, "Drop it or your friend here gets a bullet in the ear. Now!"

Tommy cursed himself for stupidity. He had no choice. And then the room was bathed in a blinding flash of white light. The photographer must have set off a flash-bulb, and both Cierli and Numia glanced in that direction.

Tommy fired at Numia's temple and missed, hitting him in the throat instead. For an instant, he stood stunned at the explosion of blood and gore from his own body. He turned slightly to face Tommy, staring at him with tiny hate-filled eyes. Tommy shot him again, catching him this time in the middle of the forehead.

O'Shaughnessy moved quickly, rolling under the gunman's arm, pulling it down toward the floor. Numia went into his death spasms and his gun went off: once, twice, three times, each bullet impacting harmlessly into the bare floorboards.

Tommy turned back toward Cierli at the window. Again the room was flooded with brilliant white light, and Tommy blinked. When he opened his eyes, Randisi was gone from the window; his scream as he fell echoed through the apartment.

Cierli was turning, reaching for his own gun, a look of feral hatred on his face. Time seemed to slow down. Tommy aimed carefully at the man; he wanted to take him alive. He squeezed off a round at Cierli's knees. It missed the man's knees and, for an instant, Tommy thought it missed him entirely. Then Cierli stood slowly up, grabbing his belly with both hands. He looked down at it with horror and surprise. He opened his mouth as if to say something, and another flashbulb went off. Cierli staggered forward a step or two, raising his gun as he did. Tommy shot again, catching the man full in the chest this time, knocking him backward and spinning him around. When he dropped to the floor, he was clearly already dead.

Tommy walked over to the two dead men. Behind him he could hear Mrs. Randisi screaming, her children crying. Looking at Cierli and Numia, Tommy felt nothing but a mild disappointment that he had not been able to keep at least one of them alive as a witness to help Nilo.

Behind him, he heard Kinnair shout exultantly. "I love this. This is great shit!"

Tommy ran forward to O'Shaughnessy, who was scrambling to his feet. The burly cop looked past Tommy at his reporter nephew coming into the room and yelled, "Shut up, you silly ass. Three men are dead."

"Are you all right?" Tommy asked.

"I'm fine," O'Shaughnessy said. "And they talked a lot when they thought they had me. I think your cousin's going to get a break."

- *Not every illegal establishment in New York City was serving bootleg liquor. On Pell Street, in the heart of the city's Chinatown, could be found two dozen opium dens. On Luciano's orders, they operated without interference from the Masseria gang.*
- *Salvatore Maranzano moved his real estate business to larger offices in the New York Central*

Building at 230 Park Avenue, near Grand Central Station. Don Salvatore's new bodyguards were Steve Runnelli, Girolamo "Bobby Doyle" Santucci, and a young man named Joe Valachi. Valachi's bodyguarding career was interrupted in mid-1925 when he was sent to Sing Sing for three years for burglary.

- *When a minor thug tried to shake down one of Masseria's gambling games, Luciano dispatched Albert Anastasia to deal with him, who killed him and dumped the body into a bed of cement at a highway project on Manhattan's West Side. Three months later, the cement heaved and the body came to the surface. Bugsy Siegel said, "Dagoes make lousy roads."*

- *Joe Cooney, a whiskey-faced young Irishman who worked for Frank Costello, went to city hall each Friday dressed in a maintenance man's uniform. He carried a brown paper lunch bag. Just before noon, he went into the police commissioner's office and dropped the bag on the commissioner's desk. The "lunch" was actually ten thousand dollars in small bills, the Masseria mob's weekly graft payment. Masseria complained to Luciano that Costello was a spendthrift and protection was costing too much. Luciano warned Cooney not to be conspicuous in his maintenance uniform. "Change a lightbulb once in a while," he ordered.*

- *After a torrent of newspaper stories by John F. X. Kinnair about the perjured testimony, Nilo Sesta received a stay of execution, pending a new investigation of his trial.*

- *In Tennessee, John Thomas Scopes went on trial for teaching evolution in school. Clarence Darrow appeared for the defense, William Jennings Bryan for the prosecution.*

- *Flapper-thin was in; a diet plan was America's best-selling book; and a new magazine called* The Reader's Digest *grew in popularity.*
- *Tommy Falcone moved out of the family's apartment on Crosby Street and, with another law student, a young man from Michigan named Tom Dewey, took an apartment closer to Columbia Law School.*

CHAPTER 7

Spring 1925–Winter 1926

Thanks to a torrent of *Daily News* stories, written by John F. X. Kinnair, Tommy Falcone—always before perfectly content to be an anonymous patrolman—had gained a sudden reputation in police circles. For Tommy's part in trying to free Nilo, Kinnair had called him "a crusader for justice" and "New York's finest hero cop," and every time Tommy saw one of the stories he winced.

On the day after the governor said he would conduct an investigation into Nilo's trial, Tommy was called to city hall to the office of the police commissioner. He was ushered into a small side office, where he was surprised to meet Captain Milo Cochran, Tony's commander at the Italian Squad. Cochran got right to the point.

"The commissioner is probably going to promote you to detective," he said. He must have seen Tommy wince, because he asked, "What's the matter?"

"Captain, can we talk frankly?"

"Sure. Go ahead."

"It's a great honor and all, but I don't want to be a detective."

"Why not? There's a raise goes with it."

"I'm not a career policeman, Captain. I've just started law school and I like my patrol beat. I can pay the rent, I work steady nights, and that lets me go to school days."

"You could work nights as a detective, too," Cochran said. "That's why I'm here. I came to offer you a job with the Italian Squad."

Tommy shook his head. "My father works for you. He works days, nights, weekends, holidays. I wouldn't want a job like that for all the tea in China."

Cochran leaned back in his chair and stared at Tommy. After a while, he said, "Okay. That makes sense." He smiled. "It's not often somebody turns down a promotion. Anyway, I'll make sure your precinct doesn't switch you off nights. You can walk a beat until you wear out your shoes."

"Thanks, Captain, I appreciate that. One other thing?"

"What?"

"Could we keep this all quiet? I'm afraid I'll sound like a nut if anyone knows I turned down a detective's shield."

Cochran smiled. "You drive a hard bargain," he said. "Sure, we'll keep it quiet. Except if you bump into this newspaper guy, Kinnair, you might tell him. Just so he doesn't go beating up on us for not rewarding you."

"I'll see what I can do," Tommy said, and both men rose.

"A lawyer, huh?" Cochran said.

When Tommy nodded, the police officer said, "Well, who knows? Maybe you'll change your mind. If you do, look me up."

———

Tonight's for wine and love and laughter.
Sermons and soda water the morning after.

TINA REMEMBERED THE VERSE as she walked among the partygoers who packed the first-floor rooms of Frau Schatte's townhouse. The early editions of the papers had just arrived, and Tina's debut concert had been more than a success. She had been called brilliant and hilarious and stunning.

It had been Uta Schatte's idea not to limit the concert to only operatic arias, so Tina had sung opera but had also done English music-hall ditties and numbers from Broadway stage hits. She had even delivered a comedy routine.

Papa wasn't crazy about that, she thought. When Tony had come backstage to her dressing room in Carnegie Hall, along with her mother and brothers, he had said, "You don't only sing opera?"

"I sing everything, Papa," she said.

He looked at her for a long second, then said, "You sing everything beautifully, Tina," and she had known how hard it was for him to change his mind and his ambition for her in the wink of an eye, and she had hugged him, and never in her life had she felt more loved. Tommy and Mario, polite as ever, had left when the small dressing room got overcrowded. Only Nilo, still in prison, and Sofia, recuperating from a difficult childbirth, had not been present.

She had to start yawning before Tony took the hint and announced that everyone should leave because Tina had to go to sleep.

"Our songbird has worked very hard this evening," he said sternly, and began pushing people toward the exit. He himself was the last to go, and after he left, Tina hurriedly dressed again in one of the gowns she had worn during the recital and left for Frau Schatte's home, where she knew the real party would be under way.

There, with the noisy crowd of Uta Schatte's friends and hangers-on, and with the two other young singers whom Frau Schatte was training, they cheered the reviews in the papers. The two new students were sullen; they did not like Tina, and their animosity toward her, and the fact that she had been given a concert, was obvious.

But I don't care about that. Everyone is my friend tonight.

Her wineglass was never empty. Everyone wanted to talk to her, to touch her. Men fell in love with her and she wanted them, wanted all of them, and their women too. *Life is meant to be a sensual feast.* Someone drank wine from her slipper; others shared in the drink. She was floating, floating, floating.

They are all here to serve me, she thought, and felt like a princess as she held out her empty glass, knowing that someone would fill it. She did not even see who. She only heard a female voice somewhere near her ear saying something like, "I hope you like it."

Tina did not even sip it. The time was past for mere sips. Life was meant to be taken in huge gulps.

She gulped and swallowed. The drink started a slow warm burn at the top of her throat. It felt wonderful, glowing as it ran down. But something was wrong. The glow should have stopped, should have grown mellow, but it didn't. It was burning now. Tina fought back the panic for a moment.

She tried to hurry toward the kitchen, toward the salvation of water, but arms held her back. People who wanted to love her. She pulled herself away. She tried running. People stared at her. She tried screaming, but no sound would come. Her voice disappeared in a terrible, terrible burning. She could feel the blackness reaching up for her. She fell.

Tina awoke in a strange bed. She was alone and she was frightened. She tried to call out for help, but it hurt so badly and only a little scared sound would come. She tried to get out of bed, but she couldn't. She was too weak. She fell back on her pillows, crying, soundlessly, and unconsciousness came again.

When she awoke again, it was full daylight and she saw she was in a hospital room. She lay there silently, afraid to try her voice, afraid that nothing would come. It was then that she noticed a small blackboard and piece of chalk on the table next to her bed. Beside them was a bell. She picked up the bell and shook it in growing terror.

The door opened and her mother came in, followed by Mario. He was unshaven and he looked as if he had not slept for weeks.

Her mother rushed to her and held her to her bosom, patting her gently like the child Tina suddenly felt she was.

Mario waited patiently by the bedside, and when Tina finally looked up he spoke.

"First," he said, "don't speak. Don't even try."

She tried to make a sound, and he shushed her by putting his big thick index finger across her lips.

"Listen carefully," he said. "If you try to speak before you're allowed to, you'll lose your voice forever."

Tina looked around frantically. She saw the chalkboard and grabbed it up.

What? she wrote. *Why?????*

Trying hard to mask the emotion in his voice, Mario explained that someone had filled her glass with some sort of cleaning agent, probably lye. She was lucky that it was too diluted to kill her or to actually destroy her vocal cords. But she was not lucky enough to have escaped injury altogether, Mario said.

She wrote: *Who?*

"They think it might have been one of the other students at your teacher's place," Mario said. "Somebody who might have been jealous of you. Papa is looking for her now."

Tina lay back on her pillow and cried softly. After a while, she sat back up again. Her mother was watching her closely, worriedly.

Where is Uta? Tina wrote.

Mario seemed to hesitate. His mother looked at the note, then said, "That woman . . ." She made a curse out of the word "woman." "That woman sent your things to our home this morning. She said she could not be part of a scandal." Tina cried anew, never making a sound.

When she had stopped, Mario said, "The doctors tell me that your throat will heal in time. They say that you will have to take it easy; most importantly, you mustn't try to speak. They say you should get your voice back."

Tina again wrote on the chalkboard, slowly this time, fearing an answer.

Sing??? she wrote.

Mario shook his head.

When Tina's eyes filled with tears again, he came forward and kissed the top of her head. "So the doctors say," he said. "But they're only doctors. That's what prayers are for. And big brothers."

But she saw that he had tears in his eyes, too.

ON HER FIFTH NIGHT in the hospital, Charlie Luciano came to visit.

BACK IN JANUARY, Nilo had been prepared to die. On the seventeenth, the day set for his execution, Sofia, already large with child, had even come to see him. She told him the details, how Tommy had tracked down the two lying witnesses but had to kill them when they resisted arrest. There had been many newspaper stories, but she had heard nothing about a new trial. She touched his hand once and said good-bye. They did not talk about her pregnancy.

Nilo had eaten his last meal and said his confession to a priest with dirty fingernails, and they were just beginning to shave his skull when a guard came hurrying down the corridor, carrying the stay of execution.

That had been six months earlier, and since then there had been no statements, no announcement from the governor's office.

Mario had come to visit him once, to tell him that Sofia had delivered a baby boy and that both were healthy. Nilo had greeted the news with a grunt. He had not forgotten that it was Tommy and Mario who had taken him into custody.

If not for them, I would not be here. The Falcones are no longer friends or family. They are just more enemies in a world of enemies, more men who are marked for vengeance when the right day comes.

Mario had prayed; Nilo had ignored him. As Mario prepared to leave, Mario asked, "Is there anything you want me to tell anybody? Tommy? Anyone else?"

"Tommy? I've got nothing to say to Tommy."

"It was Tommy who got you that last stay of execution," Mario reminded him. "Everybody else was willing to let you die, but Tommy put his life on the line for you."

"Maybe he finally remembered that we were supposed to be brothers. We took an oath once. Did you know that?"

"I think Tommy remembers it better than you do," Mario said.

Nilo answered, "Don't come back. If I need anything, I'll ask Jesus."

Tommy, my brother. Some brother. Maybe Mario doesn't know, but I do—why Tommy was trying to help me. It's because he feels guilty 'cause my wife had his baby.

Although Sofia had never told him that, he was convinced that Tommy must be the father, because he had never heard of Sofia ever being even near any other men.

He's been using my wife as his personal whore, and I'm rotting away in here and they're rolling around in my bed. A real brother might have come to see me, but he can't; he's ashamed to even look me in the eye.

On a day in July, Maranzano's driver—a hulking man who always introduced himself by all three of his Christian names, Dominick Rocco Salvatore, but was nevertheless always called just "Rock"—had shown up.

"Don Salvatore sends you his warmest regards," he had said formally.

"Thank him for me," Nilo said. "He is always in my thoughts."

Rock had looked around to make sure no guards were eavesdropping and then had leaned closer to Nilo. "Listen, Kid, it's not over yet. The governor owes Don Salvatore some favors, and the don is trying to call them in. There might still be a chance. A lot of people now figure you was framed."

"Anybody ever find out who bribed those witnesses against me?"

Rock hunched his massive shoulders and looked

around again suspiciously. "Masseria's guys. The talk we hear is that maybe it was Joe Adonis."

Nilo nodded. "If I ever get out of here, there'll be a lot of debts to collect."

"Just stay tough, Kid. Anyway, the rest of the news. Your wife had a rough time with the delivery, but she's getting better. The don goes to visit her every so often to make sure she's okay. I saw the baby once and he's real cute. He looks just like you."

Nilo wanted to scream.

Falcone blood, Nilo thought. *We all have it. And now so does Tommy's kid.*

A week later, at 9:30 at night, the door to death row opened with the groan of steel rolling across concrete. Nilo looked up casually and saw the assistant warden walking toward him. He set down his book and stood without speaking. The guard unlocked his cell.

"Might as well get moving, Sesta," the warden said in a bitter voice. "Gather up your things."

"What for?"

"You're moving out of here."

"Where?" Nilo asked slowly, wondering why they were moving him to another cell.

"Dannemora. You're going to Dannemora. The governor decided you don't deserve a new trial, but he's changed your sentence to life in prison."

"I'm not being freed?" Nilo asked. He had expected death or freedom, not some horror in between.

The assistant warden laughed.

"No, and with luck you'll die behind bars. Get packing."

Nilo said sarcastically, "I'm going to miss you."

"You think that's a joke, but you *are* going to miss me. This place is a picnic compared to Dannemora. You know what they call it? Little Siberia. Where every year seems like a hundred."

TOMMY FALCONE HEARD about Nilo's life sentence in a telephone call from Kinnair, the newspaper reporter. He hung up, feeling a grim satisfaction.

At least, Nilo will live. And probably he was guilty, and maybe in heaven I will have to answer for saving a guilty man, but for now I have no arguments with myself.

He wondered if Sofia had gotten the news. Several radio stations in New York had recently begun broadcasting news items, but he did not know if she had a radio or not.

He put on a fresh shirt and took a Broadway trolley to the Fourteenth Street stop.

When he knocked, she answered the door. He had not seen her in nine months and he was surprised to see how good she looked. He had heard that her delivery had been very difficult, but dressed now in a multicolored cotton housedress, she looked as healthy and as pretty as he had ever seen her.

"Tommy, what brings you here?"

"I've got something to tell you. Can I come in?"

"Just for a minute. It's almost the baby's feeding time."

He stepped into the apartment. "How is the baby?"

"He's fine. Even Mama thinks he's fat enough," Sofia said with a smile. "Can I make you some coffee?"

"No, thanks. I'm only staying a minute. I just came up to tell you that Nilo got a reprieve."

"What does that mean?"

"It means his death sentence has been lifted. The governor changed it to life in prison."

He had not known what kind of reaction she would

have to his news, but he had not expected her to fall back onto a stuffed chair and laugh, a bitter, angry laugh.

"So he gets life," she said. "Why couldn't they just be done with it?"

"I'm sorry, I don't understand. I thought you'd be happy."

"As long as Nilo lives, I am Mrs. Sesta. I cannot divorce. I cannot remarry. I live my life alone. My son grows up without a father. And you expected me to be happy?"

"I'm sorry," was all he could think to say. "I just thought—"

"Never mind. How is Tina?"

"She's okay. She's back home. Still can't talk above a whisper, but she's alive."

"Will she sing again?"

"No."

"She used to come and see me," Sofia said. "We would talk about old times. I read every one of her reviews from her concert. I was so happy for her. And then I heard . . . Did they ever catch who did it?"

Tommy shook his head. "She vanished. One of the other students at Tina's singing class who just got jealous, I guess. Nobody's been able to find a trace of her."

"She probably doesn't want to see me," Sofia said. "But tell her, please, how sorry I was." She began to cry softly. "I wasn't even able to go to the hospital to see her because I was sick myself after the baby."

"I know she understood," Tommy said. He rose from the sofa. "Well, I just wanted to let you know. About Nilo."

"I appreciate the thought." Sofia rose, too. "Would you like to see your . . . your cousin, I guess he is?"

"Is it any bother?" Tommy asked.

"No. He's just a greedy little thing. All he wants to do is eat and sleep. Guests don't bother him at all."

She led the way into her bedroom where the baby was asleep in a wooden slatted cradle. Tommy looked at him and saw Nilo's face on the boy. He had long eyelashes and wide-set eyes and a supple full-lipped mouth that now, in his sleep, was beginning to twist, as if the child were puzzled about something.

"He's beautiful," Tommy said. "He looks like—"

"Like me," Sofia interrupted. "Everyone says so." She bent over and lifted the baby from the crib, carefully wrapping the thin cotton blanket around his feet. With no trace of self-consciousness, she opened the buttons on her housedress, pulled one side of it back, exposing a breast, and put her son's mouth to it. Without even opening his eyes, he began suckling.

Tommy found it hard to take his eyes off Sofia's breast. It was larger, fuller, than it had been that . . . that one night.

"I'm sorry, I'm embarrassing you, aren't I?" Sofia said.

"No," Tommy answered. "It's just that I haven't been around mothers and babies much. I'll leave now."

Sofia was looking down at her son. "Suck, you greedy thing," she said. She glanced up at Tommy, and her eyes were bright, almost electric, with a curious passion, but it passed quickly and she said, "Thank you again for coming by, Tommy. Tell Tina I think of her."

"I will. And when you see Nilo, tell him . . ." His voice trailed off because he could think of no message he wanted to send to his cousin.

Sofia just shook her head.

SHE HAD NOT CHANGED all that much, Tina thought. At least not that anyone could see. She still looked the same. The face was the same and so was the body.

But the soul had changed and so had the voice. What had once been a silken rippling sound that coursed easily through three octaves was now a hoarse rasp.

Even so, the doctors said she had been lucky. Most people who suffered such a ferocious assault would never again be able to speak, but she had been the recipient of a minor miracle.

Mario's miracle, she thought bitterly. *Some miracle, God. You've taken my voice and left me with the croak of a frog.*

She tried to sing every now and then, probably more out of curiosity than anything else, but she always gave it up quickly. She could not stand the raspy, sandpapery sound that came from her mouth. The only time she sang anymore was in the shower after making love to Charlie. She couldn't help herself then; the man just made her feel so good. She laughed again: from holier-than-thou prima donna to gangster's moll in one short year.

Luciano had come to her in the hospital. She had been there almost a week when he appeared. Her hospitalization had reached that awkward point where it was obvious the patient was not going to die and so the shirttail relatives no longer had any morbid reason to visit and a patient was left with the same close relatives at bedside day after day, talking the same platitudes, recalling the same past events with each other, often ignoring Tina, until it all grew so ferociously boring that Tina just wanted them all to leave.

Frau Schatte had never visited; neither had anyone from her Greenwich Village crowd. That had hurt.

Sofia had not visited, either. Tommy and Mario told Tina that she had been ill since the birth of her son and so she had a reason, but Tina missed her nevertheless. Sofia was possibly the only person in the world with whom she could really speak. She was left instead with this unending parade of relatives, like one of those clown cars at the circus, where the same people kept coming through the door over and over and over again.

Then that evening, after everyone had blessedly left, Luciano had appeared at her door.

"Hello, beautiful," he said.

Tina still was not allowed to speak. She had written her response on the slate: *Hello.*

"I won't stay long," he said. He looked slightly embarrassed.

Tina had gestured for him to sit down, but he remained standing, running the brim of his hat around and around through his long thick fingers.

"Look, I don't know how to say this real good. I talked to your doctors and they said you're going to need a lot of help. I know your old man isn't exactly made of money so . . . well, I've arranged for the bill to be taken care of."

Tina rose up from her pillows, starting to protest, more out of form than any real desire. Luciano took a couple of steps backward, almost as if trying to retreat from his good deed, then stopped and approached her again.

"Don't worry," he said. "Your father will never know. None of them in your family. It'll be our little secret. And besides, I expect you to pay me back when you're a rich and famous singer."

Tina had started to cry then. She hadn't wanted to, but she did just the same. Luciano had tightened his jaw.

"One other thing," he said. "The little chippie that did this to you . . . she swallowed a bottle of lye herself. And nobody was around to try to save her. But nobody knows about it. So mum's the word."

Tina lifted the chalk but could write nothing. She was too horrified.

"Well," Luciano had said. "I guess I've got to get going. I'll come back and see you in a couple of days, if you don't mind. You're looking terrific, kid."

He had started to leave, but Tina had grabbed hold of his jacket sleeve. He stopped and looked at her again.

She scrawled furiously on her chalkboard in big capital letters: *WHY?*

Luciano read the note, then shrugged.

"Damned if I know," he had said. "Maybe because I never forgot the first time we met and you looked down your nose at me like I was a pile of garbage. Maybe I just want to take that look off your face. God only knows. I don't."

He had moved gently away, stopping in the doorway to smile at her once more, and to tip his hat.

OUTSIDE THE HOSPITAL, Luciano got into his car. Ben Siegel, at the wheel, looked over the seat and asked, "Did you screw her?"

"You are crude, Benny. Even for a thug, you're crude."

"I guess that means she wouldn't put out for you. You shoulda just stuck it to her anyway."

"In the hospital, right? Benny, you're not only crude, but you're a little nuts. No wonder they've started to call you Bugsy."

Angrily, Benny turned away and lurched the car forward out of the hospital parking lot.

"Not to my face, they don't," he snarled.

Luciano leaned forward, over the back of the seat, and tousled Benny's hair affectionately. "No, that's true. But do yourself a favor, Benny. Try to get a little class, will you? We're gonna go a lot of places, and you gotta be able to go there, too."

Benny grunted. Luciano sank back against the car's rear seat and then said, "By the way, I can screw her anytime I want, even in the hospital. I'm just saving it."

"For what?"

Luciano smiled. "For when I can do the most harm."

"I still want seconds," Benny said.

TINA HAD SPENT another three weeks in the hospital— with Charlie visiting her every few days—and then had moved back to the Falcones' apartment, but after a week she knew it would not work out.

Her father was in a snit because somebody had paid the hospital bill and he could not find out who it was.

"Somebody who said she was a patron of the arts," he said. "And she paid in cash. Who could that have been?"

"I don't know, Papa," Tina had lied.

He asked her every day. Every day, she lied. Meanwhile, her parents were trying to baby her all the time, and by the end of the summer Tina had moved out, found an apartment in the Village, and a job as a waitress. After a few days on the job, one evening, walking home, she varied her path so she could walk by the townhouse of Frau Schatte.

There were no lights on in the house, and attached to the brick front was a FOR SALE sign.

Tina stood there, looking at the sign for a moment, trying to figure whether anybody was still living inside, when a voice behind her said, "She decided to move out of town."

She turned to see Charlie standing at the curb behind her. His big black car was parked across the street; she recognized Benny behind the wheel. "Pretty quick decision," Tina said. "I'm surprised she didn't even let me know."

"I think it was health reasons," Luciano answered, and the look on his face told Tina everything she needed to know about Frau Schatte's decision to move. She had probably run out of town to escape Luciano.

But why? she thought. *What am I to him?*

"I never got a chance to thank you," she said. "About the hospital bill. About everything."

He waved his hand airily, dismissing it as nothing.

"You've made my father crazy," she said, smiling. "He spent weeks trying to figure out who the mystery woman, the 'patron of the arts,' was."

"Yeah, I was busy that day. I had a friend do it for me. He'll never know who." They stood awkwardly for a moment and Luciano said, "Come on, I'll ride you home."

When they stopped in front of her apartment house over on the West Side, Luciano asked her, "How's the new digs?"

"They'll do," she said. "Would you like to come up for coffee?"

Luciano mulled the idea for a moment. "Yeah, sure," he finally said.

"You too," she said to the driver.

"He's got some stuff to do," Luciano said. He helped Tina out of the car and leaned over to Benny. "I'll call you when I need you," he said. "Make sure everything goes all right tonight."

"Okay, Charlie."

She had thought her apartment, furnished with leftovers and castoffs, looked pretty presentable, but now, with company here for the first time, she surveyed it with a more critical eye and decided the whole apartment was shabby. She tried to apologize for it, after pouring coffee for her and Luciano, but he just put his hand over hers, as she stood at the table alongside him, and said, "Hey, Rome wasn't built in a day. Someday, kid, for you it's going to be money and mansions."

She put the coffeepot down on the table, then leaned over and kissed Luciano full on the lips, a long searching kiss, probing his mouth with her tongue. He slipped his hand under her sweater to cup her breast and then reached inside her brassiere to squeeze her nipple, and Tina had gasped at the touch. It had been so long, she thought, since she had had a man. Since before her . . . accident.

She pulled away from Luciano, grabbed his hand, and pulled him to his feet. She licked a forefinger and touched it to his cheek.

"I don't want that coffee now," she said.

"Oh? What *do* you want?"

"You know very well what I want," she said, and led him to the bedroom. Once inside, she turned to face him, and he said, "You sure you want to do this, kid? Once you do, there's no going back."

Tina smiled, dropped to her knees, and reached out her long delicate fingers for him.

Charlie had spent the night. In the morning, when Tina awoke, he was already on the phone. She lay in bed for a while, listening to his husky voice, barking out orders she did not understand. She was surprised to hear him identify himself as "Three-Twelve" on the phone.

After a while, she got up and made a pot of coffee, and when Luciano came into the kitchen she asked, "Would Three-Twelve like a cup of coffee?"

Luciano grinned and nodded. As she poured the coffee, he said, "You never know who's listening in on telephones. So it's best sometimes not to mention names."

"But why Three-Twelve?"

"You think about it," he said.

"I'll think while I'm cooking breakfast."

"Forget cooking. Get some clothes on."

When Tina did, Luciano took her to the Plaza Hotel, where he seemed well known, and they ate breakfast there. And in the cab, it came to her and she said softly to him, " 'Three' is for *C,* the third letter. 'Twelve' is for *L.* It's your initials."

"I always like a smart girl," Luciano said.

He came to her apartment often after that, usually three or four times a week. She never knew when he might come, and without realizing it, she managed always to stay around her apartment, not even venturing out to the movies. When he did show up, seeing him was like opening a Christmas present. Sometimes they would make love as if he had to run to catch a train, and Charlie would leave right after. Other times, he spent the night, and Tina liked those times best because they would lie in bed afterward and talk, and Tina had few people to talk to anymore.

Luciano never quite admitted to her that he was a gangster. Instead, he described himself, as "a businessman who gives people what they want."

"You sure do that for me," Tina said with a giggle.

"Aaaah, you Sicilian girls just love getting laid. If it wasn't me, it'd be somebody else."

"No, Charlie, not anybody like you," she said, and meant it.

One night, she remembered the story her father had told about how Luciano and Benny Siegel got together, and she just mentioned conversationally, "You and Benny seem very close. Did you grow up together?"

"Nahh, we met once having a fight over some woman. And we got to be friends. But Benny's important."

"Why's that?" she asked. "Important" was the last word she would ever have applied to Benny Siegel.

" 'Cause he's Jewish. So's my other friend, Meyer."

"Why does that make them important?"

"Because it's not gonna be too long before the cops and the law and everybody is after people in our business. What happens then is that everybody starts fighting to keep their own little piece. The Jews fight the Italians, and the Irish fight everybody, and we all hate each other and we all get hurt. But Benny, Meyer, I'm bringing them in with me. The Irish too. Your brother taught me that."

"My brother? Tommy?"

"No. The one who's the priest. I heard him one day in a sermon and that's what he was talking about. Everybody getting together and being one big family. And I thought it works for the church. They got Irish and Italians and every kind of priest and they all seem to get along, and I figured if it works for the church, it'd work for our business too. Italians, Jews, Irish—someday, we're gonna be all one big organization."

"I thought the Mafia already was a big organization."

"Yeah, but that's what's wrong with it. These guys at the top, they think it has to be just Italians or just Sicilians or just Sicilians from some little jerk-off village someplace, and they don't get it. Capone's like that in Chicago, fighting with everybody so just wops run everything. And it's stupid. If we all get along, we all go a lot farther."

"You've got good ideas, Charlie. Does anybody listen?"

"Nobody has to listen," he said. "Not now. When the time comes, then they'll all listen. Now shut up and fuck."

Charlie took to giving her money to pay her rent, and

with her meager savings almost depleted, Tina was grateful for it. Just before Thanksgiving, she had her second abortion. Charlie paid for it again.

She knew, of course, that Charlie had other women right along. There was one in particular whose name he would drop unwittingly in conversations—with the Russian-sounding name of Gay Orlova—and Tina knew this must be the showgirl whom Sofia had seen come into Mangini's Restaurant.

In her innermost heart, Tina was jealous of the other woman, but she knew she had no right to be. Charlie showed her more kindness than he had any earthly reason to do, and, besides, when he was with Tina he was always enough man for her. Whatever he did, that was fine with her.

Because of her abortion, she missed Thanksgiving Dinner with her family, giving them an excuse that she would be out of town.

She went over a couple of days later, at dinnertime, and found her mother and father alone in the apartment.

Her father nodded to her. "Luciano give you the night off?" he asked.

"Papa," her mother said sharply.

"Yes, he's not coming over tonight," Tina said, feeling her own anger rise.

Hate it all you want, Papa, but Charlie paid for me in the hospital, and when you couldn't even find her, he found and punished the woman who tried to kill me. You've got no right to say anything.

"Probably with somebody from one of his houses," Tony said.

"We don't discuss how he makes his living," Tina said.

"Well, maybe you ought to. He's a pimp, for one thing. He's a bootlegger, for another. He runs extortion rackets and people get killed. Innocent people. He's the lowest form of crook."

"Some people would say he's an honest crook because he's honest about being a crook. Not like some people, like some cops for instance, who pretend to be honest and steal everything they can."

Tony stood up from the table, the veins in his neck pulsing. For a moment, Tina thought he was going to strike her. Instead, he sat back down heavily.

Tina crossed the room and kissed her mother fondly. "I have to go, Mama. Give Tommy and Mario my love."

"If you ever went to confession, you could tell Mario yourself," her father snapped.

"And thank God for what he did to my throat? No, thank you." She looked at her mother. "You're welcome to visit me anytime, Mama," she said, and left. For a few days after that, she entertained her delegation of brothers who had come by "to talk sense" to her, but she quickly made it clear that she was all grown up and would live her own life. They did not come by so often now.

Things went smoothly between Tina and Luciano until just before Christmas, and then he began staying away for days at a time. When he did reappear, he seemed always in a hurry to be off again. A quick roll in bed, a change of clothing, sometimes a meal, and then he was gone. He said it was business, but Tina doubted it. She had seen lipstick on his undershirt, though even that was nothing new.

Then two days after Christmas, a Christmas that Tina spent alone, Charlie reappeared and announced that his business was all wrapped up for the time being. They made love all that day and the next and the one after that, stopping only to gorge themselves on food that Charlie had delivered. In between bouts of lovemaking and feasting, Tina showered luxuriously and sang out at full voice once, unaware of what she was doing.

That time, Charlie came to the bathroom door and opened it and seemed to be watching her. Despite the hot water, she felt a little shiver of pleasure. Charlie did that to her when he watched her; she knew he loved the way she was made.

"You're singing pretty good these days," he said.

Tina blushed.

"For a bullfrog," she said.

Charlie only smiled and went back into the bedroom.

Two days before New Year's he left in the morning without waiting for her to wake up. She had long since quit her waitressing job, and, as usual, Charlie left money for her on the kitchen table.

When he didn't call that day or the next, Tina was annoyed. She knew she had no claim on him and that she was most likely just one of a string of women, but still she thought it would have been nice, just once, to have gone out to be with people.

That afternoon, on New Year's Eve, she was in a deep depression when the telephone rang.

"This is Three-Twelve," the deep voice said, and she could almost imagine him chuckling. "I'm sending over some things. Try them on real quick and make sure they fit. If they don't, the messenger'll take them back and get you a size that does. There'll be a car around for you at ten."

The clothes fit perfectly, to the relief of the visibly nervous messenger from the women's clothing store. There was a midnight-blue evening dress with lots of sparkles and bangles—the kind of thing that would have been incredibly gauche if it had not been done exactly right.

The car was on time, with a driver she had seen before.

His name was something Adonis, and she thought, in a smooth, oily way, he was very handsome. He pulled up in front of Ross's on Fifty-second Street. Charlie's club had been a small, ramshackle affair when she had been there before, but now it had an awning and lights and a doorman and swirls of well-dressed people coming in and out.

"Good evening, Miss Falcone," the doorman said, tipping his hat as he opened the door. "Charlie's inside waiting for you. Everybody sure hopes you like the joint."

The nightclub, like the dress, had been decorated up to the edge of vulgarity and then beyond it to some sort of fantastic style all its own—all swirls and cut glass and a new polished black stuff called Bakelite, and it was all very exciting in its way.

Charlie was just inside the foyer, greeting guests, and it took him a couple of seconds before he could disengage himself from a very high-society couple and come over to her to escort her into the club's main room.

"It's marvelous," Tina said.

"I was going to name it Tina's Place, but I wasn't sure if you'd like that. So I called it Ross's instead."

"Should I ask who Ross is?"

Luciano grinned. "Me," he said. "Remember what I told you. It's not just about Italians anymore. Uptown nowadays, I'm Charles Ross." He leaned over and whispered in her ear. "And I'm glad you're looking so good 'cause the place is filled with politicians tonight. See that one over there?" He nodded toward a sleekly good-looking man sitting at a corner table.

"Yes?"

"His name's Jimmy Walker. He's going to be the next mayor."

He took her to his table and they held court with guests until after the balloons had fallen and the confetti had been thrown and the band had played "Auld Lang Syne." Tina thought that either Luciano's Russian girlfriend had been dumped or she was going to be in one terrible mood this evening.

Luciano asked her what she was smiling about, and Tina responded, "Just thought of something funny."

"Tell me all about it later," Luciano said, and gave a signal to the bandleader, who stepped to the front of the stage and announced, "Ladies and gentlemen, we are very fortunate to have with us tonight a brilliant star, back to grace the heavens of New York City. And if we're lucky, maybe she'll favor us with a number. It's an honor to present Tina Falcone."

The spotlight turned and caught them just as her name was announced. Tina gasped. She wanted to run. Luciano put his hand on her arm.

"Sing what you sang in the shower the other day."

"I can't," she said.

"You do it," he ordered sternly.

Dumbly, as if in a fog, Tina got up and walked to the stage. The crowd was still noisy. She looked at the bandleader, who said, "We'll follow you."

She started, without accompaniment, with "It Had to Be You." The band came in after the first two lines, and by the time she reached the chorus the room had quieted down. As she finished the chorus, there was a definite hush. Tina was scared. Her voice no longer sounded like it belonged to her. There were too many burrs and cracks and trembles in it, and she thought the crowd was embarrassed for her, silent only to spare her feelings. Somehow she finished the song and the audience was deathly still. She wanted to run, to get anywhere away from that stage. She looked over at Charlie in desperation, started away from the stage, and then a voice from a far table—

she recognized the man as the one named Jimmy Walker—yelled, "Bravo. Bravo."

And the whole crowd erupted into a clapping, shouting, stomping frenzy. Tina began to cry. People began shouting, "Encore. Encore."

Tina stepped back to the microphone and held up her hands for silence. She looked over at Charlie.

"Thank you, ladies and gentlemen. It is going to be a very fine New Year, isn't it?" Her smile dazzled the room. "This song has special meaning for me. It is for my friend . . . and the best man I know . . . Charlie L— Charlie Ross."

She turned back to the band.

"How about 'My Man,' boys?" she said.

SOFIA HEFTED THE BABY onto her left hip and leaned forward to pour coffee.

"He's a fine-looking baby," Mario said.

Sofia smiled and asked, "So how'd you spend New Year's Eve, Mario? Out at your favorite speakeasy?"

"Maybe I should have been. You know your cousin, Salvatore—he's calling himself Charlie Ross now— opened a new club uptown. And guess who the hit of the evening was?"

"I've already heard," Sofia said. "Tina called me." She hesitated. "She seems to be very happy with Charlie."

Mario shook his head slowly.

"You don't approve?" Sofia said. She put the baby into a playpen, where he lay quietly, looking at the overhead electric light.

"No, I don't. She is hurting herself badly. Not just here and now but in the eyes of God."

"You really believe in that stuff, don't you?"

"Of course. What else is there?"

"Well, you can worry about her soul in the hereafter, but I'd say she's got things going pretty well in the here and now. She's going to be a star again, Mario. After coming back from the grave."

"And in the process, she's become the mistress of a gangster and she's broken with her family. She and my father haven't spoken for months. It's tearing him apart."

"Italian fathers are too close to their daughters, anyway," Sofia said. The baby started to whimper, so Sofia took a cookie from a plate that she had put in front of Mario and handed it to him. For a moment, both the priest and the young mother watched the child laughably gumming the confection.

"Is there ever a chance you could talk to her?"

"Sure," Sofia said bitterly. "I'm a great example. Tina's going out with a gangster and I'm married to one who's doing life at Dannemora. I'm sure she'll love a lecture from me."

When Mario was silent, Sofia asked him, "How's Tommy? Does he have a girlfriend?"

"I don't know," Mario said. "There was that waitress who went off to try to become an actress, but I haven't seen him with any other girls since then. Tommy's got all those law-school classes and he's still walking a beat, so I don't know how much time he's got for a girlfriend."

"Yeah, college can take your time," Sofia said. "You know I'm going to NYU, don't you."

"No, I didn't know that."

"A couple of days a week. Nilo's friends pay for me. They're paying for this place too. I'm studying accounting."

"Was that Nilo's idea?" Mario asked.

"His idea? That's a laugh. Nilo's never thought about

anybody in his life except himself. No, Nilo's boss, Mr. Maranzano, told me I had to go to college. He arranges for somebody to come and take care of Stephen on the days I'm in school."

Mario smiled. "Good for you," he said. "You're young. You should get out and be with people."

"I'm young and I'm married to a man I hope I'll never see again. I think that would just about make my life finished, wouldn't you agree?"

"Of course I don't agree."

"Then you've been inside the church too long." They were silent for a moment; then Sofia scooped up the baby and carted him off to the bedroom. She was gone long enough to change him and put him to bed. When she returned to the kitchen, Mario was reading the morning paper.

"It says here that many Sicilians are still fleeing the island because this fellow Mussolini is arresting so many people."

"Yeah. And they're all coming here, and Maranzano is hiring every one of them."

"Are you serious?" Mario asked.

"Of course I am. Mr. Maranzano, for some reason, thinks of Nilo as a son, and he comes here sometimes in the evenings to sit and talk with me. He told me all these people are coming to New York without money or prospects and he feels obligated to try to give them jobs."

"See how it's easy to be wrong," Mario said. "All I ever heard about Maranzano was that he was a gangster, and it turns out that he's a philanthropist."

"Oh, Mario, don't be a fool."

When the priest looked at her quizzically, she said, "All the people fleeing Sicily are Mafia people. That's who Mussolini is trying to eliminate. So these criminals are coming here and Maranzano is hiring them for his mob as soon as they step ashore. Just the way he did with Nilo."

"Is it that bad, Sofia?"

"It's worse. I hate my husband; I hate my life." She looked at the baby. "But my son . . . his life will be different."

"Did you ever think of an annulment?" Mario asked.

Sofia laughed. "Forget it. Mr. Maranzano would never stand for it. I'm trapped."

"Nobody's trapped," Mario said.

"We're all trapped."

THEY HAD BEEN LATE COMING OUT of the waiting area, and Fatso, the guard, had been waiting for them, to put them through their paces and teach them the respect that must be shown for each and every guard at Dannemora, demonstrating on all of them the effectiveness of the steel-headed wooden clubs all guards carried, and so Nilo had missed his supper. He did not give a damn. He was tired to the point of exhaustion and he only wanted to sleep.

Fatso led them up the four flights of stairs to the narrow walkway that ran along 25 Gallery, South Hall. He roughly shoved them one by one into their cells. Nilo's was number 24. He stumbled inside and stopped.

He had heard talk on the way up about how bad Dannemora was, but nothing had prepared him for this. The cell at Sing Sing was small, crowded, almost inhuman, but this one was even worse. It had no toilet. It was filthy and smelled bad and water trickled down its cold walls. Already, Nilo's teeth were chattering.

Fatso was barking orders out on the walkway. Lights

were to be out at 10:00 and each man was to be in his bunk from then until wake-up call at 6:30 the next morning. There would be bed checks every hour, even during the night. There would be no talking anytime a prisoner was in his cell.

Nilo stretched out his arms on either side; both sets of fingers touched the side walls. He extended them overhead and he touched the ceiling. He walked the cell from front to back: three and a half steps.

It is too small, he thought. *Too damned small. They would not keep even animals in a place like this.*

He could not imagine spending the next forty or fifty years of his life in such a place. And yet it was destined to be, he thought. Maybe the old cons back on Sing Sing's death row had not been so wrong when they had said they would rather be where they were than where Nilo was heading.

What have I done, God, for you to visit this upon me? That stronzo *Selvini shot that boy, not me. It is only an accident that I was even there. Do mere accidents now condemn one to hell on earth?*

He unmade the bedding packet on his cot. It was still hours before lights-out would be called, but sleep would not wait. He took off his clothes and stacked them neatly on the floor, as far away from the toilet bucket as he could place them.

He had almost dozed off when he awoke with a start, leaping from his bed. Somebody had shot him or stabbed him or burned him with a hot poker. But of course that could not have happened. His cell was empty, and no one could get into his cell any more than he could get out. He must have been dreaming.

Nilo lay back down again and a moment later was back on his feet. Something was crawling all over him.

It was dark in the cell now, all the lights in all the cells in all the galleries having been doused. He had to know what it was that was attacking him. Cautiously, Nilo lit a match, expecting any moment for Fatso or one of the other guards to descend on his cell and inflict some sort of punishment on him.

At first he could see nothing. Then he noticed, in the flickering light, that his sheet was moving. He stepped closer to it and saw that the sheet itself was not moving; instead, it was covered with hundreds upon hundreds of tiny crawling insects, each roughly oval in shape and more or less a rusty brown in color. Nilo looked in horror at the insects covering the very place where moments before he had been sleeping. He could feel his belly tighten and a sort of panic rise in his throat; he had to fight hard to keep down a shriek.

He dropped the match and grabbed his sheet and flailed it madly up and down, shaking the insects to the floor and then taking his shoes and, in the dark, trying to smash the creatures into bloody pulp.

He had almost convinced himself that he had completed the job when he heard the hard leather heels of the guard thumping down the hallway as the man made his rounds. He hurriedly threw the sheet back on his mattress and jumped back on it. No sooner had he done so than he was attacked again, although this time it seemed as if the insects had discovered his butchery of their brethren and had decided to redouble their attack in some sort of retributory vengeance.

The battle went on all night, and by morning's light Nilo looked at the crushed blood-filled carcasses of the hordes of bedbugs littering his cell floor. He felt a fresh wave of nausea pass over him at the sight. He could not leave his cell floor like that. Shuddering, barely able to make himself do it, Nilo began picking up the dead insects—using one hand to brush them into his other—and depositing them in his toilet bucket.

After a rushed breakfast, eaten under the standing rules of silence, it was time to clean out their buckets. Nilo, along with all the other prisoners, grabbed his bucket by its long wire handle and started the march through the corridors and out into the exercise yard, where against a far wall a small, badly stinking shed had been set up. The courtyard surface had frozen over months before and was now a slick surface, partly of snow and ice, partly of human waste deposited there by prisoners unable to keep their feet under them.

Nilo waited in line. He could see the convicts ahead of him emptying their smaller buckets into one massive container and then dipping them into successive baths of disinfectant and reasonably clean water. He watched carefully, walked carefully, and when he had almost reached the shed he slipped and covered himself from head to foot with a foul combination of his own wastes and the bodies of dead insects. No one laughed. No one offered to help. He got himself to his feet and trudged on, cleaning his bucket as he had seen others do. There was nothing else to be done; there were to be no clean uniforms issued for another three days; he would have to make do with what he had.

Later that morning, a laughing guard who seemed to regard Nilo's aroma as an occasion for hilarity, assigned him a job in the weaving plant. For his first hour inside the plant, no one came near him. Finally, just before time to be marched to lunch, a paunchy prisoner with graying hair, eyeglasses, and oversize fleshy features walked toward him, his feet shuffling along in a peculiar duck-like gait.

"You're Nilo Sesta," he said. It was not exactly a question.

"Yes."

"You smell like hell. You can't work in here smelling like that."

Nilo bridled, ready to attack if attacked.

"Tell you what I'm going to do," the big man said.

"You tell me."

"I'm going to get you a fresh set of clothes."

Nilo eyed him suspiciously.

"And what's the price?"

"No price," the other man said. "I'm a friend of a friend of a friend. They asked me to look out for you while you're in here. That's why you got a job in this shop. It's the best in the whole joint. And tonight you'll get a new cell, one with no bedbugs. I'm sorry; I would've done better by you yesterday, but you people weren't supposed to get here until today."

Nilo stared at the man in disbelief. He was still young, but he had learned a long time ago to be distrustful of people who freely offered favors.

"Oh, and another thing," the man said, reaching into his pocket. "Here's fifty dollars that your friends outside sent in. You'll need it if you want to eat decent in here. You'll have to buy all your food through the commissary. You can't eat the crap they call meals here."

He grinned and held out his hand.

"My name's Harry. Harry Birchevsky."

ON MONDAY, Tommy showed up for work at his police precinct and bumped into his father.

"When are you going to resign?" Tony asked him.

"Are you that anxious to get me off the force?"

Tony drew his son into a vacant office, where they sat facing each other across a bare wooden table.

"I never expected you to stay on the job this long," Tony said.

"But why quit? The work's easy and it's a paycheck, and that comes in handy when the tuition's due."

"Yeah, but . . . dammit, if you've got to work, you should be doing some other kind of work, something important, something with lawyers."

"Police work's not important?" Tommy said.

"Not to you. It's important to me, but not to you. I'm a cop at heart. You're not."

"Papa, let's stop beating around the bush. You're just worried that some night I'm going to walk into a stray bullet."

"Okay, what's wrong with that?"

"What's wrong is that I've been a cop long enough to know how to be careful. I'm just going to hang around until law school's done, and then I'm finished. I'm no hero." He paused. "So what are you doing here anyway?"

"They hired some new patrolmen. I've got to give them a rundown on who the gang guys are that they should watch out for."

"That's a week's work," Tommy said lightly.

"More like ten minutes. All I got to do is show them a picture of Charlie Luciano. He's running everything now. If it's women, it's his. Booze is his. Gambling's his. Drugs are his. It's all his. You know, it's funny. I looked up his record and I probably gave him his first collar as an adult."

"Yeah?"

"And I don't even remember him," Tony said. "Of course, I know him now."

There was nothing to say to that, as Tommy realized

again how deeply hurt his father was by Tina's taking up with Luciano.

"Well, I've got to move on," he said, getting to his feet. He clapped his father on the shoulder and moved toward the door.

"Tommy, if you see Tina anytime, have her come home and visit Mama. If I know she's coming, I'll make sure to stay away."

Tommy again tried to think of something to say and again could not. He nodded and left.

WHEN SHE SAW THE DISMAL slushy slop that packed the city's gutters, Tina was happy that she traveled these days only by chauffeured car.

Charlie had told her, "You're a star now. No more trolleys and buses for you. When you wanna go someplace, you just call up and we'll have a car take you there."

It sounded very generous, but Tina knew that it also reflected a little of Luciano's personality, his need to control everyone around him. In his not-so-subtle way, he was telling her that she was his woman and she could go no place without his knowing, no place that he did not approve of.

Tina understood that and did not mind at all. Meeting Charlie had been the best thing that had ever happened in her life.

She was a headliner now at Ross's Club and the place was packed with enthusiastic crowds every night. She sang under the single name of "Justine." That too was Charlie's contribution.

"People like that one-name shit," he said to her while they were in bed in her apartment. "It sounds like . . . you know . . ."

"Elegant?"

"Right. Elegant. That's the word. And it sounds French too. People like French."

Tina giggled. "I know you like French," she said.

"I like a lot of things."

While she saw him almost every night at the club, Charlie still spent several nights a week with her at her downtown apartment. Several times she had been in Charlie's suite at the Plaza, but he had not invited her to move in.

Whenever she mentioned the suite to Charlie, he changed the subject. "I keep it for business. It's a good address to have when you want to do business deals. You got room service and waiters and cleaning people, and it impresses people a lot. But when I want to relax, I come here with you. No telephones, nobody pestering me for decisions all the time, and that's the way I like it, and that's the way it's going to stay."

It was not the opera stage, which had been her life's dream, but considering what had happened to her and her throat, life could hardly have been better. She rarely thought now of her family. Once in a while, when she knew her father was working, she went over to the family apartment to visit her mother, but even that conversation was strained, as if Tony's presence permeated the house. Occasionally, she would stop at the parish house to see Mario, but he tried too hard to get her to make up with her father and she was beginning to find that tedious. She talked to Tommy only on the telephone. For a while, he had seemed always to be on the run, between working his police job and going to law school, but now he seemed to be mostly bored with life. In either event, he was not much of a conversation companion.

She did not see a lot of Sofia either. In the last year,

her longtime friend had grown increasingly bitter toward the world, and a visit with her was a souring experience. Sofia hated Nilo; she hated her family; she hated everybody. When Tina invited her to come some evening to the club, Sofia said, "I doubt that Mr. Maranzano would approve. Charlie is not a favorite of his."

"Why does he have to approve?" Tina asked. "You're not a prisoner, you know."

"These mobs run our lives—yours, mine, all of us. If you don't believe it, try getting away. I told you once, we're all prisoners," Sofia had said.

The driver parked in front of the main entrance of the Plaza, and Tina waited in the car while he went inside to get Luciano. A few minutes later, the two men came out. Luciano got in the backseat and the driver took them downtown to a small building on the fringes of Chinatown.

Charlie helped her out of the car, then kept an arm on her elbow and guided her down a narrow alley, up a rickety flight of stairs, and down a long hall. He knocked on a door and waited for it to slowly swing open.

The air, Tina noticed, was strange, redolent of some sweet, spicy smell, and was vaguely nauseating. An old woman greeted them in Chinese. She obviously knew Charlie, and she led them inside through an anteroom into a bigger inner room. Tina stopped just inside the door, trying hard to impress all the sights and sounds and smells on her memory.

The room was nearly dark with only a single lamp with a red and amber shade providing a dim light. Here and there around the room, she could see the flickering of tiny flames, flames surrounded by weaving, dancing shapes and shadows, although she could not tell what the flames were or what purpose they served.

As her eyes grew accustomed to the darkness, she was able to make out numerous small tables, most less than a foot off the floor. The air was heavy with black smoke, and she could almost feel a fine powdery residue in the air.

Charlie turned to her and smiled, then leaned down and kissed her on the side of the neck. She shivered in delight. He had never done that in public before. In fact, he never made any physical display of affection. Tina squeezed closer to him and rubbed him gently with her body.

The old woman clapped her hands twice, sharply but lightly, and two Chinese boys immediately appeared. They were dressed only in loincloths and were carrying beautifully decorated silk robes. They stepped into a small alcove, and Charlie immediately began to undress, stripping down to his bare skin. He put on the robe and handed his clothes to the old woman. After hesitating a moment, Tina did the same. The two boys then each took one of Tina's hands and led her toward one of the flames, picking their path carefully.

It was only then that she realized that the floor of the room was packed with dozens of people, half of them men and half women, almost all totally naked and engaged in various arrangements of coupling, some hard and passionate, some slow and gentle, in all kinds of combinations. Tina moved slowly, watching as much as she could.

Their guides took them to a small cubicle in the far corner of the room, just slightly more private than the rest of the room. She and Charlie sat on cushions at the low table on which a small candle burned. One boy began rubbing their bodies with aromatic oils. Tina saw the other one prepare a long bamboo pipe. Around them, she sensed, rather than heard, the air fill with sound: the breathy meanderings of some strange flute playing even stranger music and punctuated occasionally by hissing, as of something boiling, the hissings followed by steady, delicate popping sounds.

Charlie stretched out on a long narrow pad and motioned for her to do the same on the one next to him. She did, with her legs pointing away from him and her head next to his. They kissed and when they stopped she realized that somehow she was no longer wearing her robe. She looked over at Charlie, but he only smiled at her, and she reached over and kissed him again.

The opium boy worked quickly now, taking a long needle and sticking it into an ornate pot filled with a sticky, darker-than-amber paste, twirling and working it into a small pill, not much larger than a teardrop. Then he held the drop over the flame of the lamp and carefully cooked it into a golden color. The boy smiled at Charlie and said, "Real good stuff this night. Number one. We mix Benares with Yunan. Try it. See." He dropped the golden pellet into the black earthenware bowl of a pipe made otherwise of brown shell and held the bowl over the lamp flame till the drop of opium glowed and a small tendril of smoke curled up and he handed the pipe to Luciano. Charlie inhaled a mighty lungful and held it down, releasing the smoke slowly, reluctantly. When he was done, he smiled at the boy. "Very good," he said.

The boy next offered the pipe to Tina. She took it, then hesitated. She had never smoked anything before, not even a cigarette. And with her throat she was frightened. She wavered just a moment, then took the pipe and gulped at it hungrily, the way Charlie had seemed to. The smoke burned its way down her throat, and she found herself fighting against panic. Then she began coughing, long noisy spasms that she was sure would stamp her as a hick in the eyes of all the other people in the room. But Charlie only smiled, so she tried again, a smaller sip of smoke, and this time it went down smoothly. And the next sip yet more smoothly.

By the time she had finished the bowlful of opium, she was transported. She felt alive as she had never felt before. Every inch of her body was sensitized to the environment around her, and she had never, she thought, been in a more beautiful place. She noticed tiger skins that covered the walls and imagined herself a Moorish princess being carried across the desert sands to be laid at the feet of the caliph, forced to capture him with her charms. She looked over at Charlie and saw his immense swelling and twisted herself so that she was on top of him, riding him hard, and him bucking like some stallion in a cowboy movie and then exploding inside her.

It was all foggy, lights and sounds. There was music; there were voices. She heard one voice say, "You're a whore now. You're my whore." And the thought delighted her so much she said, "Yes, yes, yes, yes." And the voice said, "Someday I'll have you turning tricks," and she said yes again.

Daylight came too soon, and when it did the pipes were put away and the dreamers departed.

FOR THE FIRST TIME since Nilo had been shipped to Dannemora more than six months ago, Sofia had come to visit.

Visitors were a rare occurrence in his life. Maranzano wrote long flowery Latin-tinged letters, but they mostly concerned the weather and the life of Caesar, hardly light reading for a lifer. And once a month, he sent his driver, Rock, to the prison, just to make sure that Nilo was being treated right, to give him some gossip, and to pass along the don's instructions not to give up; things moved slowly, but they were being worked on.

Nilo had no other visitors and, in fact, no other letters. Sofia had never written to him, not once. Although he had never written to them, he assumed that his parents back in Sicily had been told where he was, but they had not written, either, so all visitors were welcome, even one as unpleasant as the wife who had once admitted bearing someone else's bastard child.

The guard led him into a small room, one furnished with a rug to hide the concrete floor, and with a sofa, a couple of chairs, a big desk, and curtains to hide the bars on the windows. It was clearly the office of some prison bureaucrat, but at that it was a lot better than the usual visiting area, and Nilo knew he got the privilege for being one of Maranzano's men.

He sat down behind the desk and began idly pulling out the various drawers, inspecting their contents while he waited. He found a small penknife and slipped it into his pant pocket. In just a few minutes, Sofia was let into the room.

She entered cautiously as the door closed behind her, stopping halfway to the desk.

"Hello, Nilo," she said.

"Hello, Sofia."

"How are things going?" she asked.

"Fine," he said. "Fine. How about you? And the boy?"

She nodded slightly. "We're both fine," she said.

Sofia was still very beautiful, Nilo thought, and her figure was accentuated by a tight-fitting two-piece suit. He stared at her bosom, remembering those days when she had tutored him and he had often thought of getting her into bed. She had carefully applied makeup to her beautiful features. Was there just a chance that, in some curious way, she longed for her husband, any husband?

"I've been talking to some of the people in the church," she said. "Actually Mario's been helping me. Nothing official, but we've talked to a lot of people."

"What about?" Nilo asked. He could feel the hairs on the back of his neck start to stand on end. An uneasy feeling spread in the pit of his stomach.

Sofia took a deep breath, and then the words came out in a rush.

"Nilo," she said. "What would you think about having our marriage annulled? Through the church?"

He looked at her without saying a word but then slammed both fists down onto the desk in front of him.

"Why?" he snapped.

"Because I want to get on with my life. You know there was never anything between us. And the only reason I married you was so I wouldn't have to testify. We could get it annulled."

"Who put you up to this? The kid's father? Who is he?"

She looked at him for a long time before answering. "Stephen's your son, Nilo," she said. "I was just angry when I said he wasn't. All you'd have to do is look at him to see it." She paused to blow her nose and to wipe her eyes.

"If you don't care for me . . ."

"I don't," he snapped.

"Then care for your son," she said softly.

"Never. An annulment is for some capon, some castrato. What would people think of me?"

"You bastard," she said. "You're here, pitying yourself. What will people think of *you*? Think of somebody besides yourself for a change. I'm not old. I can get married. Stephen can have a real father, not some murdering jailbird who will make him the joke of the neighborhood. Please, Nilo."

Nilo stood up behind the desk.

"You know why we've got this office to meet in?" he said.

Sofia looked around, as if noticing the place for the first time. "No, why?"

Nilo came around the desk. "Because I've got a little influence in this place because of who I am. And prisoners with influence get a chance sometimes to use a room like this to meet their wives, just in case they want to do a little husband and wifing."

Sofia looked confused.

He stood in front of her now, and his hands reached up and grasped her breasts harshly. He spoke in almost a whisper to her. "I thought when you came up here today that maybe you wanted to see me, for me to be your husband. But I should have known. Mario sent you. Another one of my Falcone friends. Are you screwing him? Or Tommy? Or just anybody you meet?"

Angrily, she pulled back from him and snapped, "Anybody but you. You wonder what people might think of you? I will tell you. Because I will tell them. You are a useless excuse for a man. You can never satisfy a woman."

"You'll burn in hell before I give you an annulment," he said.

"Keep a spot ready for me," Sofia snapped. "You'll be burning long before I get there. I live for the day when I am the Widow Sesta."

Nilo reached for the penknife in his pocket. His hand closed around it, but with a ferocious act of will, he dropped it back into his pocket, walked to the door, and knocked. A guard came and took him back to the weaving plant.

"Must have been a lousy visit," Harry said. Nilo studied the big man for a moment before answering. There was something about him that he liked, even if the man was a Jew. He had a solid, reassuring quality. Nilo told him what had happened.

"That's just like a broad," Birchevsky said. "That's what happened with both of my wives, what happens to most guys in here. Their wives are off screwing around, and we're supposed to stay in here, playing with ourselves."

They had come to a small storeroom and let themselves inside.

"I'm going to ask you something, kid," Birchevsky said, "and I don't want you taking me wrong. Okay?"

"Sure, Harry."

The big man shifted his weight on the box on which he was sitting.

"How long've you been in? A couple of years?"

"Counting the time in The Tombs, goin' on two years."

"And you're still a young kid. What? Twenty-three? Twenty-four?"

"Twenty-five," Nilo said.

"And you ain't no punk or no sissy," Birchevsky said.

Nilo moved uneasily. He was beginning to guess what was coming.

"So you haven't been laid in a hell of a long time?" Birchevsky said. "Right?"

"Right."

Birchevsky took a deep breath. "Listen, kid," he said, "don't get any strange ideas about me. On the outside, I'm as square as the next guy. Even in here, I don't mess around."

Nilo nodded.

"What I'm trying to say is this. And I wouldn't be

saying this if you was a happily married man. What I'm saying is I need a good buddy—you know—one who won't blab to anyone. But somebody to help me work off the tensions. Somebody who's got tensions of his own, too. Not too often. No sissy, punk stuff. Just somebody to help relieve the tensions. Somebody who won't talk."

Nilo did not answer at first.

"Well?" Birchevsky said finally.

Nilo moved over beside him, and Birchevsky began unbuttoning the younger man's trousers.

"Only for now," Harry said. "Only inside."

* *Charlie Luciano bought three new touring cars, two Packards and a Buick. His prostitutes and brothels were earning him a million dollars a year, and he paid cash for the cars. Tina Falcone still headlined at Luciano's speakeasy, although she missed an occasional show when she was suffering from an opium hangover. Luciano never complained, although he spent fewer nights now at her apartment.*

* *After killing Dion O'Banion for Al Capone, Frankie Yale returned to Brooklyn and his bootlegging business. Soon Capone decided that Yale, his old buddy in the Five Points gang, was double-dipping—selling liquor to Capone, then "hijacking" his own trucks and selling the same liquor to Capone a second time. He sent a spy, Jimmy DeAmato, to New York to find out; Yale killed the spy. On July 1, 1927, one of Capone's men tried to shoot Yale, but missed. One year to the day later, Yale left a speakeasy and drove his roadster down Forty-fourth Street in Brooklyn. A large touring*

car pulled alongside and four gunmen opened fire.
Yale died immediately; his car crashed and tore
the porch off a house. The killers' guns were found
a few blocks away; one of them was a machine gun
that was bought in von Frantzius's gun shop in
Chicago. Frankie Yale was the first New York
gangster killed with a machine gun. Luciano said,
"That crazy fuck, Capone, will get us all killed.
Everybody's going to get one of those Chicago
Pianos. They'll be shooting the town up." Pri-
vately, he told Capone that Yale needed killing.
Twenty-eight hearses of flowers accompanied
Yale's body to the cemetery.

- Air passenger service started in 1926 and on May
  21, 1927, Charles Lindbergh flew the Atlantic
  nonstop to France.

- The new hot dance was the Black Bottom, but in
  every speakeasy in America, the most requested
  song was "The Gang That Sang 'Heart of My
  Heart.'"

- Father Mario Falcone was promoted to assistant
  pastor at Our Lady of Mount Carmel Church. His
  brother, Tommy, was promoted to sergeant in the
  police department.

- America wept when its greatest matinee idol,
  Rudolph Valentino, died. He was thirty-one
  years old.

- On March 18, 1927, thirty-year-old New Yorker
  Romeo LaRocca, formerly of Castellammare del
  Golfo in Sicily, was diagnosed with inoperable
  lung cancer. When doctors gave him no more than
  three months to live, he wondered what would
  happen to his wife and children and went to seek
  advice from Don Salvatore Maranzano.

CHAPTER **8**

Spring and Summer 1927

After a while, Sofia had actually begun to enjoy the accounting classes she took at NYU. There was something pure about working with numbers; it was a world in which things were right or they were wrong, and in a life in which she had found so few things coming out right, this held a powerful attraction for Sofia.

Even Salvatore Maranzano had seemed pleased with her progress, and he was certainly aware of it—of that there was no doubt. He knew, before she even told him, how well she had done in her classes, and on his regular visits to see her, he often praised both her brains and her diligence, before he got down on the floor to play with two-year-old Stephen.

She wondered if he had people spying on her, and she got her answer one day when several of the students decided to go out for coffee after one of their classes. There were two young men and Sofia and another young woman. They sat in a public restaurant, surrounded by scores of people, for no more than forty-five minutes, talking and laughing, and that night Maranzano again cautioned her against "unseemly, unwifely" behavior.

But she had no idea what Maranzano thought or knew

about her relationship with Nilo. The don did not gossip; but he often told her to be strong because Nilo would soon be freed. And he told her not to judge harshly a man who had spent so much time in prison. "He will be a different man when he returns," Maranzano said.

She could not understand why Maranzano, whose power throughout the city was growing every day, would care so much about the wife of one of his underlings, and that one no more than a useless thug. But Maranzano always talked about Nilo as if he were the heir to some kind of crown, now just briefly detained in a foreign land before returning home to take up his throne.

When her classes ended and she was ready to put her talent and education to use, Sofia had not been sure how to broach the subject to Maranzano. She decided to be direct, and one night she said, "I don't want to keep taking money from you for nothing. I want to get a job. I want to work."

Maranzano had nodded. "I agree. It will be good for you. At least until your husband returns home."

The next day, Sofia had gotten a newspaper to read the want ads for bookkeeping and accounting jobs, but before she could answer even one advertisement, the giant Maranzano henchman named Rock had shown up at her apartment with an armful of ledger books.

"Don Salvatore says you work on these," the man had said. "I pick them up Friday. I bring you new ones next Monday." Without waiting for an answer, he had placed the ledger books on the living room table and left.

The ledger books were from Maranzano's legitimate businesses, and Sofia realized as she worked on them just how far-flung the soft-spoken gangster's empire was becoming. He owned stores and warehouses and theaters. There was a boxing club in the Bronx and a women's garment manufacturer in Midtown. In New Jersey, he owned a small cereal company and garages and auto dealerships and even held part ownership in several banks.

The books were a window into Maranzano's world, and it was a much more interesting world than Sofia had ever expected it to be, so much so that she looked forward to balancing the books of those businesses.

She worked diligently every day, still often placing Stephen with a babysitter for a few hours, but one warm spring day, she answered a knock on the door to find Tina standing in the hallway with a baker's box in her hand.

"Hi," Tina said. "Still got a sweet tooth?"

The two young women had not seen each other in more than a year, and that last meeting had been cursory, a chance encounter at the Manginis' restaurant, where Tina had been driven to pick up Luciano, who was dining there. They had not had any chance to speak, because Luciano was in a hurry to leave and dragged Tina along with him. Sofia was surprised at her friend's appearance; She looked weary. There were the first faint traces of wrinkles alongside her eyes. But she was still beautiful; nothing could change that.

"Where's the baby?"

"Oh, Tina, I'm sorry. My mother took Stephen with her today to go visit one of my aunts out on the Island. They won't be back until late."

"Oh, damn." Tina took a small gift-wrapped box from inside her pocketbook. "Well, they say it's the thought that counts. Give him this from Aunt Tina. I bet he's getting big."

"Getting? He already *is* big. He's two years old, and already runs around this place like it's a racetrack. You'll love him."

A few minutes later, Sofia brought coffee into the living room, where Tina had already spread out cookies and small pastries on a fresh linen napkin on the table in front of the sofa.

"You have anything stronger for that coffee?" Tina asked.

"Brandy?"

"That sounds good."

"My friend, Tina, the drinker. That's a switch."

"Times change."

"Yeah, everything changes. Except my life. That never changes."

She brought a bottle of brandy back to the table and sat next to Tina on the sofa.

"Things aren't well?" Tina asked.

"You know, I've got a theory."

"You always had theories."

"I haven't had any in a long time. But I've got this one. I think that maybe some people are put on this earth to be victims, to be sport for other people. Like rabbits. There's no use for a rabbit, except to be hunted by dogs and wolves and coyotes and foxes and eagles and hawks and owls. That's their only purpose. I'm like a rabbit."

"Well, they've got another purpose," Tina said.

"What's that?"

"To make more rabbits."

"They just do that while they're waiting to be eaten," Sofia said. "No, they're professional victims. So am I. I've been roughed up by family, by criminals, by the law, by the governor. I ought to go out and lie down on the street with a sign that says KICK ME, I'M DIRT. Do you know I've never seen you sing? Not once since you've been at the club."

"I invited you enough times," Tina said.

"I know. But I'm not allowed to go."

"Sofia, you're twenty-four years old. You're as old as I am. You can go anywhere you want."

"No. *You* can go anywhere you want. I can go anywhere Salvatore Maranzano thinks is proper, and he doesn't think a proper Sicilian wife like me belongs in a speakeasy."

"He's told you that?"

"In just that many words. He keeps telling me that Nilo's going to get out soon and I have to be a virtuous wife and mother. He doesn't understand how much I hate your son-of-a-bitching cousin and hope he dies in jail."

"No boyfriends then?"

"Men are the least of my worries. I never liked them and I like them even less now."

"Do you think there's anything Charlie can do? Could he pull some strings for Nilo?"

"No, it's a lost cause. Mr. Maranzano is this tight with the governor's office." She clasped her hands in front of her. "But first they couldn't let Nilo out because they were running for reelection. Then they couldn't let him out 'cause they were running again for something."

"He got reelected just last year. What's he waiting for now?"

"Now he wants to run for president, and so he can't let Nilo out 'cause it'd look bad. And in the meantime, I'm sitting here, like some dried-up old prune."

"You don't look like any prune to me," Tina said. "You look like a pretty fine-looking plum."

She held her hands out in front of her bosom in a silent, joking comment on Tina's large breasts.

Sofia felt her own breasts. "The only thing these were ever good for was feeding Stephen. No, I don't think

Charlie can help. If Mr. Maranzano can't, I guess no one can. Oh, I'm tired of complaining. How's the family?"

"I don't see too much of them," Tina said. "Tommy will be finishing up law school after the summer. Mario's busy with the church. My father and mother are well."

"Do you see them?"

"Family's a funny thing," Tina said. "No matter what kind of fight you have, eventually it passes away and you're still family. At least that's the way it's supposed to be. But Papa—he just can't take the thought that I'm with Charlie. It's like I'm driving a stake into his heart every day. So I see them at big holidays, birthdays, once in a while, but we don't talk, and I get out of there as quickly as I can."

"I'm sorry, Tina. Here I've done nothing but complain, and you've got your own problems, too."

"Nothing like yours."

"Is Tommy getting married?" Sofia asked.

"I don't think so. Why? Did you hear something?"

"No. I was just wondering."

"No. He studies all the time. He doesn't have any time for girls."

"When I was young, I always thought I'd marry him," Sofia said. "Until I figured out I hate men."

Tina smiled as she sipped her coffee. "I love them. All sizes, all shapes."

"And what does Charlie think about that?" Sofia said, and watched Tina's face seem to cloud over.

"Charlie wasn't my first man. And since I've been with him, I've been with others. With women too. And Charlie's always been there. He likes it. He likes to watch sometimes."

"Oh, Tina, that's so depraved."

"You're the poet. You're the one who was always telling me that depravity was good."

"That was talk. A lot of things in my life were talk."

The brandy had seemed to heat up the room. Tina unbuttoned the top two buttons of her dress.

"Brandy does that to me," she said.

"Just brandy?"

"Brandy. Opium. Sex. I spend most of my time overheated."

Sofia looked at her and wondered suddenly if Tina was really as happy as she was trying to appear.

"And you and Charlie?"

Tina shrugged. "I don't know," she said.

"If you don't, who does?"

"It's just . . . it's not something we talk about. I sing at his club. Some nights we go out afterward. Once in a while, we have sex. But that's all."

"He doesn't talk to you?" Sofia asked.

"Oh, he talks enough. He introduces me to all his cronies. He'll talk business in front of me. I hear more sordid stories in a week than I ever imagined happened." She sipped her drink. "He talks enough. But I never know what he's thinking. Not once have I gotten a look inside his mind."

"Maybe it's just the way he is. He doesn't like to talk about what he's thinking."

"You know, it's not like I expect him to marry me. God, I know he's got other women. A lot of them. One night I heard someone say that Charlie was a philanthropist because he had given work to five thousand women. He meant all the whores in Charlie's houses. I've met some of them at the club, and it's like Charlie owns them. They're furniture. And sometimes I feel like I am, too. Maybe I'm his best sofa, but I'm still just a sofa."

"And you never ask him about any of this?"

"You can't ask Charlie things. You try to make conversation about what the future holds, about someday retiring and living on a farm, about slowing down and touring Europe, and he looks at you like you're a bug. 'That's for crumbs,' he says. 'I'd rather die than be a crumb.' End of discussion. The other night he got mad at me and said I was butting into business that didn't concern me." She sighed. "I don't know. Maybe he's just getting tired of me."

Tina finished her drink and poured another. She looked out across the living room to the street beyond, her thoughts somewhere Sofia could not reach.

She's just like me, Sofia thought. *Just another piece of property.*

She rose to get more coffee, wincing at a sudden pain that jabbed at her back.

"What's the matter?" Tina asked.

"Since the baby. My back hurts a lot."

"I had a wonderful thing the other night called a massage. It might be just what you need."

"I can just see myself getting out of here to go get a massage," Sofia said.

"No need to go anywhere. Just leave it to me." Tina stood up, took Sofia's hand, and steered her toward the bedroom. Sofia felt her heart racing.

SINCE TOM DEWEY, his law-school roommate, had moved, the rent on their apartment had been too much for Tommy to handle alone, and in the summer of 1927, he found a smaller apartment uptown in an area already being called the Upper West Side.

He would have been welcome to move back home, but

at twenty-eight, Tommy thought it was time to really start living his own life. He had only a few more law classes before he had his degree.

So without a girlfriend, without much furniture, without much of anything but his police uniforms and his lawbooks, Tommy had moved uptown—helped in the manual labor by brother Mario, who for that hot July day at least had disdained his Roman collar so he felt free to swear at the cheap help who were dropping Tommy's boxes all over the street.

Tommy spent the summer reading more lawbooks. At nights he walked his police beat, and on weekends he attended special-credit classes at the law school, and the summer ended all too soon and he was back in the full-time grind of classes, and there wasn't a day when he wasn't tired.

One drizzly night, he pushed the books aside and decided to go for a walk, and he wandered half the length of the city, down toward his old neighborhood. The drizzle suddenly turned into a pelting heavy rain, and Tommy saw ahead a small restaurant where he sometimes took meals as a policeman, and he opened its front door, forcing it to move against the wind and rain, and went inside.

Someone was sitting at the counter spot where he usually sat, but there were other vacant seats there and he walked to the coatrack on the side of the small diner, peeling off his heavy police raincoat and shaking it dry. He hung it up and saw the man at his counter seat leaving.

He started in that direction when—

"Not only are you dumb and ugly," a voice said. "You're rude and clumsy too."

Tommy looked around, surprised.

"Huh?"

"And articulate too, I see," the voice said.

The words were slowly burning their way through the fog of his fatigue. Without thinking, he reached down with his hand toward the spot on his belt where he wore his gun when he was on duty.

"Holy jumping Jesus Christ," the voice said. "Now he's going to shoot us all." The voice laughed.

Tommy turned some more and finally located the source of the voice. It was coming from a girl seated at a table nearby. With her were two other girls and a young man.

Tommy walked two steps in her direction.

"Pardon me, miss," he said softly, keeping just an edge of menace in his voice, as he had learned to do while working the streets. "Am I doing something to bother you?"

The girl stood up. She was dressed like an art student, mostly in black, covered with a few daubs of oil colors here and there. It looked as if she was several days past the time for a shampoo, but she smelled wonderful. She was tall for a girl, nearly as tall as he was, and she was slender with narrow hips and small breasts.

Like the girls of the neighborhood he grew up in, she had a Mediterranean complexion and black curly hair, but where his neighborhood's girls' eyes smoldered, this girl's eyes flashed and glinted. Her mouth was different, too: almost too wide—but even so and totally unexpectedly, Tommy wondered what she would be like to kiss.

He tried to push the thought from his mind. He had been thinking that way more and more often lately and it interfered with schoolwork.

"You sure as hell are bothering me," the girl said. "You just splashed water all over me with your raincoat, you jerk."

Tommy didn't answer immediately. Instead, he stared at the girl, his countenance softening considerably. She stared back, the anger gradually leaving her face. They kept staring at each other.

I am in love, Tommy thought. *Totally, hopelessly, completely in love. So this is what it's all about.*

"Look, lady, if you want to marry me, just say so. Don't beat around the bush," he said.

The girl flushed. Someone at her table giggled.

Tommy felt his own face redden. "Well, anyway, I'm sorry about the water. If there's anything I can do . . ."

The girl smiled at him. She had an unusually lovely, crooked smile, Tommy thought.

"No," she said, "that's all right. I just like to complain."

"You must be fun to live with," he said, but when she didn't respond he nodded and turned back toward his seat at the counter, which was now vacant. Someone was sitting next to that stool, and he was annoyed until, with some difficulty, he recognized the person as Tom Dewey.

Behind him, he heard the girl call, "Just make sure you don't do it again. Ever."

Tommy thought she had the loveliest voice in the world.

"Well, there must be a reason for the sappy look on your face," Dewey said as Tommy floated down alongside him. "You in love?"

"No, I'm in fatigue. Serious fatigue. What's that thing on your lip?" He waved to the waitress, who nodded and began to pour him coffee. Dewey carefully folded the newspaper he had been reading.

"Please. Spare me your sophomoric jokes," Dewey said. "I went on vacation to Europe and grew a mustache so I would look older."

"You don't look any older. You just look sillier."

"It might be the egg on my face."

"How's that?" Tommy asked.

"I just got fired from my law firm," Dewey said.

"Oh. I'm sorry."

"Don't be. I was ready to quit anyway. They had me doing all this peasant work that a nitwit could do in his sleep. Besides, I've got a new job."

"Better one?"

"Yes. They're paying me twenty-three hundred dollars a year and I'm doing corporate law. It's what I wanted to do."

"At twenty-three hundred per, it's going to be hard to make a million," Tommy said.

"You've got to start somewhere," Dewey answered. "I'm satisfied."

Tommy looked at him carefully. Dewey was a short, broad-shouldered, almost-chunky young man with thick dark hair, a handsome regular face, and an awkward, homely, gap-toothed mouth, now only partly disguised by his little shrub of a mustache. He spoke slowly in a Midwest twang modified by what Tommy knew was years of training for the stage and as a singer.

And he didn't come here for the quality of the food, Tommy thought. *He's got something on his mind.*

"So how are you doing?" Dewey asked.

"Fine. I've been hanging on to the cop job, but I'm taking extra classes so I can finish up law school in a hurry. Then I'm going to figure out a way to make a fortune and retire by the time I'm thirty-five."

He looked over at the girl whom he had splashed with water. To his surprise, she was watching him, too. She smiled, and he wondered what it would be like to have her smile at him a lot, forever. He nodded back to her.

He saw Dewey wave to her and she returned the wave.

"You know her?" Tommy asked.

"Who?"

"Her," Tommy said. "That girl you just waved at."

"Oh, sure. She lives just down the hall from Francie." Francie had been Dewey's girlfriend, an up-and-coming singer and actress. Tommy hadn't known whether or not their romance was still on, but he guessed it was by Dewey's casual reference.

"Her name's Rachel something," Dewey said. "I forget what. It's something Jewish, I think. I could find out for you if you want me to."

"No," Tommy said. "That's all right."

They both sipped their coffee for several minutes; then Tommy announced again, with more emphasis, "Anyway, that's my plan. I'm going to be rich."

"I told you. There's money in the Mafia."

"Stick it, friend. I'm going to make real money. Honest money."

"The job market isn't all that good."

"That's because there's about as much use for lawyers right now as there is for deep-sea divers. We're in a trade that nobody needs. Everybody's getting rich on Wall Street and nobody wants to sue anybody else, but I don't think it's going to stay that way."

"My feelings exactly," Dewey said. "Two guys as smart as us, you know, we ought to open our own office."

That's it, Tommy thought. *He's looking for a partner. He wants to go into private practice.*

Dewey was searching Tommy's face for a reaction to his seemingly offhanded comment.

"Two can starve as cheaply as one?" Tommy said.

"You never know. We might wind up stars," Dewey said. "I don't want to work for corporations. I want to work for people."

"There's always government," Tommy said. "They can always use a good lawyer."

"I don't know," Dewey said. "Long hours, low pay, and everybody hates you. I don't think being on the side of the public is a good career decision."

"You may be right," Tommy said. "The public's on its own side. It couldn't be happier. It made liquor illegal and now it has more speakeasies than it ever had taverns. But it feels real good about it. It talks about working hard and the American ethic, but it makes all its money by buying and selling pieces of paper on Wall Street. The public's happy as a clam. And just as dumb."

"Yeah," Dewey said glumly. "Maybe I'll just go back to Michigan and open a little office and do wills and mortgages for people who pay me in chicken eggs. Shut down my brain and never think again."

"Not you," Tommy Falcone said. "You're one of those pests that people will always find a use for."

"Good. Then you're in luck," Tom Dewey said. "When they call for me because they need me, I'll manage to find a job for you, too." He paused. "Mishkin," he said.

"Beg your pardon."

"Mishkin. That's her name. Her father's Lev Mishkin."

"Lev Mishkin," Tommy mused. He snapped his fingers together. "He's the guy who runs the garment makers' union?"

"That's the one. It's a shame, isn't it?"

"What is?"

"Well, here you are, an upstanding citizen, and there he is, with a beautiful daughter, but he's an old Red. I think he was in jail in Russia twenty, twenty-five years ago for being an anarchist or something."

"Sounds pretty bad."

"It's even worse."

"How's it worse?"

"Well, I don't think he'd ever allow his daughter to go out with somebody from Wall Street. Much less a goy Wall Streeter."

"Circumcision's not out of the question," Tommy said, and his roommate got up, laughing.

"About that partnership idea of yours," Tommy said. "It's not a bad thought. Together we might be a good team."

Dewey sat back down on the stool. "Think about it, Tommy. With your connections with the police and me doing the casework, we might really carve out a place for ourselves. Sooner or later, everything's going to fall apart. Everybody's going to need lawyers."

"Let me think about it. I've got some things I have to take care of first, and I haven't even graduated yet."

"Good enough," Dewey said, and rose again. "One other thing. She's an artist. A painter."

"The one in the booth?"

"Yeah. Absolutely no talent whatsoever," Dewey said. "The worst painter I've ever seen in my life. But she *is* cute."

He took a business card out of his pocket and gave it to Tommy. "Hang on to this. Let's stay in touch." Then he clapped Tommy on the back and walked away. Tommy noticed him stop at Rachel Mishkin's table and lean over briefly to talk to her. Soon everyone there was laughing. Tommy saw the girl look at him, and he blushed, turned away, left some money on the counter to pay the check, and started to go. Dewey was already gone.

Tommy was putting on his wet slicker when he was aware of someone standing beside him. It was the girl.

"Stand back. I'm putting on the killer raincoat again," he said.

"I've decided," she said.

"You have?"

"Yes. The answer is yes."

"Good. What's the question?" Tommy asked.

She flushed. "You talked about us getting married. Don't you remember? God, do you talk like that to everybody you meet?"

"Oh," Tommy said. It was his turn to blush.

"Of course, you'll have to court me properly. For a couple of weeks at least. Meet my father. We'll have to find out if we're sexually compatible."

"I wouldn't have it any other way," Tommy said.

Rachel stared at him for another moment, then leaned forward and kissed his chin.

"Bye," she said. "See you later." She turned to go and Tommy called, "Wait."

"What?"

"You want to have dinner tonight?" he asked.

THAT NIGHT, while Tommy Falcone and Rachel Mishkin were having dinner, Romeo LaRocca, the Castellammarese immigrant with lung cancer, was dying in St. Luke's Hospital. In the presence of two Italian-speaking priests, an attorney, a policeman, and John F. X. Kinnair of the *Daily News,* he made a detailed deathbed confession to the murder of Enzo Selvini and the young Roggerio boy. He said that Selvini had wronged his family in Sicily and that he had followed the man to New York to take his vengeance. He had stalked him carefully for weeks before first trying to shoot him and then putting a fire ax into his head in the theater.

He was, he knew, dying, and his immortal soul could not rest if he continued to let Nilo Sesta take the blame for a crime that he, LaRocca, had alone committed.

LaRocca died during the night. A day later, his body was returned to Sicily accompanied by his suddenly wealthy wife and their children, who traveled first-class with tickets paid for by Don Salvatore Maranzano.

TOMMY WAS HALFWAY through his shift when he stopped into a small diner to grab a sandwich. He sat alone at a table in the far corner and was surprised when Captain Cochran came into the diner and walked back to join him.

Tommy started to scramble to his feet, but Cochran, dressed in civilian clothes, pushed him back down.

"At ease, Tommy," he said with a grin. "I came to talk to you."

"I do something wrong?"

"Nope. Your father tells me you're thinking of putting in your papers. To retire."

"It can't be soon enough for him, Captain. He's been after me to quit since the first day I joined the force."

"So you're going to?"

"Pretty soon. I've just about got enough money saved to finish law school. If I'm not working, I might get done even faster."

"I've got a suggestion," Cochran said. He signaled the waitress for coffee. "I'm not telling you anything you don't know, but the thugs have had a pretty free ride in this city for a long time."

Tommy did not respond, and Cochran said, "But the times are changing. I can see it happening now. The politicians are getting afraid."

"I guess I'll believe that when I see it," Tommy said.

"Trust me. It's coming. And when it happens, well, the Italian Squad's going to be where all the action is. If the mob gets cleaned up, we're the ones who'll do it." He paused and chuckled. "I'm really working hard to convince you, and you still don't have any idea what I'm talking about."

Tommy grinned back. "My father says the Irish are that way but that they get to the point eventually."

"All right, let me get to it. I've got some discretionary money in my squad budget. What I'd like you to consider is not retiring. Everybody'll think you quit, but I'll hold your papers and carry you on unofficial leave of absence. I'll keep you on salary out of my private funds, and you work undercover."

"Undercover? What's that?" Tommy asked.

"It's a new thing they've been trying in Washington. Basically, what you do is get out and hang around with the gees. Become one of the boys. Find out what they're up to, what they've got planned. Then let us know so we can squash it. You make your own hours, set your own schedule." He stopped talking as the waitress returned with his coffee.

"Make no mistake," Cochran said when she left, "it's dangerous. If you get found out, you probably get killed."

"You make it sound appealing. What's the good side?"

"Well, you keep your pension, you build up your seniority, you get paid, and, mostly, you help us get the bastards."

"Why me? Why not somebody else?"

"You're Italian, you're smart, and you've got guts. And nobody can throw mud on your reputation. I've been thinking about you for this job ever since you turned down that promotion to detective."

"I'd want to talk to my father about it."

Cochran frowned. "I know this is tough, Tommy, but that won't work. If your father knew what you were up to . . . well, you know what he's like. Every time you turned around, he'd be following you, barging in, making it impossible for you to get anything done."

"Sounds just like Papa."

"So this'd have to be just between you and me. If anybody else knew, it might put you in danger."

"And what about the brass, your bosses? Why should I trust them?"

"All I can ask you is to trust me. I won't tell anyone. And that means no one. Only you and I will know."

Both men sat and sipped their coffee. Finally, Tommy said, "Wow."

"I know," Cochran said. "But just promise me you'll think about it. You can do a lot of good here."

"I'll think about it, Captain."

THE SUN HAD FINALLY APPEARED and was trying to burn off a chill fog as Nilo Sesta walked through the front gates of Dannemora. He stopped and waited, without turning, for the heavy iron gates to clank shut. For a moment, he was tempted to look back, but he did not.

Never again. Never look back. Never think of this place again, never talk about it, never have anything to do with it. I am free. No one will ever return me to a place like this.

His release had come with lightning swiftness. Only a day before, he had had no idea. Then he had been called to the warden's office and told that he had received a full and complete pardon from the governor's office.

"I'm not happy about this, Sesta," the warden had said.

Nilo did not answer. He was too busy trying to figure out what it all meant, and he could not yet comprehend the idea of freedom, not coming so quickly after three years behind bars.

"As far as I'm concerned, you're nothing but a baby-killer," the warden had said. "I don't care if you do have friends who lie and other friends who can get to the governor's office, you and I both know that it's only a matter of time before you'll be back in here. And I'll be waiting for you. I promise you that."

Nilo had waited quietly for the warden to talk himself out and then waited a few minutes longer to be dismissed. The guards moved him right away to an isolation cell: nobody wanted anything happening to him now that he was slated to be a free man. That would not look good in the papers, Nilo thought. He had laughed at the idea. The only time they cared about his welfare was when he was leaving their prison. All the while he had been in one of their cells, he had been treated like dirt. Like worse than dirt.

One of the guards had told him that his pardon had come from an acting governor. The full-time governor was off somewhere, talking about running for president, and in his absence an acting governor had signed the pardon.

He thought two men were approaching him, but he could not be sure. He had forgotten how to see things at a distance; in prison there was nothing far away to look at; everything was up close. These two might be walking to him or they might just be planning to walk by.

The two figures resolved themselves out of the morning fog as the lawyer Koehler and Salvatore Maranzano.

"Ah, Danilo," Maranzano said. "It is good to see you. You look fit."

"Thank you, Don Salvatore," Nilo said. He started to shake the man's hand and then stopped and instead bent forward and kissed it, as he would the hand of a pope.

But Maranzano pulled him up and wrapped the young man in a bear hug. "It is nothing. My only regret is that it took so long. Even politicians and judges who are bought and paid for sometimes take longer than they should to do what they know they are eventually going to do."

"My life is yours, Don Salvatore. Use it as you wish."

Maranzano seemed slightly embarrassed. "Come, this is America," Maranzano said. "We do not say such things here. I have brought you new clothes and we will stop at the hotel for you to change them. There is still more than an hour for the train to take us home. There is a restaurant there, too. You might like to have breakfast before we get under way."

"It might be wise," the lawyer said, looking around, "if we moved on. The press might yet be here to badger us."

"Good thought," Maranzano said, and smiled at Nilo. "You see, this is what I pay this big legal genius for. To protect me against the complications of life." He took Nilo's arm and led him toward a taxicab waiting in the fog down the street. Nilo saw the bodyguard known as Rock leaning against the fender of the cab, his arms crossed, carefully looking in all directions.

At the hotel, Nilo soaked and scrubbed himself in a hot bath until he felt he had rubbed off the last trace of prison dirt. He dressed hurriedly and then, with the other two men watching him and encouraging him, gorged himself at the hotel's restaurant. He spent the rest of the trip fighting off violent indigestion.

They sat in a private compartment in the train, and Rock took up a position in the corridor outside, guarding the door. The lawyer excused himself and said he was going to walk to the bar car. When he and Nilo were alone, Maranzano opened a bottle of red wine and they drank a toast to each other as the don explained the death-bed confession of Romeo LaRocca.

Nilo raised his glass again. "To his immortal soul. May he rest in peace."

"I'm afraid that will be up to a power greater than ours," Maranzano said.

It was the first time Nilo had tasted wine in many years. He had forgotten just how good it was. That was one of the great evils of prison. It made you a lower form of life and, after a while, you forgot that the pleasures you once cherished even existed.

"You will have work for me?" Nilo asked Maranzano eventually.

"Ah, yes, the family man. With a wife and child to support. Yes, Nilo, I have work for everybody. And I need you at my side."

"Things then are going well?"

"Exceeding well. It began with your plan to pump in whiskey past the Coast Guard boats. That gave us money. Then this Mussolini decided to assault our people on Sicily, and they have flocked to the United States to escape him. That gave us manpower. They come by the dozens, by the scores, and they are all in our organization now. We were big and powerful. Now we are gigantic and powerful beyond measuring."

"And people like Masseria? They accept this?" Nilo asked.

Maranzano waved his hand, dismissing Masseria as if he were only an annoying insect.

"Joe the Stupid who would be Joe the Boss, he just goes on doing things the same old way, as big a fool as ever he was," Maranzano said. "Without his even know-ing, our organization grew to rival his. Now we are probably larger. His day has ended. For we sons of Castellammare del Golfo, the day has just begun."

"And there will be no fight over this?"

"Oh, he makes noises about the pain he will inflict upon us Castellammarese, but it is too late. No one cares what he will accept or what he thinks." Maranzano smiled. "Still, I keep a guard on the door." He nodded to the door of the compartment, beyond which Rock waited.

"There is a place of honor for you in our new organization," Maranzano said. "You will be at my right hand. All know that you have my trust."

"It is a great honor," Nilo said.

He found his mind, though, wandering from business and thinking about Sofia. As the distance of time and temperament had widened between them into an irrevocable gulf, he had begun to think of her more and more as his wife. Of her child as his child. In some curious turn of mind, he had started to regard himself as a husband who had been away, through no fault of his own, and would be now returning to the bosom of his family.

He had understood it for the survival mechanism it was. The thought of some sort of life beyond prison had sustained him, especially during those times when he had come close to ending it all, to killing himself. Often he had thought of diving headfirst off the topmost gallery of the cells, down seventy feet to the waiting concrete floor and oblivion. But he never acted on the impulse, and one of the things that had helped him through was his growing dream of Sofia as his wife. Mrs. Sesta.

"Sofia," he began.

"I am sure she waits for you in great anticipation. She has been a faithful wife for all these years," Maranzano said. "She has attended college and studied accounting. She now does the books of businesses you will help run.

Your son is healthy and happy. Your wife does not go out at night and has no undesirable friends. The only person she sees with regularity is the one named Justina Falcone, who visits her frequently."

"Tina."

"The policeman's daughter," Maranzano said with a nod. "Sofia has been true to you in every way."

"If I could believe it," Nilo said.

"You can. I have been in charge of this," Maranzano said officiously. "It is only wrong to believe with a whole heart in things which are empty of truth. 'Quae volumus et credimus libenter, et quae sentimus ipsi, reliquos sentire speramus,'" Maranzano quoted. "Caesar, of course."

Nilo thought and remembered the passage. " 'We believe to be true what we want to be true . . . and we expect everybody else to believe the same as we ourselves do.' That's it, isn't it?"

Maranzano nodded and refilled their wineglasses. "Well done," he said. "It is a good quotation and useful to check yourself against it and remember that your enemies can always delude themselves. When they do, they are vulnerable."

Not just enemies, Nilo thought, anger creeping back into his thoughts. *Even friends can delude themselves. Like you, Don Salvatore, in believing that my wife is my wife in anything but name, at least for now.* Still, he said, "I will remember that, Don Salvatore. I will remember."

After that, Nilo dozed off and woke only when the train pulled into Grand Central Station. Twilight had just settled in and a limousine was waiting to take Nilo home to the apartment that Maranzano had rented for Sofia and the baby.

As Nilo got out of the limousine, Maranzano handed him a set of keys.

"These are for your place," he said. "A man should be able to open his own door."

It was a simple comment, but Nilo had to fight back tears. Maranzano reached into his pocket and brought an envelope from it and handed it to Nilo.

"Take this. It will help you get started. Take your wife out. Become a free man again. Sleep late. In a few days, when you are ready, come to see me. There will be time enough for work then. Now, go surprise your wife."

Nilo nodded briskly and turned away.

He took a moment to find their apartment number on the mailbox and walked up the two flights of stairs. He unlocked the door of the unfamiliar apartment and went inside.

The place was quiet. For a moment, he thought of calling out Sofia's name, of telling her that he was home, but he did not. Instead, he stood in the entrance to the living room and admired the vastness of it. He relished the unbarred windows, the clean smell, the quietness.

And then he realized the apartment was not quiet. There were sounds coming from the bedroom. Unmistakable sounds. Sofia was laughing; in a way he had never heard her laugh before.

Nilo stood quietly clenching his fist. He considered turning around and leaving.

Caesar was right. We believe what we want to believe.

He thought of that calmly and then everything inside his brain went red. Nilo went quietly into the kitchen and, using the dim light coming through the window, carefully selected a butcher knife, the biggest, sharpest one there.

He crossed back to the bedroom door, which was ajar, and eased it open. Sofia was in bed on her stomach and someone was over her, but it was not a man; it was a woman. Both women were wearing bras and panties. The woman's hands were all over Sofia, all over her back and her buttocks, and Nilo stood watching them. They were oblivious to everything except each other.

He undid the fly of his pants and took himself in his hand as he watched. The two naked women—and now he recognized the other as Tina Falcone—were twisting and moving as though they were being jolted with electric shocks. Nilo stepped back, shook off his jacket, and dropped it on the floor. He stepped out of his shoes and stood transfixed, breathing quickly. They were beautiful. He wanted them both. He stepped out of his pants and started across the soft carpeted floor, toward the bed.

Then Tina, who was on top, made a half turn and saw him, saw the knife in his hand.

She looked at him with slowly mounting terror; he smiled back at her and her face calmed. She made no effort to move off Sofia, whom she was straddling. Nilo smelled the aroma of liquor in the room and saw two brandy glasses on the end table.

He had been too long without a woman. He could not help it. He moved forward and then Sofia saw him and screamed.

The world went blank for just an instant, and when he knew what he was doing he had Tina by the hair, pulling her from the bed, fighting off Sofia, cursing and shouting at both of them.

Nilo dragged Tina from the bedroom, shoved her out into the living room, and slammed the door behind her. Back in the bedroom, Sofia was huddled in the far corner of the bed, looking like a small frightened, very beautiful animal. Nilo grabbed her by the shoulders and pulled her to him. There was no fight in her, just a strange heaviness, almost a sort of passive lethargy.

Nilo carefully opened her legs. She made no effort to fight him off. Slowly he took off the rest of his clothing, then sat on the edge of the bed and began caressing her breasts and her belly. She shuddered under his touch but made no effort to escape. He climbed on top of her and began working on her as hard as he could, hoping not to satisfy but to punish, not to give pleasure but to inflict hurt.

She lay with her eyes closed and merely accepted him. When he was done, he laid his face next to her throat and said, "Your husband's home."

"I prayed every night that you would die in prison," she said.

Nilo laughed aloud.

He went into the bathroom to wash. When he came back out, Sofia was in the kitchen making coffee.

"Do you want coffee?" she asked him.

"I want you," Nilo said.

She followed him back into their bedroom, the same half-dead expression on her face.

TOMMY CAME UP the steps three at a time. Just a small whisper in the back of his mind told him to be careful, but there was no shelter, no place to hide, and the stairway was too well lighted for stealth.

All he could do was pray that Nilo was not waiting at the top with a gun, ready to blow his brains out.

He put his hand on his revolver in his jacket pocket, then listened at Sofia's apartment door. It was quiet inside. He thought of knocking, then decided not to. He tried the door, and as the knob turned under his hand the door was flung open and Nilo was standing there, dressed in slacks and an expensive-looking white dress shirt. He seemed as surprised to see Tommy as Tommy was to see him.

"Tommy."

"Is everything all right?"

"That's not much of a welcome-home greeting," Nilo said.

"Welcome home. Where's Sofia?"

"She's inside. Could I get you a drink or something?" Nilo asked. "I'm not sure what we've got. I've been away, you know."

Tommy shook his head. "I just came to see if Sofia was all right."

"Oh?"

"Yes. Tina called me and sounded upset. She seemed to think you were about to hurt Sofia."

Nilo did not answer immediately. Instead, he poured himself a drink from the small bar in the corner of the living room, then sat in a soft armchair.

"I suppose you'd like to see Sofia to be sure she's not hurt?"

"Yes. I suppose I would."

"You're asking as a policeman?"

"Call me a friend of the family."

"I used to call you brother," Nilo said. When Tommy did not answer, Nilo walked to the bedroom door, opened it, and stuck his head inside.

"Tommy's here. He's worried that you might have been hurt. Come out here."

Tommy could hear some sounds from inside the bedroom. It seemed to be an objection to Nilo's request. It was all sort of awkward, and the longer he was in this place, the sillier he was beginning to feel.

He heard Nilo snap, "I don't give a damn. I want you out here. Now."

Tommy bridled at the words. It was not that he cared particularly for Sofia; it was just that he had always been taught that men did not talk that way to women. He started to say something, then checked himself. It was none of his business. None of this was, and he shouldn't even have been here.

Sofia came reluctantly into the room. She was wearing a sheer nightgown with a silk wrap over it. Tommy thought the white gown was very like the one she had been wearing that day, so long ago. She looked as beautiful as ever, Tommy thought, then realized he was staring.

"Hello, Sofia," he said.

"Hello, Tommy." Her voice was cool, totally without inflection.

"Tina was worried about you. Asked me to come and check in on you."

"I'm fine," Sofia said. "Tell Tina not to worry. There's nothing wrong. My husband's just come home and I want to spend some time with him."

Tommy looked around the room. "Where's the baby?"

"He's fine, too. With my mother," Sofia said.

"Oh. Okay." Tommy felt awkward and out of place and was not made more comfortable when Nilo started to laugh.

"Now you can go, Tommy," Nilo said.

"I'm going."

"All these years in the can, I thought you were bopping my wife," Nilo said.

Tommy saw Sofia shaking her head.

"I come home today," Nilo said, "and I find my wife and your sister in bed."

"She was giving me a massage. My back is hurt," Sofia said.

"Sure," Nilo answered.

Tommy walked over to Nilo's chair and loomed over him. "I don't believe you," he said.

"You've got no business here," Nilo said casually. "I'll invite you back if I decide that the four of us should have a party."

Tommy looked down at him. "Don't ever go near Tina."

"Why not?"

"Because if you do, I'll kill you," Tommy said.

Nilo's face was impassive. "I'm sorry, Tommy. I don't think you have it in you."

"I should have let them fry you. Before that liar got you turned loose."

"You didn't do it for me. You did it for that big stupid thing you call justice. Well, I've been three years in the big house and I've made my own plans for justice."

"Touch my family and you'll get more justice than you're counting on," Tommy said coldly.

"It's funny," Nilo said. "You saved me once and I saved you once. I guess that makes us even," Nilo said. "No more debts to repay."

"No. No more debts," Tommy said, and felt a wave of revulsion sweep over him. He walked from the apartment, slamming the door behind him as he left. By the time he got back to his apartment, his teeth were chattering, even though it was a warm day. He poured himself a glass of red wine to try to chase the shivers and downed it in three quick gulps.

BACK IN NILO'S APARTMENT, Sofia said again, "Tina was only giving me a massage. She's been doing that. My back hurts since having the baby."

"We will not talk about it anymore. No matter what

kind of perverted slut you are, you are my wife. You are the mother of my son. We will go on. You will do what I say, act as I tell you, perform when I order you."

He poured himself another glass of wine. "You are garbage, but you are my garbage. Don't ever forget it."

TOMMY THINKS ALL THE DEBTS ARE PAID, but he's wrong. A lot of people have to pay me back for those three years I lost. Tommy. His family. All the rest. And they're going to start paying up soon.

That thought was on Nilo's mind as he strolled into Mangini's Restaurant. Nothing had changed. He had been away for three years, but the restaurant seemed to him to have been frozen in time.

The tables were in the same location they had been years before and still bore identical red-and-white-checked tablecloths. The lights were still small hanging chandeliers over the center of each table.

Sofia's mother still stood anxious guard over the cash register; her father still greeted guests. Rosalia Mangini looked no older than she had when he had last been there, but then she had always looked like an ancient gnome. Matteo was still the same archetypically handsome Sicilian peasant, only now there were white blazes along the sides of his black hair. He seemed also to be stooped, not standing as erect as he once had been.

There was still raucous noise coming from the open door of the private back room, a room still guarded by two hard-faced men who sat at a table near its entrance. They studied Nilo as he entered; he did not even favor them with a glance.

Matteo hurried up to meet him, all waving arms and big smiles.

"Look, Mama, it's our son-in-law," he called out to Mrs. Mangini, who looked at Nilo with frank disinterest.

"I'm looking for Luciano. Is he here?" Nilo asked Matteo sharply.

Mangini was taken aback for a moment. He took a deep breath before answering.

"Just go back and tell him I'm here," Nilo snapped. He walked off to a vacant table in an empty corner of the room, and before Matteo could even move, Luciano came out of the private back room. Trailed by two bodyguards, he approached Nilo's table, smiled warmly, and shook Nilo's hand.

"I heard that you were being released," Luciano said. "When'd you get back?"

"Yesterday."

Luciano sat down, across from Nilo.

"So?" he said. "How is your baby? Your wife? It's odd, isn't it, that we are now sort of relatives, since you married my cousin?"

"A man picks his friends; he is stuck with his relatives," Nilo said, still smiling. "He also picks his bodyguards, and you ought to get better ones than those two."

"Oh? And why is that?"

"Because they saw me smiling and they instantly went to sleep. Their hands are out of their pockets, on the table. I could shoot you now and have time to shoot them too before they even got their hands on their guns. And the one with gloves is stupid. He was stupid when you used him as a spy, driving for Maranzano. I don't think he's gotten any smarter. You can afford better, Charlie."

"You seem to have gotten very smart yourself in prison."

"I learned some things. Someday I'll tell you about them. Is the linguini here as good as I remember?"

Luciano shook his head. "After you've been in the can,

nothing is as good as you remember. But it is still very good. Join me for dinner?"

"Thanks, but I haven't got time," Nilo said. Luciano, he thought, was growing impatient. *He should try prison. It teaches a man to take his time, to wait.*

"So did you want to say something to me?"

Nilo nodded. "Back in prison, I thought I would have to kill you. For turning me in, for trying to shoot me down in the street. But I was young then."

Luciano showed no expression. "And now?"

"I believe you did what you had to do. I find no fault with that." Nilo stood up to leave. He leaned over to Luciano. "We are on different sides, Charlie. But it's business. It doesn't have to be personal."

"I'm glad you feel that way. And in the meantime, if there's anything I can do . . ."

"No hard feelings, Charlie. But I'm owed for three years. Maybe someday, you'll do me a favor."

"I do lots of favors."

"The day may come when you want to do me this favor."

"Yeah?"

"I want Tina Falcone," Nilo said. "I thought you might be getting tired of her."

"You thinking of opening a nightclub?" Luciano asked.

Nilo was surprised that Luciano had misunderstood him. But he answered, "Possibly."

"It's a tough buck. I'm thinking of quitting," Luciano said. "If I do . . ."

Nilo shook his head. "You don't have to say anything now. As I said, the day might come." He turned toward the door. "And please, Charlie, do something about those bodyguards. They'll get you killed if you're not careful."

"I'm always careful," Luciano said.

————————

A FEW NIGHTS LATER, toward the end of his shift, the thought of retirement popped into Tony's head unbidden, as he sat moving papers around in his Italian Squad office.

For a long time, Tony had watched the police winning the battle over the gangs. It had seemed as if crime was on the way out. But then came Prohibition and with that stupid experiment the gangs—like some virulent seed that could lie underground for years without dying— roared back into life, worse than ever.

If the police department thought it was going to wage an all-out war against the organized criminals, he had news for them. *The war is over. We lost.*

That had become ever clearer in the last few years. When Tony had come to America as a boy in the 1880s, the Black Hand and the Mafia were riding high in the city, preying on the new Italian immigrants, demanding extortion money just to let them live. Tony's own father, a barber, had had his run-ins with the mobsters early, re-fusing to pay them anything. For someone else, this might have led to terrorism and an early grave, but the elder Falcone was such a large and powerful man, driven by an unbending sense of right and wrong, that the petty Mafia bosses in the neighborhood did not want to tangle with him, and so they left him alone. He was one of the few so treated, and from him Tony learned the lifelong lesson that evil could be beaten if a man would stand up against it.

"This is America," his father would tell him. "It should have no place for these vultures."

For a time, as Tony was growing up and then joining the police force, he thought that his father had been right.

Slowly the power of the street gangs and extortionists had waned. When he first came on the police force, it seemed to Tony that sometime during his career the last thug from the last mob would be in jail and that chapter in the Italian immigrants' life would be over.

But then Prohibition and the gangs roared back into life, worse than ever. There was just too much money to be made, and this time, the bootleggers and the speakeasy operators were not moral outcasts as they had been in the past. Instead, they were accepted into polite society. Nobody in America, it seemed, except a handful of zealots believed at all in Prohibition, and with everybody bellying up to the bar, the idea that rum-running was even a crime at all just simply melted away. It might be time to let others fight the battle.

Crime is Main Street now, and almost everybody in America is a partner in it. Even the kids growing up see where the money is to be made and they're joining the gangs again, the same kind of gangs my father and people like him worked to destroy.

These things were on Tony's mind as he closed up his rolltop desk and put on his jacket to go home. It had all been a waste of time, a whole career frittered away chasing bad guys whom the public did not want to have caught.

The telephone rang as he walked toward the door. He thought for a moment of ignoring it, but habit won out and he picked it up.

A voice he did not recognize spoke to him in a thick Sicilian accent.

"Charlie Luciano is in Mangini's Restaurant. He's been waving guns around in there. I thought you'd want to know." Click.

To hell with it, Tony thought. *Who cares?* He walked

outside the precinct building. *Oh, well. It's right across the street from my house.*

WHEN LUCIANO, FLANKED by his two bodyguards, strolled out of Mangini's toward his parked car, Tony was waiting.

"All right, Luciano," he barked. "Up against the car."

The two bodyguards reached inside their jackets, but Luciano said quickly, "It's all right, boys. This is our neighborhood policeman."

"Forget the talk and get up against the car, I said."

Luciano casually moved toward the waiting roadster. "Mind if I ask why?"

"I want to see if you're carrying a gun," Tony said.

"I never carry a gun."

"Let's see."

Tony could see that people were leaning out the windows of the apartments up and down the block to watch this little drama.

He forced Luciano to spread his legs and lean against the car. Then he frisked him up and down his body but could find no gun.

"I told you, I never carry a gun."

"That's right," said one of the bodyguards, the one whom Tony noticed always wore gloves. "He don't need no gun."

"Shut up, stupid. Who's talking to you?" Tony snapped. He turned back to Luciano. "All right, pimp. You can go."

"When are you going to stop harassing law-abiding citizens?" Luciano asked.

"You? Never. The rest of your life, every time you look around, look hard. You'll see me. Someday you'll make a mistake, and I'll be there, waiting."

"Waste your time if you want," Luciano said. He too noticed the people watching from apartment windows. He glared at them as if taking names, and some of the heads vanished back inside.

One of the bodyguards came forward to open the back door of the big touring car, and as Luciano began to move inside he turned to Tony with a smile. "I'll have to tell Tina I saw you tonight. I guess she doesn't come around to visit. . . ."

Before he could finish his remark, Tony Falcone had moved close to him, slid his hand under Luciano's unbuttoned suit jacket, and grabbed a big chunk of flesh just above the mobster's belt. He squeezed it in his powerful hand and Luciano grimaced in pain.

"Don't say another word," Tony said. "Or you'll regret it."

Luciano squirmed free and soundlessly got in the car. A moment later, it roared away from the curb.

In the backseat, Luciano mumbled, "No. You're going to regret it."

NILO SPENT MOST OF THE NIGHT in a brothel on Park Avenue. When he got home, Sofia and the baby were asleep, but she had left him a note.

"Charlie called. He said he'll do you that favor anytime you want."

Nilo thought, *It's time to start paying back the Falcones for all the years I spent in prison.*

IT WAS NOT YET NOON on a cool fall day and Tina was no longer used to being up so early. Her last show had ended not nine hours before, and she stifled a yawn as she walked across Broadway and turned left down Fifty-second Street to Luciano's club. Outside the club, she inspected the life-size wooden portrait of herself. It was beginning to look a little faded, just the way she felt.

Tina had never thought it could happen, but she was starting to get tired of singing for a living. For a long time, she had taken strength from the audiences, but that had begun to pale. More and more nights now, she found herself just going through her routine from memory, not really concentrating, not really caring what she was giving the audience or what they felt about it. And her relationship with Luciano had definitely cooled. He had not been to her apartment in a couple of months; when they talked, it was business. She went by herself now to the opium parlors on Pell Street.

She was beginning to think it was time to move on. A new movie, *The Jazz Singer,* had been packing in audiences. It featured Al Jolson singing. Everybody was scrambling now to make new talking and singing movies, and the word was that Hollywood was looking for people with voices to star in them. And then last night, in the club, a young man had come to her table and introduced himself as a motion picture agent and she had agreed to meet with him today.

Why not me in movies? I'm young enough and I can sing, and if I'm not as pretty as I used to be, I still won't scare anybody away.

The watchman let Tina in and she went back to her office to wait. The club belonged to Luciano, but for the last year or two—there had never been a definite time when it had happened—she had been running the place for him.

She ran it the way she wanted the place to be, as a

hangout for interesting people, almost a clubhouse. She served her regular customers at cost and soaked the tourists, and nobody seemed to mind. It was true that business had started to tail off, especially since Tina missed many shows now because of a liquor or drug hangover, but Charlie had never complained, and the police—thanks to exorbitant bribes—had never bothered her.

The office held a lot of memories for her. She used to be able to count on it: when Charlie came into the club late to see how things were going, they would usually wind up in the office, making passionate love on the couch or on top of the desk or on the floor, sometimes all three places, and she'd often time it so that she would go out on stage right afterward to sing her last set, with the feel of Charlie still on her body. But those days clearly had ended.

Twenty minutes later, the watchman led a young man into Tina's office. He was blond with wire-framed glasses and a bookkeeper's expression, but he moved with the wiry grace of an athlete. The name on his business card was Bill Congreve.

"I'm glad you were able to meet me, Miss Falcone," he said, and shook her hand when she offered it.

"Please. It's Tina." She offered him a drink, but Congreve seemed intent on business, so she asked him to describe his project.

"I'm working with a studio—I can't tell you which one—and we're thinking of filming *Aida*," he said. "I thought you'd be perfect."

"*Aida*'s for a soprano," Tina said. "I haven't been a soprano in a long time."

"This would be more modern," Congreve said. "With popular music instead of operatic arias. It's made for you."

Tina smiled at him, projecting all her sexuality. He seemed almost to blush.

"It's nice of you to say."

"There's a small problem, though," he said, then stammered, "I don't know quite how to say this."

"Why not just spit it out?"

"All right. Sometimes people, really beautiful like you, they, well, they just don't photograph well. We'd have to do a screen test so I can show it to the studio."

"There's nothing wrong with that," Tina said. He was a very presentable young man, she thought. Actually handsome, if he'd just get rid of those silly eyeglasses.

"We're kind of desperate for time. And I was wondering if it'd be possible for you to do the test today. It wouldn't be far from here. Just up in the Bronx."

"When?"

"Right now?" Congreve said.

She smiled. "Sure. Let's do it."

She drove with Congreve out of Manhattan, talking of classical music and opera, things Tina had not spoken to anyone about for many months. He stayed vague about which studio he might be working for—he called that "a state secret"—and the car finally stopped in a run-down area of the Bronx, an industrial section built up with only warehouses and factories.

"Not much to look at," Congreve said, "but the space was cheap."

He came around and opened the door for Tina, and she took his hand to step down from the car. She touched his arm gently with her own hand and smiled into his eyes.

"I have a good feeling about this day," she said. "I've already spoken more to you than I have to anybody else in months."

"Well, maybe we'll see more of each other," Congreve

said. Impulsively, Tina kissed him on the cheek, and she saw him blush again. She laughed merrily, took his arm, and followed him inside the nearest building.

It seemed like a warehouse. Congreve hustled Tina off to a seedy little dressing room.

"Put on your makeup real theatrical, okay? It films better that way," he said. "And here's your costume."

As Tina sat in front of the mirror, intensifying her eye makeup and lipstick, Congreve said, "The idea is that you're a slave girl being brought to the pharaoh's throne. You're scared of him, but you have to please him if you want to go on living. Okay?"

"I understand," Tina said.

"Nervous?" Congreve asked.

"Maybe a little."

He poured her a glass of wine from a bottle on a nearby table. "This'll calm you down," he said.

She sipped the wine as she finished doing her makeup, then stepped behind a screen and put on the costume. It looked vaguely Egyptian, with a long diaphanous skirt of nearly white gauze and a short halter top that barely covered her breasts.

With a grin, Congreve passed the glass of wine to her over the top of the dressing screen.

"This costume's a little risqué," she complained lightly.

"We want to be sure to show you off to your best advantage."

She sipped the rest of the wine, stepped out from behind the screen, was rewarded by Congreve's open look of admiration, and then felt herself becoming dizzy and she collapsed to the floor. She heard Congreve laugh.

She passed in and out of consciousness over the next several hours. Only bits of what happened registered on her mind.

She remembered being placed on a felt-covered table. She saw Congreve standing between her legs. He ripped off her clothing, and then she remembered he leaned forward and took her. He was big and it hurt. She remembered trying to yell but having her mouth covered by someone's hand.

Across the big room, she saw two men running a movie camera. She struggled and then passed out again.

The next thing she remembered was Congreve backing away from her, with a smile on his face.

"Who's next?" he called out. When one of the cameramen moved forward, she tried again to scream, but no sound came out.

TOMMY HAD PROMISED not to talk to his father about Captain Cochran's offer, but he had not said anything about not asking Mario's advice. He met his brother in the small study, but before they could talk, the telephone rang.

Mario answered it, listened for a moment, then scribbled something on a sheet of paper. He looked at Tommy with alarm on his face.

"What is it?"

"Somebody said Tina's in trouble."

Tommy jumped to his feet. "What kind of trouble?"

"I don't know. Just trouble. At this address."

Tommy scooped up the note. "That's in the Bronx," he said.

"The church car's out front. Let's go."

Tommy drove as if he were on a racecourse, and it was not many minutes before they pulled up beside the big warehouse building in the Bronx.

As they got out of the car, he said, "We don't know

what we're going to find here, but if there's any rough stuff, Mario, leave it to me."

With Mario following him, they entered the building through a small side delivery entrance and moved, unnoticed, through the building until they came to a large open room.

Tommy recoiled and threw out an arm to halt Mario. They saw a woman sprawled naked across a table that looked like some sort of pagan altar. She was moaning.

"I . . . oh, God. That's Tina," Mario said. The two brothers ran across the large room. In a corner of the room was a large motion picture camera on a tall tripod stand.

Mario tore off his black priest's jacket and tossed it over Tina. Then he lifted her in his arms and started for the door.

Tommy almost vomited at the sight. Tina's face and body were bloodied.

Outside, Mario was getting into the backseat of the car, cradling Tina on his lap as if she were a child. She seemed to be regaining consciousness.

Tommy hopped behind the wheel and drove quickly away.

"Where do you want to go, Mario?" he asked.

"There's a Catholic hospital only a few blocks away."

Tommy careered the car around a corner. Tina opened her eyes feebly just then and looked around blankly. When she saw her brothers, she began to scream and kept on screaming, despite Mario's efforts to calm her, until she passed out.

Inside the hospital, Mario's Roman collar was like a letter from the pope, and when a gaggle of nuns helped him get Tina into a room Tommy drove back to the warehouse.

There were still no signs of people around. He went

into the large room and opened the side compartment of the movie camera, which had been left behind. Inside was a large spool of movie film, and angrily Tommy wrenched it from the machine and unwound it onto a big pile on the floor. Then he set fire to the film and watched it burn down to ash.

All the while, he asked himself how Tina could have gotten involved in something like this. He knew none of the details, but he was sure of one thing: if she had never met Charlie Luciano, it never would have happened.

When the film was totally burned, Tommy walked through the rest of the warehouse, but it was unused and empty, devoid of even so much as a desk or a filing cabinet. The only thing he found was a small dressing room with some makeup on a table and Tina's clothes hanging over a dressing screen. There was a bottle of red wine in the room and a glass with lipstick on the rim. He smelled the wine and knew it had been drugged. So that was how it had been done.

He took the clothing back to the hospital, where he found Mario waiting for him outside Tina's room.

"How is she?"

Mario answered, "It's pretty bad. She was slapped around and roughed up by a bunch of goons, but no major damage. They're just going to keep her overnight for observation."

"She say who did it?"

"She's still groggy. I think she was drugged."

"I know she was," Tommy said.

"But she said she never saw them before. She didn't know them."

"Were they Luciano's men?" Tommy asked.

"I don't know. I think she would have said."

He took Tina's clothes and carried them to her room.

"She's sleeping," Mario said. "The nurses say there's no point in our hanging around."

"You can take the car. I'll stay. I'll get a lift back to the city."

"One thing she said. Don't tell Papa."

"Why not?" Tommy asked.

"She's afraid he'll shoot somebody or get himself shot. She doesn't want him to know."

Tommy thought, then nodded. "Just us," he said.

After Mario left, Tommy went inside and sat at Tina's bedside all night long. It was in the small hours of the morning before they finally had a chance to talk. Tina told him the whole story.

"Have you been having trouble with Luciano?" Tommy asked, but his sister shook her head.

"Charlie wouldn't do this. Not to me." She started to cry softly and Tommy patted her hand and murmured reassuringly, "You're right. Now go back to sleep. You're going to be fine."

In the morning, with a pair of dark glasses and extra-heavy makeup, Tina looked good enough to travel, and she and Tommy rode back to Manhattan in a cab. After swearing Tommy never to tell their father what had happened, she insisted on being alone in her apartment for a while.

Tommy left her, went to his own apartment, and sat by the telephone for a long time. He had been wrong and his father had been right. No one could coexist peacefully with the mob, with the gangsters. It was in their blood, and they would keep coming after you, keep poisoning everything they touched, until you were surrounded by dirt and evil. The only way to get rid of dirt was to scrub it off. But he had always thought that was somebody else's fight. Until now.

Tommy telephoned Captain Cochran at the Italian Squad.

"Tommy Falcone, Captain. Can you talk?"

"Yeah. Your father's out of the office."

"About that job. I'm your man."

"Good. Go through the motions of getting off the force. File your resignation papers."

WHILE TOMMY WAS ON THE TELEPHONE, a reel of movie film and an envelope of still photographs was delivered to Nilo at his apartment.

TINA QUIT HER JOB as headline singer at Luciano's Ross's Club. He did not protest; he announced that the club was closing.

AT THE END OF THE SUMMER, after Tommy had publicly left the police force, Rachel Mishkin moved into his apartment. She started to paint constantly, filling the tiny space with canvases of a hideousness almost impossible to describe, and lately she had developed the annoying habit of singing little songs to herself while she was painting.

She smiled a lot, too, and now she had insisted that he meet her father—her mother was dead—and no day but this one would do.

Tommy looked up at the wall clock over the counter in the diner. It was after 10:00 P.M. and they were nearly an hour late. Rachel had warned him about that. There was no counting on her father, she had said, when he was out rallying workers to more and more union militancy.

The front door of the restaurant flew open and Rachel breezed in, followed by a stocky man with water running down his face. Obviously, neither had thought of an umbrella and both were soaked to the skin. In a moment, Rachel was with Tommy, shaking her wet frizzy curls in his direction, and she smelled so pure, so fresh and sweet, that his sour mood vanished on the spot.

"Have I ever told you you remind me of this dog I had once?" Tommy asked.

"Oh, be quiet. You never had a dog. I remember you telling me all those sad stories about how deprived you were as a boy."

"Well, I intend to have a dog someday. And you'll remind me of him then."

She laughed and kissed him warmly.

"Isn't he wonderful, Daddy?" she said.

Her father shrugged elaborately, water splashing from the top of his nappy head, too.

The whole family are like water spaniels, Tommy thought. *They should go nowhere without bath towels.*

"Look at her," her father said. "Only one generation away from the old country and already she is trying to talk like the English. God save us all."

Tommy extended his hand. "I'm Tommy Falcone, Mr. Mishkin. And I'm glad to meet you. I've read a lot about you."

Mishkin shook his hand. "I just bet you have and none of it good. Sit down and do us all a favor. Don't call me Mr. Mishkin. Everybody—friends, enemies, everybody—calls me Lev. *She* calls me Lev," he said nodding toward his daughter. "Why should you be different?"

The waitress came and, unbidden, presented them with three coffees. When she left, Mishkin said, "I came to offer you a job."

"I'm living off my savings for a while," Tommy said. "While I finish law school."

Mishkin shook his head. "There are too many lawyers already. You could work for me."

"Doing what?"

Mishkin squinted at him, stood up, and leaned across the table. While he was a short man, Tommy noted he was immensely thick through the chest and shoulders. He had deep, piercing eyes that he purposely used to good effect—eyes set in a face that looked as if it had been made of leftover pieces of putty stuck together to make an approximate ball.

"You were once a policeman," he said. "I won't be coy with you. I'll tell you straight out. I know everything there is to know about you. If I didn't know it, I wouldn't be here speaking to you. So I will speak to you straight from the shoulder, as you Americans say."

He sipped his coffee and seemed to find it distasteful, because he pushed the cup away. "Sugar," he said. "People in America think everything needs sugar. Nothing needs sugar. Anyway, union organizing is a hard business. Maybe even a brutal business. Our men have spilled much blood. I warn you I am not a patient man. I believe in the Old Testament, not the New. I don't believe in turning even the first cheek. I believe in an eye for an eye. Are you following me, or does your mouth always hang open?"

Tommy self-consciously snapped his mouth shut. "I follow you," he said.

"So. So not so many years ago, the bosses in the clothing factories see that they are losing to us. That we are organizing their members, and they do not know what to do. All their normal threats and beatings do not work. Still, they do not give in. No. They find new ones to bring violence to us. They go to this man, Joe Masseria, the one they call 'the Boss,' and he does a good job. He scares many of our people, kills some. It is looking bad for us. And then I remember that every organism, every nation, everything has its own internal enemies, enemies far more subtle and dangerous to itself than anything that could attack it from the outside."

Mishkin bellowed a "tea" order to the waitress and waited for it to arrive. This time, inexplicably, he half-filled the cup of tea with sugar before sipping at it. Throughout his whole recitation, Rachel stared at him in rapt attention while fondling Tommy under the table with her near hand.

"So," Mishkin said, "I ask questions. I find that this Boss Joe has many enemies within his own organization. But most of them are thugs, no smarter, no better than Masseria. I ask more people and I learn of the one, Salvatore Maranzano, the one they call 'the Castellammarese.' I go to him, not hat in hand, but as one man to another, one chief to another. We talk. I offer him money, much money to work for me and to fight Masseria's men whenever it is needed. This he agrees to do, and within a few months everything is back where it was before the trouble started."

Rachel was trying to unbutton Tommy's fly, and he found it more difficult to concentrate.

"So far, so good," Mishkin said. "That was six months ago. But now there's a problem."

"Maranzano wants your union," Tommy said.

"How do you know that? Does this come naturally to you Italians?"

"If Machiavelli lived here in New York today, he'd be a plumber," Tommy said. "Of course he wants your union, because everything he gets is something that

Masseria doesn't have. When the war between them comes, the one with the biggest army will win."

"So I'm a pawn?" Mishkin asked. "You're telling me I'm a pawn?"

"Something like that," Tommy said. "So what's this job?"

"I don't know. Maybe negotiate. Maybe shoot them. I don't know. All I know is these people are one step ahead of me. I decide to go into a factory, they are there first. If I get people signing union membership cards, they are there with the muscle before I get them all signed up, and the next thing I know, they control the shop steward and they talk of starting a new union. They are too damned smart for me."

"There's probably a leak inside your own organization," Tommy said. "That's how they know what you're up to."

Lev Mishkin smiled at his daughter. "See? Already he's thinking straighter than I am. Why don't I figure out things like that?" He said to Tommy, "I need you. I need some *goyische kup*. Some non-Jew brain who can think like these people, who can figure out what they're doing so we can do something about it and get on with our lives."

"You deal with Maranzano directly?"

"No. Not anymore." Mishkin smiled slyly. "One of his lieutenants, Danny Neill. You know him?"

"I know him," Tommy said softly.

"Good. You talk to him. Make them go away. I don't need them anymore. Let's try to make one business in New York that these gangsters don't control."

"I don't think I can negotiate with him," Tommy said.

"Why not?"

"Because the last time I saw him, I threatened to kill him."

"Good. Don't negotiate. Murder. Whatever you want, as long as you get it done."

"Look, I'm not going to mess up law school. But let me nose around on my own time and see what I can find out. I don't know anything about unions. Is there somebody who could help me?"

There is a man I've worked with for many years. We first met back in one of the czar's prisons in 1903 or 1904. His name is Harry Birchevsky, and he knows the garment business and he's one of us Jews. You know the law and Italians. Together you ought to be unstoppable."

"You wish," Tommy said.

"I'll want to pay you," Mishkin said.

"Whatever you think it's worth. After I do something."

Rachel's face swung toward Tommy. "Good answer," she said.

"Thank you."

"But from now on, don't turn down jobs. We'll need money for the baby we're going to make tonight. And we still have to get married."

Tommy looked at her in shock, then turned his face to Mishkin. The old man said, "Get married. Please, by all means. And knock her up. Then maybe she'll stop grabbing you in public restaurants."

• *Tommy had wound up telling no one in his family, not even Mario, that he was working undercover for the police department, and he had decided that the less Rachel knew, the better. But the secrecy weighed heavily on him, and one night he decided to talk to his old friend Tom Dewey. He found*

Dewey in a Masonic Hall, giving a tub-thumping speech in favor of a Republican candidate in an election. Tommy was mesmerized. In politics, Dewey had obviously found his calling; the idea of starting a law partnership with Tommy would be the last thing on his mind now. Tommy left without talking to him and continued to carry his secret alone.

- *On October 16, 1927, Jacob "Little Augie" Orgen, who ran the labor rackets for Masseria, finished dinner at a restaurant on Norfolk Street in Little Italy, then walked outside to get a cab. When the cab pulled up, waiting in the backseat was Orgen's right-hand man, Louis "Lepke" Buchalter. He cut down Orgen with a spray of .45 caliber bullets. Also wounded was Orgen's bodyguard, Jack "Legs" Diamond, who told police he never saw the killer. Lepke took over the labor rackets; in a month, he controlled the cutters' union, whose nineteen hundred members cut all the garments being sewn in New York. Without them, more than fifty thousand workers who sewed garments would be out of work. The manufacturers paid up for labor peace. Luciano said of his good friend, "Lepke loves to hurt people." He suggested that Lepke pool his talents with those of another good friend, Albert Anastasia. Murder Incorporated became Luciano's personal army.*

- *As more and more thugs moved from Masseria's mob to Maranzano's, Nilo found out that Joe Adonis's driver had been the one who had ratted him out to the police, after the killing of the young boy in Italian Harlem. One night, as the driver, Ric-Rac Greenwald, a loud, obnoxious thug, left a Broadway speakeasy on an errand for his boss, his car was pulled over to the curb by another car. Ric-Rac pulled his gun and was so intent on the people in the other car that he never noticed Nilo step from a building behind him, open the rear door, and put four bullets into his head. Adonis was outraged. He demanded that Luciano retaliate against Maranzano just to teach them a lesson. Luciano met with Meyer Lansky and Albert Anastasia. "Maybe it's time that we let these two Mustache Petes kill each other off," Luciano said. "And if they don't, I will," Anastasia proclaimed, and hugged Luciano. "I been waiting for this for years," Anastasia said. Two nights later, the Maranzano driver known as Rock was shot to death. The Castellammarese Wars, which pitted Maranzano's forces against those of Joe the Boss Masseria, had begun.*

- *Right after Thanksgiving, Tommy and Rachel were married in a small family ceremony, conducted by Father Mario and a rabbi. Only the immediate families attended.*

- *In Hollywood, a young man named Walt Disney made his first animated film about a mouse named Mickey. On Broadway, Helen Kane was singing "boop-boop-a-doop."*

- *Beer cost three dollars a barrel to make in New Jersey. Speakeasy operators in New York paid fifty dollars a barrel.*

- *In living rooms, people played with Ouija boards, and everybody dreamed of owning a Duesenberg automobile, just like actor Douglas Fairbanks did.*

CHAPTER 9

Fall and Winter 1928: The War Years

In Dannemora, Nilo had spent many hours thinking of Maranzano's crime family and how it should be restructured. He had convinced himself that Don Salvatore was too willing to talk even when talk was useless, too slow to act even when action was the only possible course.

He vowed that when and if he got out of jail, he would not make those mistakes. The only way to fight Masseria would be to fight him every step of the way. No victory should be conceded to Joe the Boss. Maranzano's men should fight not just for the bootlegging, but for control of the drug trade, prostitution, the unions, gambling. Every time a Masseria underling turned around, he should find a Maranzano man coming after him.

I want them all to be scared to death—Luciano, Adonis, Siegel, even Masseria. When they are terrified, we will have won.

When he rejoined the gang, Nilo had the chance to put his ideas to the test. He still paid lip service to Maranzano's idea of his being Danny Neill, the next-generation lawful tycoon who would run the family, but in practice he became the hammer behind all Maranzano's operations. His natural cruel streak had also been honed while he was in prison. The lives of others meant nothing to him now, and some of the Maranzano henchmen feared going out on jobs with him because Nilo was too quick to start shooting, too ready to get everyone, including himself, killed.

The first big operation he masterminded was an attempt to smuggle in aboard a cargo ship a hundred thousand dollars' worth of heroin. When it was cut and packaged, it would sell for more than 5 million dollars on the street.

Maranzano had been reluctant at first, but Nilo told him that Luciano was making millions in drug trafficking and the money was on the streets, just waiting to be picked up.

Nilo carefully selected a three-man team to get the drugs when they arrived at the Thirteenth Street pier. But one of the team liked to drink too much and, one night, in his cups, he told his brother-in-law about the big drug deal, and the brother-in-law—who drank too much, too—wound up in a speakeasy the next night bragging about his mob connections to an affable young man named Vito.

When Nilo's team went to the dock four nights later to pick up the drugs, they ran into a city police task force that had the area staked out. They escaped through a hail of bullets when Nilo drove their getaway car straight though a chain-link fence and vanished into a Maranzano-owned garage six blocks away.

They had escaped, but the drugs would be confiscated and Maranzano would be out the hundred-thousand-dollar cost. In a fury, Nilo lined the three men up against the getaway car at gunpoint. But facing death, each one denied having told anyone about the drug shipment.

Nilo considered killing the three as an object lesson, but he was able to restrain himself.

"I'm gonna let you three live. For now. But every one of you better start looking around. We got a rat somewhere in our family, and you better get me some names."

A week later, the brother-in-law cracked, and before being buried in a pit across the river in Kearny, New Jersey, he told of how he had been pumped by a young man named Vito. Nilo offered ten thousand dollars to anyone who would lead him to the informer.

Nilo fared better with his plan to make Maranzano a force in the city's giant garment district. But again, Maranzano seemed reluctant to move.

"This Masseria man, Lepke, has the cutters' union. Should we risk a fight with him?" the don asked.

"If we fight them here, we can win. If we don't, we may have to fight them somewhere else where we've got no chance of winning," Nilo said.

Maranzano thought for a long time, concealing his face behind his steepled fingers. "All right, Nilo," he finally said. "You do it."

Still his voice was hesitant, and when Nilo left the office he thought that Don Salvatore might be getting too old to run the family.

RACHEL WONDERED if Tommy was keeping something from her. He went out frequently at night, ostensibly to the law-school library, but when he returned home after she was already in bed, she sometimes smelled beer on his breath. And she wondered where he got the money to pay their household bills. But she never asked about it. She had faith in her husband.

ON ONE OF THE RARE NIGHTS that he stayed home, Nilo got out of bed quietly and went into the next room to look at his three-year-old son, Stephen. As he looked at the sleeping boy's smooth, handsome face, his nose that would one day be long and aquiline, he thought, *He looks like me.*

Since his return from prison, Sofia had insisted the baby was his. He had not, at first, believed her. But she never changed her story, and the truth was that since he returned, she had been a good wife to him, obedient and solicitous. He did not love her, but the idea of loving a wife, or any woman for that matter, seemed strange to him. A wife was meant to run the house and bear and raise children. Nothing else. It was only important that a wife love her husband, and in that regard Sofia had given him no reason to complain.

He reached out and touched the face of the small boy who stirred in his sleep. *Well, at least I know I am the father of the next one to be born.*

He went back into his own bedroom and lay next to Sofia again. He reached out and touched her big pregnant belly. *This baby is mine.*

He had wanted Sofia to become pregnant with his child as soon as he returned home from Dannemora, but month after month passed and she did not conceive. He was beginning to worry that perhaps there might be something wrong with him when Maranzano brought the subject up at a meeting one day in his office near Grand Central Station.

"Sofia? Is she not pregnant?"

Nilo shook his head. "We are trying."

"How old is your boy?"

"Two and a half," Nilo said.

"And Sofia is still nursing?"

Nilo nodded.

"It is time to put the boy on a bottle," Maranzano said. When Nilo looked up, puzzled, the older man said, "It is well known that women do not conceive while they are still nursing. The breasts must dry before the womb will accept another child. Trust me. Do it."

It had sounded like nonsense, an old wives' tale, to Nilo, but he had insisted to Sofia that the breast-feeding time had to end. She had finally given in. Nilo did his husbandly duty. He and Sofia had sex almost every other night, and while she was not an enthusiastic partner, she was willing and pliable.

Two months after she stopped nursing, she was pregnant. If she had thought that pregnancy would stop Nilo from insisting on sex with her, she was mistaken. He wanted it known, without doubt, that he and he alone was the father of this new child, who would be a boy and who would be named Salvatore, in honor of the don.

He took his hand off her belly and rolled back onto his side of the big bed. He thought of Tina Falcone and was unable not to think of the pictures he had of her. He kept the pictures and the original movie film in a locked box atop a shelf in his clothes closet, but often he took the pictures out, just to look at.

He liked looking at the pictures, feeling them, knowing that they were his and that if they were ever made public there would be no hole deep enough for her to crawl into and hide. And all the rest of the Falcones, too. It was a hammer to be used when the time was right.

Tina had never gone back to work at Luciano's speakeasy. The big plywood figure of her was taken away from outside Ross's Club, almost as if she had never existed, and the club was closed and soon sold. Tina was working in an office in the village, a job that Mario had gotten for her.

Nilo thought, *It is time for her to work for me. She will be famous again, and the more important and famous she becomes, the more lustrous her star, the easier she will be to control with that film and those pictures. Soon I will let her know what her job will be.*

Thinking of Tina's pictures had aroused him. He rolled back toward his wife, put his hands on her pregnant belly, and roughly entered her. Sofia moaned, then tried to pretend she was still asleep.

It doesn't matter, he thought. *You are here to be used by me.*

He released himself into her and, still wordless, rolled away, onto his back, and closed his eyes for sleep.

The doorbell rang.

He became instantly alert. Sofia did, too. He slipped from bed, pulled on a robe, and took his gun from the bedside table. Sofia was sitting up, wide awake—she had not been asleep at all, he knew—and was putting on her own robe.

"Let me answer the door," she said. "I will be safe."

"So will I," he said. "I have this." He raised his gun in front of his face, then went outside.

When he looked through the peephole before opening the door, he saw two of Maranzano's bodyguards in the hall, waiting for him.

"Don Salvatore wants you," one of them said.

"So late? What time is it?"

"Almost midnight. He told us to bring you."

"I'll meet you downstairs. Give me a few minutes to dress."

The men nodded and walked away.

Although Sofia looked at him, her face filled with unspoken questions, Nilo offered her no explanation. He dressed quickly, then went downstairs, where the men were parked in front in a large black sedan.

Nilo got in the backseat, alone, feeling secure with the weight of his gun in his jacket pocket. They drove east out of the city for what seemed an endless time but was only little more than an hour.

Nilo recognized the direction and knew the destination: Maranzano's estate out near Bellmore, Long Island. While the don spent most of his time at his New York apartment, he maintained a big country house for his childless wife and assorted hanger-on relatives. But it was rare for him to do any business there, so Nilo was in the dark on what the meeting would be about. But he knew something had been planned, because the don had been away from the office for the past few days.

Maranzano's home was a white colonial-style mansion in the middle of vast lawns and thick woods. The two bodyguards walked inside with Nilo and left him in a small waiting room. Two other men—both a little older than Nilo and dressed in ill-fitting pinstripe suits—were also there.

Somebody's bodyguards, Nilo thought. He had never seen either of them before, and no one spoke.

After a long time, a tuxedo-clad man of middle years opened one of the doors and said, "Danny Neill?"

Nilo stood up.

"This way, please."

Nilo followed the man into an immense formal dining room. Down its middle was a table forty feet long and ten feet wide. It had been set for supper in the finest china and silver. Men were seated all around the table and Nilo made a quick head count of forty men. He had seen many of them around Maranzano's real estate office before, but others were complete strangers.

His escort led Nilo to the head of the table where Maranzano himself sat. He rose to greet Nilo, and when he stood, all the others at the table rose, too.

Maranzano nodded at Nilo in recognition and gestured him to a vacant seat near his right hand. The old man turned back to the others.

"For the few of you who do not know him, this is my close advisor and associate, Danilo Sesta, who is joining with us tonight. He is sometimes known as Danny Neill. He is young, but he has already suffered much in our cause. And now he is putting terror in the hearts of our enemies."

The others all mumbled something more or less in unison, which Nilo took as a greeting. He found his heart beating wildly with excitement. This was what he had been hoping for for a very long time. It would be Maranzano's formal acknowledgment of Nilo's importance, delivered in front of all these top lieutenants.

Maranzano motioned for the others to stay seated, then surveyed the rest of the room with ponderous dignity.

"We are all the children of Castellammare del Golfo," he began. "We are a family and we live by our honor and our word."

Despite himself, Nilo was awed. He had longed to become a member of the Mafia brotherhood, but he had always half-sneered at the ritualistic ceremonies he had heard about. Now he found it impressive and dignified.

"Now a new one, Danilo Sesta, comes to our family to stand with us against our enemies."

Maranzano reached into the pocket of his black formal suit and removed a .38 revolver and a deadly looking dagger and set them in front of Nilo.

"These are what we live by. If necessary, these are what we die by."

He nodded to Nilo. "Rise, child of Castellammare del Golfo."

When Nilo stood, Maranzano said "Make a cup with your hands."

Nilo did as he was told, and Maranzano took a piece of paper and set it in his cupped hands.

"Now repeat after me," he said, lighting a match to the paper. "This is the way I will burn if I betray the secrets of this family."

Fighting to control the pain of the burning paper without showing it, Nilo repeated the words.

When the fire had gone out, Maranzano reached across and carefully parted Nilo's hands, letting the ash drift down to the table.

"There are three rules," Maranzano said. "Break any of them and the penalty is automatically death.

"The first is complete obedience to your superiors.

"The second is silence, *omerta,* complete and utter about our activities to outsiders.

"The third is to never touch the wives or female relatives of members of this family of the Castellammarese."

Nilo nodded.

"Extend your right hand." When Nilo did, Maranzano picked up the dagger and stuck it into the tip of Nilo's index finger until blood came. Nilo looked at his bleeding fingertip and remembered that it was the same one with which he had once shared blood with Tommy Falcone.

"This blood means you are now one of us. You have deserved this honor for a long time." He paused. "But I thought it best to wait until the fuzz on your cheeks had turned to whiskers and all here would recognize you as brother."

He smiled at Nilo, then looked around, and the entire table broke into applause for Nilo, along with laughs and shouts of congratulations. It lasted a long time, only subsiding when waiters poured into the room carrying large trays of food of all kinds and bottles of wine and liquor.

Nilo leaned over and took Don Maranzano's right hand in his and kissed it.

"This is more honor than I deserve, Don Salvatore," he said. "But you will never regret your decision here tonight."

"I know that, Nilo. You are truly my son." He leaned close. "Do not drink. We have business yet to do."

Throughout the after-dinner drinks, individually and in small clusters men seated at the table came up to congratulate Nilo and welcome him. Finally, the conversation died down and Maranzano rose in his place and lifted his glass.

"To all in our family . . . *salute*."

Around the table men raised their own wineglasses, and Nilo did the same. Although excited, he was now getting tired; he hoped this ceremony would end soon. But to his dismay, Maranzano seemed ready to talk on.

"The Mafia is an old organization," Maranzano said, "but this is a new country. And old things must change or else they will become weak and irrelevant. But you cannot talk change to some of those in other families. You know who they are. They see the world and cannot understand it and think nothing will ever change. But everything changes. The only thing unchanging is the permanence of the grave.

"We too will change as time goes on. Right now, we are a family of Castellammarese, and that is the way it must be, because we are brothers and we must treat each other as brothers. And we are brothers under attack. The people aligned with Joe Masseria . . ." Maranzano stopped and spat on the floor at his feet.

"The people aligned with Masseria have watched our growing power, our growing strength, and now have vowed that they will destroy our family. Separately, individually, they have begun to strike out at members of our family. They believe that they can quietly pick us off one by one until there are none left who will stand together. But as your leader I tell you now that will not happen. Even this very night, we strike back against them. It will be but another early battle in a long war. But I know, if we hold true to our beliefs and faith in each other, we will be victorious.

"Still I warn you, it will be dangerous out there now. It is not a time to relax one's guard. Be alert and be careful. The war has begun. You are my chosen lieutenants, each and every one of you. If you do not let yourselves become victims, you will be the victors. You have my word on it."

The men seated at the table cheered and applauded again at the declaration of war. Maranzano let the commotion die down before he spoke again.

Nilo stifled a sigh. He was growing weary with Maranzano's endless bombast.

"The great poet Florio talked of the nine pains of death," Maranzano said. "And the last and worst was to have a friend who would betray you. Let us resolve, each of us, to avoid that pain of death." The don sat down, again to applause.

Nilo realized everyone must have been as exhausted by the hour as he was because almost immediately men got up from the table and began, trying to disguise their haste, to bid Maranzano good night and to head for the door.

Nilo stayed in his seat and watched the men—the backbone of Maranzano's family—come up to the old Sicilian and pledge their undying loyalty.

Yeah. Until someone makes you a better offer, he thought.

Maranzano seemed to linger a long time in conversation with one man, who finally nodded and turned to Nilo.

Maranzano said, "Nilo, Brother Gentile has graciously agreed to drive you back to the city."

Nilo rose. "Thank you," he said to the man, who nodded again and said, "My driver and I will be out front."

As he left, Nilo was hugged by Maranzano in a warm embrace. The old man also whispered in his ear, and the words chilled Nilo more than any words ever had in his life.

He went outside and saw Gentile sitting in the back-seat of a waiting limousine. Nilo got in, expressed his thanks very strongly, and said, "I'm tired. I'm not used to these late hours." He sat back in a corner of the seat and closed his eyes.

About twenty miles toward New York City, on one of the lightly traveled highways that were under construction all over Long Island, the driver stopped at a traffic light.

Nilo sat up and glanced around. There were no cars visible at the intersection. He drew his gun from his pocket and shot Gentile in the head, then turned his gun on the driver and shot him too. He reached over the seat and turned off the key, then shot both men again at close range to make sure they were dead.

He got out of the car and a moment later was picked up by another car, which had been trailing them without headlights since they left Maranzano's estate. A man got out of the car and drove Gentile's auto away.

The driver, the only other person in the car, told Nilo, "I'll take you home now."

"Yes," Nilo said.

"Did everything go all right?" the man asked.

"As the don wished," Nilo said. He thought of Maranzano's chilling words at the house when he had ordered Nilo to kill Gentile. *He chose to serve Masseria.*

He sat quietly on the ride back, remembering other words Maranzano had spoken. He had said, "We Castellammarese are a good family and good friends."

Unless someone crosses us, Nilo thought. *And then we kill.*

DRESSED CASUALLY IN A SWEATER and skirt, Tina Falcone looked over at her bandleader, raised her arm, and then in her signature gesture slowly let it drop. There was a split-second pause and the band lit into a slow, string-driven version of "Lover, Come Back to Me."

Tina let them go through the introduction and then came in for the verse. It had been more than a year since she had sung, not since that nightmare in the warehouse in the Bronx. During the days of recuperating in her apartment, while Mario lied to her family and told them she had gone out of town, the question came back to her over and over: *Have I brought this all on myself? Is God punishing me for my sins?*

She tried to push the thoughts out of her mind. *Keep singing,* she told herself, and somehow she managed to get through the song. She glanced back at her bandleader and he was smiling without forcing it. She had done it all right this time.

"Okay, boys," she said when she had finished. "You were great as usual. I think I'm even getting a little better."

She was greeted with affectionate boos and hisses from the band. Things were coming along, getting looser. Last week and the week before had been a horror. She had been terrible and she knew it. No voice. No control. No passion. Nothing.

It was clear the band had felt sorry for her, although no one knew why they should. The gossip said she had gone into a sanitarium to dry out. Or away to have a baby. Or she was suffering from tuberculosis. There were a thousand explanations—all of them wrong—but they had all ended with the prediction that she would never be able to sing again as she had before.

Then three days ago, it had started to come back. The atmosphere at rehearsals had changed. Nobody felt sorry for her anymore.

"Okay, boys," she said. "I want to do sort of a real low-down 'Sweet Georgia Brown.' You know what low-down is, don't you? Just think of your sister-in-law. And then we'll sort of slide into a nice, ladylike—stop laughing, you—'Bye, Bye Blackbird.' "

The band played better than she had expected them to. They were obviously starting to catch on to her rhythms and phrasing and framing them with their own tempos and volume. And when the rehearsal was done, she sincerely thanked them for their work, sent them off for supper, and began making an inspection tour of the new club.

The days with Charlie Luciano and Ross's Club were over and done with. There was no going back to that, not ever. He had denied any part in her attack, of course. He had come to see her, and when he learned what had happened, he swore he was not involved. He even offered to find the young man, Congreve, and bring Tina his penis for proof. But Tina was beyond fixing blame for the evil humiliation she had suffered. She just wanted to put it behind her, put it out of her mind. To Luciano's offer, she had said, "It won't make any difference, Charlie." And she had meant it. She was moving on.

Nilo had made it possible. After she had gotten out of the hospital and taken the job Mario had found for her, Nilo had bought a club on Forty-seventh Street, just off Broadway, and soon after, he visited her apartment.

"I need help," Nilo said.

"The new club?"

"Yes."

"You need a singer?"

"No," he said, suddenly and flatly.

Before she could figure out what she had done wrong, before she could even speak, Nilo laughed aloud and said, "I don't need a singer. I need a partner. I bought this place and all I've got is money going out, nothing coming in. I need somebody who knows something. If you're willing, it can be our place. We'll call it the Chez Tina . . . no, the Falcon's Nest, and you can be my headliner and my manager. I'll put up the money. You put up the talent and the work and we share fifty-fifty."

That was a better deal than she had ever had with Luciano, who had paid most of her personal expenses but had kept her on a straight salary at Ross's. This was a new world of opportunity.

"Well, what do you say?" Nilo asked.

"Nilo, we were never that close. And then, when you came home, that business with Sofia. It was innocent, but it looked terrible and I regretted it so much. You'll never know how much. Why have you come to me?"

"We're family," he said, and smiled again. "I'll be back tomorrow and I'll bring you the club plans to look at."

AFTER LEAVING HER ROOM, Nilo went downstairs to his car, sat behind the wheel, and laughed aloud.

He had in his pocket a set of the pictures of Tina, taken during the assault in the warehouse.

And I didn't even have to use them, he thought. *She came along without even a suspicion. So I'll save the pictures for when I need them. When I want her to do something that she doesn't want to do.*

She'll do it then. She'll do anything I want her to do.

He had business to take care of in the Bronx, and as he drove slowly back to Manhattan, he passed the warehouse where Tina had been raped. He smiled to himself. It was one of the good things about the real estate business, knowing where vacant properties were located. And Don Maranzano, who had bought the vacant building to use for a liquor storage warehouse, did not even know what it had been used for.

No one knew. And no one would ever know, unless Nilo wanted them to.

TINA STOOD IN THE MIDDLE of the dance floor, watching the band leave, and surveyed the setup. It was basically the same as the Ross's Club, only more so—better, plusher, more classy. She was proud of it, glad that Nilo had given her the chance to do it right.

"MISS FALCONE."

She turned around. It was one of the nightclub's young pages.

"Mrs. Neill is in your office."

"Mrs. Neill?" It took her a moment to realize that Mrs. Neill was Sofia. Nilo had taken to calling himself Danny Neill in public, and obviously his wife was doing the same thing. She walked toward the stairs that led to the second-floor office. It had been hard thinking of Sofia Mangini as Mrs. Sesta. It would be even harder to think of her as Mrs. Danny Neill.

The two women had barely talked in all the time since the day Nilo had come home from prison and found them together, and Tina looked forward to seeing her old friend. Maybe, at last, things were going well for her. Nilo had said she was pregnant again. *Maybe, at last, there's some happiness in her life.*

When she entered the office, Sofia was seated behind her desk, looking out the window at the traffic along Forty-seventh Street.

For a moment, she considered telling Sofia to get out of her chair, and then she dismissed the thought, settling on a casual, "Hello, Fia."

As Sofia turned, Tina sprawled out in a rocker set in a far corner of the room.

"You look wonderful. Pregnancy agrees with you," Tina said.

Sofia's face was hard and expressionless.

"I won't beat around the bush," she said. "Opening this club puts you in constant touch with Nilo."

"It's his money."

"It's his money and *my* money," Sofia said coldly. "Our money, just as it's our marriage. I don't want you doing damage to either."

"Fia . . . what are you talking about?"

"I want you to keep your hands off my husband."

Tina shook her head. "You don't have to worry about that," she said.

"Oh, no? You're holy and moral, all of a sudden?"

"No," Tina said. "But something's happened to me. I can't stand to be touched anymore. It makes me physically ill. You have nothing to worry about." She suddenly felt weary and too tired to argue. All she wanted to do was sleep.

"I don't believe you," Sofia said.

"I can't help that."

"From the time Nilo came home, he's been climbing on me day and night, all the time. And now, for the last three months, he's barely touched me. Three months. That's how long you've been working around here."

"It's not so," Tina said. "Whatever your marriage problems are, they're not my doing."

Sofia grabbed her fur coat off the table near the door and put it on. "I don't know just how much you hear from Nilo in your pillow talk," she snapped, "but let me make it clear for you: Nilo fronts a lot of businesses, but all the money is handled by me. I will give this club special attention. Don't make any mistakes, and especially don't make the mistake of thinking you can get away with something by sleeping with my husband."

"It's not so, Sofia. And I'm sorry you feel that way. Truly sorry."

"Harm my marriage and you'll really be sorry," Sofia said as she left the room.

IT WAS ALMOST 4:00 A.M. before Nilo returned home and found Sofia working at the desk in the living room.

He seemed to be a little drunk and was clearly startled. "What are you doing up at this hour?"

"I like to go over the books. And when you're out this late, I can't sleep. I just worry."

As he peeled off his jacket, he said, "You're pregnant. You should get more rest."

Sofia went across the room and hugged him. She saw a smudge of lipstick on his shirt collar, and she could smell someone else's perfume on him. She held him tighter. He stood still, with his arms hanging down at his sides.

"We should talk about some things," she said.

Nilo shrugged, walked to the bar, and poured himself a glass of wine. "So? Okay, let's talk." He sat on the couch facing her across the room.

"What are your plans for the future?" she asked.

Nilo sighed. The look on his face was a clear signal that he hated these kinds of conversations. "I was waiting for you to tell me," he said in a bored voice.

Sofia sat down at the desk again "Mr. Maranzano has had a wonderful idea in taking all his mob money and putting it into legitimate businesses. By now, everybody knows that Prohibition doesn't work. Before too long, liquor will be legal again, and those who don't prepare for that day are going to be left out."

Nilo sipped at his wine but said nothing.

"Because Don Salvatore has decided to put many of these businesses in the Danny Neill name, that puts us . . . you . . . in a wonderful position, because if anything happens to Maranzano, you control the wealth."

"Nothing's going to happen to the don," Nilo said.

"Oh, Nilo, stop kidding yourself. When you go out, you have a bodyguard. Don Salvatore has an army of them. There's a war going on out there. Before it's over,

Masseria's going to be gone and Maranzano too. But nothing has to happen to you."

"If anything happens to Don Salvatore, I will follow in his footsteps," Nilo said officiously.

He is terribly stupid, Sofia thought, striving to mask her anger. *I hate it that I wasn't born a man. Doesn't he see that if Maranzano were dead, the war would be over?*

"You can do that," Sofia said in a reasonable voice. "But you have one child sleeping inside and another inside my belly. We have to think of them and the lives they're going to have. They'll be a lot prouder of their father, the businessman, than they would of their father, the gangster. I want us to build something for our children, something that nobody can take away from them."

"I do, too," Nilo said, but his voice was listless and unconvincing. Sofia knew that she had already exceeded his usual short attention span.

"I guess what I want is for you to acknowledge that you and I are partners. We're not in this for ourselves. We're in it for our children, and we have to work together to build for the future."

Nilo came over and kissed her on the neck. "Great," he said.

"So when I ask you questions, it's all business, you understand?"

"Naturally," Nilo said.

"For instance, how's the club working out?"

"We're doing all right," he said. "We should be ready to open before the holidays."

"I stopped in today and saw Tina," Sofia said.

"She's doing a good job," Nilo said. "With her fronting this place for me, it's going to do a lot of business. You'll see."

"For me." Those were his words, Sofia thought. *He will never accept that we are partners.*

"Nilo, please don't fool around with Tina."

"Just one time," he said, "and then I don't want to talk about it anymore. I haven't touched Tina. We're not screwing. The only time I talk to her is about the club. That's the way it'll stay. Okay?"

I don't believe him, Sofia thought. *I don't believe either of them.* She said, "Okay."

"Now I've got to get some sleep. A long day tomorrow," he said, and gave her a brief nod before going into the bedroom.

Sofia sat at the desk, idly tapping the pencil on a green blotter, wondering why her husband was content to live day by day, never thinking things through, never trying to shape the future.

I cannot even tell him that our own interests would be best served if Don Salvatore were to die. Peace would come and we would thrive. But someday, perhaps, he may hear me.

EIGHT DAYS LATER, on a crisp Tuesday evening in early October, Sofia came into the Manginis' restaurant in Little Italy. She did not visit there much anymore, having no desire to see her father, but her mother had called to let her know that Charlie Luciano would be dining there that night.

She sat alone at a table in a far corner, drinking espresso, and when Luciano came in, accompanied by his usual gaggle of hangers-on and bodyguards, he saw her and nodded in a friendly fashion before disappearing into the back room.

Sofia waved to her father and told him to send Luciano a bottle of his best wine, courtesy of Sofia. The old man looked as if he were going to say something, to protest, but Sofia silenced him with a glare.

"I am here on business. Do as I say," she commanded.

The years had not been kind to Matteo Mangini. His hair was shot through now with white, and his tall, stately figure was shortening, as he was crippled over more and more by arthritis. He moved slowly and his hands often trembled, and as Sofia watched him, she thought, *Good, I hope one of his sluts has given him syphilis.*

She saw her father go into the back room, and a few minutes later, as she expected, Luciano came out alone and walked over to join her at the table.

They think nothing of women, these people, Sofia thought. *Surely, with all these killings on the street, Charlie must be taking great caution. And yet, without a guard, here he is at my table because he thinks that he is safe because I am only a woman. If I wanted to kill them all, I would round up a half-dozen pretty women, give them guns, and they would all be dead before midnight.*

"You're looking beautiful, Sofia," Luciano said.

"Thank you. I'm glad to see you."

"How long before the baby?" he asked.

"Early in the year. Maybe four more months," she said. "It's because of the baby that I hoped to talk to you."

"Oh?"

"I was wondering, Charlie, what kind of life my baby will have. Will this war ever end?"

"All wars end," he said.

Sofia could tell that her broaching the subject had made Luciano nervous. He looked around almost skittishly.

"But no one can tell the future," he said.

"I know some of the future," Sofia answered. When Luciano just looked at her quizzically, she went on: "Prohibition's going to end soon. The real money in the future will be made by people who invest in legitimate businesses. Maranzano is doing that very thing right now, getting ready for the day the bootleggers are out of work. If both sides did that, there would be very little to make war over, wouldn't there?"

"When strong people hate each other, they will always find a reason to have a war. What does your husband think about all this?"

"Nilo thinks nothing," Sofia said. "Some people think about tomorrow. My husband thinks about yesterday and considers today a great mystery. The stock market is going to crash soon. Companies, good companies, will be for sale for pennies on the dollar. Yet I could no more tell Nilo about this than I could tell him about the beauty of poetry."

"But you're telling me?"

"Because I think about tomorrow, and you are tomorrow. It is a shame sometimes that our lives are ruled by people who know only the past."

"Things change. People pass on," Luciano said casually. "You really think the stock market will fall?"

"It has to," Sofia said. "It's become just pieces of paper being used to buy other pieces of paper. All the reality has gone from it. Eventually, air leaks from even the biggest balloon."

"And fortunes will be lost," Luciano said softly, as if to himself.

"And greater ones made by those who are wise or cunning." Sofia looked at her father standing near the door of the restaurant. "What would happen if the generals left the battlefield?"

"You have something in mind?"

Sofia shook her head. "I was just wondering what you thought."

"What I think is that you should leave these problems to men who deal with them every day. Someday I'm sure peace will return because a lot of us worked to bring it about."

"I hope so, Charlie," Sofia said. "If there's anything I can help you with, please let me know. I think of you often, how kind you've been to me in the past. Perhaps I could pay you back."

"Maybe someday," Luciano said, and rose from the table. "In the meantime, take care of yourself and the baby. I'd send my regards to your husband, but I don't think he'd want to hear them."

"No, not very much, I'm afraid," Sofia said. She finished her espresso and left soon after.

Riding back to her apartment in a taxicab, she felt pleased with herself. Luciano was no fool; he understood quite well that Sofia was making herself available as an agent inside the Maranzano camp.

He might not think much of the offer now, but someday he may need something and come to me. That favor could buy my future. Mine and my children's.

Everything takes so much time. But I have time, plenty of time. I'm not going anywhere.

Rats got no complaint.

• *The one person whose advice Luciano always took without question was Arnold Rothstein. New York's secretive "Mr. Big" had fixed the 1919 Black Sox World Series; he had bankrolled scores of criminal enterprises around the city, and he had never*

*spent a single day in jail. It was on his recommen-
dation that Luciano had encouraged Frank
Costello to become the "paymaster" for graft at
city hall. Rothstein had taught Luciano how to
dress and worked to help him get rid of his coarse
New York accent, and on his say-so, Luciano had
left his old neighborhood and moved uptown to a
luxury hotel suite. Rothstein, himself, was tall and
elegant; he looked and acted like an investment
banker. And, almost as if he actually ran a bank,
the gambling money rolled in. Every night, he
would get out of his limousine at Forty-ninth Street
and stroll down Broadway to Times Square. Inside
his pocket, he had a quarter of a million dollars in
thousand-dollar bills. He would pay off losing bets
and collect winners. Then he went to Lindy's and
took more bets until the sun came up.*

- *But on the night of September 2, 1928, when
Luciano met him at Forty-ninth Street and Broadway, he knew something was wrong. Rothstein was
pale and looked ill. His clothes were wrinkled and
almost shabby looking. But he brushed off any
questions about his health. Luciano asked the mob
financier about the chances of a stock-market
failure. Should he start investing mob money now
in legitimate enterprises? Or would it be wiser to
wait until a market drop when everything would be
for sale cheaper? The usually confident Rothstein
was indecisive. At first he said Luciano should buy
businesses immediately; five minutes later, he said
it would be better to wait. Yes, the market was going
to crash. No, it wasn't; the boom would last forever.*

- *Luciano left him paying off bets on Broadway and
went back downtown to Ratner's, a small kosher*

restaurant on Delancey Street, where he found Meyer Lansky and spirited him into a back room where they could talk privately. "When was the last time you saw A. R.?" Luciano asked. Lansky answered laconically, "Couple of months ago. Why?" "He's on dope," Luciano said. "I was just with him and his mind's not straight. You can't even get an answer from him." Lansky was silent for a while. "Does he have anything that can hurt us?" he finally asked. "I'll try to find out," Luciano said coldly. "I don't trust nobody who's sticking needles in his arm."

- *A week later in an apartment at the Park Central, Rothstein got into a poker game with two California gamblers. They played for forty-eight hours. Rothstein lost over three hundred thousand dollars. He said he would pay it off the next day, then left and went to Lindy's, where he decided the game had been fixed and announced he would never pay off. On November 4, he got a phone call at Lindy's and said he was going to the Park Central again to play poker. Later that night, Rothstein was found in a service entrance of the hotel, bleeding from a bullet wound in the stomach. Two days later, he died in the hospital without identifying his attackers.*

- *Police raced to Rothstein's private office. They found a fire blazing in the office fireplace and three men going through Rothstein's files. After a few telephone calls, the men were released. One of them was later identified in police records as "Charles Lucania, a waiter." Nothing incriminating was ever found in what remained of Rothstein's files.*

- *In the closing months of 1928, ten gang members were shot on the streets of New York as the war between Maranzano and Masseria heated up. Masseria had a bigger "army," but Maranzano was willing to offer gang leaders a bigger piece of the pie, and some of the better-known thugs, like Joe Profaci and Joe Bonanno, came over to the Maranzano side. Masseria was annoyed but not yet frightened. He told Luciano, "Keep hitting them bastards," and then told Luciano that Frank Costello was spending too much money paying graft at city hall. "Tell him to cut it out. We're gonna go broke." The weekly payoffs were then ten thousand dollars. Luciano told Costello to increase the payments. "We're going to need everybody on our side before this is all over," he said. "What about Joe the Boss?" Costello asked nervously. "He's my worry," Luciano said.*

- *New York governor Al Smith, campaigning to end Prohibition, lost the presidential election to Herbert Hoover. But although he had lost, everyone knew that Prohibition's days were numbered. In Albany, Franklin Delano Roosevelt succeeded Smith as governor.*

CHAPTER 1O

1928–1929: The War

For the first time since Prohibition started, Tony had again found joy in police work.

All through 1928, Captain Cochran had come up with one amazing tip after another and Tony and his Italian Squad had made a string of spectacular arrests.

In March, they foiled a hijack by Masseria's men of a Maranzano liquor truck. They seized three thousand gallons of whiskey and arrested five bootleggers, and the leader of the hijackers—believed by Tony to be Bugsy Siegel—escaped only by hiding in a storm sewer.

Only a few weeks later, Cochran gave Tony detailed information on a burglary planned at a Midtown diamond dealer's office. When the burglars broke in late at night and started to crack the safe, Tony's men were waiting for them.

An illegal Midtown card game was held up. Two players were shot, but when the robbers left the hotel suite, they walked into a horde of plainclothesmen from the Italian Squad.

There were a string of such cases all through the year, all set up by tips received from Cochran. Tony knew his commander had an informant someplace inside the mobs, but he did not bring the subject up or question his identity. The fewer who knew about confidential informants, the better chance those informants had of staying alive.

The Italian Squad was all over the city, and Kinnair, the *Daily News* reporter, who seemed to delight in tweaking the mob, dubbed them "The Flying Squad," and wrote in a column, "The mob spends most of its time these days looking over their shoulders. Because they know The Flying Squad is coming after them."

Tony's only dissatisfaction came because city hall was so corrupt and the fix was in at so many levels that most of the gangsters he arrested were out on the street in hours, and time after time grand juries—manipulated by crooked district attorneys and judges—refused to indict them. Someday, he hoped, that would change. In the meantime, all he could do was keep the heat turned up.

One night in Tommy's apartment, Rachel looked up from the *Daily News* and told her husband, "Your father's really having a field day, isn't he?"

"He's as happy as a clam," Tommy said. He was putting on his jacket when Rachel said, "Are you going out again tonight?"

He nodded. "Up to the library. Got to study for the bar exam."

"Tommy, do you have a girlfriend?" she asked.

"What?"

"You go out mostly every night," she said. "How much studying do you have to do? You should have everything memorized by now."

"Trust me, honey, no girlfriend. I'm really working."

Rachel smiled. "I know. I'll see you when you get home."

Tommy kissed her and left, but walking away from the apartment he wondered if he was doing the right thing.

For nearly a year, he had gone out, days and nights, whenever he could, hanging out in poolrooms, in small neighborhood speakeasies, in places where he was not known and where small-time hoods congregated, listening to their bragging, encouraging them in their crackpot schemes, and then phoning Captain Cochran at home and reporting anything he thought was real.

Around the gin mills, he was known only as Vito.

He had never told anyone about his secret life, and the longer he lived it, the more heavily it weighed on him that he was deceiving Rachel. But some instinct told him that there was danger in telling anyone.

And, besides, Rachel would want to know why he persisted in it, why he had put himself in the front lines of fighting crime when his career as a lawyer waited for him. Tommy wondered how he could answer that question, especially to someone who was naive about the mob's corroding influence. For Rachel was like Tommy had been: she thought that everything would be all right and the mob would stay on its side of the street and out of the lives of normal law-abiding citizens. But how to tell her about how the mob had reached into his own family; how they had brought Nilo a new life as a murderer; how a gang leader named Luciano had tried to corrupt and twist Tina's life?

How to tell her that law, real law, didn't start in courtrooms; it started on the streets with cops fighting crime and that he could think of no more important career for a man to have. *And so, I've grown up to be my father,* Tommy thought ruefully.

Someday, and probably soon, he was going to have to own up to all of it. Probably Rachel would force him off the job, but he would not deal with that until he had to.

He pulled his leather jacket tighter around him and walked downtown, toward the city's garment district.

SOON AFTER THE NEW YEAR, Tony was called into Captain Cochran's office at the headquarters of the Italian Squad. "Luciano's been squawking that you're harassing him."

"Oh?"

"He complained to city hall and city hall's complaining to me."

"Are you telling me to lay off?"

"Look, I know there's something personal between you two, and that's none of my business. But don't you have enough to do? We're making arrests right and left and you already work twelve to sixteen hours a day. Why bother with Luciano? He's just another gee."

"No, he's not, Captain. While no one's been looking, he's taking over everything in this city. Nothing moves without Luciano's okay. The bootlegging's his; the whores are his; the shakedowns are his. It's all Luciano. And this has nothing to do with personal."

Cochran looked exasperated. "Come on, Tony. We've got Masseria and Maranzano killing each other's guys on the street, and you're worried about some guy nobody ever heard of." Cochran leaned forward across his desk. "Tony, Luciano's got friends. You keep this up and you're going to get your head handed to you. That's just friendly advice."

Tony stood. "Thanks, Captain, for your concern." He left the office, and on his way home that night picked up a retirement form from the personnel clerk. That night, after Anna had gone to sleep, he sat at the kitchen table and filled out the form.

He had told Captain Cochran that his scrutiny of Luciano was not personal, but of course it was. *The son of a bitch robbed me of my daughter.*

Tina was singing now at the new Midtown club that had been named for her. It was Nilo Sesta's club, and that galled Tony even more. She had gone from working for Luciano, one thug, to working for another thug.

What ever happened to my little girl who used to play at being a nun? Yes, Captain, it's personal. Very goddamned personal.

He finished filling in the form but left the date blank, then put it inside his jacket pocket.

AT THE END OF JANUARY, Sofia Sesta gave birth to a son. He was a healthy handsome boy of eight pounds, two ounces. His parents named him Salvatore. Maranzano, his godfather, was present at the private baptism and christening service, which Nilo decided to hold in their apartment because it was not safe to spend too much time in public, not even in church.

Tina did not attend but sent flowers and a silver cup for the baby. After everyone had left the apartment, Sofia threw the flowers and the cup in the garbage.

• *Two weeks later, in Chicago, Dr. Reinhardt H. Schwimmer, a local optometrist, walked into the garage of the S.M.C. Cartage Company at 2122 North Clark Street. He had no business there, but he knew the place was the headquarters of some local bootleggers and he liked to associate with criminals. For their part, the thugs treated Schwimmer like a mascot, letting him hang* around, in return for which he made sure their wives and girlfriends and families got the very best in the latest eyewear.

In the garage that morning were six members of the Bugs Moran gang: Adam Heyer, James Clark, Al Weinshank, John May, and two brothers, Pete and Frank Gusenberg, who had fearsome reputations as Moran gunmen.

A few minutes after Schwimmer arrived, five men—three of them in police uniforms—drove up to the garage in a black sedan, the kind often used by police. As the men went inside, walking past a German shepherd named "Highball," Moran and two of his henchmen, Ted Newberry and Willie Marks, pulled up across the street. They saw the men in police uniforms and decided to avoid the police raid by going for coffee instead.

Meanwhile, inside the garage, the men in police uniforms lined the seven men up against a bare brick wall. While the men's backs were turned, two of the "policemen" pulled Thompson submachine guns from under their uniform coats and cut down all seven men. Six of them were dead before they hit the floor; Frank Gusenberg died in the hospital, refusing to name his assailants.

The gunmen had disappeared, but in case there were any doubts who they worked for, Moran cleared it up later when he told reporters: "Only Capone kills like that."

- The St. Valentine's Day Massacre ended Capone's troubles with the remnants of Dion O'Banion's Irish gang, which had continued to oppose him. Its members drifted off and Moran himself seemed to vanish from sight. He was reduced to supporting

> *himself by petty burglaries and armed robberies*
> *and died in prison.*

"THIS IS A GOOD IDEA," Joe Masseria said, slapping the back of his hand across the newspaper. "That Capone, he knows how to deal with people who cross him."

He grinned across the table at Luciano, who sipped his coffee and then made a show of inserting a cigarette into a long holder before lighting it.

When Luciano did not answer, Masseria said, "This is what I want you to do, Charlie. Hit that Maranzano. Hit all them bastards who take his side. Let's get rid of that Castellammare *stronzo* once and for all."

"It sounds good, doesn't it, Joe?" Luciano said in his usual soft voice.

"Goddamn right."

"But there's one thing wrong with it," Luciano said, his voice patient, as if he were a schoolteacher tutoring a slow student.

"Yeah?" Masseria said suspiciously.

"Inside a year, Alphonse is going to be in jail," Luciano said.

"Bullshit. Not in Chicago. He owns that city. Like I oughta own this one for all the money we're paying those politicians." He looked across the small restaurant and bellowed, "Hey, girlie. What the hell, you on strike? Some more coffee here, huh?"

"You're right, Joe, he owns Chicago, but this is bigger than Chicago. The whole country's gonna go nuts because of this . . . what do they call it? Valentine's Massacre. I give Al a year, tops. And if we start acting the same way, I give us a year, too."

"And what do we do meanwhile?" Masseria demanded.

"Maranzano's hit, what, eight of our guys? We let him keep that shit up?"

"We've hit more than that of his," Luciano said. "What we do is we just keep defending ourselves and let this blow over. This city's asleep, let it stay asleep. Why get everybody annoyed?"

"Who's asleep? You got that goddamn Flying Squad riding around busting up everything. I thought this Tony Falcone was a friend of yours."

"Never my friend," Luciano said.

"Well, you was humping his daughter, right? Didn't that put you in the family?"

"I was humping his daughter 'cause she was good in bed and she made a lot of money for me at the club and because I knew it made old man Falcone nuts to think that his daughter was my whore. I just wanted to make his life miserable."

"Now he makes me miserable."

"Just a lot of newspaper stories. We're bigger than ever. Let things be for now."

Masseria's brow was wrinkled, as if in confusion, and then slowly he let a big smile cross his broad, stupid face.

"I got it," he said. "We try to keep things quiet and then, when they are, then we hit Maranzano. That's good thinking, Charlie."

"Leave Maranzano to me," Luciano said.

After his weekly breakfast with Masseria, Luciano went to the small office Meyer Lansky kept in a nondescript building near the city's Bowery.

"You look like you just ate a dog," Lansky said by way of greeting.

"Almost as bad," Luciano said with a grin. "I'm with Joe the Genius who thinks that we ought to buy everybody machine guns and shoot up anybody we don't like. Just like Al Capone."

"Sometimes I wonder which one of them is stupider," Lansky said. "Capone's signed his own death warrant, and Joe the Shithead likes it so much he wants to do the same thing."

"Joe signed his death warrant a long time ago," Luciano said quietly.

"But not yet," Lansky said. "We're not ready. Not till we have our meeting and get everybody lined up."

"Well, we should get working on it."

"It's set already. Atlantic City. In May," Lansky said.

"If there's anything I hate worse than a smart Jew . . ."

"It's a dumb Sicilian," Lansky said.

"And we're swimming in them," Luciano said, and both men laughed.

ALTHOUGH TOMMY HAD NOT TOLD Rachel about it, he had not forgotten Lev Mishkin's problems with the Maranzano mob trying to take over his union. Posing again as Vito, he took to hanging around in coffee shops and speakeasies in the garment district, where most of Mishkin's union men worked, but he found little to substantiate Mishkin's fears.

His first big test had come early in the year when most of the sixty-seven workers at the Adelson Coat Factory on Canal Street signed cards asking for a union election. Tommy took to loitering around the place, where he ran into a man named Harry Birchevsky, a rumpled, fattish man with a birdlike waddle, who was Mishkin's top organizer for the garment makers' union.

As far as Tommy could tell, Birchevsky's main organizing technique was to sit in coffee shops and diners, endlessly reading the *Daily Racing Form,* complaining that all the races at Yonkers were fixed, and buying coffee for all the Adelson workers who wandered in.

It did not seem like terribly effective union organizing, Tommy thought, but since a majority of the workers had asked for the election, it appeared to be a foregone conclusion that the same majority would vote to be represented by Mishkin's union.

Then, in the week before the election was to be held, an independent union that no one had ever heard of said that it would also seek to represent Adelson's workers.

No one knew who was behind this new independent union, and Tommy only figured it out one day when he was walking along the street and saw Nilo talking to a half-dozen goons who had taken to hanging around the Adelson factory's front door, where they badgered and threatened workers to vote for their union.

Again, personally, Tommy was outraged. He had come late to the fight against the gangsters, but the last year had made him a zealot. The mobsters seemed to think they could get away with anything and now they were trying to prevent a free election by working men.

Harry Birchevsky's organizing response to the goons' threats seemed to be to buy more coffee and to read more racing forms. At night, Tommy went out of his way to talk to some of Adelson's workers, and it was clear that they were frightened, afraid that they would get their heads busted if they didn't vote for the independent union supported by Maranzano and Nilo.

The day before the election, Tommy knew that Mishkin no longer had the votes to win. Something was needed, some last-minute fireworks, and that night, he had an idea and called Captain Cochran.

The next morning, just as the workers were arriving,

a police wagon pulled up in front of Adelson's factory. Lt. Tony Falcone, spiffy in his dress blue uniform, and a squad of a half-dozen policemen jumped from the vehicle and marched up to the thugs who were loitering around the entrance.

"You're all under arrest for loitering," Tony announced.

"Get outta here. We're union organizers."

"You're vagrants," Tony said. "We've had a complaint." He waved to the cops. "Bring them in." The police handcuffed the six hulking goons and pushed them into the back of the wagon. The workers milling around cheered as they entered Adelson's.

The votes were counted at 9:00 A.M. From a restaurant across the street, Tommy saw Nilo show up for the tally. He learned at lunchtime that Mishkin's union had won by a vote of 35 to 32. He felt as good about it as about anything he had done in the past year. He just resented a little bit that he could not gloat to Nilo that he had beaten him. Maybe some other time.

THEY CAME BY TRAINS and by limousine. Even though air service was being flown into nearby Philadelphia on a regular basis, none of the gang chieftains who descended on Atlantic City on May 15, 1929, was willing to trust his life to such an untried invention as airline travel.

The mobsters had the two top floors of the President Hotel, right across the boardwalk from the Atlantic Ocean beach. Every morning for three days, a gaggle of waiters came up to the top-floor conference room and set out an arsenal of coffeepots, water pitchers, trays of sandwiches and fruit and pastries, and then left, with strict orders not to set foot back on the top floor unless they were called. Ten girls, recruited from the very best brothels in the city, were on service around the clock in the two "hospitality lounges."

More than twenty gang lords from all over the United States came to the meeting, but they did not include either Joe Masseria or Salvatore Maranzano.

Maranzano had heard through the grapevine, in a story planted by Luciano, that the meeting was being called just to discuss what the mobsters would do after the war with Masseria ended. He told that to Nilo and said with a chuckle, "When the war is ended, they will do what I tell them to do. They can hold meetings from now until hell freezes over."

For his part, Masseria had been notified of the meeting by Luciano and had demanded that he participate.

"I'm the boss of New York. I ain't supposed to be there?"

"Joe, we've been losing guys to Maranzano, right?"

"Yeah?" Masseria said suspiciously.

"These guys I'm meeting with have a lot of influence. What I'm going to do is tell them that you're going to win out over Maranzano. They'll listen to me and they'll listen even better if you're not there."

"So what?"

"So, they will tell their people to make sure nobody supports Maranzano. They won't want to back a loser. And if they start putting a little heat on Maranzano, he'll be gone and this damned war will end. Joe, you got to trust me on this. I know what I'm doing."

It took a whole evening's discussion in Asti Restaurant on Twelfth Street before Luciano convinced the old gang boss that it was in his best interests to stay away. Finally, when dinner was over, Masseria clapped Luciano on the shoulder.

"Ahhh, do what you want to do, Charlie. I suppose you're gonna have all those Jews there, too, right?"

"We've got to deal with them."

"You do; I don't. I don't meet with Jews. Or Irish either, for that matter. You go do it. You tell them Joe the Boss will always be Joe the Boss."

"I will," Luciano promised. "I know what I'm doing. Trust me."

What he and Lansky had been planning for more than two years was a national crime syndicate. America would be divided into districts, and each district would have a boss who would be in charge of all the crime in his area. But no boss would go against another boss without approval from the syndicate's board of directors.

Luciano had not expected it to be easy, especially when he opened the first meeting and looked around the room at a who's who in American crime. Capone had come from Chicago, with his top advisor, Jake "Greasy Thumb" Guzik. There was Abe Bernstein of Detroit's Purple Gang and Moe Dalitz from Cleveland. Abner "Longy" Zwillman drove over from New Jersey, picking up Boo Boo Hoff of Philadelphia on the way. From Boston came King Solomon. The biggest contingent was from New York and included Costello and Adonis and Lepke, Dutch Schultz, Lansky, Albert Anastasia, and Johnny Torrio.

It took three days of meetings, many of them among small groups walking along the beach with their pants rolled up to keep them dry, but in the end, Luciano and Lansky got everything they wanted. Nobody believed that violence would be ended, but each agreed to talk to the other syndicate bosses before doing anything outside their own franchised area.

At the final night's meeting, the two big questions that

had been avoided for three days came up. "All that shoot-ing in Chicago is killing us," a Kansas City boss said. "The cops are going apeshit."

Luciano looked down the table to where Capone sat. The Chicago boss nodded and rose slowly to his feet. "You have to understand," he said. "I hit those Irishers not because they was Irish. Everybody knows I get along with everybody. I mean, look at Jake here," he said, point-ing to his assistant, Guzik. "He's a goddamn Jew from Russia and I don't have no problem with him or nobody else for that matter. I had to hit them Irish 'cause they kept trying to hit me. But I know it's stirred things up. So what I'm planning on doing is taking a little vacation." He grinned.

"Book me a room, too," Frank Costello yelled out.

"You don't want this room," Capone said. "I'm gonna go and get myself arrested for a nickel-and-dime charge and spend a little time in the can. That'll give things a chance to blow over."

Luciano smiled. "I think you're doing the right thing Al," he said. But he wondered, *Whoever gave him that lamebrain idea? Once he goes to jail, he's going to be doing nothing but be in jail.* He looked at Lansky, who rolled his eyes, clearly agreeing that Capone had lost his senses. But everybody else at the table thought it was a great idea, and Capone sat down with applause ringing in his ears.

There was still one piece of business left and Chica-go's Guzik brought it up. "We're talking a lot about end-ing all the violence, but what about it, Charlie? What about Maranzano and Masseria in New York? Is this go-ing to be one of those stupid guinea vendettas that never ends?"

Luciano got back to his feet. He looked around the

room slowly, meeting each man's eyes before he answered.

"No." There were no more questions.

- *On May 17, 1929, Al Capone was arrested in Philadelphia, only an hour's drive from Atlantic City, when he turned himself over to a policeman and announced that he was carrying an unregistered gun. He was sentenced to one year in a Pennsylvania county prison by Judge John E. Walsh. From then on, until his death from syphilis, he spent most of his life behind bars.*

SOFIA LOOKED UP from the ledger books she was working on, in a small back office at the Falcon's Nest speakeasy, to see Nilo in the doorway.

"How's everything?" he asked. "Kids okay?"

"Yes. They're with Mama."

Nilo nodded and turned to walk down the hallway to another office. He was followed by a dumpy man in a disheveled suit who seemed to waddle when he walked. Sofia had seen him around a lot lately, as he came in several afternoons a week to spend time in Nilo's office, but beyond introducing him as Harry, Nilo had pointedly failed to identify him. She wondered idly who he was. All she knew was that she did not like him. He had a leering look, and the several times she had passed him in the hallway, he had eyed her as if he were starving and she was a particularly succulent steak.

Probably another gangster. Gangsters are all we know. And we live in fear that we'll be shot by some hoodlum because we work for some other hoodlum.

And Nilo, she knew now, would never quit. Maranzano had told him to foster his new identity as Danny Neill so he could front all the organization's legitimate businesses, but Nilo paid no attention to business at all. He admitted one night that the reason he had hired Tina for the speakeasy was because she had experience in running one and she could manage the place while he was busy elsewhere.

"Elsewhere," she knew, meant out on the streets. Others of Maranzano's men often called for him late at night, and he was always eager to join them. Once, he had come home with blood on his hands and clothing. At first she thought he had been injured, but it was someone else's blood. He refused to talk about it; the next day, she took the clothes from his closet and incinerated them. When Nilo found out what she had done, he shouted at her angrily.

"They were bloody and ruined. What the hell would you want them for?" she demanded.

Nilo smiled in his disarming way and said dreamily, "A souvenir."

Recalling the incident, she thought, *My husband is a crazy man. We all belong in asylums. If it weren't that my children and I need Nilo to live, Tina could have him.*

Sofia checked the clock over the door. It was five thirty. She would finish up the bookwork quickly and leave. Tina came in at six to oversee the club and get ready for her nightly performances, and while it had never been mentioned or arranged by either of them, when Sofia came in daily to do the books Tina was never there. And Sofia made sure to leave before Tina arrived. Their lifelong friendship was indeed ended; they had not seen or spoken to each other in six months, and Tina had never seen Salvatore, the new baby.

It took Sofia longer than she expected to finish her bookkeeping work, and when she looked up, she saw it was six o'clock. She hurriedly put on her coat to leave, but in the hallway outside, she met Tina, who was just arriving.

"Hello, Fia. How are you?" Tina said with a smile.

Sofia coldly turned her face away and walked past Tina without a word. A few minutes later, Nilo walked into Tina's office and found her standing in front of the desk, crying.

"What's the matter?" he asked.

"I just met Sofia. She wouldn't even talk to me," Tina said, turning a tear-streaked face to him. And then she broke down and started to weep openly. Nilo walked to her and put his arms around her.

"Don't let it bother you," he said. He tried to joke. "Hell, most times she won't even talk to me. She gets over it. Forget it. Come on, you know you want to."

Sofia had been almost at the front door when she realized she had left her purse on the desk. When she went back to get it, she saw Tina's office door was ajar. From inside, she heard Nilo's voice. Despite herself, she stopped to listen.

"Come on," she heard him say. "You know you want to."

Unable to stop herself, she pushed the door open a little farther and peered inside. She saw Tina and Nilo standing in front of the desk; her husband had his arms around the woman.

Quietly, Sofia walked away. *I'll get her for this,* she thought. *I'll get her if it's the last thing I do.*

"IF IT WEREN'T FOR THE FACT that you think some kind of smoked pink fish served on a cement doughnut is a decent breakfast, you would be a perfect wife," Tommy said.

Rachel, who had been standing in front of the kitchen stove in the small apartment, apparently willing the coffeepot to percolate, came around behind Tommy, slid her hands down into his open shirt, played with his chest, nuzzled his neck, and said, "You really think so?"

"Without a doubt. But I'd really like bacon and eggs once in a while."

"Bacon comes from pigs and how disgusting is that? Smoked salmon comes from the sea, beautiful clean fish swimming around in the beautiful clean ocean. You'll thank me when you're ninety years old."

"All right. I'll eat your stupid fish. But this thing it's on . . ."

"That's called a bagel."

"I know it's called a bagel. That's the Jewish word for 'concrete,' right?"

She licked his ear and whispered, "It's the Jewish word for 'sex.' See the shape of it? Does it remind you of anything?"

"You're disgusting," Tommy said.

"I'm pregnant."

Tommy rose from his chair as if he had been prodded and spun toward Rachel.

"You sure?" he said with a broad smile.

"Positive. You have bageled this poor little Jewish girl one time too many."

"Yahoo," Tommy yipped. "When?"

"I'm going to the doctor today, but I think around the end of the year."

"Does your father know?"

"I saw him last week and he told me that I looked pregnant. Lev knows everything."

Tommy thought about that remark as he took the streetcar downtown to the union offices near Greenwich Village. His daughter might think that Lev Mishkin knew everything, but neither Lev nor Tommy had been able to figure out what was going on with the garment makers' union. Since their success in unionizing the Adelson factory earlier in the year, union organizing activity had ground to a halt.

While Tommy had seen signs that Lepke was trying to strangle the industry through his control of the cutters' union, Lev had been unperturbed.

"It's a good chance for us, Tommy," he said. "Up till now, the owners always figured their choice was between a union or no union. Now they're going to see that it's between a union run by that thug Lepke and one run by us. They'll support us."

"I hope you're right."

"Of course I'm right." He paused. "You've been doing good work for me. I still have a spot on my payroll if you want it. Lawyer, organizer, whatever you want."

"No thanks," Tommy said.

Mishkin fiddled with his cup. He seemed nervous and Tommy said, "Okay, Lev, out with it."

"It's about Rachel."

"She's pregnant."

"I know. That's not it. She wonders about you, Tommy. You don't take the bar exam and you don't have a job. You tell her you've been living off your savings, but she's never seen any sign of those savings. You spend most nights out. She thinks you're involved in something, but she doesn't know what."

"And you?"

"I don't know," Mishkin said. "I don't think it was just a coincidence that the police showed up at Adelson's to arrest the galoots, just before the vote there. Sometimes I wonder how that happened."

"You think I'm a criminal?"

"I think you're still a cop," Mishkin said.

"I wish I were. Then I'd be able to afford this baby."

"Okay," Lev said. "We'll just let it drop." The two men smiled at each other.

Over the next two weeks, Tommy received regular reports from Mishkin. Harry Birchevsky was having no success in getting workers to sign up to join Mishkin's union. "Something funny's going on," Mishkin said.

Tommy agreed. *Sooner or later, I'm going to find out what it is.*

IN THE AFTERMATH OF the revulsion at Capone's Valentine's Day slaughter, New York City cops had gone on a full-scale attack against the bootleggers and other criminals. And Tony Falcone, spurred on by Captain Cochran's seemingly inexhaustible supply of inside information, was in the middle of it.

He had no illusions. He knew that city hall was still protecting the mobsters and that most of the arrests were routinely tossed out by corrupt courts and prosecutors. But the arrests had, at least, harassment value and let the thugs know that someday, somehow, society would hand them a due bill for their crimes.

The highlight for Tony came after midnight on June 13, when the bodies of Red Cassidy and Simon Walker were found lying on a Midtown street, shot to death. Cassidy was a lower-echelon hoodlum, Walker apparently nothing but an innocent who wandered into the line of fire. Police quickly established that the two men had been shot in the Hotsy Totsy Club, a speakeasy on Broadway near Fifty-fifth Street, which was owned by Legs Diamond, a notorious mob gunman.

Tony took over the investigation. Eight people, both employees at the club and patrons, told police that the two men had been shot in a wild fight by Diamond and his sidekick, Charles Entratta, and that another man who was there and might have been involved was Charlie Luciano.

With unalloyed delight, Tony took a squad of detectives to Luciano's hotel.

Tony walked up to the tony-hotel clerk.

"I want the key to Thirty-nine-C," he said.

"I'm sorry. That's Mr. Ross's suite. You'll have to be announced."

Tony drew out his badge. "His name's Luciano, not Ross, and he's a goddamn killer, and this is all the announcement I need," he said. "Now give me the key or you're going to jail, too."

The nervous clerk withdrew a key from a locked box under the desk. Tony waved to one of his men.

"Keep an eye on this guy. Make sure he doesn't make any phone calls."

Half a dozen of them got into the elevator and told the uniformed operator to take them to the thirty-ninth floor. When he saw the looks on their faces, the operator said, "Look, I've got to go to the bathroom. Just pull this lever. The light tells you when you reach thirty-nine." Without waiting for a response, the operator fled. Tony sent another of the cops after him, again to insure Luciano got no sudden phone calls.

On the thirty-ninth floor, two Luciano guards were sitting on hard-back chairs in front of the elevator. The police disarmed them before they could react. With three men behind him, Tony quietly unlocked the door to Suite 39-C.

It was quiet inside, although the living room was still brightly lit.

Tony led the men across the thick plush carpets to a side door. From inside they heard sounds.

Quietly, Tony pushed open the door and saw Luciano in bed with a seedy-looking tart, who later gave her name as Nancy Presser. Holding his revolver out in front of him, covering Luciano, he strode inside the bedroom.

When he saw the men come through the door, Luciano sat bolt upright in bed and his hand reached for the drawer of an end table. Then he recognized Tony Falcone. He let his hand drop away from the end table.

"Hell of a time to come visiting," Luciano said.

"It's not a visit. You're under arrest."

"Any special reason or just the same old horseshit from you?" Luciano asked.

"For murdering Red Cassidy and Simon Walker."

"Never heard of them."

"Tell it to the judge," Tony said. "Get up and get dressed."

Luciano, naked and slim, slid out of bed and walked without apparent embarrassment toward a closet.

"You've gone too far this time, Falcone," he said. "I'm not going to play games with you anymore."

"You're lucky I'm feeling generous," Tony said. "Some cops might regard that as a threat and charge you with that, too. But I'll settle for just suspicion of two murders."

"You'll settle for nothing," Luciano snapped, even as he was drawing on a pair of trousers. "I'll be out before you even finish writing up your report."

Luciano was as good as his word. A lawyer was waiting for him when Tony brought him to headquarters, and within minutes a judge had been found who freed Luciano on his own recognizance, before he even had to give the police a statement.

As he left the police headquarters, he passed Tony. "You'll pay," he said. "You'll pay."

Legs Diamond and Charles Entratta seemed to have vanished, and Tony got warrants issued for their arrest, based on the statements of the eight witnesses.

Tony felt strong this time. Even a corrupt legal establishment would have trouble dropping murder charges, especially when there were eight witnesses. Maybe, at last, Luciano was going down.

Then the first witness in the speakeasy killings, the bartender at the Hotsy Totsy Club, was shot to death. The three customers who had given the police statements were also killed over a period of one month. But none of the reports on their killings had linked them to the Hotsy Totsy murders, and by the time Tony stumbled across the reports on their deaths, a week had gone by.

He instantly sent police out to protect the four remaining witnesses, who included the club's hatcheck girl— the one who had identified Charlie Luciano in the melee.

All four witnesses had vanished.

A week later, Legs Diamond and Charles Entratta returned to town with a story that they had been on vacation out west. Tony had them arrested immediately. The case went to a grand jury three days later, but since all eight witnesses against Luciano and the two other men had died or disappeared, the charges were dropped.

Tony took the news like a personal defeat. That evening, Tommy found him in the family apartment, sitting at the kitchen table, a gallon jug of wine on the table in front of him.

"What are you going to do?" Tommy had asked.

Tony reached into his jacket pocket for the paper he had been carrying for more than six months.

"My retirement papers. I'm filing them tomorrow."

"Do you really want to do that?" Tommy asked.

Tony poured them both glasses of wine from a gallon jug. "You got any suggestions?"

"Papa, with this Flying Squad, you're giving the mob fits. If you leave, who'll take your place?"

"What difference would it make? None of them go to jail anyway."

"No chance at all if you quit," Tommy said. "Papa, you told me once that what you did was important. I believed that. I still do. I think you should stay and fight them. Someday, Luciano, all of them, you'll get them all."

"Don't hold your breath waiting," Tony said disconsolately. "It's not just the courts, Tommy. I hear rumblings around. I think city hall might come after me."

"How could they do that?"

"The police commissioner's in the mob's pocket. If they want to hang me, they can. They'll hit me for not protecting those eight witnesses. Or it'll be because I spent too much money on pencils. Back when I was running that carnival, I met with Masseria and Maranzano's guys. I'm related to Nilo. By the time they're done smearing me, I'll look like the head of the Mafia. My pension'll be gone. I'll be lucky I don't wind up in jail."

Tommy did not answer and Tony took his silence for disagreement. "Don't tell me what I *shouldn't* do unless you can tell me what I *should* do," he snapped.

"You always told me to do what you think is right," Tommy said. "Not what you think is easy." He finished his wine, then stood. "I've got to get home. I've got a pregnant wife."

Stung by his son's attitude, Tony did not file his retirement papers the next day. But his longtime former partner, Tim O'Shaughnessy, did. He was leaving the force at the end of the week, and Anna had insisted that Tony invite O'Shaughnessy to a home-cooked farewell dinner.

"Ten years you worked with that big galoot," Anna said. "Least we can do is feed him."

Tommy had brought Rachel, and Mario had shown up for dinner, too, while Tina had telephoned her regrets that she was working at the club and could not attend. Kinnair, the *Daily News* reporter who was O'Shaughnessy's nephew, had shown up also, and even though Tony was uncomfortable around reporters, as the homemade wine flowed and Caruso records bellowed from the old phonograph everybody wound up having a good time. Tommy found himself sitting with O'Shaughnessy on the windowsill, while everybody else was out in the kitchen gabbing with Rachel about her pregnancy.

"I'm surprised you retired so young," Tommy said.

"To be a cop today, you got to be crooked or get your ass kicked," the big Irishman said, slurping noisily from a water glass filled with red wine. "As you very well know. Neither of those appealed much to me. So how's it with you? Tony worries that you don't seem ever to want to go to work."

"I'm just doing a little union work with my father-in-law," Tommy said. Abruptly, he thought that O'Shaughnessy, who had all kinds of contacts around the town, might have heard something, so he told him about the slowdown in union recruitment.

O'Shaughnessy was no real help and did not, in fact, even seem interested. He nodded and grunted a lot while Tommy talked, but when Tommy mentioned the union organizer Harry Birchevsky O'Shaughnessy's eyebrows lifted.

"What's his name?"

"Harry. Harry Birchevsky."

"Tommy, you didn't hear it from me, okay?"

Tommy nodded.

"When Nilo was in Dannemora, he was very close with Harry Birchevsky."

Tommy stared at the big cop, unable to keep the surprise from his face.

"I had a friend up there who let me know what was going on. I wanted to know in case any of it concerned your father," O'Shaughnessy said. "I remember this Birchevsky's name. Course, I don't know if it's the same man."

"Lev never told me about it. I don't know if he knows."

O'Shaughnessy laughed his musical Irish laugh and leaned closer to Tommy, glancing toward the kitchen before he spoke.

"You might try to find out. From what I heard, they were more than just friends. If you get my drift."

Tommy had nodded slowly. Birchevsky and Nilo, working together. He had wanted to talk more, but Kinnair wandered into the living room holding a glass of wine and looking more than a little drunk. He shook his head.

"You're quitting, Uncle Tim, and you, Tommy, you left the force too soon. Tony's going to have all this Flying Squad fun by himself."

"It's never fun," Tommy said.

• *All through September, the stock market drifted downward. From its high of 381 at the beginning of the month, the Dow Jones average fell to*

*370 . . . 360 . . . 330. By month's end, the market
had lost 15 percent of its value.*

SOFIA WAS WATCHING carefully, sure that even worse
lay ahead. She pointed it out one morning to Nilo, but
he was more interested in modeling for her the bullet-
proof vest he had just acquired. Safety had become a big
interest for Nilo recently. He always was armed before
going out and rarely ventured outside the apartment door
unless his bodyguard was waiting for him. He never
showed any concern, however, for Sofia, but she knew it
was because of the unwritten Mafia rule that wives and
children of enemies were not fair targets.

He made her feel the thickness of the bulky vest.
"Three guys killed this month. The next one isn't going
to be me," he said.

"Maybe if you stayed home . . . off the streets . . . spent
some time with—"

Nilo pulled away. "Now don't you start."

"But—"

"But, my ass," he snapped. "Don't go giving me any
of that wifey crap. I just don't want to hear it."

"Nilo, you're my husband. I—"

"Don't say 'love,'" Nilo snapped. "Don't even think
about saying it. What you and I got is kids. It's business,
nothing else."

He walked angrily away into his bedroom. A few minutes later, he came out, fully dressed, ready to leave.

"It's Tina, isn't it?"

"You haven't heard a goddamn word I said, have you?"
Nilo said, disgust coating his words. "Sure, it's Tina. We
screw every night when she comes to work. And most
nights when she's finished work, I hump her again. She

says she likes playing with me even better than playing with you." He reached across the table and touched her face gently.

"Happy now?" Nilo said with savage courtesy, then walked from the apartment.

Sofia sat at the table for a long time, looking at the door through which Nilo had gone. Then she looked down again at the morning paper, trying to follow the stock market reports, but she could not concentrate. She lowered her face to her hands, cupping them over her tired eyes. An old phrase sounded in her mind, over and over again . . . .

Rats got no complaint . . . rats got no complaint . . . rats got no complaint. . . .

She realized she must have dozed off, because she was startled by the knock on the door. She stood against the wall next to the door and called out, "Who's there?"

"Salvatore Maranzano," answered the familiar voice.

Before opening the door, Sofia checked through the peephole to make sure it was indeed the don, then let him inside.

He quickly made himself at home and sat with Sofia in the kitchen, drinking coffee.

"Where are your beautiful children?"

"The nurse has them out in the park," Sofia said. "One of your men is with them."

"And they are well?"

"Yes, Don Salvatore. They're well; we all are."

"I noticed you were very careful at the front door," he said.

"I always am."

"It is wise. There are rules, but there are always galoots who do not understand or abide by the rules. And I fear it will only get worse."

He stirred three spoons of sugar into the coffee and sipped it black before going on. "So I think you ought to take your children and go on vacation for a while."

"But—"

"No buts. You and the children will be safer out of town. I fear things around New York are going to be dangerous for a while. Nilo will be very busy. I do not want him to be worried about his family."

Sofia bit back her impulse to laugh, to point out that Nilo cared nothing about her and not much more about his children. She simply nodded.

"Where would I go?"

Maranzano shrugged. "Go anywhere you wish. Someplace maybe you have always dreamed of visiting. Take your nurse with you. You have been working very hard; it is time to see some reward for all that effort."

He took another sip of his coffee and stood. "Make plans quickly," he said. "If you need cash or help, please . . ."

"Thank you, Don Salvatore. I can manage."

He looked at her appraisingly. "Nilo has been very blessed. He has a wife not only beautiful, but intelligent and talented. Sometimes I don't think he knows how lucky he is."

Sofia blushed and walked with the don to the apartment door. After he left, Sofia walked to the front window and looked across the street toward the park. She could see her two boys with their nurse and the squat man in a dark suit, who sat on a nearby bench, watching them carefully.

It would be nice, she thought, to get the boys out of New York City for a while. Especially with the violence ready to escalate. Maranzano, she knew, would not have brought up the subject unless it was certain to happen.

Not for a moment did she worry about whether or not her husband would be killed. He seemed to invite occasions of violence, and there was nothing she could do about it; if he was going to be killed, it would happen, and her staying in New York City would not change that outcome at all.

Let him get shot and let his whore, Tina, mourn for him. My sons and I will be away.

The more she thought about it, the more pleasant the idea of a vacation sounded. In her whole life, she had gone on vacation only twice—both times, as a child, when she went to visit relatives on Long Island and found they lived in the same depressing conditions that she had left behind in the city. This would be a real vacation, with money in her purse, and hotels and restaurants, and it all made her a little giddy and more than a little nervous.

She might have to buy luggage, she thought. She went into the bedroom, where she was pretty sure that Nilo had stashed an old suitcase on one of the top shelves. She decided if it was too worn or threadbare, she would buy new luggage.

As she pulled the tan canvas satchel down from the shelf, a paper bag that was behind it fell, too, and spilled some of its contents onto the floor. She bent over to pick them up and then saw they were photos.

She picked up the bag to replace the pictures. Inside, she could feel a large roll of film. Then she looked at the pictures that had spilled out.

They were of Tina having sex with a tall blond man. She sat down heavily on the floor and sighed in confusion, then looked through the pictures. Not just the blond man. There was Tina having sex with other men.

She looked at Tina's face, trying to read its expression, but it was blank; her eyes were closed.

When were these pictures taken? And what is Nilo doing with them?

She looked through the pictures again. There were more than two dozen of them. But Nilo was not in any of them.

Would it be any surprise if he were? First Charlie. Then Nilo. Men cannot resist women who will do anything.

She put the pictures back into the paper bag and replaced it on the shelf. She also replaced the suitcase the way it had been.

Sofia closed the closet door.

"Slut," she said.

* *In the first ten days of October, the stock market rallied. Then the panic began. U.S. Steel dropped 7 percent in one day and then closed down twenty-two dollars for the week. General Electric collapsed at almost thirty-four dollars a share.*

TOMMY HAD STARTED tailing Birchevsky at odd times and places. And late at night, letting himself into the closed union offices with a key he got from Mishkin, he studied Birchevsky's appointments and outgoing and incoming phone calls. Gradually, the pattern had begun to emerge. More than once, he had met with Nilo in the offices of the speakeasy run by Tina. Most of the people he talked to were truck drivers who moved the clothing in and out of the factories.

It took a little while for the implications of that to sink in, and then it was obvious. There were fewer than a hundred drivers moving goods from one place to another, and without them, the garment industry would close down. Lepke had gotten a lot of power in the industry by taking over the cutters' union, but Maranzano—and Nilo—were trying to trump him by capturing the drivers.

Control the drivers and you control the industry. And Nilo figured it out, and that traitorous son of a bitch, Birchevsky, is helping him do it.

Tommy started hanging around in the neighborhood joints frequented by truck drivers. Eventually, he learned that Nilo was trying to take the truck drivers out of the garment makers' union and start a separate union for them. When he had done that, it would be a simple step to back-organize and take actual garment workers away from Lev's union.

We're headed for bloodshed, Tommy thought. *If Nilo gets the drivers for Maranzano while Masseria's man already has the cutters, they'll be machine-gunning each other in the streets. Whoever wins, it won't be the union members and it won't be Lev.*

One night in early October, Tommy sat in a neighborhood speakeasy, sipping a beer, and listened to Birchevsky, who was a little drunk, arguing with a driver a couple of barstools away.

"You worry too much," he heard Birchevsky say.

"Mishkin has been all right with us guys. I ain't gonna go with nobody else's union, especially some mob guys. Before you know it, they'll have us delivering booze."

"Hey, one union's just like another union," Birchevsky said.

"The hell it is. Tomorrow I'm gonna see Lev and tell him he's being sold down the river."

Birchevsky lumbered to his feet and tossed some money on the bar. "Don't do anything stupid," he said. "These ain't kid games."

"Go to hell."

After Birchevsky left the speakeasy, Tommy sidled down the bar to sit next to the angry driver.

"How you doing?" Tommy said. "Sounded like that guy was busting your chops."

"Aaaaah. He's a double-crossing son of a bitch."

"Let me buy you a beer. My name's Vito."

THE DRIVER'S NAME WAS EDDIE COLE, and he drove for one of the smaller companies in the garment district. He had been in Mishkin's union for more than ten years. But as hard as Tommy tried, he could not get the man to tell him the story of Birchevsky's offer. All he would say, no matter how many beers his new friend Vito bought him, was that there was "a rat bastard scheme going on, but I'm gonna fix it all tomorrow."

It was after midnight when Tommy left him in the speakeasy. The next morning, he called the garment company where Cole was employed, but the man had not shown up for work. Two days later, his wife reported him missing. It was time, Tommy thought, to tell the story to Lev Mishkin.

- *On Sunday, October 13, Tina Falcone attended Mass at Mount Carmel Church and received communion from her brother Father Mario just as Sofia Sesta and her two sons were boarding a transatlantic liner for Italy.*
- *On Monday, October 14, the stock market continued its relentless downhill slide. Tony Falcone got an envelope in the mail. Inside was another sealed envelope, with no address or name on it. When Tony opened it, he found two pornographic*

*pictures of Tina, and a block-printed note that
read: "Dear Tina, Call me sometime. I really miss
the fun we used to have. Charlie L."*

- *On Tuesday, October 15 . . .*

AT 10:00 P.M., Luciano stood on the corner of Sixth
Avenue and Fiftieth Street, waiting for his driver to bring
the new touring car around. Luciano had particularly
chosen that car this night because he was meeting a new
showgirl and he liked to make a good first impression. He
was wearing a brown tweed suit, one of a dozen new
suits he had bought that day, and all in all, Luciano was
feeling on top of the world. He had finally chased everyone else out of the prostitution business in New York
City, and the five thousand hookers in town all helped
contribute to his million-dollar-a-year tax-free income.

He had purchased a stable of racehorses and had a
hand in dozens of legitimate private businesses in the
city. Bootlegging would probably die soon, but Luciano
would go on. He had learned early in life never to put all
his eggs in one basket.

The two stupid Mustache Petes Maranzano and Masseria were still trying to kill each other, but the younger
members in each gang were listening more and more to
Luciano's talk of peace making them all rich. Since the
Atlantic City conference in May, there was no doubt
around the rest of the country that the man to see in New
York was Charlie Luciano. And with Al Capone still in
jail, where he would probably rot and die, New York was
the tail that wagged the dog.

*Run New York and you run the country. And I run New
York.*

He allowed himself a momentary feeling of satisfaction.

He was thirty-one years old.

A car rolled down the street toward him, its high beams blinding him, and Luciano stepped back from the curb. As it pulled abreast of him, the car's curtained rear door flew open and, before Luciano could move, two men with scarves over their faces had jumped out and tossed him onto the floor in the back of the car. A moment later, he felt adhesive tape being pressed over his eyes and his mouth. He could not see and he could not talk or scream.

He felt hands passing professionally over his body, frisking him for a weapon. But Luciano rarely carried a gun and he was unarmed this night. He tried to focus. The best he could guess was that there were three men in the backseat of the car facing him. Add in a driver, there were at least four other men in the vehicle.

The car drove slowly around Manhattan. Luciano tried to concentrate, to figure where they might be going, but he was disoriented and soon lost all sense of direction.

The men had not said a word. And then the beating started. They began kicking him in the ribs while he lay on the floor. When he tried to curl into a fetal position to protect himself, he felt his face and head being thumped with fists and blackjacks and gun butts.

After a while of that, he passed out and awoke when he was slapped repeatedly in the face.

That pain was just a prelude. He felt sharp pains in his back and realized he was being stabbed, probably with an ice pick. Oddly, he wondered if his suit was ruined. He could feel blood seeping down his back.

The beating went on for more than an hour. He felt the car go up a long incline and then down another long incline, and he was sure they had passed over a bridge.

The traffic was lighter now; he heard fewer noises.

Jersey. Maybe I'm in New Jersey.

Now there was no traffic sound at all. And then there was a crunch under the car.

We're driving over sand, he thought—his last thought before he was smashed hard between the eyes and blacked out.

When Luciano woke, he was careful not to groan or to move. He heard voices nearby, the first time he had heard them speak since he was abducted.

"Shoot the bastard and let's go."

"I can't."

"Why not? This was what you wanted, wasn't it?"

"If I kill him, I'm as bad as he is."

The voices were muffled, as if coming from far away, and Luciano could not recognize them. And he did not understand what they were saying.

As bad as me? he wanted to shout. *You're all as bad as me. It's how we survive.*

He thought for a moment of trying to scramble to his feet and run but realized he would not get more than a few feet. The pain in his back and head was intense.

"Well, if you won't, I will."

The voice was a little clearer now. It sounded Irish.

Luciano felt a big hand on him, spinning him over. And then, like a hot poker, he felt a knife slashing his face; he felt it slit his throat. He wanted to scream, but no sound would escape the tape. He was going to lie here and vomit in his pain and then choke on his own puke. He could feel the blood pulsing from his throat with each beat of his heart.

And then he heard a scuffle above him. His eyes were open but saw only the tape that covered them.

"No, I said." He heard a voice. It sounded like a voice he knew, but in the delirium of his pain, he could not place it.

"The world's better off if he's dead," the Irish voice growled.

"And we're worse for it. Come on. We'll leave him here."

Luciano felt the man release him and then heard footsteps scuffing through the sand. He heard four car doors slam in rapid succession.

There were four of them. At least four, he thought. He heard the car's engine start. The last thing he heard before he passed out was the sound of the car, crunching away across the sand.

When he awoke, his body felt as if it were on fire.

And I'm blind! I can't see!

He remembered then that his eyes had been taped shut. He tried to feel his hands. Then he moved them. He had not been tied up. As he raised his hands to his face, he heard waves sloshing nearby.

Carefully, he peeled the tape from his eyes. It was morning and he could see, and the sun was rising in the east. He peeled the tape from his mouth and struggled to a sitting position. When he looked down, he saw that the front of his suit was covered with blood. He remembered being cut and was afraid to touch his face and head but reached for it anyway and felt warm blood still pulsing from his throat wound.

As he was getting to his feet, he saw a sign stuck in the sand. It read HUGUENOT BEACH. He had never heard of the place.

The street was only a few dozen paces away and he struggled to walk to it. There was no traffic this early in the morning, and he limped heavily down the middle of the roadway.

After not more than fifty yards, he saw a policeman

come running toward him. Luciano fell into the officer's arms.

"Call me a cab, will you?" he croaked weakly.

"I'll call you an ambulance."

"Just call me a cab. There's fifty bucks in it for you," Luciano gasped, still unable to stand upright without help.

"Come over here and sit on the curb," the policeman said.

He led Luciano to the sidewalk.

"Where am I anyway?"

"Staten Island."

"Oh. I thought I was in Jersey."

The policeman left Luciano sitting on the curb and ran to the corner to call for help. Within an hour, Luciano was in a Staten Island hospital. After doctors patched him up and called his wounds "serious but not life-threatening," a detective named Charles Schley questioned him at his bedside.

"What's your name?"

"Charlie Luciano."

"What happened?"

"An accident."

"You're a gangster, right?"

"I'm a gambler."

"You're a pimp. What the hell happened?"

"I'm standing on the corner in New York. This car pulls up. I can't see nothing in the windows. Two guys hop out and drag me inside. They tape me up, beat me, drive me around, and dump me."

"Who were they?"

"I don't know who, where, what—nothing."

"You must have known at least one of them. Or seen him around. Or something."

"I'm telling you, I don't know them."

"Somebody you messed with, right? 'Gamblers' like you have enemies."

"Look. I'm pals with everybody. Nobody's after me. Everybody likes me. Now don't go losing any sleep over this. I can attend to it myself."

Schley and then another detective questioned Luciano for two hours but got no more out of him and finally left in disgust.

In the morning, Meyer Lansky showed up at the hospital and skeptically listened to Luciano say that he did not know who his assailants were. When he realized his longtime partner was not going to reveal any more, Lansky said, "It doesn't matter. You're lucky to be alive. You've always been lucky."

"That's me. Lucky . . . Lucky Luciano."

Later that day, the police took Luciano to a lineup at headquarters, but no one identified him as a suspect in any crime. Anxious nevertheless to arrest him for something, police dusted off an old stolen-car charge and booked him, but Lansky paid twenty-five thousand dollars in cash to free him on bail. The charges would later be dropped.

WHEN HE LEFT HIS OFFICE that afternoon, Lt. Tony Falcone filed his papers retiring from the New York City Police Department. He told himself that the time had come. *I have become as corrupt and lawless as the ones I spent my life fighting.*

WHEN NILO ANSWERED the telephone, Birchevsky was on the line.

"Listen. I'm out of the office. But Lev wanted me to find you and ask you to a meeting."

"What for?" Nilo asked, looking at his reflection in the full-length mirror on the back of the bedroom door.

"Who knows? He told me to find you. He's getting cranky because we're not signing up new members, and when he gets cranky, he calls meetings."

"All right. Did you get that mess cleaned up the other night?"

"Yes. The trouble is in the river," Birchevsky said.

"I hope so. This is too big an operation to let anybody mess up."

"I told you. Fish don't talk."

Later, in the union office, Nilo was not surprised to see Tommy Falcone, who had married Mishkin's daughter.

Giving the father-in-law a hand, he thought. *Too bad he backed a loser. They're all losers.*

Mishkin walked to the door and called for Birchevsky to come inside, then gestured to both men to sit down. Birchevsky looked inquisitively at Tommy standing alongside Mishkin's desk, as if he had seen him before but could not place the face.

"What can I do for you?" Nilo asked.

"You might drop dead," Mishkin said.

"Excuse me?"

"You and your damned Judas goat there . . ." Mishkin nodded toward Birchevsky. "I'd be happy if you both got the hell out of my life."

Birchevsky's face paled. Nilo forced himself to smile until he could feel the skin stretching at the corners of his mouth.

"I don't understand," he said. "I do something to offend you?"

"You wop bastard, you offend me by breathing the

same air as I do. I'm through with you. Does Maranzano know what you've been up to?"

Nilo said, "He knows everything I do."

"Then he's as big a douche bag as you are and your friend there. Go fuck yourselves." He half-rose from the chair as he shouted at Nilo.

Nilo reacted without thinking. He lunged forward and slapped Mishkin's face. Mishkin fell back onto his seat and Nilo reached back to throw a punch, but Tommy's hand locked around his wrist. Nilo tried to twist free but could not.

"Calm down," Tommy said quietly. He waited until Nilo nodded before releasing his wrist.

"Lev, Lev," Birchevsky said. "What is the matter?"

"What is the matter is that you and your friend here aren't going to take over this union. You're finished with this union." He turned and glared at Nilo. "And I'll see you dead before you organize any drivers or anybody else in this industry."

"Big talk," Nilo said.

"More than talk. When Stupid there killed a driver the other night, there was a witness. He'll testify. Your power grab is over."

Birchevsky laughed. "Nobody testifies in this city. Nobody lives to."

"This witness will," Tommy said, bluffing, watching Birchevsky's reaction carefully.

"Nobody lives forever," Birchevsky said.

He did kill the driver, Tommy thought. *I can't prove it, but he did it.*

"Easy, easy," Nilo said. "Look. Why don't we just talk this out? You don't like that we're organizing the drivers. Well, that's too bad. But the fact is we're going to control the industry. If you don't get in our way, Mishkin, we'll let you keep one of the locals for yourself. If you insist on giving us trouble, you won't get a thing."

Mishkin steepled his fingers in front of his face, as if he were weighing the proposal.

"Be reasonable," Nilo said. "By next week, you might not be able to make this good a deal. Tell him, Tommy."

Birchevsky said suddenly, "He ain't Tommy. That's Vito. I seen him around." Nilo looked shocked.

"You're Vito," Nilo said. "You've caused me a lot of trouble."

"I haven't even started yet," Tommy said.

Mishkin reached under his desk and pushed a button.

A few seconds later, the office door opened and four burly men came in.

Mishkin stood and pointed to Birchevsky and Nilo.

"They're leaving. Escort them out. And I don't really care if they slip and fall on the stairs on the way."

Nilo stood and stared at Mishkin.

"We can find our own way out," he said.

The muscle squad hesitated.

"You heard me," Mishkin said. "Throw them out."

"IT'S OVER," TOMMY SAID. "They know who I am."

There was a long silence on Captain Cochran's end of the phone. Finally, the police officer said, "Come in tomorrow. In the meantime, watch your back."

IT WAS TIME TO TELL RACHEL, before she heard about it anywhere else. Tommy came home early and made a big production out of cooking his wife an Italian dinner.

"I bet you didn't know I was this good in the kitchen," he said.

"I thought you specialized in the bedroom," she said.

"You're an animal. I've got to talk to you."

"About your still being a cop?"

"What?" Tommy was taken aback by what she had said.

"Lev told me. A couple of months ago. He figured it out. Was I supposed to be upset?"

"I didn't . . . I wasn't . . . I didn't know how you'd feel," Tommy stammered.

"All this while I thought you were a bookie," she said. "Trust me. I like that you've been a cop."

"I don't know what to say."

"Maybe say, 'No more secrets.'"

"What did I ever do to deserve you?" Tommy asked.

"Raw Sicilian sex appeal," Rachel said. "You've made me the animal I am."

EVERYONE DENIED RESPONSIBILITY later, but some-one tipped off John F. X. Kinnair, and the *Daily News* the next morning ran a story under his byline which read:

> A decorated war-hero New York City cop has risked his life for the past two years, working as a spy in the New York underworld. Police officials would not comment, but, privately, top brass admit that the undercover work of Patrolman Tommy Falcone has been responsible for many of the major arrests made by the renowned Flying Squad in the past eighteen months.

Tommy groaned when he read the story and immediately set out for his family's apartment on Crosby Street to see Tony and try to explain.

When he entered the flat, his father was sitting on the sofa, reading the *Daily News*. A radio played classical music softly in the background.

Tony looked up and said, "Well, well, well," and called out to the kitchen, "Hey, Mama. Vito has come to see us."

His mother came in and hugged Tommy, who couldn't take his eyes off Tony. "I'm sorry, Papa," he said.

"I'm not."

"Huh?"

"The last couple of years, I thought you had lost your ambition and turned into sort of a bum, and it turns out that you were doing something worthwhile after all. I'm proud of you."

"You're not mad? That I didn't tell you?"

Tony shrugged. "I had enough to keep me busy without worrying about you." He stared at his son for a moment, then grinned. "I talked about it yesterday with Cochran. He said it was his decision, that if anybody had told me, I'd spend all my time trailing you around to make sure you didn't get into trouble. I can't argue. He's right. I would have. No, I'm not mad. Well, maybe a little mad, but mostly proud."

Anna hugged her son more tightly. "I've always been proud," she said.

"You know how I decided what to do?" Tommy asked, looking at his father. "I asked myself what would my father do, and then I did it."

"I hate you wise-guy college boys," Tony said.

Tommy had been there only ten minutes when he received a phone call from Rachel. When he hung up, he looked at his father quizzically.

"Captain Cochran called my house. He wants to see me," he said.

COCHRAN WAS IN FULL DRESS uniform when Tommy arrived at his office a little later.

"We're not usually so formal around here," Cochran said. "I've got to talk to the chamber of commerce at lunch. But I wanted to thank you for what you did. I know how hard it was."

Tommy grinned. "Oh, you were talking to my father, too."

Cochran sighed. "Now that he's a civilian, he called me every son of a bitch in the book. But he'll get over it."

"He already has."

"Do you remember the first time we met?" Cochran asked.

"Yes, sir."

"I offered you a promotion and you turned it down."

Tommy nodded.

"I'm doing it again." Before Tommy could reply, the dapper officer said, "With Tony's retirement, the Number Two job here is open, and I don't know anybody who'd be better in it than you. I couldn't make you a lieutenant right away, but I could give you sergeant now and lieutenant probably in eighteen months."

Tommy sank down in a chair. "I came in expecting to be told to get lost," he said.

"Not a chance. I need somebody and I don't know anybody who I think would be better than you. It's no bed of roses. You know what's going on. City hall wants to look good, so they want us out there arresting everybody we can. But then they don't want to offend any of their 'friends,' so most of the cases get fixed in the courts. But it won't always be that way. If we keep arresting them, sooner or later, they're going to jail."

Tommy shook his head. "I wouldn't be any good at dealing with politicians."

"You wouldn't have to." Cochran grinned. "That's why they sent an Irishman like me down here in the first place. Nobody will interfere with you. You run the place for me, just like your father did. The political problems are mine."

"A free hand?"

"I wouldn't offer the job to you any other way," Cochran said.

"I'll take it."

"I—" Cochran stopped. "You'll take it?"

"If my wife says it's all right."

"How I've come down in life," Rachel said. "I thought I was going to be married to a millionaire lawyer. And now I'm stuck with some flatfoot."

"I'll practice law someday," Tommy said weakly.

Rachel smiled and threw her arms around her husband. "Oh, Tommy, you sap, of course I want you to take the job. Go arrest those bastards."

Thirty detectives from precincts all over the city came to the offices of the Italian Squad. While they were not technically members of the squad, the primary responsibility of each of them was gangland crime, and they filed reports of all their investigations with Cochran's office.

They waited in a big squad room on the second floor of the building, sitting in small school-size chairs, and they looked up when Cochran and Tommy, both in uniform, entered the room and walked to the front.

Cochran was brief and blunt. "This is Sergeant Falcone. He will be my second in command, running the day-to-day operation of the anti-gang squad. What he says goes." He nodded to Tommy, who looked around the room.

"Most of you men worked with my father. He had a reputation for being a tough, honest cop. That annoyed some of you. I'm just here to tell you that I'm no improvement." He stepped down off the platform and ordered, "Everyone stand up."

The detectives, all of them in street clothes, shuffled to their feet.

"Hold your hands out in front of you like this," Tommy said, stretching his hands before him, palms down.

As the puzzled detectives did so, Tommy walked up and down the aisles among the men, looking at their hands, then came back to the front of the room.

"Put your hands down," he ordered. When the detectives complied, he said softly, "Now all of you wearing diamond rings, get out of here. Go back to your precincts and tell them to reassign you. You're not working the gang squads anymore."

He looked around the room. The detectives stood in stunned silence; not one of them had moved.

"What are you waiting for? Written orders? Go on, get out of here." Slowly men started to shuffle away from their seats toward the door. In all, fourteen detectives left the room.

When they were gone, Tommy looked at the men who were left. "The rest of you get back to work. You'll hear from me one at a time. And one standing order remains in force: If you see Charlie Luciano so much as spit on the sidewalk, run him in."

Cochran stepped forward, smiling broadly, and said, "Better move it, men. The sergeant is not a patient man."

- *Inevitably Luciano heard about the high priority Tommy Falcone had placed on his arrest. He seemed unworried. "I screwed the father, I screwed the girl, and I'll screw this snot-nose kid before I'm done," he said.*
- *The stock market went into free fall at the end of October. From its high of 381 on September 3, the Dow Jones average plummeted and ended the month at 240, down over 35 percent. The market would continue to fall until the summer of 1932 when it bottomed out at 41—a three-year drop of almost 90 percent.*
- *On America's favorite radio show, Andy asked: "Is you been keeping yo' eye on de stock market?" Lightnin' replied: "Nosah, I ain't never seed it." Said Andy: "Well, de stock market crashed." Asked Lightnin': "Anybody get hurt?" Everybody got hurt. By year's end, stock market losses would be more than 40 billion dollars.*
- *While Sofia was still away with her children on vacation, Maranzano made a telephone call to Chicago to talk to a young man who looked like a college student and always carried a violin case.*
- *At the end of 1929, the most popular entertainment in America was miniature golf. New York City alone had a thousand courses. The fad soon faded. The first pinball machine, Baffle Ball, was invented.*

> *Jukeboxes became popular in small speakeasies that could not afford to hire house bands.*

- *With Birchevsky fired from the garment makers' union, Nilo's attempt to unionize the truck drivers failed. Slowly, Lev Mishkin's union began to expand. Tommy had not forgotten Eddie Cole, the young truck driver who had been missing since the night he had turned down Birchevsky's offer. Tommy assigned one of the squad detectives to try to trace Cole's last movements after leaving the speakeasy where he had been drinking.*

- *On December 2, 1929, Matteo Mangini died after suffering a massive stroke in his restaurant. Sofia was still in Sicily with her children, visiting Nilo's hometown of Castellammare del Golfo. Father Mario and Tina stood with Nilo at the graveside services. Nearby was Luciano, the knife wounds on his face and throat beginning to heal into ridged, white scars. Neither Tommy nor his father attended the funeral.*

- *A twenty-one-year-old Long Island girl quit her secretarial job for a role in Gershwin's* Girl Crazy *on Broadway, and when she held a high C in "I Got Rhythm" for sixteen measures, Ethel Merman became an instant star.*

- *Despite the market crash, Americans welcomed in 1930 by singing "Happy Days Are Here Again." On New Year's Day, Rachel Falcone suffered a miscarriage.*

CHAPTER II

1930: The War

No one knew his real name. He was just "Buster from Chicago." He looked barely twenty years old, and like a college boy he wore plaid sports jackets and light-colored shoes. He came to New York City from Chicago by train at the end of 1929 and rented a room in a cheap uptown hotel, where he registered as Leo Brothers, locked himself in his room, and carefully unpacked and cleaned the tools of his trade: a Thompson submachine gun, a twelve-gauge shotgun, and four pistols of varying calibers.

Then he took a cab to Midtown to talk to his new employer, Salvatore Maranzano. The meeting with Maranzano and Nilo was brief and businesslike.

"Nilo will tell you who we want done. You do it at your own speed, your own way. No one else will even know you are in town."

Buster smiled. He had heard such promises before and he knew that they were never kept. His presence in town would be known before nightfall. Still, it did not bother him; a little notoriety was good for business.

"All Masseria men?" he said.

Maranzano nodded. "His men are coming to our side. We want to give them even more incentive to do so."

"They'll be dying to join up with you," Buster said with a smile.

"Where will you be staying?" Nilo asked.

"It's better that no one knows that. I'll call in here every day at nine and five. If you have anything for me, you can tell me then."

After Buster left, Nilo told Maranzano, "We don't need him. I could have done this work for you."

"Nilo, Nilo, Nilo, are you ever going to stop being a shooter? Already, we have had enough trouble with that Jew killing that truck driver."

"It's all taken care of," Nilo said sullenly.

"Well, just let it go," Maranzano ordered. "We've got other bigger businesses to take care of. It was not smart to try to do dope. Or to muscle into the garment business. We are winning the war the way it is. Why change the rules?" He stared at Nilo. "And don't hang around with Birchevsky anymore. He is a hothead and will cause you trouble."

"Yes, Don Salvatore," Nilo said.

BUSTER FROM CHICAGO went to work, and it was immediately clear that the reputation he had gained in the bloody wars in Chicago had been well earned.

He was not inclined to rush into a place and start shooting it up, hoping that he would somehow hit his chosen target. Instead, he carefully followed his intended victims, made sure he knew their schedules and when they would most likely be alone. And then he struck.

Occasionally, he would need help in making the initial identification of a target, and those times Nilo sent a talky young hoodlum named Joe Valachi to act as Buster's spotter.

Buster from Chicago took his time and did not miss. Almost every week, some underling of Masseria was found shot dead in the street. Although they still outnumbered Maranzano's forces, Masseria's thugs began to live in terror.

The war went on. Meyer Lansky assigned an extra bodyguard to stay with Luciano.

SOFIA HAD RETURNED HOME from Italy shortly before Christmas, convinced that the vacation trip had changed her life.

Nilo had not even bothered to meet his family at the pier and, in fact, did not come back to their apartment until the day after Sofia had returned home. When he did, he seemed contrite and told Sofia in great detail about her father's death and funeral, how Mario and Tina had both attended, as had Luciano.

Of course, Tina was at the funeral. What would you expect your whore to do? she thought. She said nothing, however, and listened attentively as Nilo told her about Luciano's brush with death at the hands of assassins.

"He calls himself Lucky now," Nilo said. "Lucky Luciano."

"And no one knows who assaulted him?"

"There are a lot of rumors out on the street. That it was Legs Diamond's gang. Or Dutch Schultz. It wasn't us so I don't know, and Luciano's not saying anything."

"It was not Masseria himself?" Sofia asked. "A falling-out between him and Charlie?"

"No. Word is that when Luciano survived, Joe the Boss promoted him. Charlie is top dog now, right under Masseria, so I don't know who might have wanted to get him."

Sofia nodded. *You might not know, but I know. It was Tony Falcone, because I sent him those pictures of your* puta *singer. And Charlie really is lucky because if I had been here, instead of in Italy, I would have drawn out Tony's anguish, day after day, until he had no choice but to kill him.*

She was disappointed that Luciano was still alive. It had become obvious that he was the only brain left in Masseria's organization, and if he had been killed, in weeks Maranzano would have conquered Joe the Boss.

Nilo was still jabbering on about how Tony had retired from the police department and Tommy had taken his place, how Tina was keeping the speakeasy packed every night, how her mother was coping with the death of Matteo Mangini, how kind Mario had been at the funeral.

It was unusual for him to talk so much, and she let him wind down before she gave him her own sad news: that his father had died three years earlier, but his mother seemed to be well and did not appear to lack for money.

Nilo took the news stoically. In truth, he had not thought of his family for many years. It was as if Castellammare del Golfo were in another universe.

Later in bed, she saw the faint traces of healing bruises on his body, and eventually he told her about being thrown down the stairs at the union building and about being beaten afterward. More than his body had been hurt; his pride had been badly damaged, too.

"And Don Salvatore says do nothing," he complained.

"And what would you do?"

What he wanted to do was to go back to the union building and take his vengeance, first on the muscle men who beat him, then on Mishkin and Tommy too.

"I still have scores to settle with the Falcones and a lot of people," he said.

Sofia counseled patience. "The time for action is not yet. Wait for the first keen edge of their alertness to pass."

"But Tommy won't let it die," Nilo said. "He has men nosing around all over, trying to pin a crime on me."

"What crime?" she asked.

"Aaaah, somebody turned up missing in the union business. He'll try to stick me with the guy's murder."

"If it happens, *then* it's time to act," Sofia said. "But not you. Somebody else must do it, so no suspicion falls on you."

Nilo was silent a long time, finally lit a cigarette, and said, "I missed you while you were gone. You're very smart, Sofia. I am happy you are my wife."

And I am happy you are my husband, because I know better than you what your future will be and why it is so. And I will do anything to make it happen.

"THESE CRAZY BASTARDS ARE KILLING each other all over the streets." Meyer Lansky was clearly outraged; he paced up and down the living room carpet in Luciano's hotel suite. "We're going to have to do something."

"Yeah. What we got to do is make sure nobody kills us," Luciano replied. He was wearing a silk bathrobe and sipping coffee at a small glass-topped table.

"Well, you didn't do such a good job when you wound up in Staten Island," Lansky snapped. "Next time maybe you're not so lucky and you're just a memory."

"Meyer, relax. Have a cup of coffee."

"I don't like your goddamn Italian coffee."

"Have American coffee. I'll get some sent up."

"I don't want coffee."

"All right. Then listen without coffee. First of all, we don't have any worries with the cops or city hall. That's taken care of. Second of all, I don't care if Masseria and Maranzano are shooting at each other twenty-four hours a day. If it goes right, one of them will get hit. If he does, we'll take care of the other one."

"And suppose neither of them gets hit?"

"Then they'll have everybody so disgusted with them that when we do what we have to do, nobody's going to complain about it," Luciano said. "You're the one who told me you can't rush history. Meyer, we're making history."

"I just don't want to make the obituary pages."

"It's going just the way it should. You just be careful out on the street. How's it going with the businesses?"

"We're buying them up right and left. It's like we own a business on every block in Manhattan."

"Prices are right?"

Lansky grinned. "My Jewish landsmen are all in hock from the stock market. They're selling for a song. We're bigger than U.S. Steel."

"Why not? We're smarter than U.S. Steel."

"I think I will have that coffee," Lansky said. "What the hell, we probably own the coffee company."

Luciano smiled. He knew that Lansky was not nearly so worked up as he had pretended to be but simply wanted to make sure that Luciano was aware of what was going on and had a plan to deal with it. But Lansky knew that asking a question like that directly would have been insulting to Luciano, so instead he launched into his tirade to get the information and at the same time to make Luciano feel leaderly.

Meyer is very clever. He will live a long time, Luciano thought.

———

SOFIA WENT TO VISIT HER MOTHER, who insisted on taking her to Brooklyn to the graveyard where Matteo Mangini was buried. Although she had no desire to be part of a wailing graveside death scene, Sofia called Nilo, who sent a car and driver to take them to the cemetery.

The two women stood wordlessly by the grave for a long time.

"I'm sorry, Mama," Sofia said, because she felt she should say something.

"I'm not. He was a bastard."

"I hated him," Sofia said.

"Not as much as I did. I hated him before you were born."

"It's a nice grave anyway."

"Better than he deserves. If it wasn't for Father Mario, I would have just thrown him out in the street and let the garbagemen cart him away like a dead horse."

They were silent again for long minutes, still staring at the grave.

Sofia said, "Most of these graves have flowers. Maybe we should have brought something."

"I did bring something for his grave," Mrs. Mangini said. She hocked and spat. "Now you."

Sofia spat, too.

"Hell's too good for you, you son of a bitch. Good-bye and good riddance," her mother said.

"Come on, Mama, I'll take you home." She smiled. "So we can grieve."

"Anisette. A little anisette will make the grieving go better."

Sofia got home late in the afternoon, and the telephone rang almost immediately.

A male voice asked for Nilo. When she said he was not home, the man said, "This is his friend, Harry. Do you know where he is?"

"I think he's out of town today."

"Give him a message. Tell him I called and said that the cops fished some truck driver out of the river."

Sofia thought quickly, then said, "Harry, I think you ought to come up here and talk to me."

"When?"

"Now."

TOMMY HAD BEEN IN HIS POLICE OFFICE when the report came that the body found on a straggly piece of beach across the river in Jersey City had been identified as Eddie Cole. The truck driver had been shot in the head.

The detective Tommy had assigned to the case had not been able to find out where Cole had gone when he left the speakeasy where he had been drinking with Tommy. "Look again," Tommy told him. "Somebody had to see something. Get a picture of Cole. Hang out on the street late at night. See if anybody wanders by and show them the picture. Somebody saw something."

He himself could place Cole in the speakeasy with Harry Birchevsky. He had overheard the men arguing and heard Cole threaten to go to Lev Mishkin. But when Tommy left the bar, Cole was still there, still alive. He needed one more piece of evidence to grab Birchevsky for Cole's murder. *And if I get Birchevsky, he will give up Nilo.*

SOFIA SENT THE NURSE OUTSIDE with the children. When the doorman buzzed her, she answered, then stood by the door and straightened her hair. She unbuttoned her blouse just one button more than modesty allowed and looked in the mirror behind the flower-filled lavabo. If she leaned forward just so . . .

She was satisfied and opened the door.

"Hello, Harry," she said.

She leaned forward as if to pluck a piece of lint from her skirt, careful to keep her eyes modestly averted. When she looked up, Harry was staring at her bosom.

"You're looking beautiful," he said. "Nilo's very lucky."

"Come on in. Nilo's told me about this problem with the driver, but sometimes I don't think he's hard enough to deal with it." She shut the door behind him. "I think it's important for a man to be hard sometimes, don't you?"

TOMMY FALCONE ROLLED OVER in his sleep and reached out for his wife. She was gone. A flash of panic struck through him and he came instantly awake. The illuminated clock dial read 3:00 A.M.

He got up from bed and went out to find Rachel sitting on the sofa, sipping tea, staring at a partially finished painting on an easel.

"Can't sleep?" Tommy asked.

"Something like that," she said with a smile. "You know, I've been thinking."

"Oh, God, not that again," Tommy said with a mock groan as he sat next to her.

"Quiet, *paisan*. I've been thinking that I'm a terrible painter. Look at this thing." She gestured toward the oil painting, the face of a woman so hideously distorted that it looked as if the woman had been made of wax and was melting.

"I like it. It has a style all its own," Tommy said.

"You hate it. I see you grimace every time you walk past it."

"That obvious, huh?"

"I read you like a book, buddy. Anyway, I'm going to put the paints away and get a job."

"What kind of a job?"

"I don't know. I thought I might become a streetwalker out by the docks in Brooklyn. I don't know what kind of a job, you nitwit. Some kind of job."

"I don't want you being a waitress or anything like that."

"Why not?"

"I don't want people yelling at you. And anyway, you're always spilling things. You'd be a terrible waitress."

"Well, just for your information, Jewish girls don't become waitresses. We start at the top. Sewing clothes in an attic or something."

"You can't sew, either," Tommy said.

"Stop being so literal. That's just an example."

"I've got it. You can be my sex slave."

Rachel turned toward him and murmured, "Now we're getting somewhere." She kissed him hard and Tommy wrapped his arms around her before Rachel pulled away, stood, and led him back to bed.

"I'll be glad when you're usable again," he said.

"No more than me."

She turned on her side, and Tommy thought he could hear her breathing take on the rhythms of sleep. He began to doze off.

"Tommy," she said suddenly. "I can't sleep."

"Try harder."

"I was wondering if you'd be interested in a bit of sexual perversity," she said.

"Anything's better than thinking of you trying to be a waitress."

She punched him playfully in the arm, then slipped her head under the covers. Afterward, they lay together in each other's arms.

"I kind of liked that," she said.

"I'm not sure if I did," Tommy said. "You'll have to do it a couple thousand more times before I'll be able to make up my mind."

She laughed and they fell asleep.

He was never certain what happened next. He was awake for only an instant. He thought he caught sight of a male figure in the dark bedroom, and then he saw flashing light as something clubbed him on the side of the head.

Every time he struggled back toward consciousness he was hit again. He heard Rachel cry once and then her cries were muffled. He tried to yell, but there was something across his mouth. He felt a needle sting his arm and he went into a deep sleep. Later, he felt the needle sting again. And then he felt nothing.

ALL THE HOLIDAY SERVICES and the New Year's celebrations and his extra duties as assistant pastor had taken a lot out of Mario, and when his mother had seen him after Mass on Sunday, she had told him he looked like an Irisher and ordered him to come for dinner.

Now he sat at the kitchen table reading the paper while his mother fussed at the stove. "Look at the time," she said. "It's nearly six thirty. Tommy and Rachel were supposed to be here an hour ago. Dinner will be ruined."

"Your dinner is never ruined, Mama."

"It's just not like them not to call if they're going to be late."

Mario laughed. "You worry too much."

"For this wisdom, we sent you to seminary?"

The telephone rang.

"See?" called Tony, who was buried behind a cloud of smoke in the living room, reading the sports pages. Since he had retired, he was now permitted to smoke inside the house, especially since he often seemed to be in a dark, self-pitying mood and sometimes did not leave his seat on the sofa for hours on end. "That's them calling now. I bet they just forgot the time."

Anna answered the kitchen phone and when she hung up turned to Mario with a worried look.

"It was Tommy's office. They were wondering if he was here."

Mario nodded and rose. "Well, nothing to worry about, Mama. I think while we're waiting, I'll take a little walk before dinner."

"I think I'll join you," Tony said. He vanished into the bedroom, and when he came back, Mario saw his police revolver under his jacket.

"We'll be right back, Anna," Tony said.

MARIO POUNDED ON THE DOOR for a full thirty seconds, but no one answered, and finally Tony shoved him aside and slammed the heel of his shoe into the door below the knob. The door quivered and swung open.

Tommy was standing by the window in his pajamas looking out into the street. He did not even turn when his father and brother broke in.

"Tommy," Mario called, and ran to his side.

His brother did not move. He simply stared forward.

"It's all right, Tommy. We're here now," Mario said. He moved alongside so he could see his brother's eyes. He had seen them like that before, thirteen years before, in that hospital in France.

Tony walked through the open bedroom door. Mario heard him groan, and even as he held Tommy, he turned toward the bedroom.

His father had tears in his eyes. He walked leadenly toward Mario. "She's dead," he whispered. "Rachel."

"Rachel's dead," Tommy echoed in a hollow voice.

"Help your son," Mario told Tony.

"You don't want to go in there," Tony said.

"I have to."

Rachel was lying naked in bed. Her face had turned ash-dark and her tongue was sticking out like a lizard's. Her lips were drawn back in a corpse's rictal grin.

Mario pulled the bloody cover up over her and knelt at the bedside. He did not have his oils for the formal saying of the extreme unction sacrament, but he blessed her without it. He was not sure if she would have wanted it, but unbeknownst to Tommy or her father, she had talked to him and Tina often in the past few weeks about converting to Catholicism. The sacrament would do her soul no harm, he thought.

As he prayed, the tears coursed down his face.

A YOUNG PRIEST WAS CALLED in to take over Mario's parish duties so he could attend to his family, but still those winter weeks early in 1930 were nothing but a blur.

Tony had gone to tell Lev Mishkin of the tragedy, but Mishkin could not be found. As day passed into day, he was not seen or heard from. In the absence of any known relatives, Mario took over responsibility for Rachel's burial, and he shared with a rabbi the prayers at her grave.

Tommy was not at the funeral. Detoxification had been the easiest part. His body had been shot up with enough morphine to kill him, but much of it did not enter his bloodstream, and it was not over a long-enough period to addict him again.

But he had simply lost his mind. He lay in St. Vincent's Hospital, motionless, wordless, oblivious. The family kept up a vigil at his bedside, taking turns, talking to him during all his waking hours, but they might just as well not have been there. Tommy responded to no stimulus; he merely stared at the ceiling.

Even though they found it distasteful, the police's murder investigation centered on Tommy for a few days, under the theory that he had made himself crazy with drugs and then killed his wife. But the physical evidence soon made it clear that Tommy had been a victim, too. The morphine had been injected in places Tommy could not have reached himself; there were signs that Rachel's and Tommy's mouths had been silenced with tape. Tommy's head wounds, clearly not self-inflicted, were more evidence of unknown assailants, as was the sheer brutality of the vicious sexual attack on Rachel.

Sofia was not at the funeral, but Nilo came with Tina and stood with the Falcone family.

Later, he told Mario, "I don't know who did this, but I'm going to find out. When I do, they are dead men."

DESPITE A CONSTANT STRING of needling newspaper stories from John F. X. Kinnair, after a few weeks the police gave up on the investigation. Lev Mishkin was still missing, and the detectives handling the case believed that perhaps he had been involved in Rachel's murder. But on March 18, with the first glimmering of spring, Mishkin's body was found in a landfill dumping ground near Yonkers. He had been shot six times at close range and had been dead for several months. The police went through the motions, then added Mishkin's murder to that of his daughter in the unsolved file.

No one seemed to care, particularly Tommy Falcone, who was back at the convent of the Sisters of Quietude in Monticello, New York, ninety miles north of the city. He had been placed on leave of absence by the police department, and Mario had pulled some strings to get him admitted to the small convent hospital soon after Rachel's murder, just in case his life was in danger.

Tommy lay in bed like a vegetable, able to talk but not wanting to, able to move but not caring to. One of the doctors who treated the nuns at the convent told Tony that his son had suffered a great emotional trauma.

"When's he going to come out of it?" Tony asked on one of his visits.

"Maybe tomorrow. Maybe never," the doctor said. "I'm sorry. There's just too much that we don't know. He's in the right place. Prayers can help him as much as medicine."

We don't need prayers, Tony thought. *Mario has enough prayers for all of us. We need a doctor who knows something.*

The first time Tony had visited him, he had looked in on his son, then gone out into the hallway to weep. The life force had gone out of Tommy and he did not respond to questions or conversation.

When Tony got back to the city, he decided his retirement was over. Since putting in his papers, he had spent day after day sitting on his sofa, reading the newspaper, but now he was out of the house at dawn, often returning home only late at night. The police might give up on the investigation, but Tony vowed that he never would.

He went to see Captain Cochran and asked what Tommy had been working on that might have triggered mob retribution.

"If I tell you, you're going to start looking into things," Cochran said.

"Captain, even if you don't tell me, I'm going to start looking."

Finally, Cochran told him that Tommy had been particularly interested in the apparent murder of a garment district truck driver named Eddie Cole and in a man named Harry Birchevsky, who had worked for Mishkin's union.

It was a starting place. Using his old gold badge for identification, Tony interviewed everyone who lived in Tommy's apartment building several times over. Everybody who lived on the same block was grilled, as were deliverymen, mailmen, milkmen, cabdrivers—anyone who might have been on the street during the time of Rachel's killing and who might have seen something, anything. All Tony got was two reports from people who had seen a stranger in the neighborhood, a husky, disheveled man they could not identify but who walked duckfooted.

With Lev Mishkin missing, his union was in a total state of confusion, but Tony was able to find out that Birchevsky was a husky, disheveled man who walked duckfooted. Tony knew that Lepke Buchalter, who was allied with Luciano, had been making inroads into the garment makers' union. Had Luciano been behind Rachel's killing? As far as he knew, Luciano had nothing against Tommy, but was it some kind of convoluted scheme to get at Tony, for Luciano to pay him back for the late-night ride that left the gangster scarred and bleeding on a Staten Island beach?

Would I have been better off killing the bastard, like O'Shaughnessy wanted to? Tony wondered.

But he could not make himself buy that scenario. Even allowing for his belief that Luciano was the lowest form of scum, he did not believe the gang leader would have approved the brutal murder of a policeman's wife.

There was also the question of Tommy being shot up with morphine. It was clearly an attempt to pin Rachel's killing on him, but who would have known about Tommy's wartime morphine addiction?

Finally, it was Tim O'Shaughnessy who gave him the tip. Tony met with his old partner one day for lunch, and O'Shaughnessy remembered telling Tommy that Harry Birchevsky and Nilo had been in Dannemora together.

Tony went back to the union and started hanging out in the small speakeasies near union headquarters, and after one long evening of too many beers, he heard from one of the drivers about the day that Lev had ordered Nilo Sesta and Harry Birchevsky thrown out of his office and down the stairs.

That same night, Tony showed up at Nilo's apartment and rapped on the door. Nilo answered and said, in surprise, "Uncle Tony."

"Don't 'Uncle' me, you thug. I've got to talk to you."

He brushed by Nilo into the apartment and stood in the center of the living room floor.

"All right, then talk," Nilo said, turning back from the door.

Tony heard a sound behind him and saw Sofia coming out of one of the bedrooms, which was probably the nursery for their two children.

"Hello, Uncle Tony," she said.

"I've got to talk to your husband," Tony said.

Sofia shook her head. "We have no secrets."

"Whatever you want. Nilo, Lev Mishkin threw you and his own organizer out of his office. What was that about?"

"Union business. How does it concern you?"

"Because Tommy was there and his wife's been killed. Because Mishkin is missing. Because, dammit, I want to know why." He held his hands, balled into fists, tightly at his sides, trying to hold his temper in check.

"Harry Birchevsky," Nilo said.

"Yeah?"

"Harry and I were trying to organize the garment drivers. Mishkin didn't like it."

"Let me get this straight. This Birchevsky was Mishkin's organizer, but he was working with you against Mishkin?"

"He liked me better," Nilo said with a grin.

"I doubt that," Tony said. "Where do I find this Birchevsky?"

"I don't know," Nilo said. "When Mishkin found out what we were doing, that was the end of our scheme. I haven't talked to him since then."

"You don't know where he lives?"

Nilo shook his head. "We were never close."

Sofia said, "If you're thinking that Harry had something to do with Tommy's poor wife . . ." She shook her head. "Harry wouldn't do anything like that. He's not that kind of man."

Nilo glanced sharply at her as she spoke. Tony shook his head. "I'll have to convince myself of that."

"But you can't—" Sofia started.

"I can," Tony said. "Until I find out what happened."

He turned back to Nilo. "How'd you feel when Mishkin had you thrown down the stairs?" he asked.

"I wanted to kill the bastard," Nilo said. "But I didn't. And I certainly wouldn't hurt Tommy or his wife."

"For now, I'll believe you. But whoever did it knew a lot about Tommy. It was somebody family-close," Tony said. He walked toward the door.

"How is Tommy?" Nilo asked.

"He'll live," Tony said as he left.

When he had gone, Nilo went and stood before Sofia, who sat on the couch.

" 'Harry'?" he said. "What do you know about Harry Birchevsky?"

She shrugged. "I was only trying to help you."

"Harry's 'not that kind of man'? How do you know that?"

"I don't know anything," Sofia said airily. "I was just talking."

"You heard what Tony said. Whoever did this knew a lot about Tommy. Who knows more about him than you?"

"You're not serious," Sofia said, but she was unable to meet his eyes and looked down at the coffee table.

"I'm gonna find Harry myself. You better just hope that he doesn't say you—"

"I *what*?" Sofia snapped. "Tried to protect my husband? Tried to protect my children's future? I've worked hard for what we've got, as hard as you have. I'm not letting anybody take it away. Certainly not any of the Falcones. Not even you."

"Jesus Christ, you did it, didn't you? You got Tommy's wife killed," Nilo said. Sofia stared at him stolidly, then walked from the room.

———

- *The war rolled on. Buster from Chicago continued his brutally efficient work. On February 26,
in the Bronx, Gaetano "Tom" Reina, a Masseria
boss, got frightened by all the violence and
telephoned Nilo.*

"I want to come over," he said.

*"Don Salvatore will be glad to have you on
our side," Nilo said politely.*

*"It has to be quiet until it's done," Reina
cautioned.*

"It will be," Nilo promised.

*Nilo waited until he was alone in the car with
Maranzano and only his driver to let Salvatore know
that Reina was ready to defect from the Masseria
gang.*

"Should I go talk to him?" Nilo asked.

*"No. Remember, you are Danny Neill and no
part of this. Just tell him to call me to set up a
meeting. Tell him his deal will be better with me
than it ever was with Joe the Stupid."*

*Nilo nodded. Maranzano's chauffeur just
listened. Two hours later, Luciano got word and
sent Vito Genovese to reason with Reina not to
leave the side of Joe the Boss.*

*When Nilo tried to reach the Bronx boss later
that night, the operator told him the telephone had
been left off the hook. Reina's body was found the
next morning, clutching the telephone, three bullets
in his head.*

*Genovese reported the results of his meeting to
Luciano, before returning to his own club in Little
Italy. After he left, Luciano told Lansky, "I hate
that son of a bitch, but Vito Genovese is a good
dog to have in a fight."*

- *After the body of Lev Mishkin was found, Mario broke the news to Tommy. While Tommy's body had healed and he was working at the convent as a handyman, his mind seemed, to Mario, to be damaged beyond repair. He took the news of Mishkin's death with no emotion at all, as if he had never heard of the man. When Mario talked to him, Tommy was silent. It was not even clear that he knew Mario was his brother. He said few words, commenting mostly on the weather. He never questioned who Mario was or why he was there talking to him. It was as if he had lost his critical faculties, and Mario there and Mario not there were exactly the same to him. One of the priests who served Mass at the convent said that Tommy came to church every morning but seemed not to know the ritual, instead he sat awkwardly in a back pew, just watching.*

- *After the death of Gaetano Reina, Joe Valachi took Buster from Chicago across the river to Fort Lee, New Jersey, and pointed out to him a Masseria lieutenant named Peter Morello. Even in a business built on greed, Morello was exceptional, earning the nickname of "the Clutching Hand." No one could rush Buster. He waited until the summer, until he was sure, and one evening went into Morello's office, where he found the gangster and a visitor. Buster put two revolver rounds into Morello, but the Masseria man refused to fall. He staggered wildly about the room, and Buster, laughing aloud, began to practice fast draws with his gun, pegging occasional shots at Morello. Buster stopped to reload, and only after Morello had been hit six times did he drop to the floor.*

> *Buster walked to his body, fired another round into his head, then turned and wordlessly shot the office visitor, one Joe Pariano, who had only stopped by to return Morello's car keys.*

- *The shooting of Morello brought even more of the Masseria gang into Maranzano's tent. From Chicago came a pledge of five thousand dollars a week to Maranzano to finance the war. The money came from Joseph Aiello, who had taken advantage of Al Capone's jail sentence to try to install himself as a leader of the Chicago mob. Capone, freshly released from jail after the Philadelphia gun charge, called Luciano to complain. "I done my time, Lucky, and you promised you was going to quiet things down, and I come out and everybody's shooting everybody up again and I don't know what's going on." Luciano replied, "I'm taking care of it, Alphonse." Capone answered, "You do that, but I'm gonna take care of myself, too."*

IN EARLY AUGUST, Mario took a train upstate to visit his brother, Tommy. They went for a long walk in the green rolling Adirondack hills. Tommy had said nothing, and while they sat on a rock atop a hill overlooking a small valley, Mario wondered if the life Tommy faced was even worth living. *Would he be better dead?* he asked himself. He looked down at the forest floor teeming with life and death and wondered if Tommy would not be happier if he were lying there at the bottom of the hill, ready for the journey to meet God. He thought for a long time about it before he realized, *God will have to decide that. I can't.*

"Mario," his brother said.

Startled to hear his brother call his name, Mario gasped, "Tommy?"

"Birchevsky."

"Who?"

"Harry Birchevsky. Nilo's friend. It was his voice I heard. He killed Rachel."

"You have to tell the police," Mario said.

Tommy had already started to his feet. "Sure," he said.

"IT WILL NOT BE LONG," Maranzano said. "Every day, we hear from more of Masseria's men, anxious to join. The war will soon be over. I think it is time to tell our friend from Chicago to hunt even bigger game."

"I will talk to him," Nilo said. He started to his feet, but Maranzano waved him back down.

"Don't be in such a hurry," he said. "We never have time to speak anymore. How is your family? The children?"

"The children are fine. Sofia is well." Nilo wondered what Maranzano would say if he told him the truth: *Sofia wants you and Masseria both dead so that Luciano and I can control New York between us. And maybe she is right.*

"And no more *bambinos* are on the way?"

"Not now. Maybe at a later time."

"Family is the most important thing of all. It is the reason for our success. Because we are, at heart, a great family of Castellammarese. In the future, because of what we have come to learn, our families will never suffer want or prejudice or despair. It is the greatest legacy a proud father can give his children."

That and the gift of treachery, Nilo thought.

THE WORLD SEEMED to have swallowed up Harry Birchevsky, but all it meant to Tony was that he would have to dig harder. *He's either dead or hiding. Nobody covers his tracks this well just by accident,* Tony thought.

His search had continued through the summer. Police records, which he sneaked into headquarters to inspect, shed no light. No one had seen Birchevsky at his old addresses. Tony even questioned other people who had been in jail with the union man, but no one had seen or heard from him.

In early August, when Mario brought the apparently recovering Tommy home from the convent with his recollection that Birchevsky had been Rachel's killer, Tony felt vindicated. He had settled on the right man; now he merely had to find him.

Tommy offered no help. No, he didn't know any of Birchevsky's friends. No, he didn't know where he hung out or where he might be likely to hide. No, he didn't have any idea where the man might be. He answered Tony's questions in a dull voice, almost grudgingly, and Tony felt that the pain of Rachel's loss was still too much for Tommy to deal with, so he stopped asking.

There is time, Tony thought, *because I will never forget and I will never give up. Birchevsky belongs to me.*

Anna cooked a welcome-home dinner for Tommy, and even Tina showed up. Tommy was glad to see that she was making a special effort to heal the wounds between her and Tony. Tony, though, seemed distant; at odd moments, he seemed to be watching Tina, as if judging her performance. Tommy wished he knew what his father was thinking.

Is she my daughter, the little girl I raised, or is she the harlot of those photographs? Which is the real Tina? Did she do those things willingly or was she forced? Or drugged? Will she ever know how close I came to killing Luciano because of those pictures? How can I ever look at my daughter again without seeing those images in my mind? I have to believe she was a victim. We have all been victims of crime somehow. Tina, Tommy, Rachel, me. It would be so easy to give up. But we never will. Never surrender. Never surrender.

"Papa?"

"Sorry, Mario, I was daydreaming."

"We were hoping that you would play the phonograph. Some of the new tenors, maybe."

"Aaaah, the new tenors sound like fishwives. Caruso, only Caruso."

"Fishwives? Gigli? A fishwife?" Tina demanded.

"The worst," Tony said. "Just you listen." He marched off to the phonograph.

They listened to the music as they had many times before, arguing as they always did. As if by design, although none had planned it so, no reference was made to Tommy's tragedy or his plans for the future. There would be plenty of time for that later on.

For his part, Tommy offered nothing, just sat quietly in the living room, listening, watching. If there was anything on his mind, Tony could not tell it from his son's impassive face.

The party broke up early. It was only the next morning that Tony found that Tommy's police revolver was missing from the dresser drawer where Tony had hidden it for safekeeping.

• *In Chicago, rival mobster and Maranzano ally Joe Aiello offered a restaurant chef ten thousand dollars to put prussic acid in Al Capone's soup. The cook refused and told Capone about the offer. At 8:30 P.M., October 23, Aiello left the home of Pasquale Prestigiacomo at 205 North Kolmar Avenue to step into a waiting taxicab. As he opened the cab's rear door, the taxi sped away. At the same time, a window opened in an apartment across the street and a machine gun sprayed bullets at Aiello. Aiello was hit but struggled to his feet and ran into an alley. But another machine gunner waited at the end of the alley and ripped into Aiello as he tried to take cover. Doctors pried nearly sixty slugs from the gangster's body. Police said the lead weighed more than a pound. Capone told Luciano that he had Aiello hit because he was backing Maranzano while Capone was a loyal Masseria-Luciano man. Meyer Lansky told Luciano, "That guinea's nuts and is gonna get us all killed."*

- *Less than two weeks later, Maranzano struck back. Two of Masseria's top gunmen, Al Mineo and Steve Ferrigno, were struck by shotgun blasts at noon on November 5, while leaving a bookmaker's office in the Bronx. After carrying out the killings, Buster from Chicago replaced his sawed-off shotgun in his violin case and ran down the street but was stopped by a policeman. Buster said there had been a shooting down the block and he was trying to escape. The policeman went to investigate the shooting and Buster went back to his hotel.*

- *Luciano carried the news of Mineo's and Ferrigno's deaths to Masseria in his new penthouse apartment at Eighty-first Street and Central Park West where Joe the Boss had moved because it was*

safer than his old downtown apartment. Masseria
was eating dinner with his best friend, Joe Cata-
nia, and was clearly annoyed at being disturbed.
He waved off the two deaths as inconsequential.
"People get killed in wars," he said.

- *He was less sanguine two weeks later when he*
  strolled, with his two bodyguards, out the front
  door of his apartment building. Two Maranzano
  gunmen jumped from a nearby doorway and
  opened fire. The bodyguards were dropped
  instantly, but Masseria fled down Eighty-first
  Street and escaped. His bullet-riddled overcoat
  was left lying on the sidewalk. Later that night, he
  met with Luciano. "We've put up with this Castel-
  lammarese bastard for too long," the frightened
  Masseria said. "Now he is getting too brazen. I
  want him hit. I want everybody with him hit. I want
  everybody on our side to carry guns all the time
  and shoot them whenever they see them. I want
  them all dead, and I want them all dead right
  away. Start with Maranzano and go down the list
  and get everybody. And do it right away." Masse-
  ria left the city the next day for a winter vacation
  at an undisclosed location.

- *Reelected governor for a second term, Franklin*
  D. Roosevelt announced he was appointing a
  commission, headed by former judge Samuel
  Seabury, to investigate municipal corruption in
  New York.

- *A new radio show swept America by storm. It*
  began with a deep-voiced announcer intoning:
  "Who knows what evil lurks in the hearts of men?
  The Shadow knows. Ha-ha-ha." And it ended with
  the same announcer's: "The weed of crime bears

> *bitter fruit. Crime does not pay. The Shadow
> knows. Ha-ha-ha."*

IN EARLY OCTOBER, Tommy asked Captain Cochran for his job back.

Cochran greeted him warmly in his offices at the Italian Squad, but Tommy seemed to resist all his efforts to make pleasant conversation.

"I want to come back to work, Captain."

Cochran sighed. "Your job's been filled by a lieutenant from Midtown. We don't have an opening right now for you."

"I don't have to come back as a sergeant. Just a detective. Hell, I'll even come back undercover as Vito. Just let me work."

"Tommy, I looked at your records. You've still got a few months of sick time coming to you. Why don't you take the time now until you're feeling better?"

"I look that bad?"

"Worse," Cochran said.

Tommy rose to his feet. "I'll try you again in a few weeks," he said.

Cochran stood facing him. "Tommy, I know how awful this has all been for you. But I don't believe in vendetta."

"I do," Tommy said. "It's all I've got left to believe in."

AT THE END OF NOVEMBER, Tommy found Harry Birchevsky.

Since leaving the convent in August, he had gone over the same ground his father had, quizzing Birchevsky's friends, associates, and neighbors, and with the same lack of success.

But one night, lying on the couch in the apartment where Rachel was killed, Tommy recalled the image of Birchevsky, sitting at a table in a coffee shop, reading the *Daily Racing Form*. And he remembered overhearing Birchevsky remarking how his married sister lived near the Yonkers racetrack which he said was his favorite "'cause all their races are fixed and you just gotta watch where the smart money goes."

Tommy took to riding the train to Yonkers every day for the races, walking through the grandstand and clubhouse, looking for the union man. Some nights he stayed over at a cheap hotel so he could wander the streets the next day, trying to find Birchevsky's sister, whose married name he did not know.

Tommy was seedy-looking now, usually unshaven, often unwashed, and he appeared no different from the other gambling degenerates who hung around the small, dirty track. At first, he lived off his meager savings. When that was gone, he shamelessly borrowed money from Mario.

"I wish I knew what you needed this for," Mario said one day. "It's sure not for a shave and a haircut."

"It's to live, Mario."

"Can't I help, Tommy?"

"Only by giving me the money."

When he found that Tommy had never told the police that Birchevsky had killed Rachel, Mario told Tony. To his amazement, Tony would not tell the police, either.

Tony said, "I'll tell them about it after I get him. If we tell the cops now, they're not even going to look for him. All they'll do is blab about it, send out an alarm, spook him, and make him run. I don't want him to run. You stick to running the church. Leave the police work to me."

Tommy was hanging out in the racetrack grandstand when he saw a man step up to the ten-dollar window to place a bet on the final race. The man had a beard and wore a cap pulled down tightly over his forehead, but there was no mistaking his curious duckfooted walk. Tommy shielded his face with a newspaper when the man turned away from the cashier's booth. It was Birchevsky.

Tommy patted the gun he wore in a holster under his heavy jacket, then walked after his prey. He felt his heart pounding; the image of poor dead Rachel jumped into his mind, and he had to use all his willpower to stop himself from walking up and shooting the man where he stood at the rail, overlooking the track.

Too many people here. I want him alone.

Birchevsky seemed nervous at the track, often checking his wristwatch, and he left the track before the last race. He walked west on foot through a run-down industrial section of the town. Tommy followed a half block behind. It was already dark and a chill rain had begun to fall, but Tommy hardly noticed it. For the first time in almost a year, he felt alive.

As Birchevsky passed a big darkened warehouse, he turned and darted through the front door of the building. Tommy hurried across the street and tried the door, but it was locked.

Cautiously, he moved along the side of the building and found an unlocked door in the rear. He slipped inside and moved quickly away from the door, crouching low against the wall, waiting for his eyes to adjust to the darkness, holding his police revolver in his hand.

Faced with his own moment of truth, Tommy thought, *Can I do it? Can I just shoot him in cold blood? Does that make me as bad as him, as Nilo, as Luciano? As all the rest of them?*

Before he could finish the thought, something slapped the gun from his hand. It went skidding across the floor in the darkness. Tommy dove out of the way and heard a heavy clunk, the sound of a heavy piece of wood slamming into the wall near his head.

"You so smart, you think I didn't see you? You bastard, I shoulda killed you when I had the chance." Birchevsky's voice came out of the darkness, followed by another swing of the wooden club in his hand. But this time, Tommy was ready. He rolled away from the club, and as it hit into the floor next to him, he grabbed it and yanked. His force pulled the two-by-four out of Birchevsky's hands, and Tommy scrambled to his feet and swung the wooden club in front of him. There was a satisfying thud as the board made contact with flesh.

Birchevsky groaned and Tommy swung again. He hit again and Birchevsky cried out in pain.

In the dim light from a low window, Tommy could make out the man's form now, on the floor in front of him, and he smashed him in the ribs with the two-by-four. Then he swung it over his head, like a timberman's ax, and brought it down on Birchevsky's left knee. Birchevsky screamed.

He skittered away across the floor. In that moment, Tommy had his answer. *Yes, I can kill him. But that's too easy. First I'm going to cripple him, but I'm going to let his brain stay alive so it can feel hate and fear and pain, and then when he can't stand it anymore, I'm going to make it even worse.*

And then *I'm going to kill him.*

Tommy slowly walked after Birchevsky, holding the club in his hands like a baseball bat. Suddenly Birchevsky dove forward, grabbed at something, rolled on his back, and a bullet whistled past Tommy's ear.

Tommy dropped to the floor, backing away.

"I'll kill you, you son of a bitch," Birchevsky shouted, and fired Tommy's gun again into the darkness.

Again the bullet missed. Tommy heard a thud at the front door, and then, as the door opened, a glow of light from the street cast a faint glow across the warehouse floor. Tommy could see the huddled form of Birchevsky only ten feet from him.

Birchevsky must have seen him, too, because he raised the gun, and then another bullet rang out, and Birchevsky rolled across the floor. In the doorway, a man's silhouette was visible. He was holding a gun.

"Tommy," he called out.

Papa!

Tommy ran toward his father and then suddenly more shots rang out inside the warehouse. Tommy saw his father fall. He looked back and Birchevsky was still, a lump of flesh on the floor. The shots had not come from him, and then there was another shot and Tommy felt a searing pain as a bullet creased his shoulder.

Then all was silent.

Tommy ran to the doorway and knelt alongside his father, who groaned. Tommy turned him over.

"Papa," he cried.

Tony smiled up at his son. A trickle of blood appeared at the corner of his mouth. "I got him, Tommy. I got him for Rachel."

"Oh, Papa." Tommy cradled his father in his arms.

Suddenly Tommy heard the rear door of the warehouse open. He glanced back there just long enough to see a man faintly silhouetted as he moved across the open doorway. The man darted back outside and the door slammed behind him.

Was he the shooter? Maybe it was someone who was

just wandering by and had heard the noise. Tommy wanted to follow him, but Tony groaned and his eyes began to roll back in his head and Tommy held him close. Tony tried to lift his torso as if to whisper in his son's ear. His words came in a gasp. "Never surrender to the bastards. If we fight, we win. Never surrender."

His head lolled off to the side. His eyes were frozen open, but he saw no more. Tommy cried and said the prayers for the dead that he had heard Mario recite over Rachel's body.

THE YONKERS POLICE TOOK TOMMY into custody while they sorted things out. Allowed one telephone call, he phoned his father's retired partner, Tim O'Shaughnessy, who drove with Mario up to Yonkers, and, after a lot of blustering, succeeded in getting Tommy freed.

In the car driving back, Tommy sat shuddering and Mario put his arm around him. Dully, Tommy asked, "What was Papa doing there?"

"He was following you," Mario said. "He'd been following you for a long time."

"Why?"

"Because he knew you took your service revolver back. He didn't want you to make a mistake with it that might ruin your life."

"His death was a waste. You should have told me, Mario."

"Why? So you could hide from Papa and maybe get yourself killed, too?"

O'Shaughnessy put a big hand on Tommy's knee. "I know it hurts, Tommy, but your Papa died the way he wanted to. In harness. Don't cheapen it by calling it a waste." Tommy only shook his head.

MARIO SANG A REQUIEM MASS in Our Lady of Mount Carmel Church and then they buried Tony Falcone, with full police department honors, in St. John Cemetery in Middle Village, Queens. An assistant commissioner spoke at the graveside of the ultimate sacrifices Tony "and other unknown warriors have made in the battle against crime and lawlessness. While he was retired from the force, Lieutenant Falcone—at the time and in the manner of his death—acted in the highest traditions of the New York City Police Department."

Mayor Jimmy Walker sent flowers to the cemetery. Standing quietly in the crowd of mourners was Tommy's old law-school friend, Tom Dewey, and Kinnair, the *Daily News* reporter who had been covering the story and had written about the Falcones as "New York's greatest crime-fighting family." But Tommy spoke to none of them; he moved through the proceedings as if in a fog.

Nilo accompanied Tina to the funeral and caught up with Tommy as they left the cemetery.

"I haven't seen you in so long. I just wanted to tell you how sorry I am about everything."

"Forget it, Nilo."

"I didn't have anything to do with this, Tommy. Or your wife. If I had known . . ."

"I said forget it."

"I'm glad you don't blame me, Tommy. We're brothers, remember? We always were. We always will be."

Tommy wheeled around. "Brothers? We gave all that up a long time ago. Don't ever think we're brothers. As far as I'm concerned, you're a piece of garbage, just like the rest of the garbage on the streets out there. And I'm coming after you and all the others just like you. I'm taking you all down."

Nilo tried a small smile. "Do I have to spend the rest of my life looking over my shoulder?"

"No," Tommy said. "That's your way. The bullet in the back, the hired gun. I'm going to take you down the way my father would have. Face-to-face, so I can watch you fall. You and all the others just like you. No, I don't think you told your fairy boyfriend to kill my wife. But even if you had, it wouldn't change anything. I'm going to take you apart, a piece at a time. Don't ever call me brother."

He strode away just as Mario came up alongside Nilo.

Nilo glanced at the priest, then back at Tommy's departing figure.

"You were wrong, Mario," Nilo said. "Sometimes we just aren't able to choose the path of righteousness."

TWO WEEKS AFTER THE FUNERAL, Tommy closed the apartment where Rachel had been killed, the place where he had been happy so briefly, and moved back to the Falcone family flat on Crosby Street.

HOW LONG HAD IT BEEN, Tina wondered, since she had spent a New Year's Eve with her family, instead of surrounded by rowdy, drunken revelers?

New Year's Eve or not, every night is just the same. These people are the same. They . . . and me . . . we just don't have any reason for living.

During the evening, it seemed that every gangster in New York had passed through the Falcon's Nest, men from both the Masseria and Maranzano camps, as if a

New Year's Eve truce were being observed. She recognized most of them from the days when she sang at Luciano's speakeasy.

There was Benny Siegel, the one some people called Bugsy, all grown up now and still handsome, but still with a distracted air, as if he were thinking he should be somewhere else. He wished her a happy new year before leaving the club. She saw Luciano enter with his two closest henchmen, Vito Genovese and Joe Adonis, but they sat in the back of the room and left before she had to talk to them. Many of them she knew by name only. There was Legs Diamond and a doughy-faced thug from the Bronx named Dutch Schultz, who sat at a front table surrounded by hangers-on, making lewd comments to women on the dance floor in front of him.

Tina saw Nilo was busy working the floor, moving from table to table, trying to keep everyone in a good humor. She saw a tall slender man, who seemed barely out of his teens, enter the speakeasy and sit by himself in a table on the left of the dance floor. He had thick lips that seemed set in a permanent sneer, which he fixed on Schultz across the room. After a few minutes, Schultz and his party left the club and the slender man laughed aloud.

Nilo went to the young man's table and talked with him, then led him behind the stage curtain to the private offices. They were in there for almost an hour before returning.

Meanwhile, Tina had kept singing, taking only short breaks, convinced that it no longer mattered whether she sang well or poorly, since nobody listened anyway to anything except the sounds of their own voices.

I dreamed of grand opera. I achieved farce. I'm glad Papa never saw me do this.

During a break, she went over to the table where Mayor Walker was sitting like a potentate, receiving supplicants, and when he looked at her, she thanked him for sending flowers to her father's funeral. Walker smiled and told her she was in really good voice, and it was clear that he was drunk and had no idea what Tina was talking about.

Nilo and the young man came out of the offices and Nilo walked him to the front door. On the way there, Tina saw the man intentionally bump into another thug and then laugh, almost maniacally, when the other man simply walked away.

During a break, she asked Nilo who the young man was. "He seemed to be looking to pick a fight."

"He's always looking for a fight. Crazy Irisher named Vince Coll. Schultz is scared to death of him."

"He's so young."

"He's old enough that they already call him Mad Dog," Nilo said.

"You have interesting friends," Tina said with a smile.

"I have no friends. Only business associates. Happy New Year."

1931: The War

"I'M AFRAID I'VE GOT BAD NEWS for you, Tommy."

Tommy smiled ruefully across the desk at Captain Cochran. It was the first week of the New Year, and he had shown up in the captain's office asking to return to duty. "Go ahead, Captain. I'm used to it."

"I've talked to city hall. They can't keep you off the job, but they're going to make your life miserable. I guess you've made some enemies."

"So what does it mean?"

"You come back as a patrolman. You work nights in uniform. They want you on the whore squad."

"Vice?" Tommy said.

"Yeah. Midtown, rousting streetwalkers, pimps." Cochran looked dejected; both he and Tommy knew that working vice was the lowest, sleaziest duty on the force.

Tommy was silent and Cochran said, "They want you to turn it down and quit."

"I know. Who's got it in for me?"

"Nobody's talking, but I'd guess Luciano. He's the only one with that kind of muscle in city hall, and he must have figured out you were no friend of his."

"I'll take the job."

Cochran seemed to wince. "Tommy, what do you want it for?"

"It's all I know how to do."

"What about practicing law? What happened to that?"

"The law's a joke," Tommy said.

DURING THE FIRST WEEK of the New Year, Tina stopped in Nilo's office. "This seems as good a time as any," she said. "I'm going to be leaving, Nilo."

"Where are you going?" he snapped angrily. "Who hired you?"

"Nowhere and nobody. I'm just quitting the business. I've had enough of it."

"You can't just leave," he said. "This is your club. It's named after you. You're a star."

"I don't want to be a star. You can have the club. I'm going to go. I have to move on."

He drummed his fingers on the desk. "I could make

you stay," he said. Tina had wanted this to be smooth and businesslike, but instead it was becoming personal. "I doubt it," she said.

"I don't. I could—" He stopped and tried to force a smile. "Well, we can't have people working here who are unhappy. I won't stop you. But you've got to do me a favor."

"What's that?"

"The summer. You've got to stay into the summer. Meanwhile you can start breaking in a new manager and you can start finding acts to replace you. You'll give me that, won't you?"

"The summer," she said grimly. "And no more."

As the office door swung closed behind her, Nilo angrily jabbed the point of a letter opener into the wooden desktop. *So now she's giving me ultimatums? Slut. She'll stay as long as I want her to. There's always those pictures.*

TOMMY REPORTED TO WORK and went through the motions. He walked the Midtown streets at night, patrolling in front of the smaller hotels near Times Square, arresting prostitutes who were too noisy or aggressive with passersby. He tried to be polite and businesslike, and often the streetwalkers, accustomed to heavy-handed cops who swung the billy club with one hand and held the other hand out for a bribe, would offer him a bonus in trade. He always turned them down. He diligently did the paperwork on the arrests, advised the girls to leave the business before they got hurt out on the street, and when his shift was over he went home, where he usually spent his day sitting quietly in the living room, looking

out the window at busy, bustling Crosby Street, thinking
of the night his father was killed.

And every day he did the same thing.

- *At the end of January, well-tanned and even fatter
  than when he left, Joe the Boss Masseria returned
  from his winter vacation in parts unknown. He was
  upset to find that Luciano had not yet launched the
  all-out shooting war against Maranzano's forces.
  "It hasn't been a good time," Luciano explained
  patiently. "They've got that Seabury investigation
  starting down at city hall. If we stick our head up
  now, somebody's liable to blow it off, and everybody's too frightened to cover up for us."*

  *"Then why the hell are we paying twenty
  thousand dollars a week to those bastards, if they
  don't have to do anything for it? We pay graft, we
  should get protection," Masseria argued. "Do
  what I told you to do."*
- *Four days later, Buster from Chicago struck again.
  Joe the Boss's best friend, Joe "the Baker"
  Catania, was found dead on a Manhattan street-
  corner with six bullets in his head on the morning
  of February 3. Masseria added three more men to
  his army of bodyguards and stayed behind locked
  doors in his penthouse overlooking Central Park.*
- *The stock market continued its slide. The Dow
  Jones average had made a small recovery but was
  dropping again, reaching 260 by the end of the
  year. Since its peak sixteen months earlier, it had
  lost nearly 60 percent in value.*
- *In the* Daily News, *John F. X. Kinnair quoted a
  police official's report that more than fifty people*

had been slain so far in New York City's gangland power struggle: ". . and those are only the bodies that have been discovered. God knows how many others are buried out there. And the killing won't end until someone wins the war between Masseria and Maranzano." Meanwhile, Kinnair wrote, "the next generation is waiting in the wings. Behind Masseria stands Charlie 'Lucky' Luciano, the master organizer, while Maranzano's Number Two man is Nilo Sesta, who won notoriety a half-dozen years ago when he was convicted—but later freed—for a double murder in Italian Harlem. Sources say that, in a crime world not noted for restraint, Sesta sets a new standard for viciousness and brutality."

NILO CAME OUT of the bedroom, fully dressed, and Sofia pointed to the story in the *Daily News*.

"You're getting famous," she said. "The paper today calls you vicious and brutal."

"That's because they never met you," he answered with a small smile. She walked to him and put her arms around him from behind.

"We're almost there," she said. "When this is all done, you and Charlie can divide the city between you. Don Nilo Sesta. It has a ring to it."

"Until Luciano gets ambitious," he said.

"Then we'll deal with him, too."

Nilo nodded, but he seemed distracted. He kissed Sofia perfunctorily and left the apartment.

Sofia went back and read Kinnair's *Daily News* column again. Probably just by dumb luck, she thought, the reporter had stumbled onto the truth. Sooner or later,

Masseria and Maranzano would be gone. Nilo would be king and she would be queen, and she would lead the king around by his nose because she had his children and she had the brains to lead.

Her only lingering worry was Tina. She was sure, in her heart, that her husband and Tina were lovers, and that made Tina a danger to her. But Sofia knew she had a secret trump card that Tina did not have, and when the time came, she would use that to bond Nilo to her. She would be the richest woman in New York and her children would be legislators and governors. They would have all the power to control their own lives that she had never had, and she would be the one to give them that power. *And nothing can be allowed to stop it.*

BECAUSE OF HIS FAIR TREATMENT of them, the hookers in his district had taken to calling Tommy "Sir Galahad." He found it embarrassing, and one night, after breaking up a fight in a cheap brothel on Thirty-seventh Street, Tommy said to the madam, "If you all like me so much, why don't you just go somewhere else? Or leave the business?"

"Sorry, Sir Galahad," said the madam, who called herself "Cokey Flo Brown." "A girl's gotta live." He had no grounds to make an arrest, but when he was leaving the building, Cokey Flo tried to press a ten-dollar bill into his hand. Tommy refused it. "If you ever try that again, I'll book you for attempted bribery," he said.

In mid-March, he was called to handle a disturbance at a sleazy hotel on the southern fringe of his beat. In a third-floor room he found a prostitute who had been slapped around and was bleeding from cuts on her face.

"A bad john?" Tommy asked.

"John, hell. It was my pimp. That little bastard," the woman said.

"Come on. Get some clothes on," Tommy said.

He led the woman downstairs, and out on the street another policeman saw them and said, "Hey, that's Nancy Presser. She's a famous whore."

Presser stiffened with indignation. "The word is 'prostitute,' you smart bastard," she snapped. Tommy got her into a patrol car, but instead of taking her to the precinct for booking, he had the driver take them to a nearby hospital so she could be treated.

"You're the one they call Sir Galahad, aren't you?" Presser said.

"I guess so."

Presser started to cry. "I wasn't always a two-dollar whore," she said. "I didn't always look like this. I used to get a hundred dollars a night."

"Then why don't you quit?" Tommy said. "Find a new job."

"Quit?" The woman laughed. "'Cause Charlie Luciano won't let any of us quit."

"You know Charlie, huh?" Tommy asked.

"Know him? I used to be his regular girlfriend, up at his fancy hotel. The bastard used to tell me how much money he made off us whores. And then he got mad at me and he made my pimp turn me into a two-dollar trick."

"Life's tough," Tommy said as he left the woman in the hospital emergency room. "Leave the business."

"Sure, Sir Galahad," she said with a smile. "Tomorrow."

JOE THE BOSS WAS WONDERING why Luciano did not act. It had been months since he gave him the order to launch the all-out war against Maranzano, but nothing had happened yet. Maybe his lieutenant was getting "too fat, too comfortable. Maybe he likes seeing his name in the paper."

He expressed this opinion over lunch to Joe Adonis, who nodded agreeably. "I think he's making too much money," Adonis said, "and doesn't want to take chances anymore."

"That's what I think, too," Masseria said. "I like the way you think, Joe. That's what I've been looking for in my right-hand man." Although the words had never been spoken, when he left the restaurant, Adonis knew exactly what had been offered: if he killed Luciano, Masseria would make Adonis his Number Two. He went immediately to Luciano's Central Park hotel suite and told him of Masseria's proposal.

Luciano listened impassively. When Adonis was done, Luciano said, "If he asks, tell him you're working on it."

"I don't want him to get anxious and ask somebody else," Adonis said.

"He won't," Luciano answered. "He won't have the time."

"SO IF YOU WANT TO LEAVE, leave. You're free, white, and twenty-one. We don't have slaves anymore in the United States."

Mario looked across the lunch table at his sister. Tina had invited him for coffee and told him how nervous she was about her plans for quitting the speakeasy business.

"Nilo's really upset about it. He asked me to stay on and train somebody new, but every time I try to hire somebody, he turns them down."

"When the time comes to leave, leave. It's his problem."

"I guess it is, isn't it? Thank you, Mario. How's Tommy?"

The priest shook his head. "He's a zombie, Tina. If he weren't family, if he just came to me at the parish for counseling, I'd think this man probably belongs in a mental institution. He just drifts through life like a man walking through a fog."

"He's not on drugs again, is he?" Tina asked.

"No. He's on guilt. He blames himself for everything. Papa's death, Rachel's. Nilo becoming a gangster. The trouble you had that time. He thinks if he had been better or wiser or smarter or stronger, none of it would have happened. He sits on that couch, thinking of things that happened, trying to remember them exactly, trying to make sense of them."

"Oh, Mario, what's to become of our family?"

"We go on, Tina. We go on."

"It's so hard."

"But we stay the course and we will win."

• *The press did not regard the fact as especially newsworthy, but on March 31 a young man entered the former U.S. Post Office building at 270 Lexington Avenue and opened an office on the second floor of the garish old Italian Renaissance structure. Thomas E. Dewey had just been appointed by President Hoover as an assistant U.S. prosecutor.*

LUCIANO'S VOICE WAS unusually cheerful over the telephone.

"Hey, boss," he said, "let's go to lunch. All that stuff

you wanted done, it's under way. I just want you to give the final okay."

"Lunch? I just finished breakfast," Masseria said. "I don't know if I can eat lunch for a while."

"Too bad," Luciano said pleasantly. "They tell me Scarpato's just got in a load of fresh lobster this morning."

"How fresh?"

"Right off the boat," Luciano said.

"All right," Masseria said. "You want to come and get me?"

"I'll pick you up," Luciano said.

"No, wait. We take my car. It's safer than yours. There's crazy people out there."

"All right."

"Who we take with us?"

"I'll see who's around. Maybe Vito. Somebody else who can drive."

"Okay," Joe the Boss said cautiously. "But we don't talk any business until we're alone. Too many big ears around."

Luciano chuckled. "You're always one step ahead," he said. "I'll be by eleven thirty or so."

Shortly after noon on April 15, Ciro Terranova was driving Masseria's car through the streets of Brooklyn. Luciano and Masseria were in the backseat. Vito Genovese sat in the front passenger seat. It was an especially warm day and Luciano took off his gray suit jacket. Masseria noticed that his lieutenant, as usual, was not carrying a gun.

The specially built car was armor-plated and had inch-thick glass in all its windows. Its weight was twice that of a normal car, and Terranova, who had made his fortune controlling all the artichokes that entered New York City and had been with Masseria since the old days of Lupo the Wolf, seemed to have trouble steering the vehicle.

"Hey, Ciro," Masseria barked from the backseat after the driver had jammed on the brakes. "What's wrong with you? You gonna get us all killed."

"Stop the car," Luciano said. Terranova pulled over to the curb, and Luciano said, "Vito, you drive." When Terranova slid across to the passenger's seat, Luciano saw that his hands were shaking.

At 1:00 P.M., the car arrived safely on Ocean Avenue in Coney Island, on the southern shore of Brooklyn, and rolled to a stop at the Nuovo Villa Tammaro Restaurant, parking right in front of the long red-and-gray-striped awning.

"You two stay here and keep your eyes open," Luciano said. "Joe and me, we're going to have lunch."

Although the restaurant was still crowded with lunch-time diners, the owner, Gerardo Scarpato, had reserved the prime corner table for the two men. He had served Masseria many times before, and without anything being ordered, the food courses started coming to the table. First hot and cold antipasto, followed by minestrone soup and seafood salad. Lobster Fra Diavolo was the main course with a heaping platter of Milanese pasta. Masseria seemed to eat with both hands, downing large water glasses full of red wine, dribbling it down his chin and onto the napkin, which was tucked into his collar.

While Masseria ate, Luciano picked at his food and softly outlined his plan. It called for bringing in two dozen of the best shooters from other cities in the country and in one massive assault attacking Maranzano's headquarters, wiping out the Castellammarese and any of his followers who were with him.

"Why get shooters from out of town? We got no shooters?"

"Yeah, we got plenty of shooters and they all got

mouths. One of them gets picked up for something and they try to cop a plea and talk, and we're all in trouble."

Masseria shrugged, his peasant brows wrinkled. "These out-of-town shooters, they don't have mouths? They not gonna talk?"

Luciano smiled. "That's why we're going out of town. As soon as these guys are done, I'm going to put them on trains to take them back where they came from." He chuckled. "But they ain't ever going to get there. They got mouths, but they won't be able to use them."

Masseria joined in the laughter. "It's a good plan, Charlie. When?"

"You give the okay and I'll have them in town next week. Ten days outside, Maranzano will be just a memory."

Masseria wiped his mouth with his red-stained napkin. "I like the way you think." He poured them both some more wine.

It was three o'clock now and except for the two men the restaurant was empty of diners.

Scarpato, the owner, brought over a decanter of espresso coffee and a large wheeled tray of Italian pastries.

"I was gonna take a walk on the beach," Scarpato said. "Is it all right if I leave you two alone?"

"Sure," Masseria said. "But we pay the bill first."

"It's on the house," Scarpato said. "For you, it's always on the house."

"One thing," Luciano said. "A deck of cards. The tip for the waiters, Joe. I'll play you a game of *brisco* for the tip."

Masseria nodded and Scarpato brought the deck of cards before leaving the restaurant for his stroll. It was 3:05 P.M.

They played cards for twenty-five minutes. Masseria

won all the hands and was in particularly good spirits. He was shoveling pastries into his mouth and washing them down with imported wine.

"You're too much for me today," Luciano said. "I have to go to the crapper. When I come out, we'll go."

He strolled to the men's room near the front door of the restaurant, went inside, locked the door, and turned on the water taps.

At that moment, a black sedan pulled up in front of the restaurant, stopping behind Masseria's car.

Out of the second car stepped Ben Siegel, Joe Adonis, and Albert Anastasia. Genovese got out of the first car and joined them.

"What about him?" Adonis asked, nodding toward Terranova, who still sat in Masseria's sedan.

"Leave him," Genovese said in disgust. "He'll piss his pants."

The four men walked into Scarpato's and strolled past the white-clothed tables to the corner table where Masseria sat alone, idly shuffling the deck of cards. The wine-stained napkin was still stuck into his collar.

He noticed the men only when they reached his table. Before he could speak or act, the four emptied five shots each into him. His body fell forward onto the table. Then one of the men walked behind him and fired a final slug into Masseria's head.

They walked quickly from the restaurant. Ciro Terranova was in their car, but his hands shook too badly to put the car in gear. Contemptuously, Siegel pushed him out of the way, slid behind the wheel, and drove away at high speed.

Inside, Luciano washed his hands, turned off the water, unlocked the men's room door, and walked into the dining area. He waited by Masseria's side until the police arrived.

When they asked where he was during the shooting, he said, "I was in the can taking a leak. I always take a long leak." He said he had no idea who did the shooting.

With no reason to hold him, the police released Luciano and he drove back to Manhattan in Masseria's car. On the way back, he thought, *The war is over. And now Maranzano must think he has won.*

SOFIA'S TELEPHONE RANG. When she answered, she heard Luciano's voice.

"Joe Masseria is dead," he said.

"Oh."

"Since you are always so interested in delivering messages, deliver this one. Tell Don Salvatore that Masseria is dead, not because we wish to serve Maranzano, but for our own personal reasons. Tell him also that if he should touch even a hair of even one friend of ours, we will wage war to the end. If he wishes peace, we must know in twenty-four hours and we will pick out a place in which to discuss a settlement. Do you have that?"

"Yes," Sofia said.

"Deliver the message."

THE PEACE CONFERENCE WAS HELD in Mangini's Restaurant, which was closed for the occasion. Crosby Street outside the restaurant was lined with cars, and the sidewalks were lined with men who made no attempt to conceal the fact that they were all carrying weapons.

Wearing a champagne-colored silk suit and looking

like a prosperous Florida banker, Maranzano arrived with only Nilo accompanying him. Representing the old Masseria interests were Luciano, Frank Costello, and Meyer Lansky.

Maranzano declined food. "Dinner is for dinner," he said. "Meetings are for business." The business lasted only thirty minutes. It was agreed that every gang leader in the city would keep what he already had and that infringing on another's territory or business would not be tolerated. The inevitable problems that would arise would be resolved by discussion between Maranzano and Luciano. Above all, the violence would end. Both Luciano and Maranzano would be responsible for the behavior of the men they represented. Buster from Chicago, in particular, would be called off.

"There are too many people in this city already investigating too many things," Maranzano said. "What we cannot tolerate is a situation like Chicago, where that crazy fat man is shooting up the streets and calling everybody's attention to his business. Mark my words, it will bring him down and it will happen soon. We should profit from his mistakes and get on with our lives in as quiet and reasonable a manner as possible."

And the structure of the new crime organization? How would it be managed? Lansky wondered.

"I have some ideas about that," Maranzano said, "but I would like to think about them further. We will talk about it again. Soon."

Throughout the entire meeting, Nilo said not a word. When the business was done, Maranzano again declined dinner, although he did join the rest in a ceremonial glass of wine and made a toast "to the great tomorrow which awaits us all."

Then, with Nilo in tow, he left. A few minutes later,

his caravan of cars, filled with bodyguards and gunmen, raced down the street.

Back in Mangini's, Luciano looked at Lansky and Costello.

"So?" he said.

Noncommittal as usual, Costello shrugged.

Lansky said, "He'll have to go, too."

IN THE CAR SPEEDING BACK UPTOWN, Nilo said, "Should I send Buster back to Chicago?"

Maranzano shook his head. "Pay him to stay around. But tell him we have no more work for him. At least for now. And keep in touch with your friend, the crazy dog." It took Nilo a moment to realize that Maranzano meant Mad Dog Coll, gangdom's most demented killer.

SOFIA PRESSED NILO to tell her what had happened at the peace conference, and he repeated the details of the agreement between Luciano and Maranzano as if reading a shopping list. When he was done and started to turn away, Sofia grabbed his arm.

"What did they mean by this agreement?"

"They meant what they said. Isn't it clear?"

"No, it isn't. How did they act? Did you believe both were telling the truth?"

"Why would they lie?"

"No reason, I guess." Sofia fixed a broad smile on her face. "Oh, Nilo, it's wonderful news. Peace. And soon you will be boss."

Nilo did not seem excited. "What's the matter?" she asked.

"I don't know. I was just thinking I've come a long way

from Sicily. I wonder what my father would think of me now. I wonder what he would think if he knew I am considering treachery against Don Salvatore."

Sofia laughed.

"What about my father is so funny?" Nilo asked through gritted teeth.

"Sit down, Nilo. There's something you ought to know."

Nilo sat reluctantly, perched on the edge of the sofa as if ready to run off.

"Your mother told me when I visited her," Sofia said. "When she was young, she was wronged by a young thug from the village. She went for justice to Don Salvatore. Three months later, when everyone had forgotten the incident, he had the young man killed. But when your mother came to Maranzano to thank him, he treated her no differently than the thug had. She became pregnant with you, and Maranzano arranged her marriage to the man you always believed was your father. But you are Don Salvatore's son. The product of his rape."

Nilo fell back onto the couch and closed his eyes.

"Have you nothing to say? Or do you doubt me?"

"No," Nilo said softly, his eyes still closed. "It explains why he has always taken such an interest in me, even when there was no reason for it."

"You always thought it was his love for you. But it isn't. It is his guilt that drives him. Guilt because he treated your mother like a *puta*. And there is only one thing a son can do about that. That is why you can't turn back. Seize the power. That glorious power."

He turned his thick-lashed eyes toward hers. "You want it so much, I wish sometimes I could give it to you."

"So do I," Sofia said.

- *Joe the Boss lay in state in a funeral home in Little Italy for three days. His body was brought to the ceremony in a cortege of forty Cadillacs and he was buried in a fifteen-thousand-dollar coffin. Among the mourners at graveside was his close friend and associate Lucky Luciano.*

- *If Al Capone thought his brief voluntary exile in a Pennsylvania jail would take off the police heat in Chicago, he had guessed wrong. He had returned to find a city crawling with federal law-enforcement agents. Soon after Masseria's death, Capone was indicted on five thousand counts of tax evasion and bootlegging.*

AT THE END OF MAY, gang members all over New York received telephone invitations from Salvatore Maranzano to attend a meeting. Each thought he was going to a small, private conference with Don Salvatore, but as they showed up at a sprawling hall on Washington Avenue in the Bronx, they realized that five hundred men were attending the meeting.

Each man was charged six dollars at the door as a donation. For their money, they received a cardboard container of coffee, a sandwich wrapped in wax paper, and a hard-back chair facing a raised platform at the end of the room on which a large chair, resembling a throne, had been placed. Behind the chair, a huge cross was hanging on the wall.

As they took seats, Luciano said to Adonis, "What is this silly bastard up to now?"

Meyer Lansky looked at the ham sandwich he had

been given and said, "For six bucks, I would have thought we'd get chicken."

At nine o'clock every one of the five hundred seats was filled and Maranzano stepped out onto the stage, escorted by Nilo, who helped him into the throne chair and went to take a seat by the side of the stage. Maranzano was wearing a dark gray suit with a silver watch chain dangling across his vest. As he sat in the throne chair, he waved ceremoniously to the nervous crowd.

"He's running for pope," Lansky mumbled.

Slowly the crowd quieted and Maranzano rose. He said a prayer in Latin and gave a florid greeting in Italian. And then in English he said:

"The past is over. We must look to the future. We start tonight.

"We are a great army, but even the greatest army can fail if it has not discipline. We will have such discipline."

Looking around the room, Maranzano said that Joe Masseria had been a traitor to his own people, extorting money from Italians everywhere and allowing his underlings to run wild, "stealing and looting and killing, without regard for the rights of others.

"That was Joe Masseria's thing. This thing of ours—La Cosa Nostra—will be different. From now on, everything in this city will be run by five families. Each family will have a boss, a *capo*. Call him a general. Each boss will have an underboss; he will be like a major. And under the majors will be *caporegimes,* lieutenants, and under the *caporegimes* will be groups of ten soldiers.

"You ask, why this system? Because it was the system of Julius Caesar and his triumphant armies. As the children of Julius Caesar, this system will work for us, too, and it will make La Cosa Nostra triumphant also."

He paced back and forth along the stage.

"As I call out these names, please stand. Joe Profaci. Albert Anastasia. Thomas Gagliano. Joe Bonanno. Charlie Luciano."

As Luciano rose to his feet, Lansky whispered, "He's gonna give you your high school diploma."

"Look at them," Maranzano commanded. "These are the leaders of the five families of New York. These are the bosses and each of you will be in one of their families." He looked around again and then said, "You may all sit.

"These five bosses will meet together to plan for the future. They are the generals of our army. You will know them, but all you soldiers, you will never go to your boss without first getting permission of your immediate superior, your *caporegime*. You will be punished for infractions of that rule.

"There are other rules too that may not be broken. You may not violate another member's wife. You may not talk about La Cosa Nostra. You may not speak of this to your wives. You may not disobey an order from your superior. For violating these rules, the penalty will be death. Ours will be a disciplined army.

"And I will be here to oversee this discipline, because I will be your *capo de tutti capi,* your boss of bosses."

Maranzano spoke for an hour, outlining the rules that he predicted would bring order and peace to New York's warring underworld. Finally, he sat back down in the throne chair.

As he did, he said, "Whatever happened in the past is over. We have all suffered terribly, but there is to be no more ill feeling among us. From today on, our only business is business and our only goal is to make each of you rich beyond your wildest dreams. Even if you lost someone in this awful war, it is time to move on. You must forgive and forget. If you seek revenge, you will pay with your life." He looked around sternly, then said: "Now go in peace."

The American Mafia was dead; the Cosa Nostra had been born.

NILO COULD SENSE Maranzano's excitement as they drove back to Manhattan in his limousine, preceded and followed by two cars filled with armed bodyguards.

This may be peace, but he's sure taking no chances, Nilo thought.

"You're very quiet, Nilo. What did you think of the evening?" asked Maranzano.

"I thought it was fine," Nilo said

"I think the peace will hold for a while," Maranzano said.

"Just for a while?"

"There are always people with ambitions. For a while, they will be kept busy trying to put together the structure of La Cosa Nostra. After they do that, then they will start scheming again. No organization, no matter how intelligent, can overrule human nature. But that's not what is on your mind. What is it? Nilo, of all people, you can talk to me."

"All right, Don Salvatore. You named five to head families. But what of me? What is my role in this new organization?"

"You have none," Maranzano said. When he saw Nilo's shocked expression, he said, "You are not Nilo Sesta anymore, remember. You are Danny Neill. I have created this organization for today and for tomorrow. But you are the day after tomorrow. When this country rises up against what those men there tonight represent—and yes, me also—it will all come tumbling down. But people like

Danny Neill, secure in honest, legitimate businesses, will go on, rich and powerful and respected, while the rest rot in prison."

He put his arm around Nilo's shoulder. "You should not be surprised at this. I have told you so many times, even while I have been discouraging you from your youthful craziness, like that foolish business with that animal from the garment union."

"You do me too much honor."

"Should I do less for . . ." He barked to the driver, "Pull over." When the driver complied, Maranzano told him, "Go for a walk. We wish to talk privately."

Nilo saw the trailing car of bodyguards had pulled up behind them. The car in front had also stopped and was now backing up on the road shoulder to take its position in front of Maranzano's limousine.

When the driver walked away and lit a cigarette, Maranzano said, "Nilo, we must stop having secrets. I received a letter from your mother. She told me about Sofia's visit and that she told your wife the truth about you. That . . ." He hesitated.

"That I am your son?" Nilo said.

Maranzano nodded. "It was one of those things that men do, of which I am not proud, but I feel for you like a true son. That is why I want you to do business and not crime. I feel sorry that sometimes I must even ask you to meet with people at your club, but it cannot be helped. It is the only place we have where someone can walk in and be seen and no eyebrow will be raised." He leaned back in the seat. "And now we'll talk no more about this. It would not be wise to let anyone know that you are my blood. I am pleased you have gone all this long without even mentioning it."

"I only found out from Sofia a month ago," Nilo said, thinking, *This man just admitted raping my mother.*

"And Sofia kept it secret all this time," Maranzano said. "An interesting woman."

"Yes," Nilo agreed. Maranzano signaled the driver to return, and the caravan continued back to New York.

- *His brain already showing the ravages of the syphilis that would eventually kill him, Al Capone offered the federal government four hundred thousand dollars to drop the tax charges against him. When U.S. attorneys declined, he appeared before Federal Judge James H. Wilkerson in Chicago on June 16, 1931, and pleaded guilty to all the federal charges against him. But a week later, his lawyers withdrew the plea. Capone would take his chances with a jury.*

- *In New York City, the gangland ceasefire seemed to be holding. But in his office, Maranzano got word that Louis "Lepke" Buchalter was expanding his union extortion racket into the poultry and motion picture businesses. Don Salvatore knew that Lepke would not have made such a provocative move without the approval of the ambitious Luciano. Maranzano sat at his desk and drew up a list of names.*

AFTER THE LABOR DAY WEEKEND, Tina decided she was ready to leave the Falcon's Nest behind. The new manager and singer she had hired had worked out well over the last two weeks, and she was just waiting for Nilo to make one of his rare trips to the speakeasy so she could tell him good-bye face-to-face. She did not want any of the club's ownership. She had money saved and she wanted to put the club and all the people in it, that whole part of her life, behind her. Tina had no clear idea what she wanted to do, but she knew the only singing she would ever do again would be for her own amusement in the shower.

Or maybe in the choir, she thought. *They can always use a good baritone.*

She wrote herself a check for her final month's pay and heard someone walk by her door toward Nilo's office. She put the checkbook away, then went out into the corridor. Nilo's office door was ajar and she could hear voices inside. Quietly, she walked down the hallway, then stopped to listen.

She heard Nilo say, "Here's the list of names. Get as many as you can as fast as you can before anyone has a chance to react."

"Holy Christ," came another voice. "You're not kidding around, are you? Luciano, Genovese, Costello, Adonis, Dutch Schultz, Willie Moretti."

"You can start with Luciano and Genovese," Nilo's voice said. "Don Salvatore will have them in his office at three o'clock on the tenth. Get them there. Pick up the others wherever you can. There's twenty-five thousand in the envelope. There's another twenty-five thousand when you're done."

"It's good doing business with you, Sesta."

"We'll have more business soon."

Tina heard a chair slide across the wooden floor in Nilo's office and she ran back down the hall into her own office. She left the door open a bit and a moment later saw the young slender man she had seen in the club on New Year's Eve pass by. She tried to remember his name.

Coll. Mad Dog Coll, Nilo called him. And I don't want to think about what this means.

Tina left the club hurriedly. She wanted to talk to Nilo but not now, not here. It would have to wait.

September 10, 1931

"Hello, Charlie. This is Don Salvatore."

"My *capo*," Luciano said.

"We got some business to talk. I was wondering if you and Vito could come up to my office this afternoon."

"Sure, I'll get him. What time?"

"Let me look at my calendar. Three o'clock would be good."

"We'll be there," Luciano said.

He hung up the telephone in his hotel suite and went back to his breakfast.

Nilo had not been back to the club since Tina had overheard his conversation, and she wanted to tell him personally that she had quit. Reluctantly, because she did not want to talk to Sofia, she telephoned Nilo's home. He answered the phone himself.

"Nilo, this is Tina. Can I come up and see you?"

He lowered his voice. "Sofia's going out in a while. Come up at twelve thirty."

In the other room, Sofia softly replaced the extension phone.

Invading the privacy of my home, she thought. *That is too much, even for such a whore as she. This must be finished, once and for all.*

PRECISELY AT 12:30 P.M., TINA knocked on the apartment door. It swung open and Sofia stood in the doorway.

"Hello, Sofia. I was expecting Nilo."

"Yes, I'm sure you were. Come in." She stepped aside to let Tina enter the apartment and closed the door behind her.

"Is he here?"

"He went out for a while."

"Maybe it'd be better if I came back later," Tina said. "I had some business to discuss."

"Your usual business?" Sofia snapped.

"I came to tell him that I'm finished with work. The new manager is on the job. If he wants to reach me, he can call me at home."

She stepped toward the door. "I'm sorry, Sofia, that there is so much unhappiness in your life. I wish I could take some of it from you."

"Unhappiness?" Sofia said. "You Falcones had everything. You were priests and policemen. You were a star. And now you are all nothing. Less than nothing. And I will have everything. I have nothing to be unhappy about."

Tina shook her head sadly and reached for the doorknob.

"Wait! You've forgotten your souvenirs. Nilo wanted you to have them."

She handed forward a paper bag. Inside it, Tina saw a roll of film and an envelope filled with photographs. She looked at one and her heart sank.

"Oh, my God," she said.

"Just more memories of the good times," Sofia said, her face creased in a tight, thin-lipped smile. "Nilo likes to look at them at night."

"It was Nilo," Tina said. "It was Nilo who did it."

Sofia laughed and Tina clutched the bag under her arm and ran from the apartment.

Nilo returned a few minutes later. "Did anybody come by while I was out?"

"Nobody. Nobody at all," Sofia said.

FOR ALL THOSE YEARS, Tina had blamed Luciano, but it had been Nilo who had gotten her to that warehouse in the Bronx. It was what Nilo had meant when he told Tina that if he wanted to, he could force her to stay on at the speakeasy.

She ran down the street, clutching the bag under her arm. A clock outside a bank read 12:45. It was September 10 and Charlie was going to be murdered.

She darted into a candy store and found a phone booth in the back. She dialed Luciano's number, praying he would still be in his hotel room.

"Three-Twelve," he answered.

"Charlie, this is Tina. Listen. If you've got a meeting today, it's a trap. They've hired somebody named Coll to kill you."

"Tina. What . . . ?"

But she had hung up the telephone. Still weeping, she fled from the store.

TOMMY WAS ALONE AT HOME when Tina burst into the family apartment. She had expected to find him as he usually was, disinterested and daydreaming, but Tommy was dressed and his eyes flashed as she handed him the closed bag of film and pictures.

"It was Nilo," she said. "He did it. It was Nilo."

Tommy stood up slowly. "I know," he said. "I figured it out. It was always Nilo," he said. "Everything was Nilo." Finally, he opened the bag and glanced inside. His mouth tightened in anger. "Burn all this stuff before Mama comes home." As Tina ran into the kitchen, Tommy put on a long jacket and tucked his gun into his belt.

LUCIANO USED A TELEPHONE BOOTH in the lobby and found Meyer Lansky on the second phone call.

"I need some men and I need them right now. You got anybody around?"

"I got Red Levine here. And Bo Weinberg. Good men."

"Here's what I want them to do."

When he was finished with Lansky, Luciano called Tommy Lucchese. The man, known as "Three Finger Brown," had been Maranzano's driver but had always reported regularly to Luciano.

"Wander up to the Castellammarese's office," Luciano said.

"And do what?"

"Just hang around. Make believe you're trying to make peace for yourself. And if there are any visitors, make sure they find the right party."

Lucchese was not nimble-witted. He was silent for a moment, thinking, then understood. "I'll be there, Lucky."

NILO SENT SOFIA and the two boys to visit her mother. He had planned to stay away from Maranzano's office, but as the time grew nearer for the killings of Luciano and Genovese, he realized he would not be able to stay away. He wanted to be in on the kill.

He put on his jacket and opened the apartment door to tell his bodyguard to bring the car out front. But as soon as he opened the door, he was pushed back into the apartment, falling over the coffee table onto the floor. As he picked himself up, he heard the door slam and lock. Tommy stood inside the door. He held a pistol in his hand, aiming it unwaveringly at Nilo.

"Don't look for your bodyguard," Tommy said. "He's taking a rest."

Nilo smiled. "Nice of you to visit."

Tommy's voice was flat, without emotion. "That night in Yonkers when Papa got killed. It was you, wasn't it?"

"Don't you believe the cops? They said it was Birchevsky."

Tommy shook his head. "There was something wrong, but I could never figure out what it was. Until now. Birchevsky left the track before the last race. He kept looking at his watch. He was going to that warehouse to meet somebody. And that somebody is the person who shot Papa in the dark. Who tried to shoot me. Who else would Birchevsky be meeting except for you?"

"That's a pipe dream," Nilo said. "Don't go blaming it on me 'cause you let your own father get killed."

"You killed Papa. You had your stooge kill Rachel and try to kill me with an overdose. And killed Lev Mishkin. It was even you who had Tina raped."

"Try proving it. Try proving any of it."

"I can't prove it," Tommy said. "That's why I came up here to kill you."

———

AT TEN MINUTES TO THREE, four men dressed in suits and wearing snap-brimmed hats walked into Maranzano's offices in the New York Central Building at 230 Park Avenue, behind Grand Central Station.

Tommy Lucchese was sitting in a chair across the room, reading a newspaper. Behind the receptionist's desk was Girolamo Santucci, also known as "Bobby Doyle," one of Maranzano's favorite gunmen. Joe Valachi and two other bodyguards were drinking coffee near the big plate-glass window overlooking the street.

"Whaddya want?" Santucci asked the four men.

They flashed gold badges. "Internal Revenue," one said. "We got some questions for Mr. Maranzano."

"You got an appointment? You need an appointment."

"Hey, Bobby," Lucchese called. "What you getting so hot for? You know the boss always brags about paying the right taxes." He nodded to the four men. "He's inside the office there. It's a good time to ask him questions. He's alone now."

The first revenue agent nodded, and they started across the room to Maranzano's inner office. Just then, Maranzano opened his door.

"Who are you?"

"Internal Revenue."

"You people don't ever stop, do you?" Maranzano said with a smile. "Well, come on in, but let's make it fast."

"BUT I'M NOT GOING TO KILL YOU," Tommy said. "Not now. I've had a lot of time to think. If I killed you, I'd be just like you. You always laughed at justice. But justice is important. It separates the men from the beasts. It separates me from you. So I'm not going to kill you. I'm going to bring you down. From now on, every time you turn around, I'm going to be there. Everywhere you go, I'll be there. Make one mistake and I'll nail you with it. You're finished, Nilo."

Nilo smiled and looked at his watch. "Right about now," he said, "I am on my way to becoming the boss of New York. You're going to get me? Don't make me laugh. You won't get within a hundred feet of me."

TWO "AGENTS" FOLLOWED MARANZANO into his office and closed the door behind them. The other two men remained outside, then suddenly pulled guns and ordered Lucchese and the bodyguards up against the wall and disarmed them.

Inside, when Maranzano turned, he saw guns in the two agents' hands.

"You bastards," he yelled. He dove for his desk, trying to reach a pistol in the top drawer. But the assassins were quicker. While Maranzano lay sprawled across the desk, fumbling for the drawer, Red Levine pulled a knife from his pocket and stabbed Maranzano six times.

But Maranzano struggled, throwing wild punches. One connected with the head of the man holding the knife. Levine grunted and then lunged atop Maranzano, driving the knife into his throat.

When he yanked the knife loose and stood up, Maranzano lay on the desk, twitching, bubbling from the mouth. Levine watched him writhe for a full thirty seconds, then nodded to the other man, Bo Weinberg. The two men stood over Maranzano and each put two bullets into the body of the *capo di tutti capi*.

Then they ran from the office. The other two assassins who had subdued the bodyguards outside followed them. They split up and used separate stairways out of the building. Weinberg got lost, wound up hiding in a ladies' bathroom, and finally found his way to the Grand Central concourse, where he slid his gun into the jacket of a commuter waiting for a train.

As Red Levine approached the main exit, Mad Dog Coll came into the building, holding a leather briefcase in one hand.

Coll recognized Levine. "Maranzano?" he said.

"Dead," Levine said as he brushed by Coll and pushed through the door. "Better beat it, Vince. The cops are coming."

Coll turned around and walked back out onto the street, whistling. He had never made an easier twenty-five thousand dollars in his life.

Luciano and Genovese did not show up for their three-o'clock appointment.

"SO I WON'T KILL YOU. But nothing says I can't beat the hell out of you."

Tommy dropped the gun on the floor and rushed across the room and punched Nilo in the face. Nilo dropped to one knee and Tommy punched him again, knocking him flat on his back.

He straddled Nilo's body, punching him back and forth, left and right, punch after punch, until Nilo's once-beautiful face was broken and bloody.

Tommy stood up. "This is just the down payment, Nilo. It gets worse from now on. Look for me. I'll always be there."

He went back across the room, picked up his gun, and stuck it back into his belt, then left the apartment.

After Tommy left, Nilo lay on the floor a long time, gathering the strength to rise, and finally he got to his feet. Tommy had made a mistake, he thought. *He should have killed me when he had the chance. But he was too weak to do it, and now he'll die for it.*

I will run this city. Luciano's dead and all that's left now is Maranzano and me. And Maranzano goes next.

The telephone rang. When Nilo picked it up, he heard a wheezing voice. "This is Bobby Doyle. The boss is killed."

Nilo squeezed his eyes shut in pain. "What about Luciano?" he asked.

"He never showed up. It must have been his guys what did it. Be careful."

Nilo hung up the telephone. He had to get away. They might be coming for him next.

He ran downstairs to the street and saw a taxicab parked down the block.

"Cabbie!" he shouted. "Cabbie!"

The vehicle pulled up to him and, without looking, Nilo jumped through the open rear door.

Sitting, facing him, was Joe Adonis. He pointed a gun at Nilo's chest.

"Surprise," Adonis said.

Nilo felt a crack across the back of his head and sank into the blackness on the floor of the car. Adonis pulled the curtains closed.

"Don't rush," he told the driver. "I want to have time to enjoy this."

- *There is a legend that on the day Maranzano was killed, Luciano directed a nationwide massacre of more than fifty of Maranzano's strongest supporters in a vicious bloodletting poetically called "The Night of the Sicilian Vespers." But some*

*crime historians dispute this. It is known that
Jimmy Marino, a Maranzano henchman, was shot
six times that same day in the doorway of a Bronx
barbershop. And three days later, the butchered,
brutalized bodies of Maranzano faithfuls Louis
Russo and Sam Monaco washed ashore in Newark
Bay. Gerardo Scarpato, the restaurant owner who
served Joe Masseria's last meal, was also murdered. And the mutilated body of Nilo Sesta, partly
eaten by fish, was found tied to a piling under a
West Side pier. Those are the only authenticated
deaths of that day, but the rivers and landfills and
lime pits may still hold many secrets.*

IN THE END TOMMY FALCONE decided he had done
more harm than good. He had thought to emulate his
father, seeking justice, but justice had proven too elusive.
His father was dead; his wife was dead. The lives of the
Falcones had been tortured by tragedy. The criminals
had won and Luciano had survived to become the undis-
puted king of New York crime. His father had predicted
that the good would triumph, but his father had been
wrong. The blood of the evil had been stronger than the
blood of the lawful. It was time to forget about it all.

Tommy resigned from the police department and applied to take the bar examination. While he waited for
the test to be called, he found a job checking mortgage
applications for a bank. It was brainless, useless, dead-
end work, and it gave Tommy time to think, but every
thought came back to Tony's last words as he died in his
son's arms: "Never surrender," he had said. "Never surrender." The words rang in his mind like an echoing
accusation.

Never surrender. And all I ever did was surrender.

He had been at the mortgage company only a month when someone breezed into his tiny cubbyhole of an office and slammed the door behind him.

"Hello, copper," Tom Dewey said. He still looked as young as he had when he and Tommy had shared an apartment.

"Your mustache looks better than it used to," Tommy said. "It looks like a misplaced eyebrow now."

"It'll grow on you. Aren't you ashamed of yourself?"

"What for?"

"Sitting in this dismal countinghouse, doing nonsensical paper-shuffling. Do you know if you took that pile of papers on your desk and threw them all out the window, no one would ever notice?"

"This is only a way station on my road to fame and fortune," Tommy said.

"Oh?"

"Yeah. I'm waiting to take the bar exam."

"While you're waiting, you can work for me," Dewey said.

"And what kind of papers are you shuffling these days?"

"You're looking at the new assistant prosecutor for the United States Justice Department. I need a right-hand man, somebody who knows the gangsters in this town, somebody who knows the city, somebody who knows the law."

"Gangsters? Who are you going after?"

Dewey smiled. "All of them."

Never surrender, Tommy thought. *Was there still a chance?* Tommy breathed deeply, stood, took the pile of mortgage applications from his desk, and threw them through the open window.

"When do I start?"

"You just did."

They walked out of the office together.

- *In Chicago, a jury convicted Al Capone of all the charges against him. On October 24, 1931, he was sentenced to eleven years in Alcatraz. He complained, "All I ever did was sell beer and whiskey to our best people." He was paroled in 1939 and died, crazed from syphilis, in Palm Island, Florida, in 1947.*

- *The Seabury investigation showed that New York mayor Jimmy Walker had pocketed millions of dollars in graft money during his years in city hall. On September 1, 1932, Walker wired his resignation to Governor Franklin D. Roosevelt and fled to Europe with his mistress.*

- *In 1943, Father Mario Falcone was elevated in the church, and called "Right Reverend Monsignor." He died in 1961, still serving the same New York City parish.*

- *Prohibition was ended by constitutional amendment in 1933; the crime organization it created would not die so easily.*

- *Bugsy Siegel moved west and sold the syndicate on the idea of turning Las Vegas into a gambling paradise. But when he started skimming from the syndicate's construction funds, he was shot in the head in his girlfriend's Beverly Hills mansion on June 20, 1947. His closest friend, Meyer Lansky, authorized the hit. "We had no choice," he later explained.*

- *The Dow Jones stock average eventually fell to 41; 25 percent of Americans were out of work. The*

*market would not match its 1929 high until 1954,
a quarter of a century later.*

- *When his brother was killed on a Harlem street by
Dutch Schultz, Vincent "Mad Dog" Coll swore
undying enmity to the Dutchman. "I'm gonna burn
the Dutchman to hell." He hijacked Schultz's
liquor trucks, kidnapped his lieutenants for
ransom, and took over a huge section of Schultz's
gambling racket. Schultz enforcer Joey Rao came
looking for him, but Coll found him first on 107th
Street. Shooting at Rao from a moving car, Coll
missed the gangster but sprayed machine-gun
bullets into a group of five children, aged two to
four. One of them died. Coll beat the rap, but three
months later, while threatening another mobster
from a pay phone booth on West Twenty-third
Street, Coll was machine-gunned to death by Joey
Rao.*

- *Tina Falcone never sang professionally again. On
January 12, 1933, she took her vows and entered
the convent of the Sisters of Charity in Bellmore,
Long Island. No further records concerning her
can be found.*

- *Joe Adonis was convicted in 1951 of violating
gambling laws. When it was learned he had entered
the United States illegally, he was deported in 1953
to Italy, where he died in 1971.*

- *Franklin D. Roosevelt became president of the
United States. Fiorello La Guardia became the
reform mayor of New York City.*

- *Tom Dewey was as good as his word. In a succession of positions, as U.S. attorney, special prosecutor, and district attorney, he went after the mob
anywhere he found them. Bootlegger Waxey Gordon*

went to jail. Lepke went to the electric chair, and his henchman Gurrah Shapiro got life. Luciano was the next target. But Lucky proved hard to nail. Dewey could find no compelling evidence against him.

- Tommy Falcone had a desperate idea. He sent men out to the red-light districts, to which he had once been banished by Luciano, and they began rounding up prostitutes. When Tommy walked into the room where they were being questioned, two of them recognized him. "It's Sir Galahad," said Nancy Presser. "The only straight cop in the city," Cokey Flo Brown agreed. "And it's time to start telling the truth," Tommy said. "We'll protect you." The two prostitutes convinced forty more streetwalkers to testify against Luciano, and in 1936 Dewey indicted Charlie Lucky and nine of his cohorts on ninety counts of extortion and direction of harlotry. Luciano fled to Hot Springs, Arkansas, but was extradited for trial. Dewey destroyed him on the witness stand, and on June 18, 1936, Luciano was sentenced to serve thirty to fifty years. As he left the courtroom, Luciano bumped into Tommy Falcone but did not recognize him.

- With Luciano facing jail, Vito Genovese moved to take over the rackets, but when he was indicted in 1937 on a murder charge, he fled to Italy, where he spent World War II smuggling narcotics into the United States under the personal protection of his close friend, Italian dictator Benito Mussolini. In 1945, with Dewey no longer prosecutor, he returned to the United States and took over Luciano's crime family.

- *On May 2, 1957, on Genovese's orders, a thug named Vincent "The Chin" Gigante shot Frank Costello as he entered the lobby of his apartment building on Central Park West. When he survived the attack, Costello made it clear that he had gotten Genovese's message. He retired and died in bed February 18, 1973.*

- *Outraged at the attack on Costello, Albert Anastasia let it be known that he would have his revenge. He moved too slowly. He was shot to death in the basement barbershop of the Park Sheraton Hotel on October 25, 1957, at Genovese's direction.*

- *Low-keyed, quiet, and seemingly prosecution-proof, Meyer Lansky continued as the mob's money man—organizing most of the Caribbean gambling operations—until 1970, when the federal government came after him on income-tax charges. He fled to Israel but after three years was extradited. In a 1973 trial, he was acquitted and the government abandoned its efforts to put him behind bars. He died in 1983.*

- *For using his influence to help end World War II sabotage on the New York City docks, Luciano's sentence was commuted in 1946. He was deported to Italy the following February. From Italy, he directed narcotics smuggling into the United States and often traveled to Havana to oversee meetings of the national crime commission, at one of which he and Lansky decided to be rid of the dangerous Vito Genovese once and for all. They helped frame him on federal charges, and Genovese died in prison in 1969. Luciano was already dead. He had suffered a heart attack at Naples's Capodichino Airport on January 26, 1962, on his way to meet a*

TV producer who wanted to film the story of his life. Luciano had promised to tell all about the night he survived the infamous "ride" that left him scarred. "It was the cops that did it," he said. "And I know which ones." Several months later, his body was returned to New York City for interment. He was buried in St. John Cemetery, Middle Village, Queens, twenty-five feet from the grave of Lt. Tony Falcone.

- Thomas E. Dewey moved from prosecution to politics. When he was elected governor of New York in 1942, Tommy Falcone turned down a top law-enforcement job in his administration and instead enlisted in the U.S. Army. He never lived to see Dewey run twice for president of the United States. Tommy was killed in the fighting in Sicily in 1943. He had never remarried.

- Soon after Nilo's body was found, Sofia Sesta had gone to the offices of her lawyers to arrange for the transfer of his businesses to her. She found that all the stock in Danny Neill Enterprises had been owned by Salvatore Maranzano, and the government had seized the entire Maranzano estate. Left with only her savings, Sofia Sesta and her two children moved back with her mother into the apartment on Crosby Street, where Sofia ran the family restaurant until her death in 1971. One of her sons became a policeman; the other died in prison. It was in their blood, and the blood would have its way.